Turning the World to Stone:

The Life of Caterina Sforza

Part One

1472 to 1488

Turning the World to Stone

Turning the World to Stone Part One 1472 to 1488

Copyright © Kelly Evans 2023

This is a work of creative fiction. Names, characters, places, events, and incidents are either the product of the author's imagination or used in a fictitious manner. Any resemblances to real persons, living or dead, is purely coincidental.

Kelly Evans asserts her moral right to be identified as the author of this book.

All rights reserved. No part of this book may be reprinted or reproduced or used in any form or by any electronic, mechanical, or other means, now known or hereafter invented, including photocopying and recording, or in any information storage or retrieval system, without the permission in writing from the publisher, except for the use of brief quotations in a book review.

Published by Eska Publishing 2023

Cover Created by Flintlock Covers
Map Created by Lorena Cosimo

ISBN: 978-1-7780224-2-5

Turning the World to Stone

Also by Kelly Evans

Historical Fiction

THE NORTHERN QUEEN

THE CONFESSOR'S WIFE

ELIZABETH: PATH TO THE THRONE

THE BEGGAR QUEEN

UNFINISHED: THE INSPIRED LIFE OF ELISABETTA SIRANI

STUBBORN: A GREEK COMEDY

Historical Horror

THE MORTECARNI

REVELATION: THE MORTECARNI PART TWO

THE STRANGE TALE OF MISS VICTORIA FRANK

MONSTERS AND MISFITS

Turning the World to Stone

Turning the World to Stone

"Could I write all, the world would turn to stone."
Caterina Sforza

Turning the World to Stone

Turning the World to Stone
Main Characters

Milan

Caterina Sforza: Fifteenth Century noblewoman.
Luisa Tommasa: Caterina's Dama di Corte (Lady in Waiting) and friend and confidante.
Gianni 'Gian' Bossi: Caterina's advisor.
Galeazzo Sforza: Duke of Milan, Caterina's father.
Bona of Savoy: Duchess of Milan, Caterina's stepmother.
Ludovico 'The Moor' Sforza: Galeazzo's brother/Caterina's uncle.
Ascanio Sforza: Galeazzo's brother/Caterina's uncle.

Imola and Forli

Violante Riario Ricci: Sister of Girolamo Riario, mother of Raffaele Riario.
Domenico Ricci: Husband of Violante Riario Ricci, governor of Imola.
Leone Cobelli: Musician, dance master, painter, chronicler of events in Forli.
Tommaso Feo: Castellan at Ravaldino.
Bishop Giacomo Savelli: Papal governor.
Townspeople, nobles, council members, merchants, etc.

Rome

Girolamo Riario: Nephew of Pope Sixtus, married to Caterina Sforza.
Pope Sixtus IV: Girolamo Riario's uncle, Head of Catholic Church and papal states from 21 July 1414 to 12 August 1484.

Raffaele Riario: Son of Violante Riario Ricci, nephew to Girolamo.
Francesco Pazzi: Son of Jacobo Pazzi.
Caterina's Children: Ottaviano (b 1 September 1479), Cesare (b 25 August 1480), Bianca (b End of October 1481), Giovanni Livio (b End of October 1484, Galeazzo (b 18 December 1485), and Francesco, called Sforzino (b 17 August 1487).
Isach de Luca: Apothecary, healer
Ercole Miniati: Guard at Castel Sant'Angelo.
Cardinals, prelates, nobles, merchants, townspeople etc.

Main Italian families mentioned: Orsi, Orsini, Colonna, Ordelaffi, Medici, Pazzi, Visconti, Gonzaga, Bentivoglio, Riario, della Rovere, Borgia.

Turning the World to Stone

Turning the World to Stone

Chapter One
1472

"No. It's too much. I won't allow it." The voice paused. "It's unnatural." The last two words were a whisper, and Caterina, hidden under the table, strained to hear.

"He's a powerful man, and the union is important for Milan." Caterina heard the irritation in her father's voice and wished she could somehow leave the room unnoticed. But she'd chased a ball under the table just as the duke and the others had arrived, and, knowing she wasn't meant to be in the study, Caterina had frozen.

Galeazzo Sforza continued. "You know of our difficulties with the papal states. This union would protect us from any unwanted attention from Rome and guarantee added protection against the French."

"Important for Milan but at the expense of my daughter." The woman looked around the room at each of the men. "And the expense of our mortal souls."

"He's the Pope's nephew. He'll see to our souls." Galeazzo waved away the objection.

"You saw the way he looked at her last night. A thirty-year-old man lusting after an eleven-year-old girl. And only a year older than your own daughter."

Caterina knew she was being spoken of and held her breath to avoid detection.

Constanza's husband, and one of the duke's loyal retainers, tried to calm his wife. "My dear, it's not like that.

You imagined it, he was probably admiring the fine feast Sforza had prepared for us," he offered weakly.

"I can't." Constanza stood firm, her chin tilted upward in defiance. "I won't. There are many things I've done for Milan and my family, it's the painful duty of all women to suffer for their children but there are limits to the things a mother will sacrifice. And this is one of them."

From her position under the cloth-covered table, Caterina could see her father's feet pacing. For moments the only noise in the room was the crackling of the fire and her own heartbeat. A log shifted position, sending tendrils of sparks upward, making Caterina jump. Still, no one heard her.

Finally, Constanza's husband spoke. "I think..."

He was interrupted by Galeazzo. "I won't have this damage our friendship. You're one of my best generals however we need that papal partnership." He nodded; a decision made. "I'll offer my own daughter, Caterina."

"But she's only ten," Constanza whispered. "You're her father..." her voice trailed away.

"I am. And I know what's best for my family. Caterina will marry Girolamo Riario."

Caterina didn't remember anything else. She must have waited for the room to empty but had no recall except that she hadn't heard any opposition to her father's proposal. At some point, she crawled out from under the table and, leaving the ball behind, made her way to her room.

"What's wrong?" Luisa was waiting for her. Provided to Caterina as a junior maid and helper, Luisa Tommasa had become the young Sforza's closest friend. More reserved than the other girl, Luisa nevertheless joined Caterina in any adventure that presented itself. A strand of her curly black hair fell across her olive skin, and she tucked it back into her beaded hairnet as she turned to Caterina.

"I heard something I wasn't supposed to."

Luisa rolled her eyes. "You always hear things. You're always listening when you shouldn't." She returned to her sewing. "It's a sin to eavesdrop," she added piously.

"I wasn't. At least, not on purpose. My ball rolled under the table in father's study and people came in and I was stuck. What was I supposed to do, put my fingers in my ears?"

Looking up again, Luisa tilted her head. "What did you hear this time?" She expected another lurid tale of a maid and page caught in a dark corner of the palace. This time, however, the more Caterina revealed, the more she leaned forward, dropping her sewing on the ground to focus on her friend's words.

"You?" Luisa's eyes widened in disbelief.

Caterina nodded. "Yes. My father said it himself."

"I... your father..." Luisa stumbled over her words, unsure how to react or what to say. "Does your cousin know?"

"I don't know. I think they must have told her by now." Caterina glanced out her bedroom window and saw the sun had already begun to set. How long had she remained under the table, frozen in shock?

"What will you do?"

Caterina had only the same answer. "I don't know. Whatever my father says. I have no choice."

"Can you imagine a life with," Luisa paused, "him?"

"Pope Sixtus IV's nephew. Girolamo Riario. You may as well get used to saying it." Caterina thought for a moment. As a Sforza, she had access to the famed Milanese library, only second to that of the Vatican, and had grown up on tales of knights and maidens and chivalry. None of them told the story of an overweight thirty-year-old with a permanent petulant look. She swallowed. "No, I can't imagine my life from now on. But there's nothing I can do, it's my father's decision."

They were staring at each other helplessly when Caterina's stepmother rushed in. Bona of Savoy, the duke's second wife, had only been married for three years but was already admired and beloved by Milan for her kindness, humour, and love of music and food. A devout woman, she had treated Caterina, one of many of the duke's illegitimate children, as her own, ensuring both the girl's mind and soul were seen to.

"You're here. Good. I must speak with you." She sat on an elaborately carved wooden chair next to the fireplace and waited for Caterina to join her. Luisa bobbed her petite body before Bona and, with a sympathetic glance at her friend, hurried from the room.

Bona wasted no time getting to the point. As soon as Caterina was settled, she spoke. "You're to be married."

"I know."

Keeping her surprise to herself, Bona merely replied, "How?"

"I was under the table in the study when father spoke about it."

"Your spying will get you into trouble someday." Seeing the girl's face begin to crumble, she smiled gently. "I'll forgive you this time." Taking a deep breath, she continued. "Do you understand what being married means?" Her heart ached for this child, not hers yet as beloved as any from her own body.

Caterina nodded. "Father needs to keep the Pope and Rome happy."

That was more or less the gist, however there was more, and Bona felt physical pain in her chest at the idea. Before she could say anything, Caterina spoke again.

"How much am I being sold for?"

This time Bona didn't hide her shock. "Did someone say that to you?" She struggled to keep her fury contained.

"No. I heard the servants talking in the hall."

Was her stepdaughter repeating what she'd overheard, or did the child understand the situation more than she was given credit for? Seeing Caterina waiting for a reply, Bona smoothed her dress and adopted a business-like façade. "Ten thousand ducats."

Caterina considered the number for a few moments. "That's a lot."

"Yes, it is." Bona wanted to move away from this unsavoury line of questioning; unfortunately, it meant moving to something far worse. "Do you know what is expected of you? As a wife?' Seeing the confusion on the girl's face, she pushed on. "Not the palace management or entertaining, I mean at night, in the bedroom." She bit her tongue, hoping the sharp pain would stop her emotions from overtaking her. She tasted copper.

Caterina felt her face burn and looked down at her feet, embarrassed. "I do. I've heard the maids and pages telling stories." Her voice was barely above a whisper.

Bona breathed a sigh of relief. She was angry at the servants and their often simple ways but thankful that she didn't now need to explore the topic further. She stood. "The announcement will be made tonight. You must prepare yourself, for I'm not certain of the reaction."

"Why?" Caterina had stood a second after her stepmother and peered up at the tall brunette woman with awe.

Turning the World to Stone

"Never you mind. Now, let's see what we have. You need a gown and an over gown. I think the black gown with the detachable sleeves. It'll be warm next to the hall fire, and you won't need them. And the gold stitched overcoat to go over the top. I'll send Luisa back in. I'm sure she's just outside." Bona stared at the girl fondly, knowing the days of her carefree childhood were ending. The bitter taste in her mouth was no longer from the blood where she'd bitten herself; instead, it was the taste of shame that she couldn't do more for the girl.

The sounds and smells of the great hall in the ducal palace reached Caterina and Luisa before they arrived in the room. An enormous fire roared in the fireplace, ready for the traditional burning of the yule log. The kitchen, placed far enough away not to bother guests with the sounds of food being prepared, was still close enough for the aroma to escape and infiltrate every corner of the hall. Bona would normally have disapproved, for as supervisor of these activities, she believed a quiet space with no odours was sacrosanct to elevated living. But today, the smells enervated the guests and added to the already festive mood.

The music grew louder the closer Caterina got, as did the murmur of conversation as dozens of the duke's closest friends and advisors gathered to celebrate Christmas. The presence of the Pope's favourite nephew ensured that at least a few invitations had been surreptitiously acquired. No noble in Milan would dare to be absent from such an occasion.

"What are you waiting for? Let's go." Luisa nudged Caterina in the back. Her friend's enthusiasm was contagious enough for Caterina to nearly forget her situation. She knew there was no use fighting it, but at least she could perhaps discover a bit more about her betrothed during the feast. And maybe she could enjoy herself. Maybe.

They encountered a riot of colour and fabrics when they walked through the crowded room. Milan was renowned for its silk, and every hue and shade was on display. The under and over gowns were similar in style to Caterina's own, with differences only a wealthy courtier would notice. The men's fitted waistcoats could be worn with different sets of brocade sleeves, depending on the situation. Women's sleeves were broader and more voluminous, a sign of wealth, for no one could perform any manual labour wearing such a dress. And while others in Europe might wear heavily decorated headdresses, it was too warm in Italy for married noble women to cover their heads, so many wore a sheer hairnet interwoven with expensive jewels and pearls.

The room flashed with colour and material, and Caterina found it difficult to make her way to her place at the main table when the time came. Luisa was permitted to accompany her and sat at another table reserved for personal guests of the Sforza's. Caterina's brother Carlo, two years older than her, sat at the same table. Her other siblings, Alessandro and Chiara, were eight and six, respectively, too young for such a feast. Bona and Galeazzo moved to their places and stood behind their chairs, waiting for the others to settle. Pages were on hand to help people to their appointed places, all planned by Bona weeks before. The only stranger among them was a disappointed-looking man sitting to the duke's right.

"Guests and visitors, I welcome you to this feast to celebrate the birth of our Lord and Saviour." Galeazzo raised his goblet to the tables. Elevated on a dais, the Sforza family table ran perpendicular to the others so the duke could observe all his guests. "You honour my family and me with your presence." He looked down fondly at Bona. "Tonight, we not only recognise the union between the earthly and heavenly realms brought about by Our Lord's birth, but also the union between two families: the Riarios and the Sforzas."

The room erupted in noise. All knew the Pope's last name had been Riario before he'd chosen Sixtus as his papal designation. The realisation of who was sitting next to the duke dawned, and slowly heads turned toward the man.

"It is with reverence and admiration I announce the betrothal of Girolamo Riario, the Holy Father's nephew and leader of the papal army, to my own daughter Caterina."

Although she'd been warned of the reaction the announcement might provoke, Caterina wasn't prepared for everyone to now focus their attention on her. Dozens of faces, brightly lit by the beeswax candles around the room, stared at her. She saw surprise, disbelief, and pity in the faces before the embarrassment made her turn away.

Ignoring his daughter's distress, Galeazzo continued. Holding up his goblet once more, he grinned. "This marriage will unite Milan and Rome in a closer bond, and create an alliance that will be admired throughout Europe."

The prior confused and alarmed voices now turned joyous as each guest raised their goblet in reply to the duke's gesture.

"Now, enjoy the celebration!"

The room cheered, and the musicians began their unobtrusive playing once more. The food arrived, each course earning "oohs" and "ahhs" from the guests. Caterina finally raised her head and was relieved that the earlier stares had changed into discreet glances. Sitting straight, Caterina met each look with a confident nod, as she'd seen

Bona do. When Luisa caught her eye, she smiled and shrugged a little, a movement only her friend noticed.

While eating, Caterina chanced a few glances of her own: at the tables laden with food, the tapestries that decorated the walls and kept the cold from penetrating the stone, and especially at her husband-to-be. A severe-looking man, his body had objected to his love of good food and wine by making his chin and cheeks fleshy and pale, and creating delicate red veins over the surface of his nose. His eyes were deep set and dark, and darted around the room, suspicious of every shriek of laughter or private conversation. When he caught her staring at him, he frowned and turned away.

Portions of conversation reached her ears as she sat and behaved as instructed.

"He looks ill-bred. These Riarios..." The rest of the words were lost in the room's cacophony. Caterina turned her head slightly and caught another conversation.

"I don't care if he's the Pope's nephew, he's a peasant. As is that uncle of his."

"Shh, keep your thoughts to yourself." Once again, the rest of the words went unheard.

As the evening wore on, Caterina found herself growing both bored and tired, a combination which, in the past, had elicited behaviour matching Caterina's age rather than her station. She swung her feet, kicking her left against the table leg and shaking the surface. A glare from Bona stopped the movement but not Caterina's boredom. She lifted her napkin to her mouth to hide a yawn, wondering how long it would be until she could return to her room.

Fortunately, it was Bona, and not the duke, who noticed her stepdaughter's fidgeting. With a kind nod, Bona signalled to Caterina that she could leave. As soon as Caterina stood, Luisa followed. Closer to the door, Luisa waited by the entrance for her friend to join her. Caterina walked around the main table and faced her father, stepmother, and future husband. Curtseying deeply, she held it for a few seconds before rising and nodding. "Good night and God bless you on this Holy day."

    Seeing Bona's pleased smile, Caterina turned back to Luisa. Taking Luisa's hand, she held on tightly as they left the room and walked slowly down the hall.

The first winds of January were mild, promising an early end to the frigid temperatures felt in the north of Italy. Nestled between the Alps to the north and the Apennines to the south, Milan felt the temperature extremes the terrain occasioned. Cold winters led to mild springs, which gave way to hot summers. Still, Caterina shivered as she entered her room and headed toward the fire.

    "Look what arrived when you were gone!" Luisa jumped from her chair as Caterina entered the room. "You took so long, and I couldn't wait..." she let the sentence trail and pointed at an open package. A hint of gold glinted from the blue linen wrapping.

    "I'm sorry, I had a sword lesson with Carlo."

    Caterina had recently started learning sword fighting, a skill her forebears were famed for. Descended from a long line of condottieri, elite mercenary captains who served Popes and kings alike, Caterina was as encouraged as her male siblings to learn to protect herself with both sword and dagger.

    "How was your brother?"

    "Not as good as me, and he's been learning for two years longer." She smirked and turned to Luisa. "What's all this?"

    "I told you. They arrived while you were out. They're from Don Riario."

Turning the World to Stone

Caterina unpinned the small cap on her head and shook out her long blonde hair. Even at this young age, her potential beauty was commented upon by courtier and servant alike. Hurrying to stand with her friend, she looked down at the dozens of wrapped bundles waiting on her chamber table. She picked up the one Luisa had already opened and withdrew a gold chain with a large ruby pendant at the end.

Turning to her friend, Caterina held the necklace up to her throat. "Does it suit me?"

"It's too heavy for you."

Caterina nodded and placed the necklace back in its wrapping. "Pass me that large one, there, by your hand."

Luisa lifted the heavy package and put it between them. Caterina pulled at the cover, green this time with small leaves, and parted the material. Both she and Luisa gasped. Inside was the most luxurious brocade material they'd ever seen. Deep blue velvet with gold stitched flowers and vines, the raised threads catching the light and making the pattern jump from the material.

"It's beautiful."

Caterina ran her hand over the material. Turning to her friend, she smiled and nodded. Together they dived into the rest of the packages, stopping after each to show the other the contents, laughing with delight at each object. More material than Caterina had ever seen began to pile up on a nearby chair as she arranged the multitude of pendants, chains, rings, and loose precious stones across the table. Her head began to swim with the sheer quantity and weight of the objects before her.

"It's very…" Luisa hesitated.

"It is," Caterina agreed.

"Do you like anything?" She waved her hand over the table.

Turning the World to Stone

Caterina took a moment to review the table. "That," she pointed at the first bolt of material she'd opened, "and this." She picked up a gold chain, finer than the rest, with a simple drop pearl at the end. "The rest is too," she frowned, "Roman for me."

Luisa giggled and held her hand to her mouth to stifle the noise. She continued running her hands over the jewels and material. Caterina looked thoughtfully at the pile of wealth in front of her. "None of this was meant for me."

"What do you mean? He sent it to you."

Shaking her head, Caterina replaced the gold necklace. "It was all meant for my cousin, Gabriella. He thought he was marrying her, that's why he came to Milan. When her mother said no, and I was offered instead, all the gifts he brought for her were given to me."

"So? They're still gifts."

"I know." She sighed. "I just never thought, when I imagined my marriage, I would receive second-hand dowry presents."

A quiet sadness blanketed the room, interrupted by a maid carrying an armful of pure white linen. "Is that for tomorrow night?"

She nodded. "He means to lay with me after the ceremony." She turned to her friend. "I overheard father and Bona talking. When it was suggested that Girolamo only lie on the bed, with witnesses present, he refused."

Not knowing what to say, Luisa picked at a thread on her sleeve. The silence grew too deep. "Are you ready?"

"No. I don't know." Caterina's tone had lowered, and a pleading edge had entered her voice. She had been raised from birth to understand her role at her father's court: to be used as he saw fit. But she never imagined the day before her wedding would be filled with trepidation rather than triumph.

Chapter Two
1473

The rain poured down the next day, hitting Milan's buildings with such force that the citizens covered their ears as they went about their business. Even inside the palace, Caterina could hear the echoes of the violent storm washing over the city.

She hadn't slept much the previous night and was glad for Luisa's company, as her friend had denied herself her own sleep and had remained awake to comfort the young bride.

The ceremony would take place that evening in the palace chapel. A clergyman willing to perform the ceremony had been found, or at least unwilling to pass up the considerable sum the duke had paid to ignore the official laws. In Galeazzo's cynical opinion, he was marrying into the papal family, so the papal family could deal with the moral and legal consequences, seeing as they were so much closer to God than everyone else.

The day passed with a flurry of activity, most of which seemed unnecessary to Caterina. Surely she only needed to bathe, dress, and walk to the chapel? But maids and courtiers alike found a way to visit or walk past her room and stare into the open door like she was a trapped bird. Eventually, sick of the gazing both curious and pitying, she ordered a maid to keep the door closed.

Turning the World to Stone

As the dark skies outside grew even darker with the setting of a cloud-hidden sun, Bona arrived in Caterina's room. "Let me look at you." She kept her voice even, hiding her emotions. Her stepdaughter needed the strength of a mother right now.

Two maids moved aside, allowing Caterina to come forward. There hadn't been enough time for the material Girolamo had gifted her to be made into a gown. Still, Bona had ensured every detail of the girl's dress was as magnificent as anything Rome could provide.

Bona nodded. The green silk suited Caterina's colouring, and the lenza, the braided leather cord worn around her head, kept her freely hanging blonde hair in place. Her silk brocade top gown fell to her feet, flowing after her like a misty haze of colour.

"How do I look? Will Don Riario be pleased?"

The innocence and desire to please in that question made Bona bite back a sob. The sudden lump in her throat stopped her from speaking, but she saw Caterina staring at her. "He will, my darling. How could he not?" She tried to lighten the mood and ran her hand over Caterina's head in a tender gesture.

A page interrupted the moment between them. "Duchess, it's time. The others wait in the chapel."

Bona turned toward the door. Caterina, with a final look at Luisa, followed.

The mood in the palace had gone from excited and hectic to subdued. While there would be a feast to honour the night, it would be a small and private one; the usual days-long festivities that typically accompanied such an event abandoned.

Caterina followed Bona in silence, wishing she'd asked Luisa to accompany her to the chapel. She bowed her head politely at anyone they encountered through the

Turning the World to Stone

winding halls, copying Bona. To anyone who saw her, she appeared the picture of obedience.

Caterina's stomach roiled. She'd barely eaten all day, nearly vomiting the bread and cheese she'd tried earlier. It felt like something was jumping inside her, twitching and groaning to be free. Her thoughts had momentarily disappeared, and all she could do was follow her stepmother blindly to her future.

She'd been warned what to expect earlier that day, and now that they'd arrived at the chapel door, Caterina hoped she could remember the only thing she need say – volo – this is what I want. Even if she didn't want it, she would say the word.

The chapel was warm, and the smell of incense and beeswax was comforting. Ahead of Caterina, at the altar, was an unknown priest. He waited with her father, Duke Galeazzo, and Don Riario. Seeing him standing before her, Caterina noticed he was shorter than she'd initially thought. Still, she'd only seen him sitting behind a table. He also appeared a bit wider. Ignoring her sudden terror, she stepped forward to join him.

Without any delay, the priest started. "We're here this evening to bring together Don Girolamo Riario and Caterina Sforza in matrimonial union." Turning to Girolamo, the priest asked, "Do you consent and agree to this union?" His voice was emotionless and even.

Girolamo stared straight ahead as he replied. "Volo." His voice was deep, like the singers her father had brought to Milan from Venice, but not melodious.

It was her turn. Caterina barely heard the words the priest uttered. There was a moment of silence, and she realised the clergyman was looking at her expectantly.

Swallowing hard so she could force the word past her dry throat, she answered. "Volo."

Turning the World to Stone

The sense of relief in the room was tangible as the priest finished the ceremony. The rest of the words were mere formula; legalities involving the exchange of money and property. Caterina listened listlessly, realising she was part of the property being agreed upon.

After the ceremony, a few select guests were invited to dine with the family, Luisa included. Caterina sat at the head table. Her new husband was to her right, and her father and Bona were to his right. As it was a significant occasion, Caterina was permitted to have Luisa close and had her friend sit to her left. Her siblings were absent; their father had decided their presence wasn't necessary. This was Caterina's celebration. The meal was more subdued than the Christmas feast, but musicians played, and guests laughed, drank, and enjoyed the finest fare Milan had to offer. Caterina reached over and squeezed her friend's hand often during the meal, urging time to slow. But time slows for no one, especially a ten-year-old girl.

As it grew late, restlessness descended on the room. Caterina saw people glancing at her over the edges of their glass goblets. She felt a hand on her arm.

"Your husband wishes to retire for the night." Galeazzo removed his hand and stood.

The shocking stories and bawdy tales of bards about wedding nights flooded back to her, and she began to shake. Feeling Luisa's reassuring arm around her shoulder, she stood slowly. The rest of the room rose immediately to their feet and raised their glasses at the groom, who was already halfway out the door. Caterina held Luisa's hand tightly as they followed Girolamo and his grooms to the room assigned to him.

Luisa helped Caterina out of the multiple layers of clothing she wore, grateful for the added time it gave them. Leaning close, she whispered in her friend's ear, "It'll be all right. You're strong, stronger than anyone I know." As she helped Caterina into her white wedding night chemise, she added, "I'll be here for you. Always."

Caterina turned and hugged her friend, but the action was cut short by the entrance of Girolamo. He, too, wore a nightdress, not as delicate as Caterina's but expensive, nevertheless. The giant oak bed stood between them, and her husband stood staring at her. He then turned to scowl at Luisa. It was time for her friend to leave.

Gripping Caterina's hand as long as she could, Luisa smiled sadly and left the room. She waited until the door had closed after her but couldn't bear to return to her room in case Caterina still needed something. Pacing outside, she thought she heard a cry from inside the room, but it could have been the raging winds that had started battering the palace.

Luisa wasn't sure how long she lingered in the hall. Long enough to hear familiar noises in her friend's room, ones she'd heard coming from the servant's quarters. Sighing, she had just turned to go to her own room when an unexpected noise made her scramble to the side of a tapestry. Peering into the darkness, she saw Count Girolamo leave Caterina's room. Glancing down the hall, he didn't notice Luisa watching him and adjusted himself as he strode away in the opposite direction.

Waiting to make sure he wouldn't return, Luisa silently crept back to Caterina's door and slipped inside. Across the room a single burning candle illuminated the shadow of her friend's shoulders moving under the covers. Removing the blanket she'd wrapped around her shoulders, Luisa walked to the bed and climbed in. She embraced Caterina without a word, holding her as the other girl's body shuddered with wracked sobs, until her friend finally fell into a fitful sleep.

A soft knock at her door made Caterina's heart jump. She thought her husband had returned but when she saw Luisa's face she nearly cried. Feeling the unaccustomed ache of last night's consummation, she eased herself from the bed.

"I brought you water and cloths." Two maids trailed behind Luisa, one carrying a large bowl of water and the other the square linen pieces. "I got up early and didn't want to wake you."

"Thank you." Caterina would rather have soaked in one of the copper tubs where Bona regularly bathed. Still, she knew she was expected at breakfast and had slept longer than she should have. Despite her pain, she wasn't allowed the luxury of lounging in bed all day.

She soaked a cloth and ran it over her face and neck, feeling the refreshing lavender-scented water she loved. Moving to her intimate areas, she blushed as Luisa turned away to ready the clothes Caterina would wear today, delivered by an unseen servant the night before.

"Are you..." Luisa struggled for the right word. There wasn't one. "Are you feeling, do you hurt? Can I help you?"

"I'm fine."

Seeing the doubt in her friend's eyes, Luisa pushed. "Did you know what would happen?"

Caterina threw the cloth into the bowl, splashing water onto the small dressing table and over the floor. "Of course I knew!" She could say no more. Tears flooded her eyes, and her body began to shake, but she stared ahead defiantly. Despite her attempted bravado, Caterina was grateful to feel Luisa's arms encircle her, giving her strength.

"He wants to see me again tonight," she whispered into her friend's hair.

Luisa released her friend. "What will you do?" Her own eyes were wet with barely contained emotion.

Shaking her head, Caterina brought her hand to her eyes and wiped away the tears. "Think of something else. Pretend I'm not there."

"He's a vile creature. An ignorant, common Roman with nothing to distinguish himself save for the elevation of a relative." Bona waited for her maid to remove her hair net and shook out her long hair in relief. Running her hands through the dark locks to comb them out, she made an angry noise when a tangle stayed her progress.

"My dear, you know how important Riario is. Surely you can overlook his faults and be happy your daughter has made a significant marriage." Galeazzo removed his boot and stretched out his leg.

Bona turned quickly, abandoning her hair. "A significant marriage? Is this what you had hoped for your child? Not happiness? Not even contentment?"

"This alliance will help all Milan," the duke replied reasonably. His personal servant helped him out of his heavy brocade overcoat and the fitted waistcoat beneath. Groaning with relief, he accepted a goblet of wine from the servant and dismissed him with a nod. "Caterina is young," he continued, "and she will be at home for another four years. There's plenty of time for her to adjust to the idea and develop her own interests."

Bona remained unpersuaded. "Perhaps," she murmured. She waited until her maid had departed before continuing. "What kind of man would consummate a marriage with a young girl when the legal age is fourteen?" She went to the bed, where the sheets and blankets had already been turned down for the duke and duchess.

"He had the Holy Father's blessing. It was important that there be no impediment to this alliance, so allowances were made."

"But twice?! Once was surely enough to fulfil any contract?" She was satisfied to notice her husband wince slightly at her words. Seeing the stern look he immediately adopted, Bona knew she'd receive no answer. The couple climbed into bed and turned away from each other, all in complete silence. Bona had made her point, and it would have to be enough.

A few days later, Girolamo left Milan to return to his uncle and duties in Rome. According to the marriage agreement, Caterina would continue her life at the ducal palace in Milan until she was fourteen and old enough to join her husband in Rome.

"I'm glad he's gone."

"Shh, Luisa, someone will hear you." Caterina was also pleased her husband was departing but could not say so out loud, and the chastisement of her friend was half-hearted at best.

"So what? I'm happy for you."

Caterina smiled, pleased with herself. She had suffered through these trying days and had survived.

At the end of February, a papal bull arrived from Rome.

Caterina looked at it across her father's study table in awe. "What does it say?"

Galeazzo shot a triumphant glance at Bona before reading the bull. "It says we are all absolved of any sin regarding the marriage of Girolamo Riario and my dutiful daughter, Caterina." He beamed at her, and she felt the warmth of acceptance. "It corrects any irregularities regarding the previous engagement with Gabriella and sanctions your marriage," he looked at Caterina again, "despite the fact you are a few years short of the legal age."

Raising a glass of wine he had nearby, he smiled at Bona. "My dear, we are absolved. Your prayers for our souls have been answered."

Caterina watched her father as he drained his glass. If the Holy Father said what she and her husband had done was fine, then who was she to question? And if the Holy Father was right, then her father, the duke, must also be correct. And he was so proud of her! The gifts of horses and dogs that had accompanied her union with Girolamo were proof of that, surely.

Still, something in her young mind made her doubt. Shaking the feeling away, she allowed herself to feel the immense reverence the Pope's words occasioned.

Chapter Three
1473 - 1476

The week after Caterina's marriage, Girolamo had returned to Rome, and she'd been left at her father's court to further her education until she was ready to join her husband. Much of the duke's children's days were spent on their education. Even their leisure time was directed toward worthy pursuits, for both the boys and the girls. Bona took on more and more of Caterina's education herself, leaving the other children to their tutors and sword masters. As a woman soon to take over her own household, Caterina's activities increasingly included household management on top of her regular studies in Latin, rhetoric, mathematics, and grammar.

Caterina's garden was modelled on Bona's much larger one, another activity her stepmother encouraged more and more. "You see that plant? What is it?" They stood at the edge of Bona's garden, looking at a row of bushy plants with red multi-petalled flowers.

"Carnation."

"Correct. It's one of the plants I use often when preparing medicine." Bona turned to Caterina. "I want to start training you in the use of plants and herbs; it's something you'll need to know when you have your own household."

"Why? Can't the kitchen maids worry about that?"

"You're right that many of these plants will be used for cooking, but as the mistress in your own house you'll be responsible for helping the townspeople with their ailments."

Caterina nodded. "Like you do when you visit the sick people."

"Exactly. Also something you'll be doing with me." Bona plucked a few flowers and put them in the overflowing basket of plants she carried. "Come with me. I'll show you an easy treatment for your first one."

Excited at both the prospect of leaving the palace walls and venturing out into the city and this new avenue of learning, Caterina jumped and clapped her hands, then composed herself and followed the older woman to a room just off the kitchen. As she entered, the smell of drying herbs washed over Caterina and she breathed in the heady scents deeply.

Bona put the basket on a large wooden table in the middle of the room. Running her hand over the surface, Caterina felt the crisscrossed patterns and gouges made over the decades. Despite the obvious signs of use, the surface was clean. She looked around, taking in the bottles, jars, bowls, shelves of spoons, and more. A fire burned in a small fireplace at one end of the room.

"Over there, on that shelf, there's a jar marked cinnamon. Can you please bring it here?"

Caterina dutifully did as her stepmother asked, moving her eyes over the small pots and containers, reading each label until she found the one she wanted. Lifting it carefully, she used both hands to carry it to the table.

"The Venetians control the flow of cinnamon from the East. It's such a valuable spice that men have been killed over it." Bona spoke while she worked. Taking a piece of the light brown bark, she held it up for Caterina to see. "It's used for both cooking and healing." Putting it down, she retrieved the carnation flowers she'd picked from the garden.

"Carnations are called Dianthus in Latin. Do you know why?"

Caterina, completely and utterly absorbed by this new study, shook her head.

"There is a legend about the Roman goddess Diana, queen of the hunt. After a particularly bad day, Diana was returning home and came across a shepherd playing music on a pipe for his sheep. The goddess, so enraged by the lack of prey at her latest hunt, blamed the shepherd's music, even though he was leagues away and his music so sweet no animal would run from it." Bona moved to another nearby cupboard, filled with empty bowls and containers, and considered each one for a moment before selecting a medium-sized, highly polished copper bowl. Taking it back to the table, she removed the petals from the carnations and dropped them into the bowl. "The goddess would hear no excuse from the poor boy and tore out his eyes."

Caterina gasped and covered her open mouth. She'd read stories of the gods and goddesses, but their cruelty always shocked her. "And then what?"

"The legend says when she dropped the eyeballs on the ground, red carnations sprung up on the spot."

"And the shepherd?"

"Sadly," Bona finished with the petals and added the cinnamon bark to the bowl, "he died. Diana was eventually so overcome with remorse she ensured no one dared touch the carnations." She looked into the bowl and then around the room. "That bottle, there. Can you bring it here?"

Caterina followed Bona's pointed finger and saw a bottle of wine. She collected it and put it on the table within Bona's reach. "What are we making?"

Bona smiled. "This is a treatment you'll make often, I'm certain." She leaned forward conspiratorially and whispered, "It's for bad breath."

Seeing the amused look on her stepmother's face, Caterina burst out laughing. "You can cure that?"

Nodding, Bona stood straight again and opened the wine. "Yes. There are a great many ailments that can easily be treated with a garden."

The realisation of why Bona had been so insistent on her keeping her garden dawned, and Caterina now understood completely the importance of the plants she tended. Then a thought struck her. "If these cures are possible, why are there so many courtiers who, well, when you get too close and they speak," Caterina faltered, her body backing away from the imaginary conversation of which she spoke.

Bona bit her lip to stop her laughter. "I don't know. Maybe they don't think women are smart enough to do this. Perhaps they prefer an apothecary, who will charge them twice as much for half the cure." She poured wine into the bowl and stirred the bark and petals into the liquid with her finger. "We'll boil this and let it cool. After that, it'll be ready to drink."

"Who's it for?" Caterina asked.

"Anyone who wants it. I keep it on hand and use it myself." She carried the bowl over to the fire and hung it on the hooked frame made for the task. The heat was intense, and soon it started to bubble. Covering her hand with a piece of thick linen, Bona lifted the bowl and carried it back to the table. "I'll let it cool for a few minutes. Want to help me find a jar to collect the tincture?"

Nodding her head excitedly, Caterina started wandering around the room, taking everything in more detail. "This one?" she held up a small vial.

"Close, but it needs a lid,' Bona replied.

Caterina kept looking, picking up bottles and putting them down. "This one?" She held up a bottle half the size of the wine bottle, with a lid held on tightly by a wire.

"Perfect. I can make more." Bona stopped and corrected herself. "I mean, WE can make more."

"I can help?" Caterina's voice rose hopefully.

"Of course. You need to learn this. It's crucial."

Containing her glee, Caterina nodded as solemnly as she could. "I understand."

"Good. Now let's go outside and get more carnations."

Bona included Caterina more and more when she walked the palace on her daily rounds. Their visits took them into every room, and Bona spoke to every person she encountered on her way. Caterina modelled her behaviour on her stepmother, ignoring the messengers arriving daily at court. When rumours of her husband's supposed unchristian behaviour began trickling into the palace, Caterina tried as much as possible to turn a blind eye, as Bona did, and focus on her work.

The summer had ended, and a crisp and welcome coolness settled over the city. Caterina was with Bona heading to the kitchen to discuss stores for the winter with the staff, an activity she'd grown used to, but sensed Bona's mood was more subdued than usual and wondered if there was some shortage of which she wasn't aware.

As they approached the kitchen, Bona suddenly turned into a smaller storage room set off the main food area. "There is no easy way to tell you this, so I'll be blunt. Girolamo has fathered a son on another."

In her shock, all Caterina could think to ask was, "Who?"

"I don't know. All I've heard is there is a child, a boy named Scipio."

Caterina took this in. She had a stepson like she was a stepdaughter to Bona. What was she meant to do with this information?

Bona interrupted her thoughts. "There's more."

Wondering what could be worse than this son, Caterina waited.

"In Rome, your husband is called the antipope."

Staggering back, Caterina raised her arm for balance. "What does that mean? Is he evil? Has he been possessed?"

"Not by the devil, no."

Caterina waited for an explanation, but none was forthcoming. All Bona added was, "He's made many enemies." She took a deep breath and closed her eyes. Opening them again, she looked directly at Caterina. "I thought you should know. You're married now and still have much to learn of husbands and wives."

"But I already…" she stopped, her face flushing red with shame.

Bona reached out and gathered Caterina into her arms, speaking into the young woman's head. "Not that. There is more to a marriage than the physical act of consummation."

Pulling herself away, Caterina looked up at Bona. "Like what?"

"That's what I hope to teach you these next couple of years. Now come, we have work to do. After the kitchen the cellars must be inspected."

Caterina nodded, reminding herself to act like her stepmother. She adopted a blank expression and followed Bona to the kitchen.

Turning the World to Stone

Another year passed, and Caterina was kept busy with her studies and riding. New hunting dogs had arrived as a gift for her father in the spring of 1475, and she'd fawned over them so much that the duke had relented and given them to her, pleased with her interest. She continued to grow inside and out, needing to have her books and clothes repeatedly replaced and renewed.

Over the past twelve months, Caterina had adopted a more regal bearing. She now towered over many of the women at court, her figure slim and her movements more practised. The awkwardness of adolescence still accompanied her wherever she went, but with Bona's help and guidance, Caterina was developing into an elegant, refined young woman.

Caterina threw herself into her plant studies and was pleased when Bona began including additional lessons in distilling. "Some things need to be broken down to their core before being built up again stronger."

Pulling Luisa into her studies with her, Caterina was less aware of the comings and goings at her father's court. One thing she couldn't fail to be affected by, however, was the sudden disappearance of her uncles.

The early frosts made sitting in the garden less and less comfortable, but still, when the sun was shining, Caterina dragged Luisa to the stone bench. Wrapped in heavy cloaks, the young woman looked out across the fields surrounding Milan, right up to the lush pine forests that led to the mountains. Breathing in the air, she smelled the thick peaty aroma of fallen leaves giving themselves back to the earth.

"My uncles are gone from court." Caterina broke the silence.

"I know."

"My father sent them away." This much Caterina had been able to learn for herself. What she didn't understand was why he'd done it.

"Yes," Luisa replied as non-committedly as she could. She knew her friend, however, and readied herself for the next question.

"Have you heard anyone speaking to his reasons why?" she asked as evenly as she could. The news that Duke Galeazzo had banished his brothers, Ludovico, known as 'the moor' because of his darker skin, and Ascanio, the youngest son, from Milan had upset her deeply. She'd loved both her uncles and could only remember their kindness when she was younger.

Luisa shifted on the bench, feeling the cold of the stone seeping through her dress and cloak. Shivering, she pulled the material around her shoulders. "I don't know much more than you, nothing definite. Just rumours." She knew how much her friend hated rumours. So far, the story of her entire married life had been told via speculations and allegations.

"Tell me. I want to hear."

"They say your father has become distrustful lately and suffers no hint of betrayal from anyone." This was as simple and as honest as Luisa could speak.

"Including his own family."

"It appears that way, yes." Luisa glanced toward the door leading back inside the palace and then at Caterina.

"And, as far as you know, my uncles did nothing to deserve such treatment?" Caterina had grown up on tales of brothers, fathers, and cousins fighting with each other over titles, land, or perceived insults.

"I don't know that, only that your father has become fearful of an attempt on his life and sees only enemies around him." She shivered.

Caterina was silent for a moment. Then, frowning, she asked, "Do you know where my uncles have gone?"

Luisa nodded. "Yes, both to France."

"So not so very far away. I wonder how my father feels about that."

"What's keeping your uncles from returning, do you think?" It was Luisa's turn to question. Her teeth chattered slightly as she said the last word.

Noticing her friend's discomfort, Caterina stood. "I'm sorry I kept us outside so long." She saw how low the sun now sat. "Let's go inside." They walked toward the door and the welcome heat of the kitchen. Caterina replied to Luisa's earlier question as they hurried forward. "My father is a very powerful man with ties across Italy. No one would dare oppose him."

Luisa frowned at the hollow response but said nothing.

"It must be very lonely," Caterina thought aloud, "feeling like you have no one. No one to trust, no one to protect you, no one with whom to share your thoughts and to help you when you need it."

"I suppose." As they reached the door, Luisa quickened her pace to get closer to the warmth. Rubbing her hands together, she waited for Caterina to join her. "Library?" she suggested.

Caterina shook her head. "No. I wish to visit the chapel and pray for my father. Maybe God will give him peace from his suspicions."

The peace Caterina sought for her father became increasingly needed by her stepmother as well. In the last weeks of 1476, Bona had begun having nightmares, horrifying dreams eliciting screams of terror that woke the whole palace.

"Are there no cures?" Caterina asked. She clumsily plumped up one of the pillows that propped Bona up in bed.

"I've tried everything, sweet girl. I just need to rest today. My sleep was disturbed last night, and it left my head aching, that's all. It's the weather, I'm sure." She tried to wave away Caterina's concern.

"Weather doesn't give you bad dreams," Caterina replied, a small desperate challenge in her tone. "Dreams are omens. And bad dreams are bad omens."

"Where did you hear that?"

Caterina shrugged as if this was common knowledge. As she was answering, Bona spoke the words along with her. "The maids..."

Embarrassed, Caterina looked down, but not before muttering, "Well, they did say that."

She put her finger under the young woman's chin and brought Caterina's face back up. "What else have the servants been saying?"

Wondering if she should try to get out of this conversation or just tell the truth, Caterina finally opted for honesty. "They say there are portents."

Bona snorted, despite the pain in her head. "What do you know of portents? Do you even know what the word means?"

Caterina sat taller. "I am fourteen," she said, annoyed by Bona's words.

"Fine. Tell me of these portents."

With a nod, Caterina continued. "They say that birds are falling out of the sky, and cows have stopped giving milk..."

"And frogs are dancing in the streets too I suppose?"

Her forehead wrinkling, it took the younger woman a moment to realise she was being made fun of. "No, no frogs. Maybe a lizard or two." She couldn't help smiling at how ridiculous her stepmother made these things sound.

"And you, yourself. Have you seen any birds lying in the street? Have any hit the ground suddenly at your feet as you walked outside in the courtyard?"

Caterina held up her hands. "I understand. You need not continue. I've learned my lesson."

"I'm glad to hear it. These stories are the result of exhaustion, from the plague and the weather and the harvest. Preparations for winter, all of it."

Seeing how tired Bona looked, Caterina stood. "That makes sense. I'm glad I have you to still guide me." Leaning over, she placed a kiss on her stepmother's forehead, like the woman used to do for her. "I'll leave you now. Send for me if you need anything."

With a nod, she was gone, leaving Bona to smile at witnessing a glimpse of the woman she knew Caterina would be.

Christmas that year involved the usual celebrations. However, the mood at court was less than joyful. With her uncles gone, there were fewer retainers to join the lavish banquets the duke insisted on hosting.

On Christmas day, the family gathered to share a few early gifts and enjoy a private meal. The main feast would be on Epiphany, with more extravagant gifts exchanged between the family.

"This is from me to my fierce daughter." Galeazzo held up a large object wrapped in linen cloth. Rising from her chair by the fire in the main hall, Caterina bowed at her father before reaching up and retrieving her gift. Shocked by the weight, she nearly dropped it but strengthened her grip and carried the package to the table. Loosening the silk ribbons and pulling apart the linen, she gasped. Inside were

Turning the World to Stone

pieces of armour, a breast and backplate, a smaller version meant for a young person, made from highly polished steel.

"It's beautiful," she breathed, not daring to tear her eyes from the metal in case she was dreaming. "For me?" Caterina turned and looked back at her father.

"Of course for you! You're becoming a true Sforza warrior, or so I've been told by your teachers." He winked at her, and, in that moment, everything else fell away: the tales and stories and distrust, the awful truths and confusing decisions, everything about her father that hurt Caterina, all gone. Then the noise poured in, and she was back in the room looking on as her younger sister shrieked at being given another present.

Watching as her father touched a lit taper to the sides and top of the log, Caterina thought of the year ahead. Soon the moment would arrive for her to leave her home and join her husband. She tried to cheer herself by thinking about the time she DID still have with her family, but it was no use. Not even the flames roaring in the fireplace could dispel the chill she felt down to her bones.

The storm started just after midnight, and the winds were howling through the palace corridors and into every room when Caterina rose the following day. A shivering maid had stoked Caterina's fire, but still, her bare flesh puckered at the chill in the air as she dressed. Thanking Luisa for the help, Caterina descended the stairs to the main hall to join her family in breaking their fast.

"It's too dangerous. Stay here, with us." Caterina heard Bona's reasoning voice as she stepped into the large room.

"A leader of men must show himself, especially on sacred days. No weather has ever stopped a Sforza and today will be no different." Galeazzo shoved a piece of cold boar into his mouth and swallowed it with a mouthful of watered-down wine.

"No one will even be at St Stephen's, not in this." Bona waved her arm at the tapestries, gently moving in the blasts of cold air that had found its way through mortar cracks and poorly placed windows.

"It's my sacred duty as ruler of Milan to honour the town's patron saint. I will hear no more about it." He stood, and everyone rose with him. "I'll see you after mass." With a sweep of his cloak, the duke left the room with his closest retainers.

Bona shook her head and finished her meal, urging the children to hurry and do the same. They were attending mass in the palace chapel, accessible through protected corridors so none would need to step outside into the gale. Bona's personal chaplain was waiting for them as they took their places, standing at the front as close to the altar as they were permitted.

The priest blessed them and began his work, selecting a particularly long sermon. Although he delivered his words with an inner fire, Caterina felt the castle's chill and the buzz of exhaustion in her ears. She and Luisa had stayed up late giggling together, and she was paying for it now. Her eyes drooped, and Caterina felt her head falling forward slowly. Instinctively jerking her head back upright, she wondered if anyone else had seen her but was too nervous to look around, knowing the glare she'd receive from Bona if she did.

The howling wind and the priest's thin, droning Latin made it difficult to concentrate, and all Caterina could think of was her bed. Ashamed of the thought, she redoubled her focus when the doors to the chapel flew open.

A man rushed in, soaked to the bone and barely recognisable.

Turning the World to Stone

"Cicco?" Bona turned away from the altar and faced the chapel doors. "Is that you?"

"Madonna," the man gasped.

"What is it? What's happened?" Noise from outside, shouting and crying, reached their ears. "For the love of God, tell me!" Bona screamed.

Looking up, blood smeared across his face by the lashing rain outside, the duke's most trusted advisor finally spoke.

"The duke is dead. Murdered."

Chapter Four
1477

Caterina stood in the palace courtyard watching the flurry of activity around her.

"My lady, all is ready." Luisa was waiting for her.

"I know." She watched the dust fly up from the dirt each time one of the horses pawed at the ground impatiently.

It had only been four months since the duke had been murdered, and things had moved quickly. Bona had been unwilling to entertain the idea that the pope might change his mind about her stepdaughter's union, especially now that her powerful father was gone. In the first days after her husband's death, Bona had not only confirmed Caterina's marriage contract but had planned the young woman's entire journey to her new home.

It had been a difficult time for the entire city. The duke had been killed by assassins likely hired by his own brothers, but this had been kept quiet to maintain the peace. Any hint of Sforza in-fighting was bound to bring out old hurts and insults between other nobles. Instead, Bona had spread a story about fanatics who had read too much history and had decided that a return to the glory of ancient Italy was needed.

After her father's death, Caterina knew it would only be a matter of time before her life changed forever, but those few months had passed too quickly! Now she was old enough to join her husband and fulfil the duke's contract with the Holy See.

"It's time, countess." One of the armed guards accompanying her on her journey interrupted her thoughts.

April had been mild so far, and the weather today was perfect. If only one of the sudden thunderstorms that struck Milan in the spring would hit, she thought. It would only delay the inevitable for a day or two at most. Sighing, she took a last look around and headed to her carriage.

Bona arrived in the courtyard and joined Caterina. "Your route is planned, I've seen to the details, written to everyone. All is prepared." Bona still wore the deep colours of mourning, and her dark veil made her look pale. But instead of appearing ill or fragile, it made her shine like marble. Despite her thin frame, there was a strength as hard as steel in her eyes, and her posture suggested she would brook no nonsense at the court she governed on behalf of her seven-year-old son, Caterina's stepbrother, Gian Galeazzo Sforza.

Caterina's siblings had gathered to see her off, both those the duke had legitimately fathered but also her brothers and sisters from her now-deceased birth mother. She hadn't gotten to know her mother, with whom the duke had had a longstanding affair, for she and her father's other illegitimate children were moved to the ducal court when Caterina was three. Initially educated there by her maternal grandmother, Caterina's care had been taken over by Bona when her grandmother died.

Carlo was two years her senior and acted the part. An earnest young man, he nevertheless hadn't taken to the art of diplomacy like his sister and had decided young to pursue a military career. Alessandro was two years younger than Caterina and was slowly emerging as a scholar. Her youngest sibling, Chiara, was hovering behind the carriage, a ragged ball clutched tightly in her ten-year-old hands.

"The sun is rising higher, Caterina," Bona reminded her. She was heartbroken at seeing her stepdaughter leave, the young woman she thought of as her own, but kept her face firm. She had brought this girl up, and Bona hoped she'd done enough to prepare Caterina for her life as wife to the Pope's nephew.

With a small nod, Caterina looked at each of her siblings, memorising their faces. She didn't know when she'd see them again or under what circumstances. Her new life was a blank page waiting to be filled, and her stomach lurched at the thought of entering that unknown without the support of her family. Thankfully Luisa would be with her. She grabbed her friend's hand, drawing strength from the other woman's reassuring return squeeze.

Knowing she was expected to speak, Caterina cleared her throat. "I may be leaving Milan, but I take a part of you all with me." She reached up and put her hand on her chest. "I will always carry my family and home here."

She saw tears rolling down Chiara's face, and it was the final push her own emotions needed to escape the wall she'd built to contain them. Rushing forward, she threw her arms around the girl and felt the ball Chiara had been holding drop to her feet. Trembling young arms encircled her waist. They cried together for a moment before Caterina felt other arms around them both. Alessandro had gripped her legs, and Bona's own façade had crumbled, and she, too, gathered them all in her arms.

After a moment, Bona stood tall again. "It's time for your sister to leave," she said gently.

Luisa had been standing a respectful distance away and, at a nod from Bona, walked forward and put her hand on Caterina's shoulder as a quiet reminder.

Untangling herself from the group, Caterina cleared her throat and stepped into her carriage with Luisa. Putting on a happy face, Caterina stuck her head out the window and waved at everyone as the long convoy of wagons and attendants started moving out of the courtyard and onto the main road outside. Maintaining the carefree attitude, she waved until the palace grew smaller and her arm grew too heavy to hold up any longer. Knowing her family could no longer see her clearly, Caterina finally let her tears fall in earnest.

They were an hour into the journey when the thunderstorm Caterina had wished for earlier struck. They were too far from Milan now to return without wasting the day, so forged on in the torrential downpour.

Thunder clapped so loudly it seemed to shake the carriage Caterina rode in with Luisa. They'd pulled the window curtains closed and sat in the gloom as the wooden vehicle continued. The initial sway of the carriage was replaced by fits and starts as the road grew muddy, and the horses stumbled and lost their footing on the well travelled road south. Both women grew used to the motion and started getting drowsy.

"Are you asleep?" Luisa's voice made Caterina jump.

"No, just letting my mind think what it wants. Do you need anything?"

"No. Do you?" Luisa replied.

"I don't. I'm just bored." Caterina peered outside through the curtain and then slid the material back into place as rain lashed the side of the carriage. "It's too dark in here to read. I wanted this weather earlier to delay my having to leave, but now wish it would stop."

In the gloom, Caterina saw Luisa nod. They remained silent for a while, each in their own thoughts, when suddenly Luisa spoke.

"Why isn't Girolamo here?" she blurted out.

Caterina's eyes widened in surprise as she thought of a reply. In as mature a voice as she could, she replied, "He's too busy, obviously."

"It's just I heard…" Luisa stopped.

"Heard what?"

"Rumours." She waved her hand.

"That's not helpful, rumours seldom are. My husband's absence is perfectly justified." Caterina snapped, "He's a powerful man with many enemies, he's too busy to make this journey." She leaned back on the covered bench and turned away from Luisa.

Knowing her mistress, Luisa relaxed into her seat and kept quiet. They travelled the remainder of the day in silence.

Three days after leaving Milan, Caterina was already homesick. Writing to her sister, she tried hard not to cry as she imagined what the younger girl was doing at that moment. She also wrote to Bona, careful not to betray her emotions, trying to be the woman Bona had taught her to be.

Her husband had still not joined her but had sent his own retainers to accompany Caterina. Added to her entourage, the line of one hundred and fifty men and women, along with dozens of horses and wagons, made a marvellous site for those watching by the side of the roads. Their route took them through the fields and forests of the Lombardy region, where many came out to wave. As befitted her status, the Archbishop of Cesena and his thirteen men, and the governor of Imola, where she was countess, and his group of twelve also marched alongside her intricately carved wooden wagon. Their flags and livery, the red and white with the Sforza serpent, the silver and black of Cesena, and the blue and red of Imola, could be seen for miles, and thus it was a surprise for them all when they arrived at the town of Reggio, and no one was there to greet them.

"I don't understand, countess." A tall, elegant man with ebony black hair stood at the window of Caterina's carriage. Gianni Luigi Bossi had joined her only the day before, sent by Bona to watch over her stepdaughter. A trusted advisor to the duchess, Bossi provided much-needed continuity for Caterina.

"Perhaps the town council forgot we stop here today?" Tired of sitting in the carriage all day, Luisa stuck her head out the window, straining to see what was ahead of them.

"Forget?" Gian shook his head. "Impossible. Bona sent messengers well in advance of our arrival. To all the towns and cities who'll be hosting us."

Caterina nodded unconsciously. Of course, Bona had planned everything down to a list of suggested items of clothing Caterina might wear at each arrival and at every feast. Glancing up at the sun's position, she remarked, "It's still early in the afternoon. Give them a few moments."

As she predicted, the gates were opened by red-faced, stammering men who bowed and grasped their hands as they led Caterina into the city.

The council and the citizens were so aghast at their mistake that they spent the rest of the day and night ingratiating themselves to Caterina. Flushed with embarrassment at the attention, Caterina strove to convince all she met that there was no offence taken; all was well. After eating more than she could remember at the dinner feast and dancing with so many nobles she had given up on trying to remember them all, Caterina retired to her rooms in the town chamberlain's house.

"Are you asleep?"

Caterina heard a voice whisper in the dark and turned over to where Luisa's bed was. "No, not yet."

"Me neither, even though I should be. I danced so much!"

"Shh, keep your voice down." Caterina was careful to keep her own tone low. "You'll wake up the chamberlain's family."

"Has he come home yet?"

Caterina giggled. "No, he was still kicking his legs higher and higher when I left the celebration. The wine we brought seemed to inspire him."

They talked more about the dancing and the clothing, the differences Caterina had already noticed in style and food the further south she travelled. "We should try to sleep now. We've got an early start tomorrow." She started to roll over in bed when Luisa's voice, more hesitant, reached her.

"Are you nervous?"

Caterina felt a twinge of panic in her stomach and did what she always did: force it down. "No, of course not. Remember, I travelled to Venice with my father when I was young."

"I didn't mean the travel," Luisa replied quietly.

She knew exactly what her friend had meant and why she needed more and more of her reserve to keep a calm façade whenever any brought up her husband. She WAS nervous. Very. But her father had taught her that fear was something to be conquered, like an enemy, not coddled and carried like an indulgent child. "I know. And I'm not nervous. My father would not be nervous in such a situation," she huffed and rolled over for good this time.

Turning the World to Stone

Caterina listened until she heard Luisa give up and get settled in her blankets. She doubted she'd done enough to convince her friend but at least it was enough to stop the uncomfortable questions. For now.

Caterina's journey went much the same way, with long stretches of the road travelled in all weather, then a stop in the next city on her route. Most of her belongings had been driven on ahead to her new home in Imola, but the chaos of organising enough of what she did have with her for each visit was exhausting. Fortunately, Luisa was on top of everything. Along with Bossi, she had everything from Caterina's outfits to her books and toiletries ready at each destination.

The days flew by in a whirlwind of balls and feasts, with each town and city trying to outdo the others. Word of her travels had spread throughout the northeast of Italy, and hundreds of people lined the roads she took, admiring her carriages and retinue. It filled Caterina's heart so much she could almost forget what was waiting for her at the end of her journey. Luisa wisely kept her queries about her friend's feelings to herself and enjoyed their time together.

In Bologna, only twenty miles north of Imola, Caterina stayed with the famed Bentivoglio family. Giovanni Bentivoglio was a great admirer and friend to her father, probably because his own history was as mired in scandal as Caterina's own family's was. But he was kind to her, treating her like a daughter. They enjoyed a few days together, feasting and dancing and walking around the fashionable areas of the city before it was time for Caterina to make her way to her new home.

On the first of May, she set out on the last leg of her long journey with the good wishes of her host, as well as another two carts filled with lavish cloth and jewels from the city.

As they settled in, Luisa finally addressed the topic they'd been avoiding for weeks.

"Are you ready?"

This time there could be no confusion over Luisa's meaning. Caterina shook her head. "No." Her eyes clouded as she remembered her wedding night four years ago.

Luisa saw Caterina's face fall slack and reached across the carriage to take her friend's hand. "I suspected."

Caterina closed her eyes and leaned her head back against the seat. "There's no point in it, worrying. It serves no purpose!"

"I heard your father's words," Luisa said quietly.

"What other words do I have? No one can offer me any others." Tears welled in her eyes, a combination of her fear and her anger at herself for letting her terror surface.

"Then listen to MY words." Luisa crossed the carriage and sat beside Caterina, still holding her hand. "I am here for you. I will always be here for you, and that will never change. And I will always do what I can to help you." She stopped, seeing that her words were making Caterina worse. "I'm sorry," she whispered.

Tears were now running down Caterina's face, but instead of letting her anger control her, she reached over suddenly and wrapped her arms around her friend. Luisa hugged her back, and they sat like that until Caterina sniffed and relaxed. Wiping the last few tears from her cheek and rubbing her eyes clear, Caterina nodded. "Thank you."

She was cut short by shouting from outside. The carriage suddenly stopped.

"What's happened? What's going on?" Caterina stuck her head out the window and stopped one of the guards.

"My lady, we're just outside Imola and have stopped as requested." He bowed at her and walked off.

"Wait! Requested by whom?"

"By Bona, of course." Luisa gathered her scattered belongings from the carriage and opened the door. She turned back to Caterina. "Your stepmother thought you might like to refresh yourself before entering your new city." Waving in the direction of a humble farmhouse, where an elderly couple stood expectantly, she smiled. "Your hosts are waiting."

Caterina laughed. "Bona thought of everything." It was an excellent idea, stopping to refresh. Her stepmother had understood the strength of illusion, the subtle power that came when entering a room with a carefully selected outfit, wearing jewels that revealed secrets if one knew the correct language, a significant nod or look at a particular person. All without a single word being spoken.

Caterina exited the carriage and immediately walked to the man and wife. Awed by her grand appearance, they bowed and curtsied, getting lower and lower as Caterina approached.

"Please, let me help you." Smiling kindly, she raised the round woman from her curtsy. Bossi had stepped forward and helped the farmer up.

"My lady, you show us great honour in visiting us. Our home is small but it has stood for centuries." He realised he was still wearing his cap and quickly snatched it from his head. "I am Nanni and this is my wife, Maria."

Hearing the pride in the farmer's voice, Caterina took his hand. "It's I who am honoured. I know what an inconvenience all this is for you both," she nodded at Maria, waving her hand at the commotion in the small clearing in front of the main house. Behind the old stone house, Caterina saw a field with rows of green. An ancient barn stood in the distance, a witness to the passing generations of the Romagna family who had lived and toiled here.

It took a while, but Caterina finally stopped the couple's bowing. When she did, she found them both charming and funny, a much-needed lift after her travels that day. As much as she wished she could stay longer with these people who were now her neighbours, and for whom she was now responsible, Caterina knew people were waiting for her in the city.

After disappearing into a room that had been put aside for her use to wash and change, Caterina sat for nearly an hour with them. Sharing a glass of wine and some of the bread Maria had made for her visit, Caterina could finally no longer ignore Bossi's impatient looks, no matter how hard he tried to hide it.

"I've had a lovely time with you both, but I'm afraid I must leave now. I am expected at the city gates." She stood and held out her hand to Maria. "Your home is beautiful, and I promise I will visit you again."

The farmer's wife turned bright red with the praise and started to curtsey once more. Caterina stopped her and, with a nod at Nanni, returned to her carriage.

The short interlude had allowed Caterina a moment of calm before she needed to freshen herself and change into an outfit that Bona had selected. She grabbed Luisa's hand and held on tight without speaking until they arrived at Imola's city gates.

They had only been a few miles from the city, but it was enough time for Caterina's stomach to clench. Luisa gauged her friend's shifting mood by how tightly her hand was gripped and by Caterina's changing face. When the carriage jolted to a stop, Luisa shook Caterina's hand.

Caterina looked at Luisa and, with a barely perceptible nod, released herself and stood. "I'm home."

Turning the World to Stone

The sun came out from behind the clouds, and Caterina reflexively shielded her eyes from the sudden glare. Then, cursing herself, she lowered her arm, smiled, and stepped toward a tall man wearing an enormous gold chain.

The man rushed to meet her, leaving behind a woman Caterina assumed was his wife. He removed his hat as he reached her and, grasping it in his hand, bowed low. "My lady, welcome to Imola." He stood again and replaced his hat. "I am Domenico Ricci, Governor of the city and this," he turned to the waiting woman and motioned her forward, "is my wife, your husband's sister Violante."

The governor's wife was shorter than her husband but had a presence that commanded a room. Secure in her position as the Pope's niece and sister to one of the most powerful men in the country, her face had taken on a permanent look of superiority. While she was smaller than the governor, Violante stood a few inches taller than Caterina, forcing the younger woman to look up at her.

"It's a pleasure to meet you." Caterina bowed her head and waited for a response. The governor hastily stepped in when his wife showed no signs of speaking.

"The governess is at your disposal and will help you with anything you need while you get used to your new home."

"The help is much appreciated, I'm certain I'll have many questions for your wife." She looked back at Violante, waiting for a response.

After a few seconds, the woman curtsied stiffly as if unused to the motion. "It's my pleasure to see that my brother's wife is settled to her satisfaction." Rising again, she stood looking over Caterina's head.

"Well, I won't be here for very long anyway, so you won't have many responsibilities where I am concerned." Caterina's words were clipped, her sudden dislike of this woman growing. "I'll be leaving to join my husband, the count," she looked directly at Violante, "in Rome."

The older woman smiled, then hid her mouth under her hand. "Oh, did you not hear? Girolamo sent word from Rome. He says you are to remain here until he calls for you."

Caterina couldn't keep her shock to herself. "Why? What reason did he give?"

Waving a hand, Violante frowned. "I think he said the air in Rome is too dangerous at the moment, and he wouldn't want his new bride to fall ill."

Unsure how to react, Caterina was grateful when Luisa suddenly stood beside her. Drawing strength from her friend, Caterina smiled graciously. "Thank you for relaying this message to me. I'm certain that, no matter how long my wait here, I'll find many activities to distract me while I await my husband's word." Ignoring the flare of anger she saw glow briefly in the governess' eyes, she turned to Domenico. "Shall we go inside? I wish to see the city."

With a relieved nod, the governor offered his arm and led Caterina past the guards lined nearby and through the large wooden gates to Imola.

As soon as they entered the doorway, the crowds who'd been waiting patiently inside burst out cheering. The noise was deafening, but Caterina resisted the urge to cover her ears with her hands. Instead, she smiled widely and waved at everyone who lined the main street leading to the city square. Looking around, Caterina saw both Sforza and Riario banners hung from homes and across small side streets.

After walking slowly on the governor's arm for a few minutes, her path was blocked by the sudden appearance of a small boy dressed in angel wings and a white robe. Caterina stopped, charmed by the sight as the onlookers quietened. Before she could say anything to the child, he bowed low and began speaking as soon as he'd risen.

"Like famed Europa, Queen of Crete, beauty and grace in one so sweet, beloved of the gods above, we welcome you with all our love." After taking a deep breath, the boy bowed again and hurried into the crowd before Caterina could even ask his name. She supposed someone could tell her afterwards. Looking back at Luisa, Caterina raised an eyebrow, wondering if her friend had noticed the particular woman lauded in the child's verse. Seeing Luisa curl her lip to keep from laughing, Caterina knew she had. In Caterina's copy of Famous Women, Boccaccio had told the story of Europa but had injected his opinion that women shouldn't be allowed too much freedom into his narrative.

With a barely concealed roll of her eyes, Caterina continued down the crowd-filled road. Soon after the first, a second cherub stepped forward, delivering another poem. This time Caterina was compared to Penelope, the wife of Ulysses, kind and wise, who was forced by the gods through no fault of her own to wait twenty years for her husband to return from fighting in Troy. Was there an intended message, or was she just being silly? Shrugging off her doubts, she continued.

Caterina found it more and more challenging to keep her smile in place as another cherub likened her to Cleopatra, whom Boccaccio believed had nothing to recommend her except her ancestry. A fourth called her Deianira, the wife of Hercules. The obviously undisguised praise of Girolamo aside, Caterina wondered if those who organised this reception knew that, in the story, Deianira falls victim to the trickery of another. She'd have much to discuss with Luisa when this day was over.

Finally, they arrived at the main city square and stopped in front of a large stone building in obvious need of repair.

"Citizens of Imola, it is my great pleasure and honour, as governor of this fine city, to present our countess with the keys to the city." Another man, dressed in the sombre clothes of a councilman, handed the governor a blue velvet cushion upon which sat a giant iron ring with three large metal keys. Blue silk tassels hung from the ring, their soft frays spreading over the heavy material.

Caterina bowed her head at the man as she took the pillow, surprised by the weight. "Thank you, Don Ricci." She turned to the crowd who stood waiting, farmers and merchants and nobles alike. "And thank you all for being here to celebrate my arrival. I promise you I, alongside my husband Count Riario, will be a fair ruler, thoughtful and kind."

As soon as the last of her words left her lips, the crowd erupted in cheers once more. Looking around, Caterina saw that Bossi had manoeuvred himself to her side. She put the pillow and keys into his waiting hands so she could wave at the city.

Her arms had begun to ache from holding them high when the governor leaned down. "My lady, you've travelled far and must be exhausted. Perhaps we should retire to my home where you can feast with us and meet with some of the more important nobles of the city. We're not as big as Milan, but our cooks are the envy of Italy." The look of pride on the man's face made Caterina smile. With a final wave and nod at the crowd, she once more took the man's arm and allowed herself to be led to a large home off the main square.

The cooler air inside the governor's house was a welcome relief from the glaring May sunshine. Inside the entrance, Caterina ensured Luisa had the help she needed to find their rooms in the building before taking a deep breath and nodding at the governor. She was ushered so quickly to a large hall she barely had a chance to peep into the rooms they passed. From what Caterina could see, however, the governor and his wife lived well. Admiring an ornately carved bench as she passed down the corridor, her attention was pulled back to Domenico and Violante as they arrived in the hall.

"Good people, our new countess is here." He stepped aside to allow Caterina into the room. Before her were three long tables arranged in a U shape, all crowded with men and women staring curiously at her. Unsure of whether she was expected to speak, Caterina looked at Bossi with a raised eyebrow. Fortunately, the governor chose that moment to point at a large chair in the middle of the head table. "Your place awaits, my lady."

With a gracious nod at her host, Caterina walked to her place and waited as a few others joined her before sitting. As if on cue, musicians began to play, and servants entered from multiple hidden doors carrying trays of food and drink. Caterina smiled and nodded at everyone who approached her to introduce themselves, trying desperately to find a way to remember all their names and positions in the city. And not just officials either. The more successful merchants of the town had been invited, and all offered her their services.

As the evening progressed and the voices rose with the amount of wine consumed, the governor's wife seemed to take it as a personal challenge to have her voice be heard above the rest. Caterina ignored her, speaking politely to Domenico about the city and its people, when suddenly Violante pushed her chair back and rose. Her first step was unsteady, but she continued confidently until she stood behind Caterina.

"So, you are the woman my brother married. I didn't get a good look at you earlier. Why don't you stand?" she suggested, pulling at Caterina's hand. Once again unsure of the protocol, Caterina rose, glancing around the room for Bossi. Violante leaned her head this way and that, scrutinising the young woman's every feature. "Girolamo did the honourable thing when he married you. His true desire was Imola." She looked around for her wine cup. "And, of course, your dowry."

Shocked beyond words, Caterina stood there, her mouth hanging open. Then, remembering herself, she stood as erect as she could and, ignoring Violante, turned to Domenico. "The governess is tired, as am I. Perhaps one of your men could show me to my room?"

The man's face coloured the shade of the southern Italian wine he favoured, and he sputtered a few words before Gian Bossi joined them. Stepping in front of the governess, he nodded his head at Domenico. "I will take the countess; I know the way and have my own men to accompany us."

Caterina knew there was no point waiting for a reply and curtsied quickly. "Thank you for a wonderful evening and your warm welcome to my new home." With a glance at Violante, she turned and left the room, with Bossi following close behind.

Chapter Five
1477

"Who does she think she is?" Caterina held up her arms so Luisa could remove her dress sleeves then waved them angrily as she spoke.

"I don't know. I wasn't there. Tell me what she said again?" Luisa frowned as she picked at a tie at the back of Caterina's gown.

Caterina relayed the last few things Violante Ricci had said. "But it's not just what she said to me, it's how she said them. Like she's better than me."

Luisa got the last tie undone and stepped back so Caterina could wiggle out of the gown. "Well, she is your husband's sister, and I suppose when her uncle became Pope it went to her head."

"Her head and her hands and feet and legs and entire body," Caterina hmphed. "Thank goodness we're only staying here for one night."

"This is a beautiful building." Luisa smiled slyly. "But I can't wait to see your new palace, my lady." She curtsied while trying not to laugh.

"You may think you're clever but there will be times when you need to address me as such." Caterina looked around. "It's not the surroundings, it's one occupant in particular."

Turning the World to Stone

"Try not to think about it. It's late and we should both be in bed. You'll feel better in the morning. And tomorrow we can explore the town AND the palace."

Caterina smiled at Luisa's enthusiasm. Her friend hadn't been at the dinner and hadn't heard the conversation. It was only natural she'd be excited about their new adventure. If only Caterina herself could summon the strength to be that keen. Luisa was right, though. Sleep would do wonders for her disposition and chase away the feeling of inadequacy that had descended on her. She hoped.

While her surroundings and bedding were comfortable, Caterina still slept poorly and rose early, startling the young maid who had helped the day before as she entered the room with a jug of water.

"I'm sorry, my lady, I didn't mean to wake you," she stammered, flushing deep red.

"You didn't." Caterina waved her hand at the room, and the maid crept in quickly. Depositing the jug next to a washbasin, she bobbed and turned to leave. "Is anyone else awake? The governor?"

"No, my lady. You are the first." With another bob, she made it to the door before turning back. "Would you like me to bring you something to eat? The bread will be ready soon, and there is meat from last night's meal."

"Thank you, but I'll wait and dine with the governor and his wife."

By now, Luisa had woken and joined Caterina from the adjoining room. Moving her dark hair from her eyes, she stood in her shift and watched the maid leave. "Why are you up? It's barely sunrise."

Pale sunlight had begun filtering into the room, giving them a better view of their surroundings than the candles had last night. It was an enormous space, with frescoes of saints on every wall and woven silk rugs on the floor. Three windows faced onto the main square, where the sounds of merchants setting up their stalls filtered in.

"I couldn't sleep." She shrugged, wandering over to a window. Below, an olive merchant was unloading jars of oil from a wagon with the help of what she assumed was his son.

"Are you still upset by last night?"

Caterina shrugged again and continued staring out over the square. More men and a few women were arriving, some with carts and some carrying bags and pouches. She watched as food, fabrics, household and leather goods, and more were assembled for all to purchase.

"You needn't worry about her, you'll be under your own roof today."

She turned from the window and sat on the bed. "I wonder why they didn't just take me there yesterday?"

Now it was Luisa's turn to shrug. "It was late, and the celebration ended awkwardly. Perhaps they thought it best for you to see the city anew in the morning."

Caterina shook her head, both in acknowledgement of what her friend had just said but also to rid herself of the dolour she had woken with. Having seen the little she did of the governor's home, she excitedly wondered how lavish her own would be. Bona had warned her to always be realistic with her expectations, having been brought up in one of the grandest palaces in Italy. Other places were not Milan, her father had added with a sniff.

She heard shouting from outside and smiled. It was small compared to Milan, but Caterina had already fallen for the charm of the square and the friendly faces of the men and women below. Unsure of how long she'd be here before her husband joined her to take her to Rome, she decided to step into her new role and adopt the place and people as her own.

Standing, she took Luisa's hand and led her to a large wooden chest. Opening the lid, she grinned. "What shall I wear today?"

Caterina was relieved that her sister-in-law wasn't breaking her fast with them.

"I'm afraid the governess is feeling unwell. She's decided to stay in her chamber to eat and rest." Domenico's eyes flicked from Caterina to the stairs and back again. "Come, join me." He led her to a smaller, more private room where a table stood laden with jugs of wine and water, as well as platters of fruit, still-steaming bread, cheese, and cured meat.

"I trust you slept well." The governor loaded his plate with bread and took slices of three different cheeses.

"I did, thank you." Caterina thought of Luisa and the look she'd be giving her right now. There was no point in telling him the truth, though. She remembered more of Bona's words: always be gracious.

"Good, good. When we finish eating there are a number of things planned for you and your retainers."

Caterina took a sip of water to wash down a piece of prosciutto. "What I'd really like to do is see my home. I want to ensure all is set up for the count, you see." She lowered her head demurely but kept her eyes on Domenico.

Charmed by her wifely sentiment, the governor smiled widely and nodded. "Of course! How foolish of me." Put at ease by Caterina's candour, Don Ricci relaxed. "I think you'll find everything is prepared and ready." He winked at her. "And glorious enough to compare with the grandest houses in Rome."

Turning the World to Stone

Biting her lip to keep in her laughter at the man's familiarity, Caterina nodded and sipped her water. "I'm certain you've done a fine job and I am anxious to see for myself." She wiped her hands on her napkin, signalling her desire to start her day.

"I'll have a horse prepared for you, my lady." Domenico rose from the table, his bulk causing the platters and glasses to shake.

"There is no need," Caterina rose just as quickly but more elegantly. "If I'm to know my new home, I must see it from the street. I will walk."

"But my lady, it's not proper." The governor's voice rose to a whine.

"I've got my soldiers and Don Bossi will be with me the entire time." She waved a hand airily, batting away any further objections. She was her father's daughter and would not hide from her subjects.

Within an hour, she and Luisa were standing side-by-side in the main square as traders and shoppers surrounded them. Bossi ensured his charge was protected by enough men to see to her safety but not enough for anyone to mistake it as a show of force. By the time they had gathered for the short walk to her palace, Violante had emerged from her chamber. With a disdainful frown at being forced to attend Caterina, she joined her husband, and the group set off.

More Imolese citizens had joined the throng, and word had spread that their new mistress was walking to her home. While they wouldn't be allowed inside the palace, the thrill of seeing such celebrity strolling among them was enough for most to form an immediate attachment to their countess.

"Luisa, look there." Caterina pointed at a wooden stall filled with jars and containers. Without thinking, she grabbed her friend's hand and led her to the table. The vendor, an unassuming man with dark curly hair and a generously wide mouth that hinted at a sense of humour, swept his cap from his head and bowed deeply as the countess approached.

"Madonna, you do me a great honour." He bowed again.

"What are you selling?" She pointed at the bottles.

"Ah, a little bit of everything, my lady. Perfumes, unguents to keep the skin smooth, treatments for various ailments."

"And your name?"

He bowed a third time. "I am Dante Dellucci. I own a small apothecary shop a few streets away. I bring a few of my more popular items on market days to sell in the square." He gestured at the contents on his table.

"May I?" Caterina looked questioningly at the man.

"Of course, my lady."

Caterina's eye was drawn to a small clay pot with a plain lid. Opening it, she lifted the jar to her nose and inhaled deeply. "I smell, oh," she held the vessel away, "wormwood." Drawing it near again, she took another cautious sniff. "And althaea."

The apothecary clapped. "Madonna, you know your medicine!"

"My stepmother trained me." She sniffed again and frowned. "What does this mix treat?"

The man lowered his head, embarrassed. "It is to ease childbirth, my lady," he whispered.

The one word brought back everything Caterina had managed to push out of her head. She put the jar down abruptly, aware of the crowd that had gathered around them. "I'm sorry, I must go."

"Madonna, wait." Dante reached into an old leather satchel on the ground near his feet. "A gift. A perfume with exotic ingredients from the east. I've made you uncomfortable, take it, please, to make up for my rudeness."

Reaching for the man's outstretched arm, she took the small glass bottle and removed the lid. The smell of flowers and spices rose to meet her, the scent reminding her of the stories she'd loved in her father's library.

"Thank you, Signor Dellucci, I'll treasure it. And I promise to visit your shop when I have more time, I'm certain we'll have much to discuss."

With a gracious smile, Caterina moved away and along the road to her home. Her facade could not convince Luisa, who had been watching the exchange and saw the effect the man's words had had on her friend.

"I'm here." She grabbed Caterina's arm and gave it a squeeze. "Always."

Caterina and her retinue continued down a main road until they arrived at another square, this one private and surrounded by a large wall. She could see the top of the palace towering over the humbler homes they passed by, and glimpses of the massive stone structure peeked through gaps between the houses.

Caterina's father had refurbished the palace when he'd acquired Imola, and she could see similarities with her ducal home in Milan. The duke had removed the square towers, replacing them with round ones that better withstood attacks, and had fortified both the inner and outer walls. There was no safer place in all of Romagna.

The drawbridge had been lowered in anticipation of Caterina's arrival, and she followed the governor as he walked over the dry moat and into the palace. Despite the early hour, it had grown warm, and the cooler air inside was a relief. Once her eyes had adjusted to being out of the sun,

Caterina gasped in pleasure and heard Luisa do the same. The spectacle before them in the entry hall could rival any palace in Europe. Caterina took in the finely woven tapestries and hangings embroidered in silk and gold thread that hung from every wall.

More of her retainers made their way inside, and as each one entered, their utterings of astonishment echoed around the room. Even Bossi, more interested in the fortifications and protection of his mistress, had stopped to admire a large piece of furniture at the far end of the hall.

"It's beautiful, isn't it?"

He jolted at her sudden appearance beside him. "It is." He looked around the room. "All of it." Turning again to the heavy wooden cupboard, he pointed. "But this? Even Milan could produce no better."

"Shh, don't let anyone hear you say that. It may get back to Bona."

Bossi smiled and pointed at the silver goblets, bowls, platters, and jugs. "I hear the Pope gave these to your husband specifically for this palace."

Caterina inspected the contents. The pieces were all exquisitely engraved, some with floral patterns and vines with small animals peering out from behind leaves or geometric lines and crosses. Nothing in the credenza was without ornamentation. "The Holy Father is very generous indeed," she agreed.

"And my brother is his favourite nephew." Violante had joined them, a sour look on her face. "Judging by the looks of your servants, they've seen nothing quite like it in Milan." She pronounced the city name with a sneer.

Ignoring the comment, Caterina smiled politely and raised her voice. "Governess, I'm relieved you were feeling well enough to join us."

Wincing, the older woman replied. "Must you shout, girl."

Further incensed, Caterina only smiled more widely. "It's so loud in here, I wanted to ensure you heard me." With a sly look at Bossi, she added, "It would please me very much if you were to show me around the palace." If this woman were to be a part of her life, Caterina thought, she may as well make some use of her, overindulgence or not.

"But Signora..."

"You mean countess, surely?"

"My lady, wouldn't it be more appropriate for someone else..."

"Nonsense. I'm sure you know your way around. Shall we?" Caterina strode toward the nearest door. She turned and looked expectantly at the governess, adopting a stern face, when she saw Luisa covering her mouth to hide her laughter.

With a sigh and a hard look at Domenico, Violante hurried forward to join Caterina.

"You should be more careful."

Caterina flopped down on her new bed, sinking into the down mattress. She breathed in deeply, smelling the fresh plaster, new linen sheets, and paint still lingering in the air. This room was one of a dozen that made up her part of the palace, the most private place in Imola. The walls and ceiling were high and covered with gold brocade on white silk, making the room lighter and almost ethereal. A few of her belongings had been added to those that already furnished the room, creating a mix of luxury and comfort. These included her beloved books. Caterina had insisted these be unpacked first, along with her clothing. They provided a welcome sense of continuity for the young woman.

"Of what? Offending my new sister? She'd already formed an opinion about me before she even met me." She rose from the bed and, dressed only in her shift, walked to a set of chairs placed before a fireplace. Sitting, she brought her feet up underneath herself and wrapped a silk shawl around her bare shoulders. Someone had placed wine and goblets on a nearby table, and Luisa poured them both drinks before joining her friend.

"You could make an effort to change her mind?" Luisa offered weakly.

Caterina sighed, knowing the other woman was right. "I suppose. I'll try, but I won't be here very long." The last words of her sentence nearly stuck in her throat.

"Will the count be here soon?"

"I've had no word. Violante assures me he wishes to be here to escort me to Rome, but he's much too busy with papal matters." She sipped her wine and looked around the room again. How would it feel to have a man in here? Not just any man, but her husband. The thought surprised her. In her efforts to ingratiate herself with her new people, she'd almost forgotten she was one half of a pair.

"Do you think your husband has changed since last you saw him?" Luisa had kept her questions to herself as long as there was reason to. Now, however, the truth of Caterina's life was right before them both.

"I'm different, I imagine he would be too."

Luisa heard a note of hope in Caterina's voice. "Perhaps he's ready to settle down and rule, to give up his," she struggled for the correct word, "ways."

The meaning was unspoken, for both had heard the continued rumours of Girolamo's behaviour: his lax control of the papal army, his reported scheming against the families of Rome and the perceived enemies of the Riarios, and his often unchristian behaviour toward others.

"Perhaps." Caterina yawned, the day weighing on her suddenly.

"It's late. And I don't think we've even seen half of the palace yet, nor met even a small portion of the servants." She rose and held out her hand.

With a grateful nod, Caterina uncurled herself and rose. The bed did look inviting, and the room so gloriously peaceful, even in the night-time gloom. Breathing in the smell of the beeswax candles, she stretched her arms and shook her head.

As she curled up in the soft covers, she heard a whispered goodnight from Luisa. After murmuring a reply, she was asleep before any further thoughts or worries could enter her head.

For the next week, Caterina waited for news of either Girolamo's arrival or an invitation to join him in Rome. To pass the time, she explored the palace and visited the market in the Piazza Matteotti, the square made up on one side by the governor's home and the town hall. After her first two days in Imola, Caterina decided to downplay the wealth displayed by her clothing. While her outfits may have impressed the more notable citizens of the town, to the less well off, it would be an affront. And as she wandered around the town with Bossi and Luisa in tow, she began to notice the poor and the sick, carefully hidden when possible from her view by the governor. She also saw cracks in buildings and crumbling sides of homes, so different from her palatial residence. Shielded her entire life from such things, the realisation of just how privileged her upbringing had been came as a not unwelcome shock, for often these insights come with stark understanding.

"I must speak to my husband about conditions in the city. Surely more can be done to help people." By now, she had gotten used to saying the word 'husband' out loud, and it no longer stuck in her throat.

"It will depend on much, Madonna," Bossi explained gently. "Taxes and grants from the Holy See, the agreement of the nobles. You won't be involved in any of that, the count will have men to advise him."

Caterina turned from admiring a simply woven hairnet at a vendor's table to face him. "What do you mean I won't be involved? Of course I will. I'm the countess," she stated matter-of-factly.

"And you will have your own duties to perform, should the count be agreeable."

"Why wouldn't he agree to suggestions from his wife? I'm his partner, we'll rule together as equals." There was no doubt in her mind about this. Despite her husband's reputation, she believed that, once they were together, he would realise she was worth more than her dowry and see her as a partner.

"Yes, my lady." Bossi shook his head sadly, not wishing to ruin the young woman's expectations. Perhaps she was correct, and Girolamo would see his wife's value. Perhaps.

By the end of her first week in Imola, Caterina had seen most every nook and cranny of the city and the house. The governor had insisted his wife stay at the palace to help Caterina. The young woman wondered if this was truly to benefit her or if the governor was relishing the peace her absence at home afforded him.

After enjoying a rugged ride on her horse in the forests just south of the city, Caterina entered her chamber, pulling her hair net from her head and shaking out her long locks.

"Oh, it's you." A voice surprised Caterina, and she cleared the hair from her eyes. The parted locks revealed Violante.

The shock of seeing this woman in her room left her momentarily speechless. Her eyes narrowed, and she finally found her words and delivered them evenly. "What are you doing here, sister?"

"I, um," her words came quickly, "I was looking for something."

"Looking for what? What is so important that you couldn't wait for my return?"

Violante suddenly smiled. It reminded Caterina of the faces of the small lizards who scurried among the rocks near the Milanese palace. "A book. I left a letter in it and can't find it."

Now over her disbelief at the woman's intrusion, Caterina continued into the room, throwing her gloves and hair net onto a chair. "There are only my books in my room, governess." Caterina had never seen Violante with any book or letter and wondered if she could read.

"My mistake. I'll leave you." She headed to the door as Luisa entered, shaking her own hair free from its restraint.

"Sister? A question before you go. This letter you seek, is it from Girolamo? Will he be here soon?"

Violante's face flushed with irritation as she turned back in the doorway. "No, it's not. And no, he won't be here soon. You married a very important man with responsibilities to his uncle."

Caterina waved her hand, dismissing the governess. "Thank you, I'll see you later in the hall to dine."

Violante hurried from the room without replying, her quick footsteps echoing down the stone floor.

"What was she doing here?" Luisa asked. She went to one of Caterina's dress boxes and searched for something for her friend to change into from her riding outfit.

"She said she was looking for a book."

"Do you believe her?"

Caterina shook her head. "I don't believe anything she says. Except for the fact that Girolamo may not appear for some time."

Luisa found a simple but elegant green overdress and a set of darker green sleeves. "We'll just have to be patient and wait for word."

Caterina allowed Luisa to help her out of her riding gown. "No, there's another option." She lifted her arms and stepped out of her dress before turning to Luisa. "I don't care what anyone says, I can't stay here another day. Tomorrow, we're leaving for Rome."

Chapter Six
1477

The journey took twelve days, most of which Caterina spent complaining about Violante to Luisa. Luisa listened without comment, suspecting her friend's frustration helped Caterina justify her hasty decision. Gian Bossi had tried for hours to dissuade the countess, to no avail. Once he saw that she was determined, he gave up and arranged her travel as best he could, and had one of his men ride ahead to Girolamo in Rome, advising the count of his wife's decision.

"You can't take all your belongings," he tried. "There's no time to arrange to transport everything to Rome on such short notice." He had hoped the idea of leaving behind most of her belongings would persuade Caterina to at least wait a while longer.

"The count will see to my needs." She was sure of this, one of the only things she was certain of. It was a husband's fundamental duty to provide for his wife and see to her comfort.

So Bossi had surrendered and had kept any further concerns to himself as they travelled the old Roman roads to the Papal city. He even hid a smile at the exchange he'd witnessed between the governess and his mistress in the open courtyard.

"I will take as many men as needed to travel with me, and any supplies."

Violante had stood her ground, her arms crossed over her chest. "If you leave, you'll take your own people. Imola needs her men to protect it and I'll not risk any of them on such a foolish venture."

"Are you calling me a fool?" Caterina had countered.

"Of course not," she'd stammered, "it's this sudden uproar you've caused." She had waved a hand at the wagons and servants exiting the palace carrying boxes and crates.

Caterina had had enough. "I am the Countess of Imola and my wishes will be honoured or else the count will hear of it."

Bossi hadn't stepped in. He'd stood by, along with the men Caterina had brought with her from Milan, waiting to see what the governess would do. To his satisfaction, Violante had seemed to grow smaller. "Of course, countess," she'd said the words through a clenched jaw, "I will see that you have all you need." With an abrupt turn, she'd stormed back into the palace.

The next day Caterina's Milanese guards smiled at Caterina as she walked by and bowed respectfully.

"They've heard of your fight with the governess," Bossi whispered as they passed another bowing soldier. "Many of them have quietly voiced their dislike for your husband's sister."

Caterina giggled and put her hand to her mouth to hide her pleasure. She already felt freer; these men were loyal to Milan and now, loyal to her.

After the fifth day of travel Caterina found she had relaxed enough to enjoy the voyage, and the vast countryside of Italy through which they travelled. Bossi rode ahead each day and arranged lodging where he could, at towns small and large. As they rode along the coast south through Umbria toward the north of Rome, Caterina was charmed by the differences she observed in clothing, customs, and accents. The weather was accommodating, but at times when they rode through the middle of dense forests, she could almost believe it was autumn and was grateful Luisa had thrown spare wraps in the carriage.

When it rained, they covered the windows to keep dry, talking and playing word games to stop themselves from getting bored. But when the sun was out, Caterina looked at everything and everyone, taking in all the details she could.

Finally, on the twenty-fourth of May, she and her reduced retinue reached Castel Novo, an afternoon's ride outside of Rome.

"We'll stay here tonight," Bossi announced.

Caterina looked up and saw the setting sun. It would be too dangerous to risk travelling at night, so she reluctantly agreed.

"It will give us time to prepare your outfit, like we did outside Imola." Luisa peered into a wagon, looking for a specific wooden storage box she knew contained Caterina's more luxurious overdresses and gowns.

Caterina nodded. She had been delighted with Imola, but this was Rome, known around the world for its vast wealth and limitless power. She must look like she belonged. "Let's find some food. The castellan is waiting for us."

After they'd eaten a meal of pheasant and pastries and washed it down with spiced wine, they retired to the rooms set aside for their use. Caterina was bewildered to see that, even though so close to Rome, the castle was not as well built or decorated as her new home in Imola, nor the ducal palace in Milan. She had expected buildings to get larger and more elaborate the closer she got to the holy city. Maybe once they'd entered the city itself, she thought, pushing her surprise aside to focus on what to wear the next day.

"The blue damask, I think. With the red brocade sleeves."

"Perfect. I'll get everything ready while you do your hair."

"Let one of the maids do it, just let them know what I want. There's no need for you to always be fussing. You're my friend, not my servant." Caterina pointed to a chair that sat by the bed. She was already in her sleeping chemise and only needed to run a comb through her hair before pinning it up and settling down.

Luisa sat and watched as Caterina ran the wide wooden comb through her long blonde locks. She reached over to take the comb but was rewarded with a slapped hand and a grin from her friend.

"When we arrive in Rome tomorrow, I want you close."

"I will be." Luisa bit her lower lip, considering her words. "How are you feeling?"

"I'm excited. I'm finally starting my life. And Bona prepared me well, you know that. Both of us are ready."

"And Girolamo?"

"He is my husband and I will obey and serve him, as any wife should. I'm certain when we get to know each other better, we'll find much in common and many causes we can work together on." She said the words firmly, convincing herself with each syllable that they could be true.

"And you will meet your uncle."

Caterina crossed herself and nodded solemnly. "My union with Girolamo will be officially blessed by the Holy Father," she whispered in reply.

"It will be a fine ceremony I'm certain." Luisa reached over and squeezed Caterina's hand.

Gripping it back, Caterina smiled gratefully. Her look changed to one of mischief. "And who knows, perhaps we'll find you a handsome count of your own in the great city."

The mood lightened. Luisa bid her friend goodnight, her hopes lifted and anticipation growing for their day tomorrow.

Castel Novo was a flurry of activity the next morning as Caterina prepared for her entry into Rome. Her clothes chosen, she took her time selecting her jewels, ensuring she completed her ensemble with the finest Milan had to offer.

"How do I look?" Caterina turned in front of Luisa.

"Perfect. There isn't anything I would change."

"Well of course not. You helped me assemble everything." She turned and admired herself in the half-length travelling mirror she'd brought with her. Her blonde hair was held back tightly in a new sapphire studded hair net pinned to the back of her head, leaving her long curls to cascade down the back of her deep blue gown. She had applied a small amount of vermillion to her lips to make their natural rosy colour stand out against her pale skin. Smiling at herself, she turned to the right and left, admiring how her bust and hips had begun to fill out. Feeling like a true woman, Caterina adjusted her dress to make her developing cleavage more noticeable. Then, frowning, she pulled the neckline up again, suddenly uncomfortable.

"Are you sure this is the outfit? I don't want to look too Milanese." She remembered the day four years ago when she'd received clothing from Girolamo as part of the dowry meant for another and her dislike of the heavier Roman fashion. But now she wanted so much to fit in she'd agree to dress as a jester if it would make her more accepted by Roman society. There was also the fact that her new uncle was the Pope, and because of this, she'd face more scrutiny than others, particularly where her modesty was concerned.

It was a difficult line to tread, a combination of being decorative but also illustrating the decorum expected of a noblewoman and one with such close contact with the papacy.

"I'm positive." Luisa busied herself with collecting ribbons and hair nets. Caterina had had some last-minute indecision about her appearance, and the results were the colourful mess Luisa now tidied and packed away. After waiting a few moments for another reply, Luisa turned to see Caterina still scrutinising herself in the mirror.

"What about my husband?" she asked.

"What about him?"

"Will he approve of my outfit?"

Luisa heard the hopeful note in her friend's voice. "Of course he will, how can he not?" She was matter of fact, putting to rest any lingering doubts Caterina may have had. There was no point encouraging idle speculation, and also no more time. The day had arrived. "I want to check that your things have been loaded on the wagons."

"You don't need to do that, I've already told you." Caterina still stood before her reflection.

"I don't mind. I'm anxious to set out and can't just sit and wait."

"I understand. Be back as soon as you can."

With a nod, Luisa left. As she hurried down the hall toward the courtyard, Bossi stepped out of a room and stopped her.

"Signora, if I may have a word?"

Curious, Luisa followed him into a small room with a desk and shelves lining the walls. Leather-bound books and manuscripts filled the space.

"Please, sit." He waved at a chair.

Settling herself, Luisa waited for the man to state his business with her. "Dona Tommasa, you're closest to the countess than anyone and I wanted a few moments with you before we depart."

"Of course, Signor."

"I watched my lady grow from a child to a young woman and have come to understand her well these past few weeks. I fear she may need help adjusting to her role as wife."

Luisa smiled, relieved. "Bona has ensured Caterina knows all she needs to support her husband and be a fair ruler."

Bossi shook his head. "No, that's not what I mean."

Embarrassed, Luisa looked down. "Do you mean the marriage bed?"

The older man turned bright red. "No, no, that's not it either."

"Then what, Signor?"

Gian sighed. "I feel the countess may have expectations about her role, her partnership with Girolamo."

The use of the count's first name surprised Luisa, but she heard the worry in Bossi's voice and realised there was no need for formality between them, not here in private. "She believes her union is one between equals. Her illegitimacy wiped away through her dowry, and his inferior rank diminished through his uncle."

"Yes, exactly," he agreed. "But I fear she will be disappointed. I've been in touch with Bona and her contacts in the holy city and, if a fraction of what we hear about Girolamo is true, Caterina needs to be more prepared for a life of possible subservience."

"Subservience? That is a strong word. Surely the count..."

"Surely the count what? Is a completely different man than described by these stories?" He shook his head again. "I don't think so."

Luisa thought about the advisor's words. "What would you have me do?"

"Manage her expectations in any way you can. Divert her attention away from unpleasantness when possible. Make her aware that, even though she was born a child of Galeazzo Sforza, she is still a woman."

While she didn't like the sentiment, Luisa had to admit the man was right. It would be tragic to see her friend let down so badly and so wrongfully, especially if there was something she could do to prevent it. Speaking solemnly, she rose. "I promise I'll do all I can." Walking to the door, she turned back to Bossi. Stinging a little from his words, she felt she needed to defend her friend. "My lady is headstrong. You must also be aware of this." She waited for his nod of acknowledgement before curtsying to him and hurrying to finish her list of self-imposed tasks.

They set out in the afternoon after enjoying a light meal at the castle. Leaving the bowing castellan, they headed out into the May sun, Bossi leading the way in front of Caterina, guards riding on either side of them both. Luisa rode just behind, and every so often, Caterina glanced back to reassure herself that her friend was near.

Halfway to the city, they heard drums, then shouts, and the sound of men marching. Peering into the hazy distance, Caterina saw a company of horsemen wearing black uniforms with a yellow rose embroidered on their sleeves and carried on their standards. It was the Riario rose, and her husband approached.

Her stomach leaping, Caterina felt nauseated but sat tall in her saddle. Riding forward, she was met by Girolamo and his retainers. She barely had a chance to scrutinise him before he had leapt from his mount and held out a hand to help her down from hers. Aware that all eyes were upon her, she accepted his aid. Their horses were led away as they held hands before the onlookers. Caterina felt her husband move closer, and suddenly she was being held tightly by this man, her husband, and a stranger. As he released her, he placed a chaste kiss on her lips before moving back quickly again.

The late afternoon sun glared down at them, and Caterina instinctively shielded her eyes with her hand. She managed to get a closer look at Girolamo but was not quick enough. He turned back to his soldiers and signalled for his horse.

"I have arranged a small repast just up ahead. There is a grove that will provide shade. Once we've refreshed ourselves, we will ride into the city." Girolamo said matter of factly, like a soldier stating battle plans.

Nodding respectfully, Caterina allowed herself to be helped back on her horse and followed Girolamo and his retainers for about half an hour before they stopped again. This time, in the shade of the trees, she could see more clearly and was delighted to find so many fine-looking soldiers attending to her husband. Caterina looked for Luisa and, satisfying herself that her friend was nearby, sat beside Girolamo at a table laden with meats, cheeses, and pastries made in the shape of the Riario rose.

As they sat eating with their retainers, Caterina could view Girolamo properly. He had aged in the four years since they'd last been together and was heavier. Others of his standing might carry the extra weight with the confidence that went with their position, but the count looked uncomfortable, occasionally shifting his shoulders as if his fitted waistcoat and sleeves were too tight. The light wind caused the branches under which they ate to move, allowing more light into the grove, and Caterina also saw that her husband's face was sallow and tired looking. She hadn't truly scrutinised Girolamo as closely when they'd first been joined, but Caterina was certain there were more wrinkles on his face and a hint of shadow beneath his eyes.

"Are you enjoying your meal, countess?" Girolamo's voice was deep and pleasant enough, and his tone polite.

"I am, thank you. You've arranged a wonderful feast." She bowed her head graciously.

Seemingly satisfied by her reply, Riario turned to speak to someone standing behind him, an advisor Caterina guessed. She looked around once more, at the grove and through the trees where more of the count's retinue waited patiently. More guards and nobles appeared out of nowhere, many peering into the shade to catch a glimpse of the couple. Caterina was content to see Bossi standing nearby, speaking with another stranger, and Luisa sitting at a chair at the end of the table.

When they had finished, Girolamo helped Caterina back onto her horse, and they started the final stretch into Rome. As they approached, more and more people joined them until Caterina couldn't guess how many their party now made up. Along the way, farmers and other workers crowded the road to welcome her, and she waved at the excited children who trailed behind her horse.

Luisa had urged her mount forward a few steps and now rode beside her friend.

"I think my husband has most certainly changed. Look around us," she waved her hand, indicating the throngs of followers. "He is obviously a powerful man and must love me, for surely he would not have taken the time to accompany me in such a manner." She nodded to herself happily. "The rumours are obviously false, made up by his enemies, as I've said. And now, here is the proof before us."

"I'm happy for you, my lady." Luisa was clever enough to know that her familiarity with Caterina only went so far when they were in public and before so many obviously important and wealthy people.

They rode up the gentle slopes of the Monte Mario, the high hill north of the city and into Rome. A mix of old and new awaited her, with crumbling ancient buildings existing beside new palatial homes of cardinals and other high church officials. By now, the roads were so packed that Girolamo's guards were forced to dismount and hold the crowds back so the couple could move forward. The fresh winds atop Mario were replaced by more humid air, scented with the humanity of the holy city.

They finally stopped a short distance from the hill at a large stone building. The front was decorated with columns of the finest marble, and a passage led to an inner courtyard where Caterina caught a glimpse of a sparkling fountain raining down on what looked like an ancient Roman cherub.

Girolamo swung his right leg over the saddle pommel and slid from his horse. Dusting himself, he once again helped Caterina from hers and walked her to the courtyard.

"This is the villa of the Cardinal Giovanni of Urbino, who has generously offered to host a lavish dinner for us," he explained as they walked toward a thin, older man wearing the bright red of his office.

He held his arms wide and, stepping unevenly forward, embraced Girolamo. "My dear count, I welcome both you and your bride to my humble home." Stepping back, he lowered his head in a pious gesture. A nearby servant took his arm to support him as he stood tall again.

"Your Eminence, it is good to visit with you again. Allow me to introduce my wife, Caterina Sforza Riario." Girolamo stepped aside, leaving Caterina waiting alone.

"My dear, I have heard much about you. Indeed, all of Rome has, and we've been anxious for your arrival." He was about to move toward her, but, seeing the weakness of his age, Caterina rushed forward. Kneeling before him, she took his hand and kissed his ring. "Cardinal Giovanni, it is my great honour to meet you."

"Please, rise, rise." He put his hands on her shoulders as she stood.

Caterina stood and looked into his face. She had grown taller, and he had shrunk with age, evidenced by the crisscrossing of lines across his sagging face. But his eyes, still startling blue, shone kindly as if amused by a joke known only to him.

She stepped into her role as a wife with ease and bowed her head respectfully. "My husband and I thank you for your generosity. I'm looking forward to seeing your beautiful home and enjoying the feast you've troubled yourself with."

The cardinal's face lit up, and he grinned as he looked at Girolamo. "Charming and polite. The Holy Father will be pleased." Offering Caterina his arm, he leaned heavily on his helper and ushered her from the courtyard into the building.

Inside, the smell of cooking boar filled the halls, and Caterina breathed in deeply, reminded of the feasts in Milan. Boar had been a favourite, and her father used to enjoy boasting his prowess in killing these fearsome creatures to his guests. As they made their way through a long hall, servants and maids hurried around efficiently, carrying jugs, cloth, and platters, ignoring the young woman who watched them. The cardinal stopped when they arrived at a long flight of marble stairs.

"There are rooms set aside for you and your retainers. At the top of the stairs, to the right."

Caterina took a deep breath. "And the count?"

Cardinal Giovanni patted her hand kindly. "He will not be staying tonight. His uncle has decreed that a blessing of your vows be performed by him before you join your husband in your home across the river."

Squeezing the old man's frail hand carefully and gratefully, Caterina made her way up the broad staircase, marvelling at the whiteness of the marble and its sheer size. She felt someone at her side and was relieved to find Luisa climbing the steps with her. Together they stared in wonder at the frescoes and tapestries covering every room they passed until they reached Caterina's. Upon entering, they found the same lavish decorations as the rest of the palace.

"This man is like no churchman I've ever seen," Luisa said.

"Shh, don't say such things," Caterina frowned. "At least not so loudly." She walked over to a wall hanging depicting a hunting scene. Lords and ladies in bright colours rode horses while dogs chased deer through a green forest. Running her finger over one of the ladies' dresses, she felt the roughness of the gold thread used to make the outfit shine. Turning back to her friend, she nodded. "You're right. Such wealth for a holy man, and a cardinal too."

"Perhaps this is the way cardinals in Rome live."

"I'm certain we'll find out. Girolamo seems to be on good terms with this cardinal, and more than likely others. The size of his guard surprised me, I'll admit it. I now realise just how important my husband is, and I imagine we will be in demand at many events."

"And you'll share all the details with me when you return home each night." She was interrupted by a servant carrying in one of Caterina's trunks.

"Don't be silly, you'll be by my side as often as possible." She walked to the box. "Let's change out of our travelling clothes and prepare for dinner."

Chapter Seven
1477

The faint sound of music accompanied the wafting smells of their feast as Caterina and Luisa hurried down the staircase. Running her hand over the curved railing, she enjoyed the cool smoothness, the almost calming surface of the marble. The cardinal must feel the same way, she thought. Maybe he feels closer to God with such beauty around him. It certainly soothed her.

When they reached the bottom, a servant showed them the way to the banquet hall, the largest of the many rooms that made up the cardinal's home.

"My lady, come in, welcome." The cardinal rose slowly from his chair and waved her forward.

Seeing Girolamo already seated beside the cardinal, she bobbed her head at them both and made her way fully into the room to join them. Rectangular in shape, the hall had high ceilings painted with frescoes of scenes from Roman mythology. The longer walls were painted with rows of columns in the trompe l'oeil style, making the pillars appear as though they existed in the room. At the far ends of the hall, on the shorter walls, were more realistic paintings, this time of decorated stone archways and distant lakes.

With a glance at Luisa, she walked confidently forward, ignoring the stares from the other guests who sat at one of two long tables running along the walls. She sat on the cardinal's left in the chair he had indicated. A servant stood behind her, waiting for Caterina to get comfortable before gently pushing the high-backed wooden chair forward.

"Who have you brought with you?"

Caterina nodded for Luisa to sit beside her. "Your eminence, this is Luisa Tommasa, my Dama di Corte, my Lady in Waiting." She smiled, mainly because it amused her to surprise her friend so. If Luisa wouldn't give up some of the duties that maids could perform, she would at least ensure her friend's importance was recognised.

"Dama Tommasa, you are also very welcome here." He looked up at a servant dressed in black standing in the corner. The man nodded and stepped swiftly from the room. Turning to Caterina, he held up both hands in front of him. "I have invited friends here tonight, those who would wish to know you." He leaned toward her. "Don't worry about remembering them all, my dear. I can barely remember them at times," he whispered conspiratorially. "There will be time for learning names, and tonight isn't it." He stood, waving away a servant who rushed forward to help him. "My guests, I'm deeply moved that you were all able to attend my small celebration this evening. You already know the Holy Father's nephew, Girolamo Riario, however I can see by your curious looks the real reason you are here tonight."

A few guests shifted uncomfortably in their seats, their secret suddenly exposed. But Cardinal Giovanni burst out laughing, and Caterina knew she would get along with this man.

"Do not worry. You cause no offence. It is only due to my position that I could meet our guest before you all." He smiled down at Caterina, who was growing warm with the focussed attention of everyone in the room. "As I say, you know Count Riario but not this exquisite young woman who graces us with her beauty and charm this evening. My friends, this is Countess Caterina Sforza Riario."

Every neck strained to get a better look at Caterina, daughter of a famed warrior, and she felt beads of sweat forming on her forehead. Thankfully the food arrived at that moment, filling the already-scented hall with a rush of new smells. Darkly dressed servants carried in platter after platter as the evening wore on. After the first dozen courses, Caterina decided to just sample enough to be polite. In her excitement, she'd forgotten the main rule of surviving a feast – small portions. But the cardinal's fare had looked and smelled delicious, and both Caterina and Luisa had difficulty not piling more onto their plates than decorum dictated.

When the meal was finally over, the tables were pushed to the room's edges to make space for dancing. As the musicians moved closer, Girolamo suddenly stood and cleared his throat.

Bowing at the cardinal, he addressed the guests. "Please forgive my interruption but I wished to present my bride with a gift."

Caterina's eyebrows raised momentarily before she remembered herself and smiled. She loved presents as much as anyone, but the surprise ones were the best. It boded well for their union, she thought. Standing, she made her way to the centre of the room where her husband stood waiting, his hands held behind his back. She stopped before him and curtseyed. "My lord."

Without a word, he walked around her until he was standing right behind her. She stood still but looked up as his hands came down over her head, a string of large pearls held between them. His rough hands brushed the delicate skin on her neck as he attached the necklace, then stood back.

Spinning to face him again, Caterina felt the weight of the pearls bounce on her chest. They were just long enough for her to grab and raise so she could see the details more closely. The pearls were large and held in place by intricately tied knots in the silk thread. Each knot had a small ebony bead woven into its pattern, the interplay between the pure white and the deep dark evident.

"It's beautiful, my lord. Thank you." She curtsied to him again and was gratified to see him bowing back.

The room erupted in a chorus of approval before the signal was given for the musicians to start. Caterina watched Girolamo move to a far corner with some of the men who'd been invited and assumed he was discussing papal business. She had expected at least one dance with her husband, but before she could concern herself with any possible meaning, she was pulled aside to share a dance with a short, elegant man who spoke so quickly she couldn't hear his name. Noble after noble offered themselves as her dancing partners, and she was happily exhausted by the end of the night.

As she'd been told, Girolamo left the cardinal's home to return to his papal residence once most of the guests had retired to their own homes or rooms in the cardinal's palace. He offered a curt good night before mounting his waiting horse and riding into the darkness. Caterina and Luisa returned to her rooms, followed by a handful of maids Cardinal Giovanni had made available.

"You danced a great deal, you must be tired."

Caterina beamed at her friend. "You must be too. I saw you with more than one handsome curly haired Signor."

"I have you to thank for that. Your introduction was overheard by most of the room. I have gone from a nobody to a lady." Luisa laughed, enjoying the clout the title offered, as evidenced by the attention she'd received that night, more than ever in her life.

"You were never a nobody, anyone who knows me is aware of that. And soon all will know you as my closest friend and advisor. That will bring more gorgeous Romans to the door I'm certain."

Luisa flushed bright red, still enjoying the new attention. Perhaps Rome wasn't as bad as the court in Milan thought. She voiced her opinion. "I believe you will make a home here, a happy one." Such was her enjoyment of the day that she dismissed her conversation with Bossi earlier about managing Caterina's hopes as overly cautious. How could she do that when her own were so high at that moment?

Despite the late hour and the hectic night, Caterina stepped lightly into her room and rushed to the bed, throwing herself onto it. Lying on her back, she admired the tiny gold stars on the ceiling and started giggling.

"What's so funny?" Luisa threw herself onto her back beside her friend.

"I don't know. Nothing. I'm just happy."

"Me too."

The following morning Girolamo arrived at the cardinal's house as Caterina rose. Washing herself in a tub filled with hot water by a line of maids carrying jugs from elsewhere in the house, she re-entered the bedroom and found her dress waiting. Bona had made a few suggestions about her gown for this day in particular and had strongly urged the outfit now waiting for her on her stepdaughter.

Luisa had instructed maids which items to unpack, and Caterina was soon standing before her travelling mirror in a gown of black with a crimson skirt covered by a silk over gown of blue and gold brocade. The over gown mostly covered the skirt, but an occasional red flash was revealed when she walked. With the rings and necklaces she wore, along with the pearls from the count, Caterina was not only trying to impress the papal court but also making a statement, even if she wasn't aware that Bona had planned it. See, here, the wealth of Milan. Even our under gowns are made of the finest materials. And the colours, the hint of red, a symbol of power, revealing itself carefully beneath the more virginal blue.

They ate some figs and cheese before joining Girolamo in the courtyard. Caterina smiled at him as she was helped onto her horse but received no response. Shrugging it off, Caterina assumed her husband was thinking about the day ahead and began the ride to the Vatican with a nod at both Bossi and Luisa.

As they made their way through the streets, more and more horsemen joined them until they numbered over one thousand when they finally arrived at the Basilica of Saint Peter. Caterina took Girolamo's proffered arm, and together they ascended the steps leading to the basilica's courtyard. While she knew to keep her head straight and look ahead, she couldn't help but glimpse the row of arch-topped columns that made up the open space, making her feel like she had entered a Roman temple. As they continued, they passed a fountain in the shape of a pinecone that was at least as tall as three of Caterina, reminding her of the heavily scented forests near her childhood home.

Ahead was the holiest spot in all Christendom, and Caterina took a breath as they entered the basilica. Like the courtyard, simple columns ran in a double row the entire length of the building. As they moved slowly to the front, Caterina could see chapels set into the walls, each glinting gold in the candlelight. She also saw the others gathered for mass today, staring at her and her husband as they passed. Keeping her eyes focussed forward, she barely noticed the polite nods and smiles but still knew they watched.

By the time they reached the tomb of St Peter at the front of the basilica, Caterina's dress felt uncomfortably warm, and her skin prickled with the added heat of attention. Sweat rolled between her shoulder blades, and as they finally stopped and took their places at the front of the gathered congregation, she lifted her hand to surreptitiously wipe her neck. Her movement was interrupted by loud whispers that moved through the crowd like a wave.

Turning slightly to see what was happening, she understood. The Holy Father, Pope Sixtus IV, had arrived.

The mass lasted three hours, during which time Caterina was able to surreptitiously look around, not only at her surroundings but at those who surrounded her. And while she gathered her nerve to glance to her sides, she focussed on the Holy Father.

Sixtus, born Francesco della Rovere, had lived a life devoted to the church. Rising from simple monk to cardinal, he disdained the displays of wealth some of his colleagues enjoyed, preferring to maintain his widely recognised reputation for simplicity and piety. A man of middling height and slender frame, with a nose that dominated his face and piercing blue eyes, at age sixty-three he could still command the entire basilica with a voice from the pages of the Old Testament.

Caterina thought he looked uncomfortable in his pontifical clothing, as if they were ill-fitting somehow. She found it easy to imagine him delivering the mass wearing a plain monk's robe and looked forward with some trepidation to meeting her new relative.

Shifting her attention away from the Pope, Caterina flitted her eyes sideways, then up, taking in the details of the old building. There were so many paintings they were almost overwhelming, and she wondered how anyone could concentrate on the mass surrounded by such splendour. She forced herself to stare straight ahead, promising she'd find a way to return when there was time to walk around. But even the altar before her offered sufficient distraction, with its twisted columns reportedly put in place by Emperor Constantine himself, taken from an old pagan temple dedicated to Solomon. The enormity of the history where she now sat overwhelmed her, and she imagined the first Christian emperor walking these aisles and staring up at the ceiling. Charlamagne himself was crowned the Holy Roman Emperor here. While she obediently followed the mass, crossing herself and kneeling when required, it was these thoughts of history that Caterina amused herself with as the hours went on.

She'd allowed her mind to wander when suddenly the mass was over, and the Holy Father was looking in her direction.

"Come. My uncle would meet you." Girolamo looked at her expectantly.

Nodding silently, Caterina allowed herself to be led into the sacristy, where the Pope had just exited. Gian Bossi followed closely behind.

Entering the small room, they found Pope Sixtus surrounded by clergy members. The room was a hive of activity, with some helping the Pope remove his vestments and others carrying liturgical objects like the chalice, the paten which holds the body of Christ, and the various cloths used in the service.

"Ahh, Girolamo, come here, help us with this." The Pope waved his nephew over and stood waiting.

Caterina watched as her husband approached the most important man in all Christendom and helped him shrug out of his chasuble, the heavy garment worn over his usual clothes when mass was performed.

"Ahh, that's better." Sixtus rolled his shoulders and moved his head from side to side. Then, looking directly at Caterina, he smiled. "Now, who do we have here?"

Nervous and forgetting herself, Caterina rushed forward and knelt on the floor before the Pope. Without a word, she leaned forward and kissed the toe of his foot, the only part of his slippers visible under his long white alb.

"Rise, my child."

She felt a surprisingly strong hand on her shoulder and stood while Sixtus held her arm.

"Uncle, this is Caterina, my wife." Girolamo stood to the side, watching the exchange.

Looking her up and down, the Holy Father smiled gently again. "Come with us." He looked around the room. "All of you." Leading them through another door and down a corridor, Sixtus moved like a man who could navigate these corridors in the dark. They entered a larger and more lavishly decorated room, with heavy wooden chairs that looked like thrones, and tapestries depicting saints hanging from the walls.

"Sit. Let us get to know each other better." He waved one hand airily towards the group of chairs while indicating to a prelate with another. Before each could settle, platters of food and jugs of wine arrived.

Caterina curtsied toward the Pope. "Holy Father, may I serve you?"

The man's face broke out into a wide grin. "Of course, my dear. We would be honoured."

Blushing at the praise, Caterina took the jug from a waiting prelate and poured out four cups. She frowned at the plain silver vessels, unadorned and worn thin with polishing.

"Your Holiness." She lowered herself and carefully handed the goblet to Sixtus as the prelate gave the others to the remaining guests.

"We thank you. Now, tell us about yourself." The Holy Father settled back into his chair and brought his wine to his lips.

This was Bossi's turn to perform one of the duties for which he'd been sent. Standing, he placed his cup on a nearby table and approached the pontiff. Kneeling to kiss the shoe, he stood and began.

"Holy Father, it is my pleasure to sing the praises of the Countess Riario and I hope my humble words will not detract from my noble sentiments."

Caterina, unprepared for this, looked on in surprise as Bossi continued.

"I have known the Lady Caterina since she was a child; when she was full of the joy and charm so often robbed from us later in life. But no thievery has occurred to my lady, like it has for the rest of us, and she remains the most serene and happy woman the Holy Father could hope to meet. She descends from a long line of brave, clever condottieri and is as bold and astute as any of her ancestors. Her patience and kindness serve as an example to us all. Her benevolence, exhibited from her early days, is known to every citizen in Milan, the city who loves her."

He finished with a bow and stepped back.

"Bravo. A fine speech. You are also obviously just as astute as your mistress, and it makes us glad to see how fortunate our new niece is in her counsellors." Nodding to the prelate holding the jug of wine, the Pope continued, his voice grown serious. "My dear, we would see you married to our nephew again."

Startled, Caterina nearly choked on her wine. What did this mean? Had she slept with her husband all those years ago out of wedlock?

Seeing her worry, Sixtus shook his head. "You misunderstand. You are already married, it is indisputable, but we would feel better if we, ourself, blessed anew your union with our nephew."

Nodding her silent acquiescence, Caterina stood and, together with Girolamo, knelt before the pontiff and bowed their heads. In the room's stillness, she could feel the movement of the Pope's hand above her head as he performed the blessing.

"In the name of the Father, the Son, and the Holy Spirit, we bless this union and pray it will be a happy and fruitful marriage."

Caterina waited until she saw her husband rise, then quickly followed. The Pope smiled at her kindly. "My children, it is time for you to depart for your celebration and for us to allow our old bones to rest." He chuckled. "But before you do, we have a gift for the bride. From our own treasury in the Castel Sant'Angelo." Another nod at the ever-waiting prelate, and a moment later, a silk pouch was in the Holy Father's hands. "If you'll allow us?" he asked. Without waiting for a reply, he stepped behind Caterina and untied the clasp holding the pearls Girolamo had presented to her earlier. She reached up as the necklace slid off her neck and held it tightly as a new one replaced it. "There. Much better."

Turning to Sixtus, Caterina looked down at her chest and saw another chain of pearls, larger and more lustrous than her other. Every pearl was a perfect globe, and she marvelled at the uniformity.

Dropping to her knees, Caterina held her head down. "Thank you, Your Holiness, for such an astonishing piece."

Rising, she saw her gesture had pleased him. Her husband, however, was anything but. A fleeting look of anger had crossed the count's face, directed at his uncle before it had faded to cold indifference. Trying not to frown, Caterina curtsied a last time as the Holy Father nodded to them. "Enjoy your feast, my dear. We will speak with you again soon." He swept from the room, calling out from the hall, "Nephew, we will need you here first thing tomorrow morning." The only sound after that was the soft padded footsteps fading as the Pope headed to his private rooms.

Chapter Eight
1477

The wedding feast lasted five hours, and Caterina barely had time to eat a portion of one course before the next was announced by music and fanfare. Small children recited verses every five courses, to the delight of all. With over twenty-two courses to feed the two hundred nobles, ambassadors, and high-ranking clergy invited, every dish had to be unique and display the grandeur of Roman cuisine. Fish with silver and gold scales elicited applause from the guests, but the sugar-coated oranges were Caterina's favourite.

Looking around, she was able to relax for a moment as she enjoyed the company. After the pope's blessing, Caterina and Girolamo had ridden to their new home and Caterina had barely had time to look around before the dinner, organised by the pontiff's staff, required her presence.

When the dishes had finally been cleared, a table was brought to display the gifts for the newlyweds. Piled high by the end of the night, Caterina tried to thank every guest but was so tired she was sure she'd forgotten some. Hoping not to cause offence, she spoke at the night's end.

"My new friends, thank you for your evening reception and attendance at our feast. I know I haven't had a chance to speak with you all, something I will remedy in the coming days. In the meantime, I hope you all have a pleasant and safe journey back to your homes, and to those gracing us with your presence overnight, I wish you a peaceful slumber inside these fine walls." With a gracious wave of her hand around the room, Caterina sat again as the guests applauded. As she and Girolamo bid their guests goodbye, Caterina's stomach began to clench and try as she might, she couldn't drag out the farewells forever.

Luisa had left the celebration early to prepare her friend's room and now stood as Caterina entered.

Seeing the worry on Caterina's face, she desperately thought of something to say. "I put your linen from Milan on the bed." She turned to a nearby table. "And here, your own jewellery box." Circling back to the bed, she went to the side where another table sat. "Here are your books." Along with the books was a jug of wine and a glass, already filled and waiting.

"Thank you." Caterina's voice, so filled with joy only hours ago, was now a whisper. She took the wine and gulped it down, feeling the burn in her stomach despite the amount she'd eaten that night. There were no more excuses to put off the night, no more guests and all the cleaning would be done by the servants. She couldn't claim exhaustion, no matter how true, for she knew what was expected of her.

With few words between them, Luisa helped Caterina out of her dress and into a silk chemise. Luisa was about to secure her friend's hair in a sleeping net but felt a hand on her wrist.

"Leave it to hang freely. My husband may prefer it."

Blinking back her tears at Caterina's bravery, Luisa put the hair net aside. With a glance up and down, she nodded, the unspoken words hanging in the air above them. She was ready.

"Perhaps this time will be different," Luisa offered meekly.

Caterina had the same hope but dared not voice it in case she was wrong.

As she collected Caterina's clothing for storage, Luisa saw Girolamo enter and hurried to gather the gown sleeves. With a polite curtsey to the count, she smiled sympathetically at her friend and quickly exited the room. Luisa remembered the last encounter between Caterina and her husband. There had been a storm blowing, and Luisa couldn't tell if the noise she'd heard was the shrieking wind or the screams of her mistress. Tonight, there was no storm and no mistaking the sounds. Wincing each time she heard Caterina cry out, Luisa hurried down the hall toward her own rooms, hoping her friend's ordeal would not last long.

The next morning Caterina woke to find herself alone. She hadn't heard Girolamo leave and guessed he had either gone to his own chambers or had been called to aid his uncle. With an immediate sense of relief, she lifted herself from the bed, grimacing at the pain she felt, the result of Girolamo's clumsy act. With no regard for her, he had performed his husbandly duty without a word to his new wife or any enquiries as to her wellbeing. Caterina had stayed awake long after he had fallen asleep, disappointed that her hopes for a different experience had been so brutally shattered.

Once standing, she tried a few steps, using the bed to balance, feeling the pain between her legs throbbing at the same rhythm as her heart. Taking a deep breath, she paused for a moment then stood tall and walked again. At least it wasn't as bad as the first time, she convinced herself. When she was at the end of the large wooden bed, Luisa had arrived with enough maids to make the chamber suddenly feel crowded. She waited for each to perform a duty: one carried a pitcher of water, another a platter of bread and meat, and yet another wine.

Turning the World to Stone

Once they'd gone, Luisa approached her friend. "Are you well?" she asked, her face a mask of worry.

"I'm fine. Nothing bad happened, he just, he put..." Caterina flushed deep red and paused for a moment. "He did what a husband is meant to do, and I did as a wife is expected." Not like in the stories, she left unspoken. The last part of herself that was still a child had retreated to a small corner of her mind to reside alone.

Caterina's tone suggested she would rather talk about anything else, so Luisa changed the subject as she went to a chest and searched through the gowns. "I've looked around a little bit, there are dozens of breathtaking rooms that look out over the courtyard. You won't have to worry about noises from the street while living here, that's for certain."

"We can explore today, see what we can see."

Both women knew they were feigning cheerfulness, and each hoped the artificial mood would eventually turn to real pleasure in their new surroundings. "What would you like to wear?"

"Something light, I think. And fewer jewels than last night. I nearly fell over with the weight of those pearls."

Luisa smiled at the comment, which made Caterina smile. The joke had suddenly lightened the entire room, and both women continued in this vein as they prepared to step out into the holy city of Rome.

As Caterina straightened her sleeve, she turned from the mirror to Luisa. "Do you know if the count is downstairs?"

Luisa shook her head as she tightened the fastening that held the sleeve to the gown. "He is not. The Holy Father sent word the count was needed." She kept her voice even, unsure how this news would be received.

Turning back to the mirror, Caterina smiled. "Then it shall only be us today."

Finally finished with the sleeve, Luisa grabbed Caterina's hand and squeezed it quickly as she stepped away to admire her work. Her friend wore a pale green gown with a light overdress and a simple woven cap at the back of her head. Luisa had woven silk ribbons in Caterina's hair as she braided it, and the result was an elegant but powerful young woman enjoying some time alone with her retainers.

"You have a lot of people waiting for you to visit."

"I know." Caterina took a last look and walked over to the table, popping a chunk of bread into her mouth. "Today I want to view my new home and neighbourhood. I want to explore!" She smiled and took another piece of bread, this time adding some cheese.

Caught up in the enthusiasm, Luisa joined her, and after a while, they had finished the platter. Brushing the crumbs from their laps, they grinned at each other like they had when younger and had shared a secret. Caterina grew serious, barely able to keep her face stern. "Now, we must act like Roman women and behave. Let's walk around the palace first. I'm certain Bossi will join us. He'll never let us explore outside without him."

Linking her arm in Luisa's, Caterina felt relief. The night she had long dreaded was over, and she had survived. And now, she was in a new home and city. What would the heroines of her beloved stories do? Step gladly into the adventure. And Caterina had already taken that first step and then some. Now she could have some fun.

The heart of the palace was the courtyard, still decorated with luxurious hanging tapestries with beautifully sowed gardens and lush forests.

"They tell me the theme is 'Our Earthly Paradise'."

Caterina turned to see Bossi standing nearby. She hadn't been surprised because, as she'd predicted, he'd been waiting for her to rise.

"They're beautiful. We can't leave them out here, they'll get ruined the next time it rains. I'll need to ensure they're brought in," Caterina noted aloud. Bossi nodded approvingly, knowing Bona would be proud of moments when her stepdaughter displayed her readiness to run a household.

As Luisa had already said, dozens of rooms looked out over the courtyard, and Caterina noticed that she could stand back unseen while observing the comings and goings of the servants below. She saw men and women swiftly passing under her, carrying jars, goblets, cloth, and anything associated with the emptying or cleaning of the banquet hall.

"Let's go and look at more inside." Caterina led the way, wandering through the maze of halls and corridors and through large and small rooms. She didn't want to admit it, but this palace was more opulent and more extensive than her home in Milan.

"Is there a library?"

Luisa smiled. "It's the first place I asked about when we arrived yesterday. Let me see if I can remember how to get there. We'll need to go back to the courtyard; I only know my way from there."

After starting down a few wrong corridors, and startling several maids, they finally found it.

"Someone will need to draw me a map," Caterina joked as they stepped into a large, quiet room. Breathing in, she smelled the leather, candles, and mustiness she'd loved in her library in Milan. Entering, she looked around at the shelves that lined the walls, following them to the far end of the room where a giant fireplace stood ready for the cold days of winter. Beside the fireplace were carved wooden chairs with pillows on the seat for comfort and a table upon which sat an empty Venetian glass jug and a set of matching wine glasses. Whomever Girolamo had purchased this home from, they had good taste.

The room wrapped itself around Caterina, and she claimed it as her place of refuge should she ever need to escape from the city for a while. Running her hands along the spines of the books, she saw many she recognised from her father's library and was glad to have his memory here with her.

"My lady, I know how much you wish to spend the day here, but we should really leave now if we want to walk around the neighbourhood safely."

Caterina turned toward the door. Bossi was right, and she did want to get a sense of the neighbourhood around the palace. They entered the courtyard and crossed quickly, their eyes not having enough time to adjust to the sudden bright light before they were inside again and at the main entrance. Once truly outside, it took a few moments for Caterina's eyes to adjust to the bright May sun once more.

Looking to her side for both Luisa and Bossi, she noticed a few of the household guards had also followed her outside and stood ready to accompany them. Unused to such protection, Caterina nevertheless kept her questions to herself and stepped out into a large square. Like her house in Imola, the front of her Roman palace made up one entire side of a large square where vendors had set up their stalls.

Wandering over to a few, Caterina was surprised to find similar items for sale as in the markets of Imola and Milan. Soaps, perfumes, leather goods, foodstuff, everything you could hope for, just on a larger scale than anything she'd seen before. The other three sides of the square were made up of rows of smaller buildings and, peering into the shadows cast by the covered colonnade which ran along the building fronts, Caterina could see they were shops. As she strolled around the outer edges of the market, where numerous small streets spread like a spiderweb joining the various areas of the city, she smelled something hidden the night before by the burning torches, beeswax candles, and incense: the smell of decay.

Wrinkling her nose, she looked down one street and saw refuse, rats, and other waste lying there. It had been pushed to the side of the road toward the household doors to allow merchants to pass. Caterina imagined the stench still followed them home to their families.

Frowning, she continued her walk, taking in not only the market and people but also the buildings around them. Some had been rebuilt but many urgently needed repair. Caterina wondered if all of Rome were like this. And the guards! They were everywhere, dressed in different family colours, and accompanied every shopper in the square that day. But unlike her father's soldiers, these men were scruffy, their uniforms unkempt and in need of repair.

She could no longer hold back her puzzlement. "Why are there so many soldiers?" she asked the air.

Bossi was at once by her side. "They are all private family armies, my lady."

"I don't understand. Does Rome not have its own fighting force?"

"It does, my lady. The papal army is one of the strongest in Italy. Sadly, however, there are so many rivalries and vendettas in the city that families retain their own men, particularly the old families."

"Are such measures necessary?" Caterina nodded surreptitiously as yet another grandly dressed couple passed a short distance away, followed by four men with daggers tucked into their belts. The couple noticed her anyway and smiled warmly, eliciting a polite curtsey back.

"It is, my lady. Not only are there the old enemies but God forbid, if the Holy Father were to die, anarchy would be unleashed on the city. Anyone related to the Pope who was foolish enough to remain in the city would be attacked. Their home would be ransacked, and their belongings taken by anyone who cared to join in the chaos."

Gian had painted such a horrific picture that Caterina shivered. "Is this true?"

Bossi nodded. "I'm sorry to say it is. This unsavoury part of the city's behaviour is one of Rome's great shames, and one which it wishes to keep secret, so obviously all of Italy knows." He raised a wry eyebrow.

"This is the city God has chosen to be his own?" Caterina shook her head sadly, aware her words could be deemed blasphemous.

Luisa thought the same thing. "My lady, you mustn't say such things. You're no longer out in a forest in Milan, where there are very few ears. Here," she waved her hand around, "everyone hears everything. In only a day I've learned secrets from the other maids so shocking I blush to even think about them."

Luisa was right. She'd have to be more careful. And quickly determine the loyalties of those around her.

Chapter Nine
1477 - 1478

Over the weeks and months that followed, Caterina's days were kept busy visiting the wives and families of Roman nobles and her nights with banquets and more dances than any fourteen-year-old girl could hope for. She was gradually getting used to this city and its people and felt more and more accepted by all, including the Riario side of the family and the della Roveres. The Holy Father had once had the simple name of Francesco della Rovere. When his beloved sister Bianca had married into the Riario family, the Pope had taken all his nieces and nephews to his bosom, elevating the men to positions of authority within the See.

The Pope's sister Bianca was Caterina's mother-in-law for only two years before she passed away, while Caterina still resided in Milan waiting to join her husband. During this time, she'd met her brother-in-law, Cardinal Pietro Riario, who had travelled north on papal business. Caterina had found him a delightful man, full of warmth and cleverly erudite. Sadly, he had also passed away on his return to Rome after his visit, but he'd given Caterina hope that not all the Riarios were as dour as her husband.

After meeting Girolamo's sister, Violante, she wasn't as confident anymore. She knew Violante had a son studying canon law in Pisa and wondered how long it would be before she could meet him, a relative more her own age, even if she was his aunt and two years younger than him. There were so many Riarios and della Roveres in the holy city Caterina wondered how two families could be rich enough to offer dozens of their children to the church without thinking about the lack of income these offspring could bring in, especially in the forms of land, property, and coin. And to display their pride openly for all to see. So many of her husband's family had been elevated to cardinals and filled other important positions within the papacy. A more pious family would send their son or daughter to follow God's path without fanfare or celebration.

But here in Rome, everything was different. Families paraded their wealthy church relatives before everyone, throwing lavish celebrations whenever someone was elevated or even came to the particular notice of the Holy Father.

Caterina had finally gotten used to her surroundings and had memorised everyone's names, knew where their homes were, who their children were, and their different likes and dislikes by the end of the summer. She had discovered, to her delight, that advice given to her by Bona worked exceptionally well: to sit silently and never rush to fill a gap in a conversation. Instead, she was to wait, for someone else will eventually speak out of sheer discomfort with the silence. And this is where people often reveal their true selves if one is patient enough to listen. This revelation and Caterina's ability to remember small details made her popular with everyone. Soon, friends began to emerge from the gaggle of nobles, those whom the young countess could relate to and befriend.

"Who is that?"

Caterina stood at the stone railing, looking down on newly arrived visitors. Her nephew and new cardinal Raffaele stood with her, as did Luisa. The cardinal had finally finished his studies abroad and had been introduced to Caterina only a few weeks ago after a brief visit with his parents in Imola. Whether through her constant efforts, or his coming to some decision, the young man had finally started warming up to Caterina and Luisa.

"That is Francesco Pazzi."

"Why have I never met him before?" She shivered and pulled her cloak more closely around her shoulders as a gust of January wind blew into the courtyard.

"He lives in Florence with his uncle Jacopo. They are an old family, very prideful. Bankers." Raffaele listed off the things he knew about the family. Although he was still young, he'd learned much during his travels and his stay in Rome. The intelligence that would ensure his success also allowed him to understand the country's prominent families and their grievances, particularly when those criticisms flew close to the papacy.

"He's very handsome," Luisa added, peering over the railing with her friend.

Ignoring the remark, Caterina asked, "I thought the Medici were the bankers in Florence?"

"They are. They were even the papal bankers until four years ago."

Caterina frowned. "What happened four years ago?"

Without a thought about her personal history, Raffaele continued explaining. "Duke Galeazzo of Milan was going to sell Imola to Lorenzo Medici for one hundred thousand florins but instead sold the city to the Holy Father for forty thousand florins."

"Why would my father do such a thing?"

Suddenly realising to whom he was speaking, the cardinal turned as red as his robes. "I'm sorry, Madonna. I should not be speaking of such things."

His words had the opposite effect to what he'd intended. Instead of putting Caterina off, it only fuelled her curiosity. "Tell me. Why would my father offer the land for so little?"

Stammering, Raffaele cleared his throat. "For you, my lady."

"I don't understand."

"Part of your dowry was the city and surrounding lands. The duke sold it to the Pope, who gifted it back to his nephew, Girolamo, so you and he could rule."

Keeping her surprise to herself, Caterina merely nodded as if this was not new to her. "I imagine Lorenzo Medici was angered by such a move."

Encouraged by Caterina's nonchalance, the young man warmed to his topic. "Oh, he was. Very. He refused the Holy Father's request to finance the purchase."

"His holiness persuaded my father to sell Imola to him instead of the Medici, and for much less, and then asked Lorenzo to loan him the money?" Her voice was incredulous, and her shock was no longer hidden.

"It's all true. The Pazzi family," he bobbed his head toward the courtyard, "offered to finance the deal, even after the Medicis forbade any banker in Florence from doing so."

"These Medicis sound ruthless." Caterina wondered if her father had ever dealt with them.

"They are, Madonna. After that, the Holy Father took great offence and terminated the family as the papal bankers. Instead, he appointed the Pazzi family."

Realisation dawned on her. "That must be why my husband is meeting with this Francesco. To discuss some financial issue on behalf of his Holiness."

"It would seem so, Madonna."

Money. All the world's woes seemed to come down to money. Who had it, who didn't, and who wanted more and more. She sighed. When she had dreamed of adult life as a child, never had Caterina imagined the confusing and ever-changing tangle of families and loyalties she had encountered so far in this city. And here she was at the centre of it. It was too early for her to decide if this was a good thing or not.

Caterina was left to lead her life alone, except for the rare meal with the count. When he was required to attend a feast, he sat uncomfortably and left as soon as he was able. He visited her bed at night but performed in only the most perfunctory manner then left immediately afterwards. Most of the time, she only glimpsed him hurrying down a hall from his rooms or escorting a guest from the courtyard.

"You've been busy these past few weeks," Caterina remarked. She was with Girolamo on one of the few occasions he decided to dine with her. March had brought a splendid spring with it and, most nights, the palace no longer needed fires in the rooms.

"My uncle prefers to keep me close." He didn't look up from his plate as he spoke.

"Is there anything I can do to help?" Before he could object, she hurried on. "You already know I can read, but I can also keep books, and arrange meetings or correspondence." Her voice slowly started to creep up at the end, making her statement sound more like a question.

"I have all the help I need. You have my household to run. That should be enough to keep you occupied."

He spoke abruptly and Caterina thought he sounded impatient, like he would rather be someplace else. He confirmed this by suddenly standing and throwing his napkin on the table.

"I must get back to work." Without a further word, he left Caterina sitting at the table, staring after him. A moment later, hushed voices reached her from Girolamo's rooms, then the sound of a door closing firmly.

The next morning Girolamo was gone before Caterina was up. He often enjoyed hunting as the sun rose before heading to aid his uncle or continuing his secretive meetings with Francesco Pazzi and others.

"A letter arrived for you." Luisa entered and put the document on a table before helping Caterina from bed.

"From whom?"

"Bona."

"Wonderful! Let me see." She reached out and, taking the letter from Luisa, smiled as she read. "Bona is well, as are my brothers and sisters. Ooh, and she's heard news of me from visitors at the Milanese court. She writes, *'Many have told me of the honours and gracious reception accorded to you by His Holiness and all of Rome. And of you, my stepdaughter. They speak well and with many compliments, for your charm and wit have enraptured them all.'*" She continued reading as Luisa sat down nearby. "She also says she misses me and wishes we could see each other. *'Be of good cheer and brave of heart. I assure you this will give me the greatest pleasure any mother could hope for, as you, yourself, will hopefully soon discover. For in motherhood, you will discover a bond so deep that I have not the words to describe it.'*"

Sighing, she put the letter on a nearby table. "I'm brave of heart. Or at least seem so to others?"

Luisa nodded. "As long as I've known you." She glanced toward the window. "Have you any errands to run?"

Caterina shook her head. "Not today. A box of new books arrived yesterday, and I had it taken to the library. Come and help me unpack it."

They made their way to Caterina's favourite room, ordering food and drink on their way, and arrived as a servant was lighting a few candles close to the sitting area. A fire had already been started in the hearth and the women sat together as their food was carried in by a maid. Losing track of time, Luisa and Caterina unpacked the crate, admiring each book in turn, as they ate pieces of bread, smoked meat, and cheese. Caterina was flipping through a new history of France when the sound of someone entering stopped her.

"My lady, I'm sorry to interrupt you." Bossi hurried into the library, a harassed look on his face and sweat dripping from his forehead.

"Gian, come in." Caterina poured a cup of wine and handed it to him. "Sit. What's happened?"

Bossi drained the cup in one gulp but stayed standing. Taking a deep breath, he spoke, his words hurried. "There was a plot to kill Lorenzo and his brother, Giuliano, Medici. Giuliano has been murdered, stabbed nineteen times, at the Duomo in Florence."

Caterina and Luisa both covered their mouths in horror as Bossi took another lungful of air. Caterina finally spoke. "And Lorenzo?"

"He managed to flee to the sacristy with minor wounds."

"I can see why you were so disturbed when you arrived." Caterina looked at the man sympathetically. "And their poor wives," she muttered.

"Madonna, there is more."

"What? Tell me."

Gian now hesitated, and it was the first time in Caterina's life she'd ever seen the man nervous. "It's your husband, my lady. He has been implicated in the murder."

Chapter Ten
1478

"Where is Girolamo now?" Caterina had taken a few moments to absorb the news from Gian Bossi, waving any further comments away with her hand while she composed herself.

"No one knows, my lady."

Caterina frowned. When she'd first heard the news, she'd done nothing but pace the halls, shoving poor maids out of the way as she thought. Her efforts only exhausted her and provided no further information except for a guess at where her husband might be at this very moment.

Finally, she returned to the library and re-joined Luisa and Bossi. "I know. He has hidden in the papal palace. It's probably the best place for him." She looked at the empty jug on the table close to where the three sat. Bossi jumped up and went to the hall. Caterina and Luisa heard voices, and Luisa gave her friend a sympathetic glance as Gian returned. Within minutes the old jug and glasses had been swept away to make room for fresh wine and a small tray of sweetmeats, cheese, and fruit.

"Tell me everything." Caterina was now prepared to hear all the details, including any sordid elements involving the count.

Bossi took another long draught of wine and leaned forward. His voice was now back to its ordered, confident tone, and he delivered his words like a chronicler.

"People have begun calling it the Pazzi Conspiracy."

"What? Pazzi? As in Francesco Pazzi?"

"Yes, my lady. He and his uncle Jacobo. As you know, the Pazzis are an old family, and their pride grew when they were given the papal accounts. They assumed any vacant position within the church or Signoria would be given to a member of their family, and when these were blocked by the Medicis they decided to take matters into their own hands."

"And how does my husband fit into all this?"

"The count is aware of the enmity between the Medicis and the Holy Father, particularly as it pertains to your new home of Imola."

Caterina stood suddenly. "Do you mean I am to blame?"

"Madonna, no. Please, sit. Let me continue."

Mollified by his tone, Caterina sat again.

"Girolamo never felt safe with the Medicis still yearning for Imola. Lorenzo desperately needed the city for its key location between Florence and Venice."

Caterina nodded, remembering what Raffaele had told her. "Cardinal Riario! My nephew. He was in Florence, is he..." She dared not speak the words.

"He is, my lady. But he also has a part in this. He was sent to Florence to try to arrange a peace between the Medici and the Holy Father. One of his duties was to perform mass for the holy day of Easter. On that holiest of days, as Cardinal Raffaele held the host aloft, the conspirators acted. You know enough of the rest. I will not repeat the details."

"I still do not understand how my husband is involved."

"Madonna, it was he who orchestrated the entire plan. He met with the Pazzis in secret, along with the Archbishop of Pisa, a man named Salviati, who also had a grievance with the Medicis. He sent Salviati to take over the Signoria while the Medici brothers were being murdered."

"Does His Holiness know all this?"

Bossi shifted in his seat uncomfortably. "My lady, the Holy Father sanctioned it."

Now both Caterina and Luisa stood, knocking over the tray from the table. "No. It can't be possible, it's a slanderous lie!"

"Please, my lady." Gian looked at Luisa. "Both, please let me finish."

Not satisfied, they sat and waited for him to continue.

"I'm afraid it's true, to a certain extent." He held up a hand when he saw Caterina about to interrupt. "Girolamo Riario approached his uncle but was told by the Holy Father that His Holiness could not sanction such an action because of his holy office."

Caterina closed her eyes, relieved. "Then it is untrue."

Bossi ignored her remark and continued kindly. "Sixtus did, however, say that it would be a great benefit to the papacy if the Medicis were removed."

Caterina fell silent, unable to form words. Luisa finally spoke up. "What happened next?"

Relieved to be able to finish his report, Bossi smiled gratefully at her. "Francesco Pazzi killed Giuliano himself while Saviati took soldiers to take over the Signoria. The citizens of Florence did not rise against the Medicis as the Pazzis had hoped, and they soon found themselves on the receiving end of the crowd's vengeance."

"What happened to Raffaele?"

"Lorenzo Medici himself saved the cardinal from the mob however he is still being kept as a 'guest' of the Medicis."

"And the conspirators? What of them?" Luisa asked.

"Archbishop Salviati was hanged from the window of the Signoria for all in the palazzo below to see."

Caterina had now recovered from her initial shock. "But the count. What proof is there of his involvement?"

"Just before he was hanged from the same window as Salviati, Francesco Pazzi revealed the whole plot, complete with dates and times of meetings and the name of everyone involved, including his own uncle."

Shuddering as she imagined not one but two decaying bodies hanging in Florence's main palazzo, Caterina's lips grew thin. "And this uncle? Jacobo?"

"He has fled the city and remains in hiding. There are many in Florence who want him found and brought to justice, I'm certain it's only a matter of time before the lure of gold makes someone betray the man."

Caterina sank into her chair, suddenly exhausted. So it was true, all of it. She'd seen the meetings, witnessed Francesco Pazzi here, under her very roof. What she thought was papal business turned out to be so much more that it made her feel ill. And Caterina had not said a word. About the meetings and how often she saw Francesco leaving with Girolamo, patting each other on the back and laughing. Why would she? She had no idea what they spoke about.

"What do I do? How can I bear it?" She rose and began pacing around the library. "What will people think of me?"

This time she'd asked a question neither of her closest advisors could answer.

Girolamo returned home after a week of living in the papal apartments. During that time, Caterina found herself the subject of looks both pitying and angry, and often she found herself dismissed from a crowd of Roman women gathered in the nearby market square. Some vendors even refused to sell to her, although the ones she'd made friends with were sympathetic and treated her with respect.

Caterina received few visitors, and those who did dare to enter her courtyard made hasty excuses as to why they couldn't stay long. After dining alone one evening, she went to her husband's room, knowing Girolamo was still up.

She knocked and waited until a voice from the other side of the thick wooden door replied. "Come in."

Entering, Caterina was astounded by the chaos that surrounded her husband's desk. Papers and scrolls, books and ledgers covered every surface, including chairs, shelves, and the windowsill. "I would speak with you."

Girolamo looked up, and Caterina saw the dark circles under his eyes as he narrowed them. "About?"

Taking this as permission to step further into the room, Caterina walked to his desk and stood there. "The conspiracy."

"There's nothing to discuss."

"There is everything to discuss! Do you not realise the shame you've brought upon us? Upon me? Do you not understand the disdain my presence elicits from the nobles?"

"And do you not understand, wife, that any respect you were shown was because of me." Enjoying Caterina's frown, he smiled. "It's true. Did you think the bastard child of a soldier could ever earn the admiration of citizens in the greatest city in the world?"

Speechless, Caterina stood there gaping. Before she could even think of a reply, she found herself dismissed.

"Go now. I have business to attend to. Keep your opinions and laments to yourself." He returned his attention to the page in front of him.

Caterina held back her tears until she had at least left the room and closed the door behind her. She felt their burning presence in the hall as she ran to her rooms, not caring who saw her.

Caterina spent the next two weeks in bed, ignoring everything and everyone around her. Luisa tried to get her friend to speak about what was happening, but all Caterina could manage was to describe the dark cloud that had descended on her, one she could not find her way out of. Luisa had a temporary bed set up beside Caterina's so she could be there to help her friend find her way through the darkness.

News of the conspiracy spread through Italy and Europe until the heads of state and high-ranking officials spoke of it in dozens of cities and countries. There was no chance of the story not reaching Milan.

"Caterina." Luisa shook her friend gently, trying to rouse her from her stupor. "Caterina. There is a letter."

Caterina opened her eyes and blinked a few times, forcing her mind to clear a path so she could engage for a while.

Seeing Caterina awake, Luisa didn't hesitate. "Here. It's from Bona."

Even hearing the name elicited a spark of hope in Caterina's breast, and something flared to life again in her mind. She took the letter and read it to herself as Luisa waited.

"My dearest daughter,

It can be no surprise to hear that news of your misfortune has reached us in Milan. The truth is difficult to come by, and I am still piecing together the various strands of this cloth, but I know enough to understand what you're going through.

I've never told you this, but I, too, struggled when your father was still alive. His sins were many, some of which you are blissfully and thankfully unaware of. After he passed, I feared for his immortal soul, such were the gravity of his deeds. I wrote to the Holy Father, begging for advice, for such a spiritual matter was beyond my understanding.

His Holiness replied with the only solution available to me: pray for my husband's soul. This was the only way to ensure your father would be saved. Yet I still fought with my own guilt at not doing more. The release I sought could only be found in helping others. Doing good works, healing the sick, and helping the less fortunate. In this way, I felt that my soul, too, was healing.

You are clever and kind but also fierce. Do not let others determine your value. That is for you alone to decide.

Yours ever in Christ, Bona of Savoy."

By the time she had finished reading, tears were streaming down Caterina's face. She heard the sadness in Bona's voice through these words. Handing the letter to Luisa, Caterina wept for a long time, allowing herself the release her body so desperately needed. Then, breathing deeply and wiping her face with the back of her hands, she rose from bed.

"Call for a bath to be prepared and help me decide what to wear today. I'm going out."

Overjoyed that her friend had miraculously recovered, Luisa still frowned in confusion. "Are you certain you're well enough?"

Caterina smiled grimly. "I am. I know I'm the topic of Roman humour right now, I've heard the whispers and laughing of the servants when they think themselves unnoticed. Don't think I have no idea what is being said about me. But Bona's letter has acted like a balm to my broken soul."

"What do you want to do?" Luisa's frown vanished, and she was now excited to leave the room with her friend.

"The market, I think." She walked to a box and opened it, looking for a gown. She had been made to feel inadequate and at fault for something she'd had no part in. It had taken her back to her first meeting with Girolamo's sister at Imola and her fear of not being accepted. Caterina now fully understood the importance of knowing everything going on under one's own roof. And that included as much as was possible of her husband's business. The more she thought about it, the more determined Caterina was to never stand by passively again, to never be caught out with news such as this. She would ensure she'd never be kept in the dark again.

Four guards stepped forward wordlessly as they appeared in the courtyard and followed them into the market square. Used to most aspects of her life in Rome, the constant guard was something she doubted she'd ever find normal.

"Here we are." They'd arrived at a small, dark shop set behind the colonnade that ran around the square. Stepping inside, Caterina let the familiar smells of the apothecary envelope her.

"My lady, welcome to my business." A large man with a friendly, wizened face stood behind a counter filled with jars and bowls. The entire shop was lined with shelves, top to bottom. Each was stacked with containers of all shapes and sizes, from clay to fine glass, and every vessel held something.

"Signor, I am..."

"Madonna, I know who you are. All of Rome knows. It's an honour to have you here." He came out from behind the counter, and Caterina could see from his bulk how successful his trade must be.

"You know who I am, tell me about yourself and your shop." She pointed at the shelves.

"I am Isach de Luca, son of Tobia. This, as you can see, is my family business." He smiled proudly.

"It's a pleasure to meet you. May I call you Isach?" Caterina had already decided that she liked this man.

"Of course, Madonna. Now, what can I help you with today? Something to soften your hair? Or perhaps a beauty tincture for your skin?" He held up his own hand, and she could see the smoothness of his olive complexion, belying the roadmap of wrinkles on his forehead and around his eyes.

"No, thank you, Signor." How to explain to this man that she wished to set up her own physick room. "I studied healing before I moved to Rome, and now wish to continue my work. I require supplies that will allow me to mix my own treatments and cures."

Instead of the disapproval she'd expected, Caterina was delighted to see a wide grin spread across the man's face. "Another healer! My lady, it will be my greatest honour to see that you have everything you need. We can even exchange recipes if you deem it appropriate."

Barely able to contain herself at having found a kindred spirit, Caterina set about listing the items she required. "I will write to my stepmother and ask for her advice, for she is also a talented healer."

"And I will be here for you anytime, my lady." Isach bowed again, and his curly black hair fell forward over his forehead.

"I would appreciate your sending word when everything is ready."

"I will, Madonna. I wish you and your lady a good day." He nodded at Luisa.

Outside, she breathed in the Roman air once more, so different from in the apothecary. She'd noticed the city's unsanitary conditions before but hadn't any ideas of how to help. Or if it was even her place to do so. Bona had always taught her to be gracious to her citizens, but she didn't rule Rome. She was a guest here, like many others. An important visitor, but a visitor all the same. The smell of the apothecary took her back to her childhood and the lessons her stepmother had imparted.

"When we get back, I must write to Bona." Caterina started working on her letter as they walked the rest of the way home and was so deep in her mental composition that she barely had enough time to stop herself from bumping into a group of Roman women standing at the edge of the square. She heard their whispers as she passed but held her head high and slowed her step to a more confident pace.

Chapter Eleven
1478 - 1479

By the end of the summer, Caterina and Luisa had set up a reasonable copy of Bona's workroom, complete with everything Rome had to offer any healer. Caterina was delighted to find ingredients she'd never heard of before. It seemed everything could be obtained in the holy city, even items from Arabic regions if one knew where to look. Caterina had also been spending more time in the papal library. Now used to coming and going freely through the Vatican halls, Caterina found medical resources she could have only dreamt of in her father's library in Milan.

She'd also kept her eyes and ears open, relying on both Luisa and Bossi to provide information on the conspiracies of the city. There were always rumours, and Caterina was quickly learning to discern fact from fiction, even with the most tangled of family intrigues.

Luisa had accompanied her friend to the Vatican library and then left to run errands. Caterina breathed in the air, so much like her family library. The smells of Rome disappeared here, and one could almost believe the world's sins had dissolved into nothing. Two guards stood outside waiting and would stand there as long as their mistress was in the library, no matter how many glares they received from the priests who ran the place. There were two of them, and they never spoke other than to deliver terse replies to her questions. She never even learned their names and referred to them by nicknames she had assigned.

Today she was here to browse, seeking shelter from the early Autumn heat outside. Running her hands over the stacked books, she hummed a tune to herself, one she'd learned as a child at her father's court. She picked up a book she recognised and flipped through the stunningly decorated pages while still singing.

"What song is that?"

Startled, Caterina turned to find Sixtus standing behind her. "Your father, I mean My Holiness." In her shock, she dropped the book. Unsure what to do, she reached down slowly and picked up the heavy tome. "Your Holiness." Caterina dropped into a deep curtsey, the book clutched to her chest.

"We are sorry, my dear. We didn't mean to startle you. Here," the Pope raised her up. "There, that's better." Looking down, he saw the book. "What have you discovered in our collection?"

Caterina held out the tome.

"Ahh, Bocaccio. Quite a racy fellow." He winked at Caterina. "We think you'll enjoy that one."

"I've already read it, Your Holiness."

The Pope's smile lit up his face, chasing away the years of worry. "Would you care to join us for a meal? We would enjoy your company."

"It would be my honour, Holy Father."

"Excellent. We will send a messenger to your home." They walked out of the library. Sixtus dismissed Caterina's guards, informing them their mistress would be safely accompanied home. He found a passing maid and sent his request to the kitchens. When they were alone in the corridor, the Pope leaned toward Caterina. "When we are alone, you may call me uncle if you like." He looked at her fondly. "Or Papa if you would honour me so. And we'll dispense with the other formalities."

"Holy Father, you honour me like a true daughter."

Sixtus waved away the comment and led her to his private apartments. Few saw these rooms; only family or beloved members of the college of cardinals were ever permitted past the door. The room was just as extravagant as the rest of the Vatican, with gold trim on every piece of furniture, silk cushions on each chair and silver thread woven into every tapestry that covered the high walls.

"Sit here, my dear." Sixtus led Caterina to a table beside a large window overlooking the Tiber and the city beyond. As they settled, servants efficiently delivered food and wine, then disappeared as quickly as they'd appeared. "Eat, drink. Enjoy the best of what our beloved country has to offer." As Caterina picked her meat and cheese from a large platter, the Pope poured rich dark wine into finely engraved glasses. He gave one to Caterina and held his up. "To the glory of God and Rome."

Caterina smiled and sipped from her glass, her eyes widening at the strength of the drink.

Seeing her look, Sixtus laughed. "It's from Tuscany. One of my favourites."

While they ate, the Pope pointed out different city areas and places where ancient ruins still stood. They talked of light matters: how she found Rome, if the air agreed with her, and her hobbies and activities.

"I hear you are often in my library."

Turning red, Caterina rushed to defend herself. "I am, Papa. But I also enjoy walking around the city, speaking with people and finding new merchants."

Sixtus nodded his approval. "I was teasing, my dear. You may visit any time you wish. And I admire your kindness while on your walks, if only more in this city were like you."

Emboldened by the Pope's compliment, Caterina suddenly had an idea. "Uncle, may I suggest a way to help people in the city and keep it cleaner?"

"My dear, I am all ears. Tell me what plans you've made on your walks."

"The water. Something everyone needs. The wealthy in Rome have the means to obtain it but the poor do not. If you were to repair the water passages of the ancients, fresh water would be channelled to Rome as it did long ago." Caterina hoped the image of a glorious past would intrigue the Holy Father.

Sixtus sat silently, considering the proposal.

Caterina continued. "With fresh water once again available throughout the city, the people would be happier and the streets cleaner."

The Pope smiled. "It's true." He took his glass and sipped slowly, staring at Caterina. Putting the glass back, he nodded. "I'll speak to the cardinals about it. I'm certain some monies could be diverted for such a worthy project."

Caterina could barely keep still in her chair. She'd grown much over the last year, but often her excitement threatened to take over. Her face suffused with happiness, she grinned triumphantly and took a mouthful of cherries sprinkled with sugar.

"You will be a good influence on my nephew, I can tell." Sixtus reached over and patted Caterina's hand. "Give him a child. Let him see what being a father means." He looked out the window.

Caterina waited to regain his attention and thought briefly of a rumour that Girolamo was actually the Pope's son, not his nephew. She shook the idea away. Surely the Holy Father wouldn't lie.

The quiet between them grew heavy, and Caterina wondered if she should make an excuse to leave the pontiff with his thoughts. As she considered her options, Sixtus spoke.

"There are some who argued against the Pazzis, did you know that? They warned of trouble to come, but I didn't listen. For that I'll be sorry the rest of my life."

"So it wasn't my fault?" Caterina whispered.

"No, child, of course not. No one can stop evildoers, they are like weeds in a garden, they always find ways to grow and expand and push out the beauty." The pontiff sighed deeply, and Caterina wondered if he was talking generally or about members of his own family.

"Why did you give your permission?"

The glimpse Caterina had had of sadness was gone. "Is that what people are saying?" He shook his head. "Like the misunderstanding that led to the martyrdom of England's beloved Thomas a Becket, my words were twisted to suit someone else's purpose, and death was the result." Sixtus suddenly looked his age again, the joy at having Caterina visit now fading. "Your nephew Raffaele, innocent of any part in this plan, has only just been released from his jailers in Florence, who still live with an interdict for assuming papal justice and murdering the Archbishop of Pisa." He smiled kindly. "My dear, I am afraid I have much work to see to, as you can tell by my ramblings, and I'm certain you're being missed at home by now."

Standing along with him, she curtsied and kissed his ring. "Papa, thank you for your kind words and sage advice." She watched as he left the room, and a papal guard appeared a moment later. Caterina thought of the conversation as she returned in the carriage provided by the Pope, dissecting every word and expression. He'd given her much to think about and share with Luisa.

After his part in the Pazzi conspiracy, Caterina hoped her husband would avoid intrigue. He did not. If anything, the failed plot had only encouraged him that his power was endless and that he was above any law created by man. Caterina was not the only one paying attention this time. So was the Holy Father.

"Raffaele, it's lovely to see you." Caterina reached over and placed a kiss on the blushing cardinal's cheek.

"It always makes my day when I receive an invitation to dine with my favourite aunt and uncle."

A cold October wind blew through the courtyard, making Caterina shiver. "Let's go inside. There is food and spiced wine waiting and a warm fire." Leading the young man inside, Caterina snuck a sideways glance at the cardinal. He was thinner, his experience in a Florentine jail still reflected on his frame, but his eyes sparkled with the wit she had grown to love, and she adored the way his face lit up when he saw her.

Caterina had arranged a private meal for Girolamo, herself, and the cardinal, and they sat in one of the smaller rooms at the end of a table meant for six or more. A chicken and bread soup made with Milanese almonds was followed by a bresaola prepared with veal and a breast of beef served with hot orange juice, cinnamon, and sugar. Caterina had received a few bottles of Tuscan wine from the Holy Father after one of their lunches and had been saving them for a special occasion.

Girolamo sat quietly through most of the meal, letting Caterina make most of the conversation. He'd add a question or comment but, for the most part, sat impatiently as he ate.

"How is my sister?"

"My mother is well. She writes to ask when you will next be in Imola."

Girolamo grunted. "I have business here that keeps me from travelling."

At this comment, the cardinal looked down, suddenly uncomfortable. "Uncle, this business you speak of is one of the reasons I am here this evening." Raffaele now had Caterina's and Girolamo's undivided attention.

"Go on." Girolamo's voice was low and menacing.

Raffaele cleared his throat. "The Holy Father is disturbed by rumours which are continually dripped into his ears. When he heard I was visiting this evening he asked me to pass on his suggestion that you focus less on your military plans and those of the papacy and more on your family."

The room grew quiet. Any servants within hearing distance of the cardinal's speech had found ways to slip away until only Girolamo, Caterina, and Raffaele sat.

"He said what?" Girolamo's voice had dropped even lower. The threat was unmistakable.

"I'm sorry to be the one reporting this, uncle, but His Holiness does not want the papacy to be brought into disrepute."

Girolamo rose slowly and looked down in disgust at his nephew. "Is that it?"

The cardinal now looked nervous and glanced at Caterina for support. At her almost imperceptible nod, he finished. "The Holy Father suggests you stay away from the Vatican and get more comfortable in your own house. You spend so little time here," he waved a hand around the frescoed room.

"I see."

Caterina heard the anger in his voice and noticed that his words had emerged from a tightly clenched jaw. Swallowing hard, she sat as still as possible, preparing for anything. Instead of the expected outburst, Girolamo bowed his head at the cardinal.

"I'm suddenly tired and will retire. Stay as long as you like, there are rooms prepared should the evening grow long." With that, he strode silently out, leaving Caterina and Raffaele to stare at each other.

Whether the Pope's words truly affected her husband or if he was just good at hiding his frustration at not being allowed back at the papal court, Caterina couldn't tell. But for the remainder of the year, Girolamo grew more attentive to both her and the palace. He presented a calm exterior and attended Caterina's dinners with polite interest. Relieved that she had also somehow been forgiven by Roman society, Caterina enjoyed her home life more than ever.

After a long evening of music and dancing on a cold night in February of 1479, Caterina had retired well after midnight feeling excited and exhausted. She was content with her new life, and even her husband's frequent visits to her bedchamber had became more tolerable, if still not the romantic meeting of souls a small part of her yearned for. Snuggling into the covers, she had fallen asleep looking forward to the next day's scheduled hunt, something Caterina and Girolamo, despite his coldness, could enjoy together.

The next morning, however, she woke feeling ill. Wondering if she'd perhaps had too much fine Sicilian wine, a gift from a well-wisher last night, she rose to sitting in her bed. Immediately a wave of nausea rolled over her, and she scrambled to reach a nearby basin before the contents of her stomach were expelled.

Luisa rushed in, a look of alarm on her face, and hurried to Caterina. Holding the strands of Caterina's hair that had escaped her net back from her friend's forehead, Luisa waited until the heaving finally finished. Helping Caterina to stand, she walked her back to the bed and helped her climb in. As she made Caterina comfortable, she instructed a maid to take away the basin and bring another, as well as a jug of water and glasses.

"What happened? How do you feel?" Luisa stood beside the bed, looking down worriedly.

"I don't know. I woke feeling ill. Perhaps something I ate." Caterina frowned. "Is anyone else unwell?"

Luisa shook her head. "No, not as far as I know."

Staring for a moment longer, Luisa finally stepped back. "I'm summoning a physician. I'm certain Bossi will know if one is nearby."

"No!" Her own voice startling her, Caterina composed herself. "Please. I don't need anyone. Just some rest."

Her forehead wrinkled with worry, Luisa considered her friend's words.

Caterina took advantage of the pause. "I've been exerting myself. We both have. The visiting and our walks around Rome and rides in the fields beyond the walls, not to mention the feasts and dancing most nights."

Although she'd never say it out loud, Luisa felt the same. It had been months of frenetic activity and a day doing nothing except reading in quiet, like they used to, sounded like bliss. "Should I call off the hunt?"

"I don't think so." Caterina noticed a guard patrolling the hall outside and called to him. "Send word to the count that I am unwell today, that it is nothing serious, and that he should go on the hunt without me."

The man nodded and hurried off.

"There. All done." The effort had made Caterina nauseous again. Luisa, still peering closely at her friend's face, saw the sweat break out and the skin grow pale and rushed over to the maid who'd just entered with a clean basin. Returning to the bed, she was just in time to place the bowl near Caterina so she could vomit again. This time it took less time as the countess' stomach was empty. Still, listening to her friend's heaving raised her own gorge as well as her sympathy.

Caterina was ill for the next few days, and even Girolamo, who had shown little interest in his wife's well-being that summer, visited her room.

"You need a physician."

She knew she should keep quiet and agree. But Caterina had grown tired of Luisa's hints about healers. The energy it took to keep persuading her friend that she needed only sleep was exhausting, and caused Caterina to address her husband more sharply than she intended.

"I need rest. Why must I keep explaining this to everyone?" She burrowed down in her bed, trying to disappear.

"Your woman tells me you've been ill for days now. I must insist you get over this northern stubbornness and listen to reason." Girolamo's face showed no emotion as he waited in the doorway.

Sighing, Caterina admitted defeat. "Fine. Send for someone." She looked out from beneath a blanket. "Someone trustworthy," she added.

With a slight nod, the count left. Luisa moved around the room, tidying areas she'd already tidied twice over and rearranging objects on shelves just to use up the nervous energy she felt. At least Caterina had agreed to see someone.

"You had better not be feeling smug right now." Caterina's voice came floating across the room.

"I'm not. I'm relieved you're finally seeing sense. Rome supposedly has the finest physicians in all the world and it's foolish not to seek them out when needed."

Feeling even more deflated, Caterina sulked. "I know. But I'm a Sforza," she explained.

"You are also the Pope's niece, and it would not look good if any found out you refuse treatment. It may seem like an excess of pride on your part."

Caterina preferred to think of her reticence as caution but could understand what her friend meant. They settled into a more comfortable silence until a noise and flurry of footsteps announced the physician before the harried-looking man appeared in the room, accompanied by Bossi. Bowing deeply to the countess, he spoke in a kind voice. "My lady, I am the Holy Father's personal physician. His Holiness sent me to attend you."

With a surprised glance at Luisa, Caterina sat up in bed, hoping her stomach wouldn't betray her in front of this man. Fortunately, there was nothing left, and apart from a moment of uncertainty as to whether her body would take over, she was able to prop herself up with help from Luisa.

The doctor retrieved a nearby chair and sat close enough to question and examine her if necessary.

"What are your symptoms?"

"I am tired yet am unable to sleep soundly most nights. In the mornings I feel the lack of sleep in my stomach, and when I try to rise from my bed, I expel anything I was able to eat the evening before."

The man nodded. "And you are able to eat in the evenings and keep food down?"

"Yes, although certain foods that I loved I find repugnant now, and others I barely noticed I crave more than anything."

"For example?"

Caterina thought for a moment. "Mushrooms. Any kind, from any area of Italy. I had no love for them before but now I feel great urges to consume as many as I can."

Lowering his eyes, unused to speaking directly with a woman, he asked, "Your courses, have they stopped?"

A look of shock passed over Caterina's face. How could this stranger have known? Her courses had never been regular, making management difficult at times, but she had noticed its disappearance for longer than ever before. "Yes."

The physician nodded again and smiled gently. "I believe I know what ails you, my lady."

Caterina glared at Luisa and grabbed her friend's hand as she sat on the edge of the bed. "Tell me."

"You needn't be alarmed, it's not bad news. In fact, you'll be pleased. My lady, I am overjoyed to tell you, as will the Holy Father be I'm certain, that you are carrying a child."

The physician obviously expected an overjoyed response, but Caterina's was anything but. "What?"

"Madonna, you are pregnant."

She shook her head. "No. You're wrong." She thought back to Bona and the cures she'd imparted. "It must be something else. Give me some candied ginger, I'm sure that will help me."

As the Pope's physician, the man wasn't used to delivering such delicate news to a woman, never mind a young woman. In his experience, the creation of a child was a direct sign of God's pleasure, and no one would dare question that.

"I assure you my diagnosis is correct. You show all the signs and I'm assuming more. Have your gowns perhaps felt a little tight lately?"

Caterina was about to deny any such thing, but Luisa nodded instinctively. The healer noticed and held up his hand. "You see?" He took her hand, patting it awkwardly. "Rejoice, my dear. Your husband will be proud and his uncle even more so. In the meantime, rest and God will guide you to a successful delivery."

He turned to leave, but Luisa stopped him. "What about her vomiting? How do we stop the sickness?"

"Pray for relief, for only the Almighty will provide it. And remember that all you endure is because of Eve's original sin." He bowed at a frowning Caterina and left the room.

"Pray? That is his advice?" Even raising her voice made her feel ill again.

Luisa adjusted a pillow. "Never mind that right now, how do you feel about this news?"

Caterina sat quietly, breathing in stomach-calming air and allowing herself to become used to the idea that she was carrying a babe. She reached down to her stomach and ran her hand over the barely swelling surface. A child, only a layer of skin from her hand. The deep breathing she'd gotten used to using to chase away her nausea had the effect of clearing her mind until there was only her and the unborn child. Her child. She smiled unconsciously. Perhaps a daughter, someone she could raise as she'd been, to be fierce and clever.

"The count will be pleased. He must be told, my lady." Bossi had been standing in the corner of the room. While he knew all of Rome would be delighted by this announcement, the husband must be informed first. For him to find out from a courtier or servant would be a grave insult.

"Yes, of course. Is he here?"

"I believe he is with the Holy Father. He sent the physician alone, but I'm sure the healer will head right back to whisper the news. It's seldom anyone carries good tidings, and I don't imagine the physician is immune to the possible rewards associated with delivering such a message."

"Once he hears from the healer, I'm certain the count will come home immediately." Caterina thought of writing a heartfelt note to her husband, like heroines in her stories did, but the idea was fleeting. She was not a heroine, her husband was not a prince, and their marriage was a contract. And now, here was the first fruit.

Caterina's pregnancy progressed with the weeks. The northern winter winds that chilled the walls of Milan lost their ferocity by the time they reached Rome, but the winter evenings were still cooler and the clothing required was heavier. Caterina's dinner parties were now celebrated with perhaps less energy, but with all the grace and wit the Roman elite had come to expect from the countess.

She put her feet up on a stool, took a sip of wine, her book open and balanced on her belly. With only a couple of months to go, she was tired of carrying the extra weight and the restrictions her condition forced on her. Like less riding, hunting, or fewer long walks around the city. Even in the cooler weather, she enjoyed her freedom and chafed at being forced inside at times.

Her confinement had been used productively, however. Caterina and Luisa had continued their work on Caterina's healing room, expanding it, and adding shelves and bookcases. Come spring, they would be setting up a garden inside the palace walls.

"Do you remember when Bona started teaching me herbs?"

Luisa looked up from her own book. "I do." She waited for more but went back to her story when no further discussion was forthcoming.

Caterina sat contentedly and picked up her book, an ancient treatise on medicine from an Arab healer.

"Caterina? I'm sneaking to the kitchen. Do you want anything?"

Caterina had been so involved in her medical book she hadn't realised any time had passed. She yawned sleepily. "Yes, some of the honey that was collected this morning and a few pears, please." Her stomach growled in anticipation.

Luisa hurried away and quickly returned holding a tray with Caterina's pears and honey and a dish of dates. They ate together in companionable silence, enjoying the peace.

"Have you ever noticed a feeling, I mean when people are here for a feast and it feels like a few of the guests share a secret, and they keep it from others, who want to know the secret but also have their own secrets and strive to keep them hidden?" Caterina knew she was doing a terrible job of explaining the strange sense of unease she felt at some of her banquets, one she'd started detecting after months of immersion in the city.

Luisa's eyes widened, and she nodded so vigorously that she nearly spilt the plate of dates. "Yes! On the surface, everyone smiles and is friends but underneath their eyes shift quickly, watching all in a room."

"Do they really do that?"

Nodding, Luisa continued. "One of the benefits of being your dama di corte is no one notices me. When we dine, all eyes are on you. I am free to sit and observe."

"I wish I could do that too. Rome will soon get tired of me, but not until this babe is born and someone new arrives or some scandal is uncovered. When that happens then I, too, will be free to just watch all."

"I don't understand how anyone lives like this. Do you think your father's court in Milan was the same?"

Caterina had been raised to adore her father, but in her time here in Rome, she'd learned of his reputation, and with enough proof for her to realise he wasn't the idealised man she'd worshipped as a child. Like many, he had faults that she was too young to see. Now, however, with her eyes opened by the politics of Rome, she understood more about her childhood than ever.

"Probably. I think all courts are the same." She wrapped her arms around her belly protectively, shifting the book to a nearby table. Leaning closer, she whispered quietly, "But I won't let any of that affect you, mia cara. I will protect you with my life."

Chapter Twelve
1479

When he'd found out his wife was pregnant, Girolamo had decided that their house wasn't big enough and had built a larger one in the newly popular Piazza Navona area of Rome. Close to the Tiber, Caterina could look out the window from her second-story rooms and see the Castel Sant'Angelo just across the water. The house was more lavish than their previous one, and Caterina wondered at the size of it as she and Girolamo wandered around on a visit to the site. The courtyard was three times as large and had colonnades made of highly decorated marble, with a covered walkway around the entire space.

  Now, months later, Caterina was seeing her new home for the first time and was startled by the gaudiness of the decoration. Girolamo, believing his wealth had imbued him with taste, had hired the most expensive painters he could without his wife's opinion or the artists' ability considered. After walking around a bit, she decided she could live with it, but insisted on adding her own suggestions to the nursery and her own rooms.

  "I'd like something calming, perhaps with tapestries showing nature and the beasts of the forest."

  "Speaking of the forest, I'm going hunting tomorrow. Will you be joining me?"

  Girolamo's efforts involved inviting Caterina to hunt with him more often. It was the perfect way for them to be involved in an activity together, one they both enjoyed, but with little opportunity to speak directly about anything of consequence. Luisa would join them often, her presence no longer a seeming irritant to the count.

"I would like that very much." She rubbed her hand over her stomach, relishing the ride despite her swelling size.

"I'll have the grooms prepare your favourite horse to be ready at dawn. I was thinking the Janiculum Hill."

The hill on the west side of Rome was close enough to escape the crowded city but far enough that one could imagine themselves in a distant forest instead of being within eyesight of one of the largest cities in Europe. The Riarios hunted there often, either together or on their own. This pleasure and planning (or, in some cases, replanning) her home's decorations made her pregnancy seem easier. After she'd gotten used to sitting with her extra weight, she rode out a few times a week, sometimes with the count and at other times with just a small guard. The countryside was the one place she could truly feel free from any responsibilities.

Caterina continued hunting and riding until it began to get unwieldy. Yielding to Girolamo's and Luisa's requests, she retired from horseback for the time being. There were still months to go before her child was born, but, seeing the contentment her decision had given them both, she relented.

As the final few months of her pregnancy approached, Caterina lay back in her chair in the library and wondered if this was finally it. The life she'd always dreamed of, an end to their troubles. Sighing deeply, she allowed herself to believe it.

Caterina had dragged Luisa to the papal library to look through the shelves, despite knowing her friend wasn't as comfortable as she was in these surroundings.

"What if the Holy Father should need something? Will he send someone to collect it or visit the library himself?" Luisa looked around as if she expected the Pope to jump out from behind a table.

Trying hard not to laugh, Caterina adopted an uninterested look and kept searching through the stacks of books. "Sometimes he sends someone, at other times he visits himself. One never knows. He could show up at any moment." The look on her friend's face at her words was too much. "I jest! Besides, even if His Holiness does enter the room, you'll hear the four bookmen of the acropolis flutter with excitement. Plenty of warning for us."

Luisa's worry turned to mirth as she giggled at Caterina's nickname for the priests who ran the library, including the two young monks who had joined recently. It was true. This room was like an ancient temple, only one devoted to knowledge instead of God.

After noticing the glares of the librarians, Caterina shushed her friend. "Let's go before they ask us to leave."

Knowing no one would dare ask her friend, a countess and woman whom the Pope treated like a daughter, to leave, Luisa nevertheless agreed.

Stepping out into the bright summer light with Luisa, Caterina looked around, unprepared to return home on such a glorious day. A new building had been erected nearby, and the open door was too tempting. "Let's sneak inside and take a look." She began walking toward the structure before Luisa could reply.

"This will be the new chapel, designed by the Holy Father himself," Caterina whispered as they entered. They passed through a small square room into a longer one, much like an enormous banquet hall. Looking around, Caterina noticed marble stones and the mortar and tools used by the masons scattered at the room's edges. Then she saw a lone figure standing halfway down the room, his back to her, staring at a wall.

Suddenly feeling like an intruder, Caterina signalled to Luisa and turned to exit. Her foot hit a piece of marble, and she tripped, prevented from falling by Luisa's quick reflexes. The noise was enough to attract the attention of the staring man.

Now that she'd been discovered, Caterina quickly recovered and stood tall. "I'm sorry Signor, I didn't mean to disturb you." She curtsied and started to leave once more.

"Wait! Madonna, please, you are welcome here."

Uncertain of what to do, Caterina glanced at Luisa. Her friend just shrugged and raised her eyebrows. By now, the man was walking over to her, so she turned to face him.

"I'm Caterina."

"I know who you are, my lady. All of Rome knows your name." He winked at her, his brown hair falling into his eyes.

She laughed. "I imagine they do." Especially after her husband's intrigues, she thought to herself, wondering if this person was thinking the same thing.

They stood in awkward silence. The man hadn't yet introduced himself, and she knew it would be rude to ask. "What are you doing here?"

"Excuse, my lady, I'm being impolite. I am Sandro Botticelli. I am working on a commission for His Holiness."

"Ahh, the Holy Father won't tell me what he has planned for his great chapel, no matter how much I pester him."

Sandro leaned in conspiratorially. "I will tell you if you promise not to share with anyone." He stood back and eyed her critically. "Are you interested in art, Madonna? You would make a wonderful model."

"I am, yes. My father was a patron of many artists and musicians."

"I'm glad to hear it. Now, let me describe to you what this chapel will look like, close your eyes if it helps."

Caterina looked back at Luisa, who was still standing nearby, listening, before focussing on the artist's words. Closing her eyes, she let his description fill her mind.

"Picture this, Madonna. Along the walls will be vast frescoes depicting the life of the Saviour and the life of Moses. Other artists and I have been selected to create these works. These focal pieces will be offset by portraits of past Popes above the frescoes and drapery done in the trompe-l'oeil style beneath."

Caterina could see the large chapel taking shape in her mind. "And the ceiling?"

"Blue with gold stars spaced evenly."

She nodded. "If it's anything like I'm imagining it will be magnificent."

A noise at one end of the room interrupted them. Caterina opened her eyes and saw another man enter. Another painter, she guessed. "I must go."

But Sandro was off in his own world.

Smiling, she joined Luisa and left him as they had found him, staring at a wall.

Caterina found the rest of the summer hot and uncomfortable, and watched in envy as Girolamo went out riding and hunting most days. He often took Cardinal Raffaele with him, and Caterina was glad that they seemed to have reconciled. She was also grateful the young man chose to dine with them often.

"Did you enjoy your ride today?" Caterina asked at dinner. As it was a Friday, Caterina had arranged a salted and smoked pike along with mock ricotta made from almonds and pike broth, followed by a dessert of plum crostata tart. She always observed the non-meat days but insisted that the food be fresh and well-seasoned, something she'd become known for in Rome.

"We did. The weather was very fine and the countryside around Rome is glorious." The cardinal beamed as he dug into his tart.

Girolamo had been silent for the meal, lapsing back into a habit tolerated by Caterina these days.

She continued, keeping the mood light. "You're not getting up to anything I hope."

Raffaele laughed delightedly at the thought.

Her husband, on the other hand, took her comment seriously. "No, just trying to mend my family."

He sounded positive, but the look on his face left Caterina wondering.

She was still puzzling over the dinner a few days later. "You don't think Girolamo is up to anything, do you?"

"I haven't seen anything out of the ordinary in the duke's demeanour," Luisa replied.

Nodding, Caterina walked to her mirror. "Neither have I. And I hate to be so suspicious..." her words were cut off by a sudden pain. Caterina winced.

"What's wrong?" Luisa was now standing.

"It's nothing. The babe has been moving so the past few hours." Her face wrinkled in pain again, and she took a deep breath as she grabbed her belly and leaned over.

Dropping any pretence of formality, Luisa grabbed her friend's shoulder. "Caterina, I think your time has come."

"No," Caterina shook her head, "the physicians said it would be another few weeks yet." She straightened. "I just need to sit down."

Luisa helped her to the chair she'd just vacated. Caterina was so large she could barely squeeze herself into it. As she lowered herself down, pain seized her again, and she felt a wetness between her legs.

Looking down, Luisa nodded. "I'm calling for the physician." Without waiting for any argument from Caterina, she rushed into the hall and found a maid. "Get the doctor. Now." The maid hurried off, and she returned to the chair. "Can you stand?"

Caterina nodded, now fully aware of what the earlier pains had been. "Yes."

After dressing her only moments ago, Luisa helped Caterina out of her clothes and back into bed. As expected, it didn't take long for the doctor to arrive.

"I hear we're ready to bring this child into the world, Madonna." Maids followed carrying towels and jugs of water, and Luisa directed their activities as the physician approached Caterina.

"You need more pillows; it will ease the child's journey and your own efforts."

Luisa was again on top of everything, gathering cushions from the chairs and benches in Caterina's bed chamber and adjoining rooms and arranging them around her friend.

"Your lady may leave us; she'll not be needed."

Caterina's eyes widened in horror. "No! She will stay." She reached over and took Luisa's hand, dragging her down so she sat on the opposite side of the bed.

"Your husband wishes your trial to be private."

"And so it shall be." She nodded at the maids and servants in the doorway, scattering them with a glance.

"See? Just us." Caterina started to wave at them but grabbed her stomach instead as another surge of pain hit.

The physician decided there was no time for further argument. "Now, my lady. You must bring your knees up." He positioned the sheets to ensure maximum privacy for Caterina and full access for himself. "When you next feel the pain, you must push with all your might."

Breathing heavily, Caterina nodded as the next contraction began. She tightened her grip on Luisa's hand, but rather than pull away at the pressure, she felt her friend's other hand envelop hers.

"Why is your husband not waiting someplace in the house?" Luisa asked.

"I don't know. But he sent me these." Caterina pointed to a nearby box. "Candied oranges."

Luisa made a hmphing noise. "That's the least he could do. He should be home."

"To do what?" Caterina managed as she blew out air. "I don't want him here." She screamed as another agonising wave of pain washed over her.

"Push, Madonna. You must push to help the child!"

Caterina had thought the pain of her marriage night the worst she'd ever felt, but now it consumed her, focussing her body on a single objective.

"Keep going, my lady. You can do it." Luisa released Caterina's hand and dipped a cloth in cold lavender-scented water from a nearby basin. She wiped her friend's face and arms in a business-like manner before sitting and taking Caterina's hand as another contraction started.

"There is the head! Push again, my lady. The child is almost here!" The physician had noticed Luisa's ministrations and had decided his patient was being well looked after enough for him to focus only on the baby.

With a final effort, Caterina screamed as the babe tore her open. The agony suddenly subsided, and Caterina laid her head back in the bed for a moment, letting her mind clear itself of the pain-infused fog.

"Madonna, you have a healthy child."

"What is it? A boy or a girl?" She knew without their having ever discussed it that Girolamo would prefer a boy. What man in Rome did not?

"A boy, Madonna."

Caterina fought the pain in her hips and legs and, with Luisa's help, sat up as much as she could. She reached out her arms, ignoring her exposed thighs and fluid-stained sheets. All she wanted at that moment was to hold her son.

The physician wrapped the child in soft linen and handed him to Caterina. Gazing down at the small angry face, her heart swelled to a size she never knew was possible. Bona had been right; this was a love unlike any other. Caterina knew Girolamo would be pleased. She didn't care. As she stared into the face of this helpless creature, she knew she would give her life for this child.

Caterina named her son Ottaviano, the birth name of Julius Caesar, who had brought peace to war-torn Rome. She hoped the name she'd chosen would bode well for the child's successful future. Over the next month, Caterina spent her time in the nursery when she wasn't eating or sleeping. Girolamo bragged to anyone who would listen about his son and made it evident that his prowess was responsible for the boy's existence.

There had never been an expectation that she would breastfeed Ottaviano herself, but Caterina was present most of the times the wet nurse fed her son.

"Are you ready to go?" Girolamo stood in the nursery doorway.

"We are." With a nod at the wet nurse, Caterina picked up her son and walked with her husband to the waiting carriage outside. The ride to the Vatican took only ten minutes, but Ottaviano was still too young to be carried the distance, and Caterina still too sore.

"The papal vice chancellor will be acting as godfather for our son, a high honour," Girolamo reminded Caterina. She already knew of this man, Cardinal Roderigo Borgia, for she had often seen him hovering around the Holy Father's quarters. Before her lying in, Caterina had spent more time with the Pope, finding him kind as a father but also challenging.

"Cardinal Borgia is in charge of requests for papal favours, is he not?"

Girolamo nodded. "Yes. So you see why today is important for us."

Caterina sighed. Despite her husband's attentions, none of his decisions were ever about her or their family, only about him and his standing and connections. Today was a special occasion for Caterina, and she was disappointed Girolamo saw it only as a way to regain his uncle's favour. And there were certain to be guests invited that she hadn't approved, wealthy nobles with influence.

They arrived at St Peter's and passed through the courtyard into the cathedral. The early Autumn winds had cleared out the foul air in much of Rome, and all Caterina could smell as she made her way to the far end of the building was beeswax and incense.

They waited only moments before Sixtus entered. He smiled at the three of them, a seemingly perfect family unit. Prayers and readings were said for both the child and his parents then they rose from the benches and carried the boy to the baptismal font, where the Pope stood waiting.

"Do you both renounce Satan and his works?"

Caterina and Girolamo replied at the same time. "Yes."

"Do you believe with all your heart and soul in God the Almighty Father and creator of all things?"

"Yes."

"Do you believe in Jesus Christ, the son sent to save mankind?"

"Yes."

"Do you believe and trust in the Holy Spirit?"

"Yes." They spoke in unison, as if rehearsed.

Sixtus held out his arms for the baby, and Caterina gently placed her son in the Pope's care. His Holiness made the sign of the cross over the child, then scooped water from the font with a fine silver baptismal cup and poured it over Ottaviano's head three times.

"Who will stand as godparent to this child?"

Cardinal Borgia stepped forward and stood still long enough for Caterina to finally get a decent look at him. Tall and thin, he would have had the appearance of an ascetic except for the heavy gold cross he wore and the jewelled rosary, sparkling in the candlelight, which hung from his belt. His face was pale and sharp, with small brown eyes glancing around as if he expected an attack of some sort.

"Do you promise to raise this child in accordance with the Holy Mother Church and all her teachings?"

"I do, your Holiness." He bowed before both pontiff and child.

As the ceremony was completed, Caterina briefly wondered about this man who would raise her only son should anything happen to her or Girolamo. A man, it was rumoured, who had been in a long-established relationship with a courtesan and who had numerous children by her. Was it even possible for such a person, cardinal or otherwise, to teach her child the morality he was meant to practice?

Shrugging the thought off, she spent the rest of the day as the centre of attention. Gifts for both her and the child arrived all afternoon, some useful, others an obvious ploy to gain the patronage of her growing family.

As the year marched closer to its successor, Caterina spent her time between her garden, her work area, and her family. She had gotten into the habit of letting the Holy Father know when she needed a book from the Vatican library, as he would often invite her to dine with him. Now seventeen, Caterina has been living in Rome for nearly two years and believed that she'd changed dramatically. She felt more capable of discussing Rome and its needs with Sixtus, even if Caterina felt like he humoured her much of the time. But she didn't mind. She was learning: the politics, the players, the hidden messages in their words and body language, everything.

Chapter Thirteen
1480

Early in the new year, Pope Sixtus announced grand plans to restore Rome, the eternal city, to its formal glory, starting with repairing the aqueducts and moving ancient sculptures and wall murals to a central location so all could visit them and wonder at the magnificence of the past.

"You listened to me," Caterina remarked excitedly at lunch with the Pope.

"You may not think I pay attention, not many do. But it's my secret power you see. I appear an old doddery man but then I surprise all by proving them wrong," Sixtus joked.

Mortified at the suggestion she'd been disrespectful, Caterina flushed red. "Your Holiness, I was not one of those," she stammered.

"Hush, child. I jest. Your idea was inspired and will do much good for the citizens of Rome."

"I still don't understand how it got to be so bad."

"When the church left to lead from Avignon, Rome was left defenceless and without trade. Structures already ancient crumbled into disuse and poverty took root and spread. When the papacy returned to the great city over sixty years ago, nothing was done to improve the lives of Romans."

Caterina shook her head. She'd never say it out loud, but the affluence she saw in the church and its servants shocked her. In Milan, they had wealth but saw to it that all in the city were looked after. Here, those who claimed to represent the poorest on behalf of the Lord seemed to only represent themselves and their own interests. At least something good was finally happening, she thought.

She was still pondering to herself when Sixtus brought up an unexpected subject. "I hear your uncle now rules Milan."

Startled by how well-informed he was, Caterina struggled with her emotions. "Yes." Her voice caught as she relayed what she knew. "My stepmother was ruling on behalf of my young brother, Gian Galeazzo. She took a lover, someone called Antonio Tassino, whom one of my father's advisors found distasteful and unworthy of the duchess' attentions. I don't know for certain, as I have not heard it from Bona herself, but they say she shared secrets of government with the man."

She stopped to take a long drink of wine, clearing her throat of the sudden lump she found there. "This Tassino invited my exiled uncle Ludovico back to Milan, where Ludovico seized control and imprisoned my father's advisor, Cicco Simonetta." Caterina looked down. "My uncle tortured Cicco and killed him because Cicco would not swear allegiance to him. When she saw the extent of her husband's injuries, Cicco's wife went mad," she choked.

"And now he rules on behalf of your brother?"

Caterina nodded meekly. "Yes. As soon as he returned, he found fault with Tassino and banished him." She picked up a date and threw it back on her plate. "I don't know what to do. I must support my stepmother, even if I do not understand her actions. But Ludovico is my uncle and family."

"I understand your dilemma. Will you take some advice?" Sixtus offered gently.

"Of course, Holy Father. Anything you can offer that will sooth my conscious would be a blessing."

After thinking for a moment, the pontiff spoke matter-of-factly. "You must write to your uncle and praise him for his actions."

"But why?" Caterina blurted out.

"Your young brother is still a minor. His safety must be assured. Were you to disapprove of your uncle's actions, Gian's life would be at risk, would it not?"

Aghast at an idea she'd never even considered, Caterina threw her hands over her open mouth. "Do you really think my brother's life is in danger?"

Sixtus stared at her. "You've been in Rome for long enough. What do you think?"

Caterina closed her eyes. What a fool I've been, she thought. When it came to her family and their safety, all personal considerations must be secondary, no matter how painful. "You're right. I should have realised it myself." Standing, she curtsied at the Pope and spoke sadly. "With your permission, I'd like to return home and write the letter. The sooner I can have it dispatched the better I'll feel," she said sadly.

"Go, child. We will both feel better once this task is completed, as distasteful as I know it is for you."

She rushed over to him, a sudden feeling of devotion washing over her. She was grateful to have someone who could offer advice. And, instead of kissing his ring, she hugged him without fear of reproval. Feeling him embrace her back, she didn't care if that advice would serve more than one purpose. It didn't matter to her at that moment.

Content with her relationship with at least two Riarios, the Pope and Cardinal Raffaele, Caterina's happiness increased when she realised she was once again with child. By now, she knew what to do and had even made her own treatments for the nausea which plagued her. With a perfect understanding of what her body was capable of doing, she continued with her usual activities, dividing her time between her first child, studying new remedies in her workroom, hunting, and helping the Holy Father with his grand plans for the city.

Now that Girolamo was back in his uncle's good books, his accolades rose once more. He was made the chief warden of the Church of Santa Maria del Populo, a new building on the same side of the river as their new home and another of the Pope's pet projects. Every Sunday, Caterina and her husband rode their carriage to make the twenty-minute journey to the church. Their carriage rode along the newly created roads around their palace and into the Roman countryside littered with old buildings and long-since fallen columns that once witnessed pagan rituals. As they neared the church, Caterina enjoyed gazing at one of these decrepit buildings. The Holy Father had told her it was a mausoleum for the emperor Augustus and his family, and she wondered how the ruler would feel if he knew his resting place was now used as a garden and a place where children and dogs played.

When they arrived, they took their place at the front of the church and were greeted by everyone when they left. It was a powerful appointment for Girolamo and a source of networking for Caterina. Many dinner and hunting invitations were offered from nobles as she walked the short distance from the church to her carriage. Most Caterina agreed to purely for social reasons. Others were more strategic acceptances. But despite her association with the upper echelons of Rome, she still enjoyed visiting her favourite vendors whenever possible and while she was still able to get around easily.

"Madonna, how lovely to see you!" Isach stepped out from behind his counter, wiping his hands on his apron as he approached. He bowed and reached for Caterina's hand, finding it readily given.

"Signor de Luca, I've told you before such formality isn't necessary. We are equals here." She waved her hand around the apothecary. A noise from behind the counter made her frown. Peering over Isach's shoulder, Caterina saw a small face staring back at her. "Who's this?"

"I'm sorry, my lady. This is my daughter, Sarra. She spends time with me, I hope she'll take over for me when I'm too old to practise any longer." He turned. "Come here, child."

The girl came forward shyly, staring at the floor.

"This is Countess Riario, a very important patron." Turning back to Caterina, he smiled as he put his arm around his daughter's shoulder. "She was told to return upstairs to work on her studies." His voice grew louder as he spoke. But his mock frown fooled no one. "Say hello," he urged her forward.

"My lady, welcome to my father's shop." She curtsied and stepped back.

Caterina leaned down, so she was level with Sarra. "Thank you. I hope I'm more than just a patron, though, for I trust your father as much as I would any true friend."

Sarra turned to her father, uncertain of how to reply. Isach nodded at her, and she ran to the back of the shop. Caterina laughed at the footsteps scampering less-than-daintily up the stairs. "Thank you for your kind comments, Madonna." He watched her struggle to rise. "I see your own child is nearly ready to join us."

"Yes, another month." Feeling at home here, Caterina stretched her arms up and sighed.

"What can I do for you today? Is there anything you need for your own work?"

"No, not really. The babe was as restless as I, so I decided to take a walk. I enjoy stopping by and saying hello."

"And to see if I have anything interesting to share, no?" Isach winked at her.

Caterina laughed. "Am I so obvious? I thought I had improved after my years in Rome."

A flash of a frown passed over Isach's face before being replaced with a more even look. Caterina, however, had noticed it. "What's wrong? I can see there's something troubling you."

"My woes are not for you to worry over, Madonna." He returned to his place behind the counter and started grinding an herb he had been working on.

"Signor de Luca." Caterina put her hand on his, stopping them. "You have heard me mention my trials in the past. Let me do the same for you."

Flushing red, Isach put the wooden pestle he'd been using down. "Your mention of your years here, this city." He stopped to gather his emotions. "I know you are a favourite of Pope Sixtus and, as such, above the concerns of many. I also know you are protected everywhere you go." He glanced at the soldiers waiting outside.

"Signor! I can easily ask my guards to move so your shop is not seen in any negative light!"

Isach shook his head. "No, Madonna, you misunderstand." He sighed. "This city, with its guards and warring, it's barely safe for the Christians who live here. But for us..." he let his words trail.

She held up her hand. "I understand." Despite feeling she'd learned much, every day introduced her to things she hadn't even realised existed.

"My daughter. I just don't feel it's safe for her to grow up here. A less crowded place perhaps, someplace more open."

Caterina thought for a moment, considering his words. "Imola," she announced suddenly.

"My lady?"

"You introduced me to your daughter as a countess. I am that, and would see that all in my land are protected as best I can." She saw he was listening earnestly. "I offer this as a choice, for you to think about." Not wanting to put Isach on the spot, she smiled and pointed at a jar on a shelf. "Now, tell me about that, I don't recognise the name on the label."

By August Caterina was again suffering the exhaustion her swollen body caused. Still, her discomfort was alleviated by more news: the Holy Father was conferring the territory of Forli to Girolamo.

Feeling particularly awkward, Caterina adjusted her dress as she and Luisa prepared for the ceremony.

"Where is Forli?"

Looking in the mirror, Caterina nodded. "It's just south of Imola, a little closer to the coast. There's a small town called Faenza between our two cities." She turned to Luisa and spoke knowledgeably. "There are only two roads which run from Milan and Venice to the papal states in the south. One goes through Tuscany, the other runs through both Imola and Forli."

"A strategic city."

"Yes, and important." She glanced outside, seeing how high the sun sat. "We should get going, I don't want to be late." Caterina winced suddenly, leaning over.

"Are you well enough to go?" Luisa's forehead wrinkled.

"Yes. This one has been very active lately, that's all. His time is in a couple of weeks and he's enthusiastic about joining his brother." She stood fully. "There, he's quiet again. Shall we?" Caterina offered Luisa her arm, knowing her friend would help her. It was an important day, but rather than feel cowed by the ceremony, Caterina felt elated. More honours for her husband meant more security for her son.

Still uncomfortably warm, Caterina sat at the front of the church at St Paul's while the Pope praised his nephew's leadership abilities and wisdom. Caterina was certain no one in the place believed a word of it, not even the Holy Father, but there was a convention of duplicity in this city to which all adhered. As Sixtus blessed his nephew as the new Count of Forli, Caterina felt a painful cramp and suddenly understood. The child was coming early.

Trying to keep the pain a secret, she couldn't help but wince and grab her stomach as a strong contraction gripped her. The resultant commotion around her caught the attention of even more people. The Pope and Girolamo turned, the pontiff with a worried expression and her husband with an annoyed one.

The Pope nodded at her and hurriedly finished the ceremony as Caterina was ushered from the chapel by Luisa and Bossi. Helping her into the carriage, they both turned to see if Girolamo was close by.

"He's not here, my lady," Luisa whispered into the carriage window.

"Go. Please. Get me home. My husband knows the way." She grimaced again as more pain hit.

Luisa climbed inside and grabbed Caterina's hands in her own. The jostling of the vehicle made Luisa feel ill, and she had no idea how her friend could still sit upright. They arrived home, and Caterina was accompanied up to her bed. A messenger had been sent on ahead, and her room was already filled with servants making preparations. After her first child had been born, and with her closer relationship with the Holy Father, Caterina insisted that a midwife, rather than the papal physician, be present. The midwife, an older short woman with greying hair and strong arms, stepped forward and curtsied.

"Madonna, my name is Maria. I'm here to help you and your child."

As if acknowledging her words, another contraction forced Caterina to the ground. Maria and Luisa helped her up, got her changed, and into bed. The pains were still far enough apart for Caterina to drink sips of wine, but after nearly spilling her glass when a strong one engulfed her, she handed the cup to Luisa.

The palace was filled with Caterina's screams for the next two days, followed by the murmured words of encouragement from the midwife and Luisa. Even through her exhaustion, Caterina could see the worried looks on the faces of anyone who entered. The baby was already weeks early, and now the protracted labour meant many had already decided the child's fate.

Cesare Riario was born as a muddied August sun woke the citizens of Rome.

"I must write to Bona." Caterina sat up in bed a week later as Luisa entered the room.

"Have you received any news from her lately?"

"No. But I'm sure she must be very busy. She enjoyed working as a healer for the palace, perhaps a fever is spreading." Despite her attempt at cheerfulness, Caterina was worried. It wasn't like her stepmother to not write for so long.

"You're right." Luisa had Caterina's clothes ready. It was still too early for her to ride, but she had persuaded her friend and the midwife that she was fine walking around her home. "We must stop by the nursery first."

"Of course." Luisa smiled as she dressed Caterina. After her first son's birth, the countess had been sad for a while, for reasons unknown to Caterina. But this time Luisa saw only true happiness in her friend's face.

Chapter Fourteen
1480 - 1481

The weeks passed, and Caterina returned to her favourite activities as soon as her body permitted. Her walks around the palace had grown more vigorous, and soon she could order new clothes in her usual slim size.

"I want to work in the garden today."

Luisa nodded. "It has been a while since we worked outside. The fresh air will do us both good." Luisa tided Caterina's room as they waited for their breakfast. "Is there anything in particular you want to do?"

"Just gather supplies, I'd like to make a few treatments."

"Speaking of treatments, that reminds me, we need to prepare more tincture for burns."

"My most popular treatment at the palace it seems. We can make more today. I think I have the ingredients in the garden." She mentally noted the ingredients. "Can you get an onion from the kitchen?"

A maid carried in a tray with food. "Where is the count today?"

"With the Holy Father, my lady," the maid replied, bobbing and hurrying from the room.

They sat to eat. Caterina was silent for a moment, eating a piece of bread dipped in olive oil. "Did you know my husband tried to trick Lorenzo Medici into poisoning him?"

"What?" Luisa sputtered, spilling wine on the floor. Reaching down to wipe up the mess, she looked up, frowning. "What do you mean, trick him?"

Caterina sighed. While recovering from Cesare's birth, she'd been frustrated by people's reticence to share negative news with her. Now she was frustrated when they did. "He bribed a priest from Imola and tasked him to move amongst the citizens of Florence and spread hatred of Girolamo. This priest was told to speak against the count to the Magnificent himself and offer to poison my husband if the Medici would provide the poison."

"The count is still alive," Luisa added wryly as she sat up again.

Nodding, Caterina swallowed a slice of pear. "Lorenzo somehow found out about the plot and had the Imolese priest arrested and tortured."

Luisa shivered. She knew torture existed but, as with many in Rome, chose not to acknowledge it unless it confronted them directly. "Why would the count do such a thing?"

"I can only guess he meant to discredit the Medicis. My husband harbours resentment over the failure of the Pazzi conspiracy."

"So, he still schemes. For himself, or his uncle?"

"I don't know anymore." Caterina threw up her hands, scattering crumbs on her dress. "And who knows what else he's involved with. Girolamo is mired in so many plots there's not a family in Italy who hasn't got at least one member seeking retribution."

"What will you do?"

Caterina stood, ready to work. "I don't know. But the conferring of Forli couldn't have come at a better time. I know Girolamo has already ordered the outer defences of the city strengthened, an unusually wise decision. Once we finally leave Rome to live there, I'll be more confident of the safety of my children. Until then, we wait."

"Is it true you've filled all of the high offices in Forli already?" Caterina was eating with Girolamo after an afternoon of hunting. She'd kept her words to herself all day, judging his mood while they were out and waiting for an opportunity. "And that you've told the people of Forli they need no longer pay taxes?"

"It is." He looked at her, his eyes narrowing. The habit of viewing everyone and everything with suspicion, one he'd picked up after so many years in Rome, extended to his own family. "How do you know?"

Caterina stopped herself from sighing. They'd been married seven years and together for three, and he still didn't understand that she was more than a broodmare. "I had some cousins of the Orsini over yesterday. They mentioned the nobles of Forli were here in Rome and had sought an audience with you." Despite the count's meeting having been a private affair, the entire encounter was somehow still shared and dissected by the whole city.

"They should mind their own business." He banged his goblet on the table and waited as a servant rushed over and refilled it. "As should you."

Knowing she had to tread carefully, Caterina adopted a gentler tone. "My lord, as your wife and Countess of Forli, it is my duty as much as it is yours to greet the people we now rule over and to see to their comfort." She focussed on her food as she spoke, hoping the nonchalant tone would disguise her anger. Because it was true: as count and countess, they should have both been there to formally greet the Forli representatives.

"I had my uncle's servants see to their comfort, as you so eloquently describe it." He picked up a slice of deer with his knife and stuck it in his mouth, chewing noisily.

Caterina knew he thought she was finished. She wasn't. "When will they return to Forli?"

Girolamo looked at her, annoyed, but nevertheless replied. "Tomorrow."

"And when will we be going to Forli? As rulers, should we not at least have visited by now?" Caterina kept her voice even and reasonable like she did with Ottaviano.

Sighing, he turned to her, his face exasperated. "You obviously don't know, I can't leave Rome right now. The Turks have occupied Otranto and their ships are visible from the town's shores, waiting to invade Italy."

Of course she knew! All of Europe knew! She was also aware that Pope Sixtus had, so far, done nothing about the Moorish threat, instead leaving the situation to King Ferdinand of Naples. So why her husband believed he was necessary for the security of the land was a mystery to her. More hyperbole about his importance to Rome and its well-being, she guessed.

Girolamo drained his wine cup and stood. "There's nothing stopping you from leaving. Go, if you want. It'll be one less thing for me to worry about."

Again, Caterina was reminded how little her husband knew her. "Nothing stopping me?" she asked incredulously. "There is one thing stopping me, husband. There is always one thing." She lifted her eyes to meet his. "You. Do you think I'd be foolish enough to leave you alone in Rome? Relying on messengers and unreliable stories no better than rumours to inform me of your failed plans and ever-increasing list of enemies? People who are also my enemies now, and those of your children, because of your endless scheming?"

For some reason, whether the wine or the earlier hunt, Caterina's words had the opposite effect of what she imagined. Instead of the rage, she thought she'd provoke in him, she saw only a twisted arousal.

"Fine. In that case, stay. But keep out of my business," the count delivered flatly, "or there'll be consequences." He raised an eyebrow, challenging her to reply. When she said nothing, he turned and left. She breathed out, not realising she'd been holding her breath until that moment. There were very few things she could be sure of when it came to her husband. But she had recognised that look. He would visit her bed that evening, of that she was certain.

The weather had turned surprisingly cold by the end of September, but this didn't stop Caterina from riding out as often as she could with Luisa and a few of her most trusted soldiers. She was fortunate that most of the guards who had accompanied her originally from Milan had decided to remain under her employment. Bossi would often join them, to keep an eye on her, he claimed, but Caterina occasionally saw a look of pure joy on his face when they rode hard and he thought no one saw him. The older she grew, and the more experienced, the more Caterina would insist he stay in the city. She needed his eyes and ears. Today that insistence proved fruitful, for the man himself was waiting for her as she arrived back at the palace.

"There is news, Madonna." He helped her from her horse, a lean grey mare that had been a gift from the Pope.

"There's always news, Bossi," Caterina joked.

"This time it concerns you."

Caterina turned from her horse. Still removing her gloves, her smile faded when she saw the look on her advisor's face. "Tell me," she said as she hurried into the palace to her rooms.

Bossi spoke as they walked the corridors from the stables at the back of the house to her chamber. "Your uncle, Ludovico, has forced Bona into an abbey and forbidden anyone contact with her. No visitors, letters, or messengers."

Caterina stopped and turned suddenly. "Why? She can't have done anything wrong, not with my brother's safety at risk."

Servants were starting to get curious about the group, slowing their passing and leaning in, so Luisa took Caterina's elbow and led her friend into her rooms.

As soon as the door had closed behind her, Caterina's voice rose. "What do you know? Why has this happened?"

Bossi picked up on Caterina's earlier question. "Madonna, it's your brother who is the cause."

Caterina grabbed the older man's arm. "Is Gian hurt?"

"No, my lady, your stepbrother is well." He gently removed Caterina's arm and led her to a chair. "From what I've been able to determine, your uncle Ludovico had been growing increasingly fearful of Bona's influence over her son."

Caterina did a mental calculation. "He's just turned eleven, a long way from his majority."

Bossi nodded. "Yes, my lady. And now Ludovico rules as regent."

"With no one left to protect my brother, will he even reach an age to rule?" Caterina stood again and walked to a window. She stared north in the direction of Milan, her heart aching for her family.

"Madonna, the young duke still has friends, thanks to Bona's efforts. And I have people placed at the Milanese court who will keep me apprised of events." Bossi's voice was even, despite knowing his words would provide scant comfort.

Turning from the window, Caterina sighed, her face a mask of misery. She could reveal her feelings to these people with the doors closed to the world. "I'm as ashamed of my own family as I have been of the one I married into." It hurt her to admit these things, but her misery turned to anger as the seconds crept by. "My uncle thought he could use me, as did the Holy Father. He advised me to write to Ludovico supporting his actions in torturing and driving mad one of my father's closest advisors." She shook her head, the dawning realisation of the part she'd played in this, inadvertently or not, washing over her and fuelling her anger. "I've been played for a fool. Merely a chess piece in an elaborate never-ending game with ever-changing players."

She strode angrily to the fireplace mantel where logs were positioned and ready to light. "If I had been born a man, none of this would have happened."

"Madonna, no one could have foreseen..."

Caterina cut him off. Something inside her had suddenly snapped into place, and a calm assurance crept in and soothed her rage. "I should have. My father would have." She turned and stood taller. "I am no man's pawn. And anyone who cares to challenge my position from now on will find themselves dealing with a Sforza."

In late November, representatives from the most prominent families in Florence came to Rome. They came to beg the Pope's forgiveness for putting Cardinal Riario's life at risk then holding him hostage instead of allowing him to leave

Florence. They were also there to ask the pontiff to lift the indictment that still sat upon the city so the people could once again be blessed with the holy sacraments. After humbling themselves and kissing the pontiff's feet, the nobles left with their humiliation visible to all.

"I feel sorry for them." Caterina was having a late dinner with Girolamo in his rooms. Both had been there to witness Sixtus' triumph. The count's rooms were a visual illustration of how disordered his mind must have been, for there were books and papers on every surface and dirty armour tucked in corners. A young maid had tried to tidy some of the mess and would have been killed had it not been for Caterina's intervention. Even the table where they dined that night had been abruptly cleared to make room for her. A set of candlesticks still sat between them, and Caterina had to stare around the ornate silver sticks to talk to her husband.

"You shouldn't. They got what they deserved." Girolamo spat out the words.

"How can you say that? Their children were dying unbaptised and the old and feeble unshriven in their last days." She poked at a piece of fish and threw her knife down, her appetite gone. "It wasn't their fault, and they were brave enough to come forward for their children's sakes."

Girolamo laughed condescendingly. "They were enemies and enemies must pay. All must be made to understand that there are consequences for denying the Holy Mother church."

You mean denying you, she thought but kept her words. Her husband sounded so assured that she wondered if anyone fell for it anymore, if, in fact, they ever did.

The following May, the Sultan died, and the Turkish fleet suddenly disappeared from Italy's shores. A few soldiers still held the city of Otranto, but the threat of any real attack from these dwindling forces grew less and less as the days passed. Caterina was as relieved as the rest of Rome. More so, because the Pope had finally given her and Girolamo permission to leave the city and visit Forli.

With all the planning she had, Caterina had no time to visit old friends and say goodbye. Girolamo was suddenly interested in getting to his domains as soon as possible, leaving Caterina little time to prepare. Added to her responsibilities was that of her unborn child. Five months pregnant with her third child, she felt the weight more keenly this time and wondered if she might finally have a daughter. And they still had to sit for Botticelli, who wanted to include both Caterina and her husband in a fresco for the Pope's new grand chapel. People had already started calling it the Sistine chapel after Sixtus, and the scope of art had expanded to include the Holy Father's relatives and friends.

"We must go this afternoon," Caterina warned her husband. "It's the only time Sandro has available."

"If he's as talented an artist as you and my uncle seem to think, he can paint me from memory." Girolamo was in his office, packing up last-minute papers and journals.

"It's at your uncle's insistence that we do this. You must attend."

Sighing deeply, he threw a rolled document on the desk. "Fine. But I'll stay no more than half an hour. There are much more important things to see to right now. This timing is terrible."

Caterina nodded and remained silent, savouring this small victory.

When they arrived, the artist had two chairs set up for them. "Madonna, so good to see you again." Botticelli rushed over and bowed, then kissed Caterina's hand and held it as he looked at her. "Your face is flushed, you glow like an angel."

"Sandro, you flatter me."

"I have an artist's eye, my lady, and try to see only the beauty the world offers." He turned to Girolamo. "My lord, we haven't met but your reputation precedes you." He bowed again, holding his arms wide.

"Let's get this over with. I'm a busy man." The count looked around. "Do I sit there?" He pointed at one of the chairs.

"Yes, my lord, and your wife beside you. I only need finish a few sketches and can complete the painting." He waved an arm at the wall beside them. "As you can see, the fresco is nearly finished. It shows the purification of a leper."

Caterina turned to stare at the wall, trying to take everything in. In the background was a depiction of Christ being tempted and various smaller scenes of buildings that looked like Caterina's Rome. In the foreground, a priest accepted an offering from a newly healed leper dressed in a pure white robe. Various well-dressed individuals stood on either side of the priest.

"That's you, just behind the priest." Sandro had grabbed a piece of red chalk and, addressing Girolamo, pointed it at an unfinished figure. "I'll add your face once I've done the sketches." He walked a few steps and pointed at a woman, visibly pregnant, wearing a flowing white dress with a blue cloak. On her shoulders sat a cord of wood tied tightly with metal bands. "And that, Madonna, is you and your unborn child." Turning to them, he smiled. "Now, if you will sit, I can begin, and you'll be on your way."

They sat in their respective chairs and allowed Botticelli to position them so he could best capture their images for the fresco. Girolamo sat still for a few minutes, then started sighing and glancing around impatiently.

Caterina tried not to frown at her husband's behaviour and sat unmoving the entire time.

"That's enough. I must go." The count stood and suddenly walked out.

Caterina stood, her eyes wide. "Sandro, I'm so sorry." There was nothing else to say.

"It's fine, Madonna. I have all I need." He nodded his head at her, inviting her to see his sketches.

She walked over and looked carefully at his work. Seeing her face emerge from the scratches and scribbles of chalk the artist had made was a wonder. She stepped to one side to the sketches of her husband. Botticelli had captured his likeness perfectly, especially his face today: unhappy and impatient looking. "You've added a cap. What colour will you paint it?"

"I haven't decided yet, Madonna. What do you suggest?" Sandro smiled warmly at her.

"I think red, he hates wearing the colour. Claims it makes him look pale."

The artist's smile grew more expansive, and his eyes twinkled conspiratorially. "Red it is, then." With a wink, he picked up a brush. "I'm done for now. I know how busy you are."

"Thank you, Sandro, for everything. I hope to return to see your finished masterpiece soon." She grabbed his hands in both of hers and shook them before turning and walking out.

Caterina returned home to find her husband in a worse mood than before. Ignoring his wife's carefully laid out plans for their travel, Girolamo insisted on getting involved.

"I don't understand why it's so shocking that I wish to travel with my sons." Caterina had come out to the garden after sitting with Botticelli and looked around sadly. She had no idea when she'd see it again and had left instructions for its tending.

"Because that's not the way nobles do things," Girolamo's replied impatiently.

She turned toward him angrily. "You forget I come from a noble family. More noble, in fact, than your own."

"You boast of your nobility?" he snorted. "You? From Milan?"

Caterina felt her face burning and started walking back to the house. "I'll leave now, my lord," her voice dripped with scorn, "for I'm busy but would also spare you the shame of saying something unforgivable to your wife."

In the end, Caterina had finally acquiesced to her husband's wishes, if only to save herself from Girolamo's inevitable sullenness and silences on their journey. Ottaviano, now two, and his younger brother Cesare were sent ahead with their nursemaids and servants. They travelled in heavy carriages protected by armed guards the count had sequestered from the papal army.

"The safest children in Italy," the count remarked curtly, his lips curled triumphantly. "They'll be fine, and we'll see them in a couple of weeks."

After bidding her sons goodbye and ensuring all who travelled with them understood their roles, Caterina and Luisa finished packing.

"I think all is ready, my lady." Luisa closed the lid on the last box of clothing and locked the box. Turning, she watched Caterina wander around the nearly empty room.

"I don't know when we'll be back, but I certainly won't miss this place." She smiled at Luisa. "Let's go."

Chapter Fifteen
1481

With the fine June weather, it only took them eight days to travel from Rome to Forli. Arriving two weeks after her children, Caterina missed them terribly, and the first thing she did was insist on seeing them.

Cesare was still too young to understand what was happening, but his large brown eyes stared at everyone and everything. Ottaviano tottered toward her when she arrived in the nursery, falling at her feet as his balance gave out. She took an hour to investigate the rooms and change her clothing before going back outside to greet the people she now ruled over.

As with her arrival in Imola, the citizens of Forli had dressed the streets and squares with arches and tapestries. Taking Girolamo's proffered elbow, Caterina accompanied her husband through the lanes to the main market square, where they were handed the keys to the city.

The noise of music being played, bells being rung, expensively draped horses snorting and pawing the ground, and the people, in general, made it difficult to hear the speeches given.

"Can you hear anything?" Caterina spoke through her smile as she leaned toward Luisa.

"Not at all," Luisa shouted back, laughing.

After the presentation of the key, the Count and Countess of Forli made their way to the Church of Santa

Croce for a Te Deum. It was difficult to remain focussed in the darkened building when the sun and festivities were just a few feet away. Caterina glanced at Luisa and saw that her friend was also struggling to keep her face solemn. Knowing more than one set of eyes was upon her and Girolamo, Caterina forced herself to look forward until the service was done.

"Now we can have some fun," she whispered to Luisa as they headed back out into the sunshine. "There's a dinner planned at the palace for us."

Luisa stifled a yawn. The atmosphere in the church had made her drowsier than she realised, and the sudden sunlight had made her sleepy.

"Wake up!" Caterina joked. "I need you with me tonight."

Laughing along with her friend, Luisa stopped when she saw Girolamo glaring at the two of them. Still smiling, she accompanied Caterina and Girolamo through streets packed with excited people to the palace.

Music reached their ears before they entered the building, and a cheer went up as they stepped through the large stone entrance to the interior courtyard. Somehow the city's nobles had managed to settle themselves inside the house before Caterina's arrival, and she wondered if any of them had actually gone to Santa Croce at all.

The music died down as the couple were led to a large room decorated with freshly painted frescoes. Two chairs, almost thrones, sat at one end, and as the Riarios sat, the nobles filled the room before them.

A man emerged from the crowd and stepped forward. Dressed in brightly coloured silk, his hair hit the floor as he swept his arm forward and bowed deeply. "My lord, my lady, it is my great honour to welcome you to our beloved city. We are all grateful to God for your safe arrival and pray for the health and happiness of both you and your children."

The applause that followed was deafening, and the man turned bright red.

"Thank you, Signor?" Caterina asked.

"My apologies, Madonna. I am Leoni Cobelli, musician, dancing master, painter, and chronicler. I arranged tonight's festivities for you." He bowed again so earnestly that Caterina had to curl her lips in to suppress a giggle.

Before she could reply, Girolamo stood. "I thank you, Signor, for your words." He nodded to Cobelli and then addressed the nobles. "And thank you all for our welcome. I know we'll have many meetings in the days to come but I want to reassure you that all the promises I made to you in Rome will be kept." The crowd erupted in cheers, all pretence of superior reserve gone as they turned to each other laughing. Girolamo smiled widely, enjoying the adulation, and held up his hand. After a few attempts, he finally managed to speak. "And it is my intention to do even more for the good of all in Forli."

As the nobles pushed their way forward to meet with her husband personally, Caterina stood waiting and watching. The wives made their way to her, and she had to focus on them, but it always interested her to see Girolamo in a public way, as others might see him. When she was first married, Caterina had managed to convince herself that there was a rough handsomeness to him, but now viewing him through the eyes of others, she saw a tired grey-looking man who carried his mistakes on his shoulders.

The music started again as they entered the main dining hall, and Caterina was surprised to see Signor Cobelli sitting with the musicians playing a beautifully engraved lute. With a puzzled expression, she smiled at him as she took her place in the middle of a long table. Without warning, food started arriving, dozens of dishes from all corners of Italy and beyond. Caterina sampled as much as possible and was surprised by the difference from Roman food. The boar was more earthy, and the sauces more delicate and more faithful to the herbs they were created from.

After the meal, they were shown to another room large enough for dancing. Delighted, Caterina tried to get Girolamo to agree to at least one dance for show, but he refused. The nobles all seemed too nervous to ask to dance, and she wasn't sure if it was because of her new role in their lives or her husband's frown. Fortunately, Cobelli had been lingering nearby and stepped in.

"My lady, you will do me the greatest honour if you agree to be my dance partner." He bowed and, once again, Caterina held in her mirth at the man's hair hitting the floor. She'd have to remember to ask Luisa how often she thought he needed to wash it.

"I would be delighted, Signor Cobelli." She handed the man her hand and allowed herself to be led to the centre of the room. She had changed between dinner and dancing and had selected a lighter dress, one more suited to movement.

As they stood facing each other, Caterina had the opportunity to see this man up close. Like most of the guests, he had removed his overcoat and sported a bright blue waistcoat with silver brocade that fitted his slim form to perfection. The red sleeves had been deliberately arranged to display their fullness, and the hose Cobelli had chosen was the same deep red to match. She couldn't remember if he'd been wearing a cap earlier, but he certainly wasn't now, and she could see that every effort had been made to keep his sleek dark hair smoothed down and curled in at the ends.

A basse danse began, and Cobelli and Caterina started the slow, graceful steps, sliding across the floor without lifting a foot. The evening would begin with slower dances so all might digest their meal. As it got later, the wine would flow, and the dances become faster and more exciting.

"I saw you told the truth about being a musician. And I can see by how well you dance you haven't lied about being a master of that craft either. But you also write AND paint, Signor Cobelli?"

"Please, Madonna, if you will allow me to be forward, call me Leoni, as my friends do."

Caterina smiled. "Signor Leoni it is."

"My lady, you misunderstand..." Cobelli stopped when he saw the laugh on Caterina's lips. His face lighting up, he bowed to her. "A wit, I see. I will have to come better armed next time." Picking up where he'd left off in the dance, he smiled.

After her arrival, the presentation, the Te Deum, dinner, and dancing, Caterina was exhausted. Knowing her guests wouldn't leave until given permission, she looked over at Girolamo. Fortunately, he understood.

"My new friends, it's been a welcoming night. The countess and I thank you for your good will and gifts, and bid you enjoy yourselves as long as you wish." He turned to Caterina. "The countess is retiring. I will still be available for some time, however, to meet with you."

All heads turned to Caterina, who glanced at Luisa before bowing her head at the nobles. "I bid you all a good night." Turning away, she strode forward and was relieved to see Luisa beside her.

"A successful evening I'd say," Luisa whispered as they exited the room.

She nodded her head, grateful that the noise of the party was fading and she could finally hear her own thoughts. "I think so too. I suppose we'll see in the coming days."

The following days were filled with more celebrations, culminating in an elaborate tournament in which an enormous wooden castle was taken in a siege. The fear of the Turkish occupation still lingered enough to warrant boos and hisses from the audience as the Turks appeared and deafening cheers when the castle was retaken.

Caterina's time over the next few weeks was filled with decorating the palace during the days, followed by feasts and dances in the evenings. The rooms had all been freshened with plaster and frescoes, but the placement of her own furniture took some consideration, given the size and shape of the building. With Luisa there to offer suggestions, soon the palace was done, and everyone invited into the house to view the enormous shelves filled with precious plate and china, the tapestries, and the statues she'd brought from Rome.

"I must start a garden next," Caterina announced as she and Luisa had a midday meal.

"The soil is similar to Rome, a bit more acidic I think. I've been exploring the grounds." Luisa pointed to her left. "To the side of the palace is an empty plot. There are stones but once cleared I think it would be a perfect spot for a garden."

"I have time now. I have no plans this afternoon. Shall we go and look?" Caterina stood and brushed off her gown.

They made their way downstairs to the side of the building. Using an experienced eye, Caterina viewed the area critically, noting the placement of the surrounding trees and shadow from the palace. Finally, she nodded. "You're right. This spot is perfect." She wandered the plot's perimeter, imagining the rows of herbs she knew she needed.

"Have you found anywhere for your workroom?"

Caterina shook her head. "No. Not yet. I've tried to talk to Girolamo about how important it is to me, but he told me to deal with it myself."

"He left you to run the house in Rome on your own, it's not like this is new behaviour," Luisa pointed out.

"I know. I'm foolish to think he'll ever be more involved. I don't know why a part of me, no matter how small, keeps trying."

"You are his wife," was all Luisa said. She hesitated, bending down to pluck one weed of a hundred near her feet. "Do you know you have an admirer here already?"

Caterina frowned. "I don't understand."

Luisa smiled. "It's true."

"What do you know?"

"The master of all arts and self-proclaimed chronicler of Forli, Signor Cobelli."

"What of him?"

"He's enamoured by you."

Caterina pulled her friend into the shade of the palace. "How do you know all this?"

"The servants here, like in Rome, are free with their gossip." She nodded in the direction of the building, glancing that way.

Laughing, Caterina's voice was gleeful. "I hope he writes nice things about me. He does know I'm married?"

"Oh, he doesn't lust after you, not in that way." Luisa leaned in close. "I understand from the bedroom maids that he lives with another painter and that they are quite close."

Nodding her understanding, Caterina laughed. "It's always good to have admirers."

"It is. Just be warned he enjoys the company of all the nobles of Forli." Luisa started listing them on her fingers. "The Ordelaffi, the Orsi..."

"So, the same names as Rome." She rolled her eyes. Still, here was an opportunity that would pass her husband unnoticed due to his distrust of any non-noble. This man Cobelli might be helpful and someone in the city she could trust to convey news and other goings on. And with such connections, it made him perfect.

"Indeed." Luisa suddenly clapped her hands, sensing her friend's mood was growing more serious. "Now that we've found a garden let's go and find you a workspace."

Excited again, Caterina grinned. "Let's."

By mid-summer, the rumours that always seemed to involve Girolamo, which Caterina had thought she'd left behind in Rome, had started.

"He never leaves his room, Madonna. And most of the city have noticed." Bossi rode beside Caterina as they explored the countryside surrounding Forli. She had insisted on looking at the main fortress, Ravaldino, on her own. With only Bossi and a single guard as protection, Caterina could ride hard and efficiently survey the area to see if any improvements were needed to the structure. Since her arrival at the city, she'd not only conducted her own research into the needs of Forli, she'd insisted on walking out and being seen by nobles and merchants alike.

"I know. He barely comes out to eat with me either."

"Is he well, my lady?" Bossi asked hesitantly.

"He is. His health is not an issue." She sighed. "He's afraid for his life." She stopped her horse and put her hand over her eyes to shield out the sun as she stared at one of the citadel's crumbling towers. "My husband has made so many enemies it's difficult to keep up with their grievances." Turning her horse, Caterina started walking it back to the palace. "I'll speak with him. I don't know if he'll listen to me, but I'll try."

Bossi kicked his horse to catch up to her. "Madonna, watch out for yourself. Be careful."

She smiled gratefully at him. "Always."

After they'd returned to the house and Caterina had washed and re-dressed, she dined with a few of the noblewomen who were constantly clamouring for her attention. Her time in Rome had imbued her with particular manners and habits she hadn't even realised she possessed and which the Forlesi found both charming and sophisticated. After bidding them goodnight and seeing them off, Caterina went to her room.

As Luisa started to help her change, Caterina turned suddenly. "I need to speak to my husband." She had had a few glasses of wine with dinner and felt as prepared as she could for any confrontation the meeting might provoke. She wanted to get it over with before she slept.

Luisa silently backed away, leaving space for her friend to go.

In the hall, Caterina hurried to Girolamo's rooms. She had changed into her soft slippers and glided noiselessly through corridors until she arrived at her husband's suite door. Knocking, she was admitted by a servant in livery and shown to the count's office.

"What do you want?" Girolamo had his head down over a paper, his quill scratching angrily on the surface.

"Can't a wife visit with her husband, my lord?" Caterina removed a book from a chair and sat.

He looked up at her. "As you can see, I'm busy. What do you need?"

Sighing, she got to her reason for being there. "Come out with me tomorrow when I visit the market."

Girolamo's eyes widened. "Why would I do that? If I need something, I'll send you or a servant." He returned to his page.

"The people need to see their ruler."

Looking up at her again impatiently, he waited.

Caterina continued. "You made yourself loved before you even arrived with your concessions and tax gifts."

"The people adore me."

"They adore your money," she replied flatly. Seeing Girolamo's narrowed eyes, she hurried on. "They want to see their ruler," she repeated.

His voice low, the count replied. "You're doing a good enough job for us both."

The way her husband's words were delivered grated on Caterina. She stood. "Someone has to." Without waiting for a reply, she turned and left.

In August, the count decided to ride to Imola to check on the city. He had instructed architects to improve the buildings in the town as well as the fortifications.

"He wants to see what his money has bought him." Caterina and Luisa were packing the last boxes for the short trip north.

"How long do you think we'll be there?"

Caterina shrugged. "I don't know. Not too long I imagine, we're settled here in Forli, it would be too disruptive to keep moving back and forth between both cities, no matter their importance."

The ride took less than a day, and they arrived before their belongings did. Girolamo's sister was there to greet them.

"My dear brother, how well you look!" She turned to Caterina. "And my sister, you are again with child. Another strong son for my virile brother?" Violante laughed at her own attempt at humour. But the words had a sharp edge.

"I believe this one may be a girl, a welcome addition to my family." She wrapped her hands around her belly. In her seventh month of pregnancy, Caterina was tired but exhilarated at the thought of a daughter. The sudden sour look on Violante's face at her emphasis on the word 'my' was enough reward for Caterina. "Shall we go in?" She addressed the entourage who had accompanied them from Forli. As they began to move, Caterina turned back to her sister-in-law. "Oh, and you may join us if you wish." She walked away before seeing the older woman's reaction but nearly laughed when she imagined it.

They settled in quickly, everyone used to packing and unpacking wagons and boxes by now, and soon Caterina was out visiting merchants in the main square and hosting acquaintances at her home.

Girolamo met with his architects and spent time reviewing the city's improvements, all of which Caterina approved of, as did the citizens of Imola. But once he'd finished his inspections, the count returned to his previous behaviour: that of hiding in his room. As the days passed, Girolamo grew more and more suspicious of those around him. Caterina could see no reason for her husband's increased wariness and worried he may have gotten himself into something she was unaware of.

Ignoring his behaviour as best she could, Caterina continued her outings and entertaining, realising she enjoyed herself more on these occasions when her husband wasn't there to create an atmosphere.

Two weeks after they'd settled in Imola, an ambassador from Milan arrived to see Caterina. Following her earlier disgust with her uncle, she treated the tall, thin man with polite coldness. Inviting him to sit in her private reading room, Caterina served him chilled wine and fruit and sat across from him.

"Madonna, I am Antonio Appiani, councillor to Duke Ludovico of Milan."

"My brother's title," she spat.

The man looked uncomfortable and shifted in his chair. After wiping his head with a linen cloth he'd removed from his pocket, Antonio took a long drink of wine and continued, ignoring Caterina's comment. "My lady, your uncle the duke wishes to extend an invitation to his favourite niece to visit the court of Milan."

Taken aback, Caterina nevertheless kept her expression blank. "And does my uncle say why he is making this offer?"

Feeling on steadier ground, the ambassador smiled. "The duke knows how long it has been since you've visited your home and wanted you to know you are always welcome to join him at court."

Still surprised, Caterina mulled over these words. Was there some ulterior motive? How could there not be? She nearly snorted at the thought but saw the ambassador staring earnestly at her. "Thank you for delivering this invitation. I will think on it."

Later, in her room, she spoke with Luisa.

"I still don't know if there is any purpose to it."

"If there is, you'll figure it out. How do you feel about returning?"

"I miss Milan. It will always be my home, the place I spent my happiest days." She turned to face Luisa. "I wonder if my uncle will let me visit Bona. Surely, he would not be so cruel as to invite me then deny me access to her?"

Luisa kept quiet, letting Caterina work out the possibilities for herself.

"It would be nice to visit my brothers and sisters again, to see if Gian is really doing well." She sighed, picturing their reunion. "And to hug Bona and discover if she's happy where she is. I could speak with my uncle about her. If she's truly content at the abbey, perhaps I could bring back Bona's equipment with me." The excitement of visiting her family and riding out to the hunting grounds she loved as a child grew.

By the time she crawled into bed, Caterina had decided. "I miss Milan. I'll speak to Girolamo about spending a few weeks there." She fell asleep enjoying her imagined reunions, smiling to herself.

Chapter Sixteen
1481 - 1482

"No."

Caterina was surprised by Girolamo's vehemence. "Why not?"

"I have my reasons."

She had been forced to visit him in his rooms again and now competed with another document for her husband's attention. "Do you fear my uncle?"

These words worked. Girolamo looked up suddenly, his eyes narrow. "I fear no one. You are needed here. Your place is by my side."

"How can I be by your side when you never leave your rooms?" she demanded. Before he could reply, she hurried into the corridor where Luisa was waiting.

"I heard." Luisa saved her friend from having to repeat the verdict.

Caterina rushed down the hall toward the library. "I don't understand what the issue is."

"Perhaps he's worried about your health and that of his unborn child," Luisa offered, knowing her words rang hollow.

Caterina snorted, not caring who heard. "No, there's something else." She stopped and thought for a moment. "Come with me. I must see Bossi."

They found her advisor in the stables, brushing down his horse. It was a pleasure they shared, tending to their own beasts, no matter the objections of the stable staff. She tried to lighten her own mood. "There are people who will do that for you."

"My lady." He bowed at her over the back of his horse, a fine black palio, a breed said to go back to the ancient Romans. He glanced over at a lingering servant and sent the man away with a flick of his head. When they were alone, he came out from behind the horse. "What do you need?"

She held up a hand to calm him. "It's nothing urgent. It's just, I've had an invitation from the Milanese ambassador, as you know. The count, however, will not give me leave to travel."

"I wondered if he would allow it."

"Why would you even think to wonder such a thing? Why won't my husband let me visit my home?"

"Madonna, I told you not so long ago to watch out and be careful."

Caterina nodded. "I remember."

"I fear my advice is more necessary now than before." He hesitated. "Your husband's distrust is known to all. But I fear it's extended even to members of his own family."

She knew Girolamo's doubts couldn't stretch to his uncle. His nephew, perhaps? Was the cardinal involved in something Caterina didn't know about? Then the truth of Bossi's words hit her, making her stagger back. "You mean me," she said flatly.

"I'm sorry, Madonna, but yes. I've gotten friendly with a few of the less objectionable papal soldiers, and they delight in discussing their master's business."

"But why? What have I ever done to deserve such mistrust?"

Bossi smiled kindly. "Because you are more popular than him."

"What?" Luisa looked from Bossi to Caterina and back again. "I don't understand."

"I do." Caterina walked from the stables to a stone bench just outside one of the palace doors. Once again, she found standing for long periods difficult and accepted Luisa's help to settle herself. She continued. "My husband has always longed to find a place for himself. Until his uncle became Pope, he had a less than illustrious career open to him, a soldier sent to fight for whoever would pay. When he came to power, he was so desirous of recognition that he convinced others, and himself, that he was a leader of men, a fierce warrior."

Bossi finished for her. "Then you come along, an unknown commodity and one with an impressively military family. And you delight them all. Your grace and the ease with which you befriend everyone has made you far more admired than the count."

Luisa nodded her understanding. "I imagine staying in his rooms doesn't make his reputation any better."

"Exactly." Bossi, still standing beside the bench, looked down at Caterina. "Speak to the ambassador. Perhaps a way can still be found."

Caterina invited the Milanese ambassador to dine alone with her the following evening. She walked him around the palace, pointing out her favourite spaces and tapestries, before entering a small room where food and drink waited for them on a table.

"Don Appiani, I've invited you here to inform you that, sadly, I will not be able to make the trip to Milan at this time." Caterina watched his reaction before helping herself to a piece of cow tongue cooked with onions and cloves.

"My lady, I'm saddened to hear it, as will your uncle Ludovico. May I ask why you are unable to visit? Is it your health?" His eyes widened in alarm, and he glanced down at Caterina's swollen stomach.

Stopping herself from being insulted at such an assumption, she took a sip of wine before replying. "No, not at all. My health is excellent. I find," she struggled for a reason, "I find I have no clothing fine enough for my uncle's court."

The ambassador's face lit up. "Is that all? I will see that cloth is sent from anywhere in Italy if you so desire. The duke would insist on it."

Curse him for his curiosity, she thought, then cursed herself for the flimsy explanation. Caterina saw him beaming at her, waiting for her to smile and agree. Panicked, she blurted out the real reason. "The count will not allow me to visit."

The man's face fell as all visions of reward and acclaim for satisfying the Sforzas disappeared from his mind. "Should I meet with the count?"

Alarm met with her panic. "No!" She waved her hand in front of her. "Please, he'll think I sent you to beg for me. It will not improve my situation."

Bowing his head at her in acknowledgement, the ambassador ate in silence. Caterina hoped the man would keep his words to himself and not try to do what he thought best for her, whether she wanted it or not.

The ambassador was scheduled to meet with the count and countess over dinner as part of his diplomatic duties, and Caterina pasted a smile to her face, praying the man would keep his word to her, such as it was.

"It's a shame the countess will not be able to make the trip to her home, but I know she's much beloved here." He ate a piece of braised tuna and waved his fork in the air.

"It will be Milan's loss; the city will be a poorer place without her light to shine upon it."

Girolamo frowned at the man's ambassadorial phrasing. "Yes. She is needed here. I cannot be parted from her." He smiled at Caterina, but the look was obvious to her and chilled her to the bone.

"We're returning to Rome."

Caterina jumped at the sound of her husband's voice. Returning Cesare to his ornately carved wooden cradle, she nodded at a servant before walking out into the hall with Girolamo. "Why?"

"It's safer."

She waited, but he offered no further explanation, and she was too tired to guess his reasons. "Is it?" He glared at her in reply. "It's not good for the children, all this travelling." It was late September, and the travel would still be pleasant, and Caterina desperately wanted to settle down in Forli and truly make it her home.

"So leave them behind."

Shocked by his words, those of a father, she shook her head furiously. "No. I could never do that."

Girolamo stared at her, his head tilted as if considering his words for once. "Then you stay behind."

Her anger rising, Caterina kept her face blank. She could not trust her husband on his own in Rome. She needed to be there for first-hand information about the count's activities rather than remain here and rely on day's old news. "Oh no, my lord. It wouldn't be appropriate for a wife to leave her husband's side." Her words were delivered through a clenched jaw. "You said as much to the Milanese ambassador. That you couldn't live without me." She watched his face and, seeing no reply coming, added, "I'll prepare," before turning and walking toward her rooms.

They took the same familiar route from Imola to Rome and stayed at the same places. All were happy to see Caterina again but kept their pleasure to themselves when greeting the count.

They arrived in good time, and Caterina had barely two weeks to unpack and get their house in order before her third child was born. Her much hoped-for girl arrived at midday at the end of October 1481 after an easy delivery. Smiling down at the tiny sleeping face, she whispered, "My daughter, Bianca."

Even the count was pleased, in a way. After Caterina and the babe had been cleaned, Girolamo visited. He peered at the newborn, lying next to her mother in the countess' large bed, and said, "She'll be useful."

While she healed, Caterina gradually permitted more and more guests to visit. All the old Roman families clamoured once again to present the most luxurious and highest-value gift to the Pope's smallest relative. Now that the Riarios were back in the city, the avenue to the Holy Father they presented was too tempting. Many of Caterina's visitors asked to be remembered to the pontiff the next time the countess and Sixtus met.

November blew into Rome overnight, bringing cooler temperatures from the north. Caterina had grown up with the less temperate climate of Milan and enjoyed the heavier dresses and the opportunity to show off some of her finer cloaks the season occasioned. After the requisite time allowed for her recovery had passed, an invitation from the Holy Father arrived at their palace.

"He's invited me to have lunch with him in his private rooms."

"Back to the same old schedule I guess," Luisa replied. She was ensuring her friend needed nothing more that night. "The green and silver gown with the darker overdress? Your figure isn't quite back to your preferred measurements yet."

Anyone else pointing this out would have been met with a tongue-lashing. Luisa could talk freely when no one else was around and had developed a habit of speaking honestly, whatever the topic or pain it might cause, something Caterina was grateful for.

"It'll have to do." Caterina looked at herself in the mirror. Dressed in her night dress, it was difficult to see her figure in the mirror, but she could feel by the way her clothes fit and the ease with which she could now move that she'd almost returned to her usual size and weight.

"Did the Holy Father deliver any other message?" Luisa asked as she picked up a stocking from a wooden bench.

Caterina shook her head and climbed into bed. "No, just a messenger with the lunch invitation."

"Then it should be a pleasant visit."

"I think so too." Caterina watched as Luisa blew out all the candles in the room except for the one she carried and the one on her friend's bedside table. Breathing in the familiar smell of Rome, she fell asleep.

At her first lunch with the pontiff, Caterina was served the exquisite food she had come to expect from the papal kitchens. But rather than the fatherly conversation she'd looked forward to, the Pope seemed more concerned with her uncle and the goings on in Milan. After repeatedly denying she knew more, their lunch had been cut short.

"Perhaps he had a bad day?" Luisa suggested helpfully.

"Perhaps." Caterina had nodded. When their second meeting proved just as puzzling, she still tried not to take it personally. But Caterina's feelings were bruised when their lunches occurred less over the months, and each one more rushed than the last.

"Your uncle seems different since we returned to Rome." Caterina scooped some honeyed pears onto her plate. The new year had come and gone, and as much as they'd settled back into their old Roman routines, Caterina still felt like she was constantly holding her breath. Being cooped up against the cold hadn't made things easier, and at least the spring breezes had arrived, welcoming the sprouting herbs and plants in Caterina's garden.

Girolamo nodded distractedly. "He's a tired old man."

That tired old man to whom you owe everything, she thought. Changing topic, Caterina frowned. "I hear there is trouble in Romagna." Bossi, her constant source of information, had updated her on the developing situation.

"Salt?" she had asked incredulously.

"Salt is very important; many would die without it and many grow rich controlling it." He had explained that Venice, controllers of much of the salt mining in the north, had discovered the city of Ferrara extracting salt from Venetian lands. When the Doge forbade them, the city refused.

"So now Milan and Florence have joined Ferrara against Venice?"

"And Genoa, yes. These coastal regions always support each other."

Girolamo cleared his throat in disgust, bringing Caterina back. "You mean how Milan are supporting that little nothing of a city Ferrara?" He spat out the words and glared at her with such hatred she could feel the heat of his emotions. "What of it?"

"What is the Holy Father doing about it? I haven't been able to see him for ages, I might have been of some use."

Raising an eyebrow, her husband frowned. "What do you know of such situations?"

Feeling defensive, Caterina nevertheless kept her tone even. "I could have listened or offered advice."

"You? Offer advice to a Pope?"

"He listens to me," she said, forcing her chin up a little. "It was my idea to make repairs to Rome, to clear the streets and fix the ancient waterways so fresh water now flows into the city."

Girolamo laughed, a choking sort of bark. "That may be, but none of it was done because of you." Caterina looked at him, waiting for an explanation. He laughed when he saw her. "So you really don't know? He used your idea as an excuse to persuade the rich and poor alike to give money to see their city glorified as it was in ancient times." Girolamo stared into her eyes, ensuring he had her full attention. "He took most of the money for himself."

"No." The barely whispered word was all she could manage.

"Yes." His single word was filled with as much pleasure as hers had been thick with pain. He shook his head. "I know by your disdainful looks that you think yourself my intellectual superior, but even I know that my uncle only does what's best for him and his family."

Caterina felt her face burning with shame and humiliation and was relieved their meal was nearly over anyway when she stormed out. One of the two Riarios she thought she could trust had failed her miserably, and the realisation weighed her down as she hurried through the palace to her rooms.

"Do you remember saying anything that would bring you harm?" Luisa sat across from Caterina in her rooms, a pitcher of wine and two glasses on the table between them.

Caterina shook her head. "No. I don't think so. Sixtus asked me questions, usually ones I couldn't answer, then mostly talked about himself." Realising how he manipulated their conversations brought on a fresh wave of shame. "I feel so foolish. I was so free with my trust."

"Who wouldn't be?" Luisa almost shouted her defence. "He's the Pope, the most powerful man in the world. No one would dare question him or his motives."

"Still." She stood suddenly, unable to bear the weight of her disappointment. "I need to leave. I can't stand being in this place anymore."

Luisa's eyes widened for a moment before she calmly placed her wine glass on the table in front of her. "Where will you go?" she asked reasonably.

Caterina thought. "My uncle will take me and the children in. Girolamo is too involved with Venice right now." She paced the room, the movement calming her. Reality finally replaced her panic. "I can't flee," she admitted. Sitting back down, she finished her glass of wine in one long gulp and watched as her friend refilled it.

"Your absence is certain to be noticed."

Caterina thought of the added humiliation the plan would bring, and the gloating of her husband as he dragged her back to Rome. "If not now, then someday. I'll keep trying to find a way."

The salt situation had grown worse, with Naples now joining the fray. The ruler of Ferrara was married to the Napolitano king's daughter and had sent word to his father-in-law of his plight. Naples had responded immediately by sending an army of seasoned soldiers north, led by the king's son

Alfonso, to aid the small city. They had requested permission to pass through papal lands on their trek north and, despite them answering the Pope's call to fight the Turks, the Holy Father said no. Undeterred, the army had marched anyway, destroying property and crops until they reached the outskirts of Rome itself, where they now camped out.

Caterina, Bossi, and Luisa stood on the balcony in Caterina's favourite spot and watched the activity in the courtyard below. As head of the papal armies, her husband was sent by the Pope to defend Rome against Naples and was preparing to leave.

"Maybe he'll die in battle," Luisa whispered.

"And leave me a widow with children in Rome, where wolves and jackals prowl every street?" She shook her head. "No. I need him." Caterina's words made her cringe inside. But what choice did any woman have? She could decide to disobey and fight with him and risk repudiation, or act the part of a supportive wife for the sake of her children and herself.

They stayed until the last soldiers had marched out of the courtyard, then turned back to the house and their respective activities.

Caterina waited at home anxiously, knowing that at any moment, her entire future could be at stake. For days no word arrived, and even spending time tending to the spring shoots in her garden did nothing to calm Caterina's nerves. She was kneeling in the dirt, pulling up weeds as Luisa sat reading nearby when Bossi appeared from around the corner of the palace.

"My lady, there is news."

Caterina stood and wiped her hands on her apron. She looked at his face. "What's happened?"

"Perhaps you should sit, Madonna."

She frowned at him. "Tell me. We know each other too well to play games of propriety."

Bossi nodded and, glancing at Luisa, who had risen along with her mistress, accompanied Caterina into the house. "You know Alfonso and his men were camped just outside Rome," he reminded her.

"Yes, of course. My husband was summoned to deal with the young prince."

The older man shook his head. "That's just it, my lady. Your husband, instead of seeking out the enemy and engaging him, gathered his army and hid them inside the walls of a church."

Caterina stopped walking, the fresh dirt drying on her hands and making them stiff. She rubbed them on her apron again. "Why? Why would he act in such a way?" The word 'cowardice' immediately sprang to her mind, the worst thing a man could be to a Sforza. She brushed it aside and listened to Bossi.

"The count claimed he was ensuring the citizen of Rome wouldn't revolt during the conflict."

"The citizens? Was this..." Her thoughts abandoned her as they arrived at her rooms, and she sank into a chair. There were no words strong enough to describe the depths of her shame.

"There is more, my lady."

She threw up her hands in despair. "What else could there be?" Caterina saw the kindly look in her advisor's eyes and stilled herself. "Go on."

"It seems that the count and his men played dice on the main altar of the church as they hid inside."

Ignoring his confirmation of her suspicions, that of Girolamo hiding rather than protecting, she kept a small wail to herself as a maid arrived with a tray of wine for them all. Caterina signalled to the young woman, who hurriedly handed the countess a glass filled with rich red liquid. Draining it to half full in one gulp, she shook her head. "Does my husband care nothing for the state of his immortal soul?"

The more Bossi shared, the more ill Caterina became. "He gambled away the papal army's wages and, when the soldiers demanded their pay, he sent them to pillage houses in the area to make up for their losses."

Caterina suddenly held up her hand. "No more." She dreaded to think of the fates of those who dared to fight back as their homes were ransacked and worse. Shuddering, Caterina stood. "I must go to the chapel."

Bossi made to follow, but Luisa stopped him. Their mistress needed to be alone. As Caterina hurried to the private chapel downstairs, she thought to herself. If God would not forgive her husband his sins on her behalf, perhaps He would still protect her children.

Chapter Seventeen
1482

For the next two months, Caterina followed her stepmother's example and prayed for her husband. Dressed in penitential clothing, Caterina started wearing only plain brown dresses and cloaks and eschewed all jewellery. Even her hair nets were of plain-woven silk, unadorned with the usual pearls or precious stones. To the growing dismay of Luisa, who tried her best to help her friend, Caterina stayed up most nights on her knees in the chapel praying and saying her rosary. During the day, she distributed alms to the poor and food she denied herself. The only time she slept was when her exhaustion forced her to.

For weeks she travelled from church to church and shrine to shrine, praying and lighting candles at each one. Like Bona before her, she visited the sick and infirm, praying with them all. She finally understood her stepmother, and the questions she had wanted to ask about how Bona could stand by a man such as the Duke of Milan were now answered. As much as she'd loved her father, it had been his wife who'd seen to his soul. Something Caterina now did for her own husband.

"You must stop." Luisa had watched her friend grow thinner and thinner, and the circles under Caterina's eyes alarmed her.

"I must do nothing of the sort." Caterina tried to rise from bed but felt a hidden pressure forcing her back. With effort, she finally managed to stand. Walking to a tray, she ate a few chunks of bread and swallowed them with water before collecting a grey linen dress.

"You're not well, my lady." Luisa hoped the formal tone would make its way through the fog her friend seemed to be under.

"My body is not my concern. It's my soul and that of my husband." She waved Luisa away and dressed herself, slipping the gown on and tying the waist with a plain leather thong. "Did you know he continues to gamble and drink?" Caterina threw the words out as if this were explanation enough for her actions. "Are you coming with me?" She knew her words sounded harsh.

"I'm needed here, there is a delivery for the kitchen," Luisa replied.

"Of course." Caterina nodded her head and left without a backward glance, leaving her friend to stare after her in worried silence.

The following week news reached Caterina that the Pope had finally had enough of Girolamo's tactics and had asked the Venetians to send help. Their response came in the form of Robert Malatesta, a seasoned condottiero who controlled a well-maintained and ready army.

"Let's go see him when he marches in tomorrow," Luisa suggested.

Caterina considered the idea, intrigued by the stories she'd heard of the man's bravery. "Yes, I'd like that."

The next day they lined up with the rest of Rome's nobility, cheering and waving Malatesta and his men. Caterina had woken feeling light-headed and was grateful to have Luisa beside her to keep her steady. She stared at the leader intently, admiring his dark hair and assured demeanour. When he caught one of his men's eyes, Caterina saw that the soldiers respected their leader, a very telling detail.

"They look so... clean." Luisa leaned over and whispered, interrupting her thoughts.

Nodding, Caterina agreed. "And see the way they march in formation? So different from the count's troops. My husband's men are a dishevelled, unorganised rabble." They watched the men march by, each wearing the yellow, red, white, and black crest of the house of Malatesta. As the army passed, Caterina suddenly felt dizzy. She reached out a hand in panic for Luisa as her vision blurred.

"My lady?"

It was the last thing Caterina heard before the noise of the crowd, the snickering horses, and the steady beat of the soldier's march died away to nothing.

"She has quartaine fever," a male voice announced.

"Are you certain?"

"I am. Her symptoms are clear: a high fever, shaking, vomiting, headaches." The speaking stopped.

"Who's there?" Caterina's voice sounded like someone else's to her dull ears.

"My lady!" Luisa rushed over and sat on the side of the bed, taking Caterina's hand. "You're finally awake!"

Caterina opened her eyes and saw she was in bed. Attempting to rise caused a wave of dizziness to wash over her. "What happened?"

"You've been ill." Luisa put out a hand. "Don't move, let me get you something to drink." She hurried to a corner of the room as an unfamiliar man entered her exhausted view.

"I am the Holy Father's personal physician," he announced with such gravitas that, had she felt better, it would have made Caterina laugh. Instead, she wondered how many physicians considered themselves a 'personal' one to the Pope, for she'd never seen this one. He continued. "You collapsed and were brought home. I was sent to tend to you." Shaking his head, he frowned. "I was told you'd been fasting and not sleeping. It's no wonder you fell ill."

Luisa came back carrying a glass of water. She sat and, holding her friend's head, helped Caterina to take a small sip. "You've been delirious for over a week. Sometimes you slept for more than a day and we struggled to wake you."

Caterina reached out a weak hand and was comforted when Luisa grabbed it immediately. "Thank you for looking after me," she whispered, knowing instinctively that the younger woman had remained in the room the entire time Caterina had been ill.

Luisa leaned closer. "Always."

The doctor cleared his throat. "I suggest we leave the countess to rest."

"Wait." Caterina's voice was faint, but there was no mistaking the tone, one that would brook no argument. "What of my husband? The papal army?"

Luisa looked at the doctor, who shook his head. Caterina glimpsed the exchange through half-closed eyes. "I must know."

The doctor shook his head again, this time in exasperation. "See that's she given the medication I prepared, the arrogan."

Caterina's usually clear mind struggled to remember the ingredients of this familiar treatment, and all she could recall was marjoram and rue.

Luisa nodded at the healer and watched as the man left. He had the good sense to close the door behind him. "It's over."

"What do you mean? What's over?" Caterina had given up moving anything but her mouth; the dizziness and pain that engulfed her were too great.

"The battle between the papal forces with Malatesta and the Napolitano prince Alfonso has been fought and won."

Caterina waited for her friend to continue, preparing herself.

"The field where they fought is now called the Campo Morto, the field of death." The words came pouring out of Luisa. "On the morning of the twentieth of August, the forces met each other and fought for seven hours under the hot sun. When it was over, two thousand men were dead and multitudes more are now suffering the effects of the bad air from the nearby marshland."

A tear rolled down Caterina's face. "Continue," she whispered.

"The count, who was supposed to lead the Pope's army, instead stayed at the camp during the whole time the battle was fought. Afterward he claimed he was protecting the tents, but all of Rome is shocked by his actions. There are many unable to decide if your husband's cowardice is the worst sin, or his treachery in leaving the noble Malatesta to fight alone in battle."

"Is the general dead?"

Luisa rushed to calm her friend. "No, he lived and won the day for Rome." She hesitated.

"There is more. There is always more," Caterina said.

"Your husband met with the Holy Father and claimed the victory for himself." Before Caterina could say anything, she added, "Don't worry, the Pope didn't believe his nephew, for there were those who had gotten there first and told Sixtus the truth."

Caterina yawned, and even that movement caused her head to ache. Luisa, sympathetic to her mistress' plight, smiled kindly. "You must rest. You've heard all the important details. I'll share more later."

Hearing her own insistent tone echoed in Luisa's, Caterina gave in. "Thank you," she said again. She was asleep again before Luisa could finish her reply. "You're welcome."

Caterina was still recovering in bed when the Pope announced plans for a triumphal march rivalling those of ancient Rome to celebrate the hero, Robert Malatesta. Girolamo hadn't been home since he'd left to fight, and Caterina barely had time to wonder at the anger he must be feeling at his uncle when news arrived that Malatesta was dead.

"They say he succumbed to a fever, my lady." Bossi stood near Caterina, who sat wrapped in blankets on a bench in the garden, despite the summer heat.

"A terrible end to a proud warrior." She shook her head. Another two weeks had passed, and the bedrest had done much to relieve Caterina of many of her symptoms. Then she had a terrible thought. "Where is my husband?"

Bossi looked down at his feet. "At the papal apartments, Madonna."

"Tell me the truth. Did the count poison Malatesta?"

"There are rumours, my lady," he admitted, then rushed to reassure her, "but there are always rumours."

"Girolamo is a jealous man. Such a deed is not beyond him."

"No one knows for certain, take comfort in that. The general was suffering from symptoms of breathing bad air soon after the battle."

She nodded, trying to feel reassured by his words. That kind of comfort embraced her less and less, and happened so infrequently, these days.

Girolamo returned to his home a week later and left Caterina alone after a cursory visit to her chambers to check on his wife's health. Following his usual pattern of behaviour, he locked himself up in his rooms.

The weather decided to be kind to Rome, and the October winds were mild and comfortable. On one of his rare forays outside his room, Girolamo decided to finally acquiesce to his wife's requests that they dine together.

"How are my sons?" He stuffed a piece of agnolotti pasta into his mouth, inhaling the scent of the broth and butter in which it was cooked.

Surprised by his interest, Caterina smiled proudly. "Ottaviano is a strong boy, and his tutors say he is bright for his age. Cesare already enjoys holding a toy sword in his tiny hand." She hesitated, looking up at her husband before continuing. "And your daughter is only one but smiles and laughs as happily as any child I've seen."

"Good." The word was thrown out like a bark. Caterina waited, but no further inquiry came about their children. They ate in silence for a while, each enjoying the food the fine harvest had produced that year. Suddenly Girolamo spoke again. "My uncle requires me to travel to Rimini."

"What for?"

"I am to seize the lands and belongings of Robert Malatesta." Girolamo took a drink of wine.

"But the father's inheritance must surely go to his son? Hasn't it all been decided?"

The count snorted dismissively. "A child. What good will a child ruler be? The papal state needs land in that region, it will be an important stronghold." He stood and threw his linen napkin on the table in front of him. "I depart in the morning."

She watched him leave the room and finished her meal calmly, preparing for the waiting she knew would come.

Over the next few weeks, Caterina was well enough to work in her physick room. It was one of the places she felt most comfortable. Just entering the large shelf-lined room and breathing in the earthy plant scent took her back to her childhood and happier days.

"Let's go to the market, I need supplies." Caterina looked around, mentally noting the empty and near-empty jars.

Luisa smiled. "The walk would do us both good, I think." She untied the apron she wore and flung it across the back of a chair. "Do you want to bring the children?"

Caterina thought for a moment before shaking her head. "No. We won't be too long. I'll ask Bossi to remain here while we're out."

"He won't like that."

"I know. But one man can't be in two places; he knows that. He also knows he'll be more important to me here." She took off her own apron and left the room with a final wipe of her hands.

With the weather still mild, Caterina wrapped herself in a light cloak and stepped into the courtyard after assuring Bossi he was needed at home more than with her. Taking a deep breath, Caterina had a moment of sadness as she remembered the rich mulchy scent of Milan at this time of year. Shaking it off, she waited for Luisa to join her before heading to the market.

The unexpectedly sunny day had brought more vendors to the square than Caterina had expected. She stopped more than once to gaze at wares crafted from leather, jewelled hair caps, pendants and rings made of copper, silver, and gold, and anything else that caught her eye. By the time she'd crossed the square, Luisa had made arrangements with half a dozen merchants for something Caterina had liked.

"Oh no!" Turning a corner on the far side of the market, Caterina raised her hand to her face. "What happened?"

The apothecary rose suddenly and turned, his eyes wide. "Madonna! It's good to see you again." Isach glanced down at the shattered glass surrounding his feet. "An accident." He dismissed it with a wave of his hand.

Caterina frowned. "What kind of accident?" Suddenly remembering Isach's daughter, her eyes widened. "Sarra? Is she hurt?"

He waved his hand again, this time in protest at her words. "No no no, nothing like that." Seeing her staring at him, he sighed. "A rock was thrown through my window. Perhaps someone didn't realise..." his words trailed off as his excuse fell short of his belief.

Too shocked to speak, Caterina walked over and picked up a piece of the broken window.

"No, Madonna, please." Isach gently took the shard from her hand. "This isn't the first time such an event has happened."

Ignoring protocol, Caterina grabbed the man's arm. "Isach! Why didn't you say anything?"

"To what purpose, my lady? What could you have done to prevent an action such as this? Have your guards stand in front of my shop day and night?" He shook his head sadly.

Caterina realised his words, although perhaps exaggerated, were true. There wasn't much she could do to help him.

Using his foot, the apothecary shoved a few last pieces of glass toward the shop so no one could step on it. "Let's go inside, Madonna. I'm sure you've come for more than to discuss my life with me."

Frowning at his back as he pulled open the door, she followed him into the shop. The glass had already been cleared from the inside, and there was no sign of the rock that had caused the damage. "Are you sure no one was hurt?" She wasn't accusing the man of lying, just hiding the truth from her.

"No, my lady. You're kind to ask. Thankfully the attacks happened at night when we were all upstairs."

"And how is your wife?" She'd known the apothecary long enough, through her visits every time she was in Rome, to know he wouldn't object to personal questions.

"She's scared."

His words made Caterina shiver. "That's understandable." She fought for the right thing to say, but found her vocabulary lacking for such an occasion. Fortunately, Isach spoke.

"What is it you came for today, Madonna?"

"It hardly seems important now but if you have these," she reached into her basket and withdrew a piece of paper upon which her list had been hastily scribbled.

Isach read the note, nodding as his practised eye ran down the items. "I have everything. Let me see..." He wandered toward a far shelf mid-sentence.

"Don de Luca, is it still your intention to move your family out of Rome?" She called across the shop.

Isach reached up and took a jar from a shelf before turning. "It is, Madonna. I remember you told us Imola would be safe, but I've heard rumours."

Caterina nodded, annoyed that rumours had such an insidious effect on those who least deserved it. "I've had another idea. South of Imola is Forli, where I am also countess." She remembered telling the man that anyone who moved to Imola would be protected. Sadly, she'd had higher expectations of her husband's abilities then. But now she'd matured, and understood more, saw more. And was able to speak knowing more.

"All who follow the Jewish faith are welcome there. It's my intention to visit often, even if my husband is required to stay in Rome." It was her plan, despite the uphill battle she knew she faced convincing Girolamo. "Already many families have set up businesses and are raising their children in a city that treats them fairly."

Isach finished gathering Caterina's supplies and began to tally their value at the counter. "It's does my heart good hearing stories of the happiness of others, Madonna. I'll speak to my wife when we next discuss our plans." He smiled gratefully as he placed each item in her basket. "There. That's everything."

Luisa stepped forward and gave the man more than the herbs and other ingredients were worth, as she always did. Don de Luca knew the countess well enough to acknowledge the gift with a smile. He'd tried many times to protest her generosity, to no avail.

On their way back to the palace, Caterina had a grin on her face. She felt she'd done something worthwhile today, something that may help a friend, and it filled her with happiness.

"She spoke! Luisa, quickly, Bianca spoke!"

Luisa rushed into the nursery, where Caterina sat with Bianca on her lap. "Are you sure?"

"Of course I'm sure. Listen." Both women watched the child as it sat, silently looking from one to the other. "Go on, Bianca. Say it again. Mama."

"Mama," the girl whispered. She jumped at her mother's subdued squeal, then smiled as she saw Caterina laughing.

Picking up the baby, Caterina leaned her nose into her daughter's hair and breathed in deeply, then turned to Luisa. "See? I told you."

A sudden noise in the hall made them both turn. Luisa walked to the nursery door and peered outside. "It's the count. He's back from Rimini."

"He's only been gone a month." Caterina handed Bianca to the ever-hovering nursery servant and hurried toward the courtyard. Before Caterina could make it halfway there, Girolamo rushed past her and headed for his rooms. The only acknowledgement she received from her husband was a glance as he slammed his door.

Luisa was now beside her. "What happened?"

"I don't know. He said nothing to me." Caterina shook her head. "It can't be good. Bossi will find out, I'm certain."

They headed to Caterina's favourite waiting place, the library. During her time in Rome, Caterina had been honing her healing skills and amassing one of the largest collections of books in the city. Most of the nobility weren't interested in old historical tomes or books of philosophy or history, so when one came their way, they often gifted it to Caterina. She also found them at markets and shops, and had befriended many booksellers, all of whom knew her tastes, especially her interest in military history. Any such book would earn the seller a handsome reward.

After letting a maid know they'd be eating their midday meal in the library, Caterina and Luisa settled into their favourite chairs. When the food was brought in, it was arranged so each woman could eat and read at the same time. Caterina smiled, reminding herself to thank the servants later for the thoughtfulness.

It didn't take long for Bossi to find them. "My lady," he said as he bowed before her.

"Sit and eat. There is plenty." She waved at a nearby chair, then at a servant who had accompanied him. "Another glass and more wine, please." When the young man had gone, Caterina turned to Bossi, who had moved the chair closer and settled himself into it. "You've spoken to the count's men?" There was no need for a preamble; the entire household had heard the count's angry footsteps and the slammed door.

"It didn't go well in Rimini, Madonna."

"I assumed." More wine and another glass arrived, and Caterina stood to pour for Bossi, who continued.

"The count's efforts to seize Malatesta's son's inheritance were thwarted by the Florentines, who were disgusted by both the count and the Holy Father's greed. They swore to protect both Malatesta's widow and her infant son until the boy comes of age."

Caterina felt a twinge of pleasure at her husband's defeat. She believed it best to strengthen their ties with Florence, not antagonise the great city further. Was she being selfish, she wondered? Perhaps, but Caterina had realised that she thought more strategically than most men. She was learning from their mistakes, so many to choose from, and she was an eager student.

Chapter Eighteen
1483 - 1484

The months flew by, and after a mild winter and early spring, summer blazed golden across Rome. Still stung by his defeat in Rimini, Girolamo spent most of his time avoiding people by hunting, riding, or staying in his rooms. But his ongoing distrust continued, and soon he imagined schemes against him in Forli.

"He's decided to punish the conspirators of a supposed plot by forbidding the entire city to harvest their grapes." Caterina added a few roots from a white lily plant to a granite mortar and started grinding. "I'll need to speak to him, make him see that no grapes mean no wine, a major source of the city's income."

"Will he listen?" Luisa ground her own pestle into slivers of ginger and cedar.

"Who knows? I'll plan my moment carefully, perhaps after a large meal with much wine, when he visits..." she left the words hanging, knowing Luisa would know what her husband's visits meant.

Luisa suddenly laughed, remembering something she thought would cheer her mistress. "I hear you and the Holy Father are more than just friends." She snickered again.

"What? I don't understand." Caterina stopped working.

"Rumour has it that you and he are, well," Luisa shrugged and raised an eyebrow suggestively.

Instead of the rolled eyes, she'd expected, her friend nearly dropped her pestle. "Please tell me there is no such rumour."

Adopting a more serious expression, Luisa nodded. "Yes. Your visits have been seen by those who don't know when to keep their mouths shut."

Sighing, Caterina put her tools down. "It's blasphemous. He's the Pope. And nearly seventy years old." Frustrated, she walked to a shelf and took down a jar. Picking up her pestle again, she put her frustration into the grinding, angry at herself for forgetting that there were eyes everywhere.

The Vatican library was a place Caterina could never stay away from for long. Sixtus was continually buying new books and having the monks in the scriptorium copy others, and the space was the world's envy. She'd been reading much more history the past year, leaving behind the romances and mythology of her youth. Wandering the shelves, she wondered how such a man could condone the acts that the Holy Father had, yet still be a man of art and literature? Perhaps he swapped one for the other as a warped penance.

By fall, the Pope was ill.

"How serious is it?" Girolamo had accepted his wife's invitation to dine in her rooms.

"No one is sure."

Caterina took a mouthful of her roast boar, the rosewater and spices used in the basting leaving a subtle but lingering taste. She thought through the various scenarios involving the Holy Father's illness. "What will we do if the worst happens?" She didn't want to ask but needed to know.

Girolamo looked up from his plate, his face lined with worry. Caterina knew that without Sixtus, they had no safety in Rome. Their property would be attacked by their enemies and any citizens who were tired of her husband's misuse of power. She recognised these truths but what scared her more was the look of fear on Girolamo's face.

"We'll buy another house," she suggested.

"What difference will that make?"

"None, if it's in your name. But put it in Ottaviano's name and that will protect it." She remembered how he'd tried to take away another boy's rightful inheritance and hoped Rome wouldn't follow his example. She stood, signalling their dinner was over. "Think about it."

While his uncle was ill, Girolamo placed extra guards around the house. No one was allowed out as the crowds that gathered outside the palace day and night could become unruly at the slightest provocation.

"I must see the Holy Father." Caterina walked the halls with Luisa, trying to burn some nervous energy she'd usually dissipate with a ride or visit to the market.

"Why? He won't want to see anyone right now," Luisa replied.

"I'm a healer and I'm certain I can treat Sixtus."

Luisa nodded her agreement. "It's not possible to leave the house right now, you know that." She waved vaguely in the direction of the courtyard, where, even now, her husband's borrowed guards from the papal army held back any who tried to enter.

"I've been thinking of that. I have a way, but I need your help."

Luisa raised an eyebrow at her friend. "It's not like you to be so mysterious. What do you plan on doing?"

Turning the World to Stone

"We're not allowed out, but someone still has to leave to buy food and supplies for the palace, correct?"

"I believe so, yes."

"Well, if I were to borrow a servant's clothing and cover my head, I could sneak to the Vatican unnoticed and help the Holy Father."

It seemed reckless to Luisa, but she agreed with her friend that they shouldn't be made to suffer because of the count's foolish vendettas. "I'm going with you."

Caterina tried to keep her smile to herself, but Luisa caught her eye, and she beamed. "I'm glad." Then, remembering the reason for their intrigue, grew solemn again. "I must gather up some remedies from my herb room. Will you see to our disguises while I do so?"

"Of course. I'll meet you back in your bedroom." She squeezed Caterina's arm as she hurried towards the kitchen, happy for the unexpected adventure.

Half an hour later, they both wore the plain blue dress of kitchen maids. The Riario emblem was emblazoned on the shoulder of each dress, and their heads were covered with linen veils, making it easier for them to walk past the guards at the back of the palace with little fuss.

"That was easier than I thought it would be," Luisa whispered as they continued around the building to the main concourse.

"Did you want a confrontation with the guards?" Caterina asked.

Luisa blushed. "No. It's just, I had a story all prepared. You're Serafina and I'm Palmira and we've been working for the count and countess for nearly a year." She smiled proudly.

"Doing what, exactly?" Caterina was enjoying herself but kept a close eye on their surroundings as they headed toward the Vatican.

She stopped and sighed. "I hadn't actually got that far yet," she admitted.

"It's just as well because you're a terrible liar." They'd arrived at the Vatican, and Caterina mounted a set of back steps that led directly to the papal apartments. "Sixtus may let me in, but I think you'll have to wait for me. I'll make sure I find a guard I know to keep an eye on you. Otherwise, someone is likely to send you to the kitchens." She smiled kindly at her friend.

It was easy enough to get into the Vatican; there were always many servants coming and going. And luckily, Caterina found a friendly guard right away, one who laughed when he saw her.

"This is Nino. He'll see that no one asks you to bake them a loaf of bread." She smirked at Luisa, then turned and entered the Pope's private rooms.

Those inside recognised her, from both her frequent visits and her familial connection, and while a few raised an eyebrow at her appearance, none stopped her from entering the pontiff's bed chamber.

The smell hit her first, like something had died under the Pope's bed. A cardinal looked up as she entered, then frowned at her. "Madonna, this is no place for a woman."

"Nor for you either, judging by the smell in this room." She walked to a wall and pulled aside a tapestry, revealing a window. Lifting the metal hinge, she pushed the glass open and felt the cool fall air drift into the room as the cardinal stood and sputtered at her. "What do you think you're doing? The Holy Father is ill and not able to withstand any change of temperature." He started toward her, his face now the colour of his robe.

"Wait." A weak voice came from the direction of the large walnut bed. "She stays."

The cardinal glared at Caterina but backed away. "On your head be it," he threw at her as he opened the door and let himself out.

"My dear, what are you doing here? You shouldn't have come. You may become ill." He struggled to speak, and Caterina had to force herself not to finish his sentences.

She called to him from another side of the room. "I'm a healer. We've spoken of this before." Pushing aside another tapestry, Caterina frowned when she saw dirt on the second window. She'd have to talk to someone about that, she thought, then pushed this one open as well. The stream of air from the first window rushed toward the second, and soon, the room smelled like the fresh air around the Vatican. If they had been in the centre of Rome, Caterina would have erred on the side of caution and kept the windows closed for fear of some miasma sneaking in and making the Pope worse. But Hadrian had been clever when selecting a site for his tomb and had chosen a less swampy area set outside the city proper. Over the centuries the Popes had rebuilt the buildings, but all were still protected from stifling Roman air by their location.

Caterina turned and glanced around the room. From the looks of it, the cardinal hadn't allowed maids in to clean the place and had thought the job too low to perform himself. Busying herself with picking up pillows, sheets, and undergarments, Caterina kept talking and taking occasional glimpses at Sixtus.

"I thought I would try to see if I could help your Holiness." She decided to leave out the part of the story where she had disguised herself to escape her guarded home, as the pontiff had apparently not noticed her state of dress anyway. He had pushed himself upright a little, and Caterina could now see how ill he really was. Every one of his seventy years showed on his face, and more. He was thinner than the last time she'd seen him, and there were bruise-like smudges under his half-closed eyes. His frailty terrified her. It made her realise how close she was to the collapse of her life.

After picking up as much as she could, Caterina pulled a chair toward the top of the bed and sat, pulling her basket toward her. "If you are able, tell me what hurts." She sat matter-of-factly, like she'd seen Bona do with terribly ill patients, and prepared herself to listen closely.

Sixtus' voice was hoarse, and he waved his hand a little. Immediately understanding the gesture, Caterina poured water from a glass jug into a small cup and held it to his lips. After taking a few sips, the Pope relaxed into his bed. "I hurt all over. My head aches so badly I cannot think. I shiver one moment and wrap myself in my blankets then sweat the next and expose my body to the air." He paused, catching his breath. "God will not grant me any respite from my suffering," he whispered.

Caterina wasn't sure if he'd said the last line out of habit, for often, he'd stop mid-sentence to bemoan some aspect of his fate, either to prompt a pitying reaction from his listener or out of genuine piety. Either way, she had to try her best. "Is there anything else? Can you eat?"

After a slight nod and a quick wince, Sixtus slid back down into his bed a little. "I can eat very little and just plain foods."

She shook her head. These symptoms sounded like a fever, and surely the papal physicians were practised enough to treat an ordinary fever. Even in one so elderly, where the danger was amplified? Sighing, she then remembered the state of the room when she'd entered and wondered.

"I will give you a few things that will at least help with your symptoms, making it easier for you to sleep. Your body will be better equipped to fight this ailment if it can rest between battles."

"You sound like a soldier."

Smiling at what she hoped was a compliment, she rummaged through her basket and removed a treatment for aching heads that used oil of roses and pomegranate, another to help him sleep made with mandrake, and a third to balance his humours. Placing the vials on a small table close to the bed, Caterina took Sixtus' hand and held it gently. "I have left you medicine my stepmother used to treat others successfully. I am confident they will help you, but you must follow the instructions I wrote on the side of each bottle. If your medical cardinals," she spat out the words, "deny you these treatments or dismiss them, you must insist that you know your mind and take them anyway." She looked into his aging face and felt pity, despite knowing his true character. "Will you promise me this?"

He nodded weakly, and she could see in his eyes how exhausting this short visit had been for him. Releasing his hand, Caterina picked up her basket and walked to the door. "I'll visit again when I can." She didn't know if he'd heard her words and didn't care, for they were as much for the Holy Father as they were for herself.

Through the rest of the autumn and into the new year, Caterina found ways to sneak out and visit the Pope. She changed her dress, never using the same one twice, and always borrowed from her own servants. It became a badge of honour in the household, having the mistress visit your room to ask to borrow an item of clothing like a sister or cousin might. Because of the reasons for her doing so, she endeared herself to the staff more than she had already.

As like-minded members of a large household will inevitably find each other, inevitable also were the secrets shared between them. Caterina didn't know if it was a maid or a cook, but somehow a few of the soldiers discovered her intrigue. Fortunately, they were already more loyal to her than Girolamo and decided to help keep her activities hidden from not only Rome but her husband.

Her plans nearly fell to pieces at dinner one evening. "Did you visit my uncle yesterday?"

Caterina's fork stopped halfway to her mouth. She recovered quickly and ate the piece of trout before replying. "No, of course not."

Girolamo glared at her suspiciously. "One of my men says he saw you near the back of the Vatican."

Caterina rolled her eyes. "Are you certain the man wasn't drunk? It's not unknown." She let the insult hang between them, knowing it would further aggravate her husband but unable to stop herself from taking advantage of the opportunity.

"He swears he wasn't."

"If you already questioned the man, you must have had doubts about his words." She cut a slice of boiled egg and chewed it slowly before taking a sip of wine.

"Nevertheless, I want an answer. Did you disobey my orders and leave the house?"

Looking up from her plate, Caterina stared right at him. "No, my lord. I did not."

Frowning at her sincerity, Girolamo took a few more bites, then picked at the rest of the food on his plate with the tip of his knife.

Anxious to get away in case he should ask further questions, Caterina stood. "I'm going to say goodnight to our sons and daughter. Do you wish to accompany me?" She knew the answer before he replied.

"No." He waved her off. "You go." His head was still wrinkled as she left. Hurrying through the halls, she found

Luisa with the children in their nursery. They were already settled into their beds, Ottaviano and Cesare on miniature versions of her own bed and Bianca still in her wooden cradle.

She stood beside her friend, both staring in silent wonder at the tiny sleeping forms.

"I lied to my husband today. The first time since we were married." Caterina kept her eyes fixed on her slumbering daughter.

Luisa turned to her. "How do you feel?"

Caterina replied without turning. "I feel nothing. But I'll pray extra hard on Sunday for forgiveness." From the corner of her eye, she saw Luisa's confused face and broke out laughing, the tension she'd been carrying at nearly getting caught dropping away. Startled, Luisa now frowned before the sudden realisation that her friend's words had been said in jest. She started giggling, but Cesare chose that moment to turn in his bed and make an unintelligible noise which stopped both women immediately. Smiling at each other, they turned and walked out of the room silently.

As the weeks passed, the Pope grew healthier and, by March 1484, was well enough to perform the investiture of one of Caterina's relatives to the college of cardinals. Ascanio Sforza, Caterina's paternal uncle, stood tall and proud as the Holy Father spoke of his virtues and pure soul. Caterina's chest swelled with pride as she stood nearby watching, grateful to have a true friend and blood relative in the Curia.

Girolamo's nephew, Cardinal Raffaele Riario, had unsurprisingly risen to the rank of Camerlengo and now administered the Vatican's properties and monies. Caterina understood he got the role because of his name, but she also knew he had more honesty than the other family members and hoped he'd wield his power well.

Summer arrived late and cooler than expected, keeping Caterina inside more than she preferred. It also meant she was privy to the meetings her husband had resumed, more so than she would have been if she'd been out in her garden or riding with Luisa.

"Who is that man I've seen my husband with," Caterina asked Bossi as they sat in the library reviewing plans to expand the building. Girolamo had decided he needed another wing to keep up with other Roman families and the fashion for rebuilding.

"Virgilio, Lord of Bracciano."

She thought for a moment, remembering the heavy-set man's fleshy face and veined nose. "Head of the Orsinis. Why would my husband be conducting meetings at all hours with this man? I thought them enemies?"

"Men are only enemies until united against a common threat. In this case, that threat is the Colonna family."

Caterina knew the Colonnas, and had had members of the family over to dine and dance at the palace. They were one of the oldest and wealthiest families in Italy, with vast land holdings across the country. Respected by Rome, they nevertheless made as many enemies as any other family, more so because their lofty position in society was too tempting for some younger families not to attempt to knock them from their ancient pedestal.

She tried to keep as on top of her husband's intrigues as much as she could, but it wasn't easy, and some of the webs in which he entangled himself were edged with danger. Suspicious of everything and everyone, he rarely spoke to Caterina, and she found it more and more difficult to perform her wifely duties when all she received from him was a cursory hello and if she was lucky, an enquiry about their children.

"Anything I should be concerned about? With the Orsinis?" She folded a sketch of a fresco the count insisted be painted on the entire wall of one of the new rooms. A gaudy classical hunting scene, Caterina had disliked it on sight and had decided to try to talk her husband out of it.

"No, I don't think so. Not that I know of anyway," Bossi replied.

Still her closest advisor, if Bossi knew of no plans then she would push her worries aside and focus on the building work, decorations, and furnishings.

The construction continued, and the new wing was soon completed. Caterina, despite all her work, rarely ventured near that end of the palace. Ignoring his wife's wishes, Girolamo had gone ahead with the hated fresco, and seeing it only reminded her of him. Content that nothing undue was occurring within the walls of her home, Caterina busied herself with her children and her herbs. Ottaviano would be five in a few weeks, and, as the autumn closed in, she decided it was time for him to have his own sword master. Not that he'd shown any interest in fighting, but she'd send to Milan for someone suitable nonetheless.

Cesare was a year younger and, idolising his brother, emulated Ottaviano's behaviour in all ways, making it difficult to see any of his own personality traits shining through. But Caterina was sure his wishes and desires would emerge in their own good time. Bianca, her baby, smiled whenever Caterina entered the room, and each time she saw the child, her heart felt fuller than she thought possible.

Early in the Spring of 1484, Caterina was in her workroom with Luisa. They were taking an inventory of herbs and other materials that were left after the usual winter illnesses had finally subsided. Caterina stopped suddenly, feeling a wave of nausea. Barely making it to a copper mixing bowl, she vomited the food she'd eaten to break her fast that morning.

"Caterina! What is it? Should I call someone?"

Caterina stood and wiped her mouth with the edge of her apron before taking a sip of water from a nearby jug. "No, I'm fine."

"You're not, from what I just witnessed. Are you certain?"

After taking a few deep breaths, she smiled at her friend weakly. "I'm positive. That is, I'm positive I'm with child again."

Chapter Nineteen
1484

Over the spring, Caterina took it easier than she had for her previous pregnancies. The cool weather found ways to seep into her bones, and the child she carried somehow worsened the feeling. The servants knew they could find their mistress sitting in front of any of the large, ornately carved marble fireplaces, either sewing or reading.

"Can I get you a blanket?" Luisa asked as she entered her friend's room.

"I'm feeling a bit warmer today, I suspect because the weather has finally turned." Caterina stood, stretching her arms behind her back, grasping her hands and enjoying the slight pull. "How do you feel about a ride in the fields behind the palace?"

"Are you sure?" She immediately regretted the question.

Caterina felt so much better today she kept silent about knowing her own mind. This pregnancy was different, as they all were, and had sometimes made her angry, snapping at all around her. Today she was more like her old self. Smiling, she lowered her arms. "I am. It's a beautiful day, the April sun has blessed us, and it would be an affront to God to stay inside."

Luisa sent word to the stables that they would be riding, and informed Bossi of the same. Together they proceeded down the stairs and out of the back of the house.

Bossi was already there waiting for them, with three saddled horses and a small group of handpicked soldiers for additional protection.

"My lady." He bowed, handed Caterina the reins to her brown Calabrese mare, and led a smaller horse of Arabian descent to Luisa. "Yours is spirited today, be watchful," he advised. His own horse, an enormous stallion, stood patiently waiting. When he'd helped the three-month-pregnant Caterina into her saddle, Bossi ran his fingers through his horse's mane and patted its neck as he settled into his own.

They set off at a walk, but Caterina, cooped inside for so long, urged her horse onto a canter, then a full run. She laughed as she felt the wind, with its last hint of winter, nip at her cheeks as the horse understood its mistress and went faster. Leaving her responsibilities behind, Caterina gave the mare free rein to run and let the beast continue until foam dripped from its mouth. Finally, she slowed and turned, finding Bossi riding just behind her and Luisa a few paces back, their faces sporting grins as large as hers.

She knew how far from the city they'd ridden and headed back in that direction at a leisurely speed. Bossi kicked his horse and, riding beside Caterina, matched her pace.

"Is there anything I should be aware of? Any hints of intrigue which might amuse me?" Caterina felt so good she laughed at her own joke. Then, seeing Bossi's face fall, she grew serious. "My husband, I presume?"

"Indeed, Madonna." Bossi bowed his head at her. Without waiting, he explained. "You remember asking me about the count and his dealings with Virgilio Orsini?"

Caterina nodded. She'd noticed that the man had been in and out of Girolamo's rooms with increasing frequency lately. Each time she happened to catch him leaving, she felt a sense of déja vu as she remembered similar assignations that had led to tragedy years ago. "I remember."

He continued. "You'll also recall that he and the count have joined forces against a perceived common enemy: the Colonnas." After a second nod, he hurried on. "It seems to be another dispute over land."

"Of course it's about land, it's always about land," Caterina said bitterly. "Our family's current position is precarious at best, and my husband continues making enemies instead of much needed allies." She shook her head, her exasperation evident by her rising tone.

"The Colonna family owns vast tracts of land all over Italy," he reminded her.

"They've had centuries to acquire it," she responded.

"Girolamo wants to claim that land for himself and, with the help of the Orsinis who follow their own agenda, intends to take it by force."

"But how can he imagine that's possible?"

Bossi nodded, reaching down once more to pat his horse's neck, finding the rough hair soothing. "The count has already accused the family of treason, on what grounds I'm uncertain, but it involves their behaviour at Campo Morto."

"Is there any truth to my husband's charge?"

"No, Madonna. All accounts state the contrary, that all Colonna soldiers acted honourably, even those under the direct command of the count. The denouncements are false."

They rode together in silence. Caterina glanced over her shoulder and gave Luisa a grateful smile for allowing her and Bossi privacy for this conversation.

"What can we do?" Caterina finally asked.

"Wait. With the Pope's ailments still fresh in people's minds, your husband may not have the support he believes. We need to see who moves next." He smiled grimly at Caterina and urged his horse on, leaving her to her thoughts.

She rode thinking about his words, tumbling them around in her mind as she always did, looking for a sliver of a solution. Unable to think of anything, she hoped it would come to nothing.

Over the next few weeks, the Colonna family moved themselves and their belongings to a large property outside Rome. It did little to help: at the end of May, Girolamo and two hundred men stormed the palace and dragged Lorenzo Colonna, Lord of Marino, from his home. When the pope wouldn't summon the man to the Vatican to account for his supposed treason at Campo Morto, Girolamo imprisoned him in the Castel Sant'Angelo and gave his men permission to ransack the house and its belongings. Word spread of the count's approval. Soon, most of the family's Roman properties had been pulled down to their timbers, and anything reusable was taken away by soldiers or opportunistic citizens looking to take advantage.

"Is there nothing you can do to persuade Girolamo to be reasonable?" Caterina had invited Cardinal Raffaele to dine with her. She'd also asked Bossi to attend; despite knowing how uncomfortable the older man was with formal meals, she wanted his opinion should anything arise that she wasn't already aware of. He knew who to trust among the soldiers who protected the palace, making his information network invaluable.

"I've tried, many times. He won't listen, despite the generous offers the Colonnas made to re-establish peace."

"What offers?" She looked at Bossi, who shook his head. He hadn't heard either.

"The family sent a representative to my uncle, begging for the release of Lorenzo and offering two of Italy's finest fortresses, that of Marino and Ardea. But Girolamo's greed knows no bounds, for he sneered at the suggestion and stated that he would have everything and take it by storm if need be."

"I pity the poor man who had to face my husband."

The cardinal crossed himself. "He no longer needs anyone's pity, my lady, for Girolamo ended his life."

Caterina mirrored the cardinal's action and made a quick cross over her chest. She sighed, feeling suddenly tired. Horrified, disgusted, shocked, yes. But mostly exhausted.

Rumours, the fodder of Rome, reached Caterina's ears, but nothing she heard was ever verifiable. Bossi reported whispers of Lorenzo Colonna's treatment at the Castel Sant'Angelo, but Caterina shut down the part of her that, knowing her husband, believed them. She instead tried resorting to the wilful ignorance that seemed to serve others so well, to no avail. The hints and suggestions followed her everywhere, including her sleep.

"Why does the Holy Father not do anything?" she demanded one morning.

Luisa jumped at her friend's sudden exclamation, nearly dropping a piece of wafer dipped in honey in her lap. "What do you mean, 'do'? You've been visiting him; you know how weak he is." She lowered her voice, fearful of sounding sacrilegious.

"I know. You're right. I think even he is afraid of my husband." The admission did nothing to quell the anger that had been growing in her for days. With no one else apparently able to resolve it, she felt she should try again to solve her husband's problem. The resentment she felt at fighting Girolamo's battles further riled her. But this time, there was no avenue for her to follow, no one she could meet with to discuss terms.

Bossi joined her in the library at the end of June, where Caterina had decided that she was going to hide from the world today. "My lady, shall we venture outside? Your garden, perhaps?"

Hearing a tone in his voice, she rose from her chair and put the book of French history on a nearby table. "Of course."

Luisa was out running errands, so Caterina sent a young maid to her rooms for a light shawl. The sun hit the palace marble and nearly blinded Caterina with its brilliance. Once in the garden, they sat on a stone bench beneath an olive tree out of the direct sunlight.

"Lorenzo Colonna has been executed, Madonna." He waited, and when she said nothing knew her silence was a tacit request for him to continue. "His head was cut from his body two days ago, on the Feast of Saints Peter and Paul. He had to be carried from the Castel Sant'Angelo because his legs could no longer bear his weight, so devastating was his torment while imprisoned. As head of the papal army, the count saw to the man's torture. He forced a false confession from the man and, based on that alone and despite Lorenzo's later repudiation, had him killed."

Caterina nodded, seemingly deep in thought. But she was preparing herself. "There is always more when my husband is involved."

With a sigh, he told her the rest.

"Why did you torture Lorenzo Colonna?" It was two weeks after the man's death at her husband's hands, and Caterina had insisted that Girolamo join her for dinner in her rooms to explain himself. The anger she'd begun to feel had only grown worse, casting a dark shadow over her and her daily activities. Even playing with her children could barely raise a smile.

The count had laughed at the resolute tone of Caterina's invitation and sent the servant relaying the message away with a black eye. But he had nonetheless arrived at her door as maids were carrying in trays. Staggering in without waiting, he'd gone to the table and poured himself a glass of wine. She could see he'd already been drinking and, with a quick head tilt, ordered Luisa from the room before Girolamo had even known she was there.

"Because it was necessary." He bit into a chunk of beef boiled with citrus juices and sugar and, chewing noisily, washed it down with more wine.

Caterina remembered the details of the man's condition when his body had been sent back to his mother, as reported by Bossi. Every limb had been dislocated, and his feet and thighs had been sliced open, not enough to kill but enough to cause maximum pain. "Did you know his poor mother died of shock when she saw her son's body?"

"What's that to me? Perhaps the shock was of her son's treason." He tore some bread off a loaf and popped it in his mouth. "You should be happy that mother and son are reunited."

After that, she had no other comment, and husband and wife ate in silence for a while. Finally, Caterina spoke, hoping to glean information from Girolamo. "I'm worried about the Holy Father."

"All of Italy is."

His lack of concern inflamed her already smouldering ire. "How can you be so unmoved? You know how serious our situation is."

He replied with the same uninterested tone. "I'll take care of it."

Caterina's pique overwhelmed her. "What? Like you have been? Emboldening our enemies and making new ones when we need friends right now?"

Girolamo glared at her, and Caterina felt slightly smug at finally pushing him into revealing himself. Mocking her tone, he lashed out. "What? Friends like your Bossi? Your closest advisor, always around to do your bidding." He glanced around the room. "I'm surprised he's not lurking in the shadows, waiting to whisper in your ear? I've often wondered if he whispers about himself and you, and if my children are even mine."

This was the best he could do? Insinuations? She was grateful Bossi wasn't around to hear such slander.

Her husband went on. "Or friends like that little *puttana*, your lady? Where is she? She's always sniffing around." He glared at her with such disdain it felt like she'd been hit by him. "You need to mind your own business, arrogant Milanese whore that you are."

Caterina stood, her body trembling. "How dare you?"

"I dare because I can. You have been too free with me, wife. You should watch yourself." Girolamo moved his hand to his knife hilt threateningly but knocked over his glass of wine in the process. His face a deep red, he picked up the glass and threw it across the room before storming out.

As he exited the main door to the hall, Luisa entered through another just in time to see Caterina stare open-mouthed and then collapse on the floor.

She spent a few days in bed, at times speaking her depressed and black thoughts aloud without a care what anyone thought.

"There are moments when small shards of despair invade my soul and cause me to envy the dead, for they are beyond the woes of this world, and I wish my cares were over like theirs."

"Hush, Caterina, I'll not hear talk like that." Luisa had taken on the role of nursemaid, as she usually did, but this time there were no ointments or oils. Her only task was to sit near her friend's bed and listen. And, if the need arose, to gently chastise. "Those thoughts are sinful." With these kinds of comments, and her presence during the nights when Caterina would toss and turn in bed, weeping, her friend's mood improved. When Caterina finally rose above her darkness, it was with a renewed determination.

"I must move. The children and I." Caterina was in her healing room with Bossi and Luisa, where she knew no one would disturb them. While the servants felt comfortable enough to visit this room when they were ill, superstition at her healing abilities kept them away when her services weren't needed. "I no longer feel safe here. The crowds grow bigger outside every day, and the men my husband hired to protect us more often than not forget their duty and start fights with each other."

"To where?" Luisa was ready to follow her mistress anywhere, and knew Bossi felt the same, but she recognised that their options were limited.

Caterina sighed. "That's just it. Sadly, the only place I'll feel more secure is a place sure to be haunted by the ghosts of recent history." At their confused looks, she continued. "The house once belonging to the Colonnas, near Paliano. Girolamo and his men have set up a camp nearby."

"So, because of the count's enemies, you and your children, though popular among the citizens, are still in danger of harm." Bossi spat out the words, then turned and lowered his head. "I am sorry, Madonna. I mean no disrespect. I just," he faltered.

"I know," she acknowledged. "Will you prepare the horses?"

He nodded and bowed his head again.

Caterina turned to Luisa. "How quickly can you arrange to have our belongings ready to go?"

Luisa thought for a moment. "Necessary items only? Give me two hours." At a nod from her friend, she reached over and squeezed Caterina's arm before joining Bossi and hurrying to complete her task.

They'd gone for a walk through the fields behind the house in Paliano, enjoying the late summer heat, and Caterina had come back flushed with the exercise and smiling. "I believe I'll sleep better than I have for a while tonight. The fresh air did me good." A yawn interrupted her words, and she raised her arms, feeling the stretch through her back. She was in her seventh month of pregnancy, and this baby sat more uncomfortably than his or her elder siblings had. "I think I'll visit the Holy Father tomorrow."

"Didn't you see him last week?"

Caterina nodded and slipped into her sleeping shift, feeling the cool linen brush against her stomach. "I did. But he needs me." She shrugged. "Can you help me?" Climbing into bed, she reached for a pillow and arranged it under her belly to better support herself. Once she was comfortable, Luisa pulled the light sheet up and ensured Caterina was covered. Yawning, she snuffed out most of the candles. As Luisa left to go to her own bed, she threw a whispered 'good night' into the gloom. She received no reply.

The following day Caterina woke to the sound of a scream. Wondering if she'd been dreaming, she sat up and listened. In the distance, raised voices reached her, as did the tolling of bells. One set followed another as the entire city of Rome cried out. It could only mean one thing: the Holy Father, Pope Sixtus IV, was dead.

Chapter Twenty
1484

Rising quickly and grabbing her silk dressing gown, Caterina slipped her arms into the sleeves as she hurried to the window. Before she could get there, Luisa flew into the room, her eyes wide in panic.

"What's happened?" She joined her friend at the window and leaned out as far as she could, staring in the direction of the city.

"It must be Sixtus." As if in reply, a banging on the front door made them both jump. Slipping her feet into a set of soft indoor shoes, Caterina wrapped her dressing gown around her unwieldy body more tightly and walked as calmly as she could to the door. The banging increased in urgency, and Caterina moved more quickly in response. Wondering where the servants were, she pulled open the door to find a young man of about fifteen standing there in a shabby papal uniform.

He bowed awkwardly as soon as he saw Caterina, more used to fighting than flattering. "My lady, your husband the count sends me to tell you that his uncle, Pope Sixtus, has died." Caterina glanced over her shoulder at Luisa, standing nearby, to ensure she'd heard the man's words. Their worst fear had been confirmed.

The soldier continued. "My lord has been given orders by the Sacred College of Cardinals to return with the papal army to Rome to help maintain the peace."

She nodded, imagining the scenes in the city right now. With no spiritual advisor overseeing its actions, even temporarily until a new pontiff could be elected, the city exploded. Old vendettas were avenged in the bloodiest possible ways, and new ones started between the younger but rising noble families. Personal armies paraded through the streets, taking what and who they wanted.

"Thank you. You may go to the kitchen if you wish, you'll find food there."

The man nodded eagerly and turned to leave. Remembering himself, he turned back to Caterina and bowed before running around the side of the building.

Shutting the door, Caterina turned to Luisa and stood there, thinking.

"What can we do?" Luisa interrupted her thoughts.

Caterina started walking back to the room she'd chosen to use as her bedroom. "I can't sit here and wait. I'm certain the reason Girolamo was sent back to Rome is because it's his enemies who will be the main cause of any trouble. With no protection, his banished enemies will see their chance and flood back into the city."

"We're in no position to fight anyone," Luisa pointed out reasonably.

Passing a maid in the hall, Caterina ordered food to be sent to her room as she returned. Arriving, she removed her dressing gown and night shift and began wriggling her thick body into a dress. When she was finished, she turned to Luisa. "My husband is the country's disgrace, but I am not prepared to be a widow, not yet and not here." She took a piece of bread from the tray the maid carried in. "If I must see to my own future and that of my children's, then that's what I'll do."

Feeling more energised than she had for weeks, Caterina donned her riding boots. Collecting her long hair at the back, she tied it up and bundled it neatly and efficiently under a hair cap. The cap fit more tightly than she preferred, but she needed to ensure her locks wouldn't get in her way. This was too important.

She was so caught up in getting herself ready that she barely heard Luisa until her friend placed a hand on her shoulder. "Caterina?"

Turning, she nodded at the other woman. "I'm sorry, my mind was elsewhere. I have a plan, but I need your help. First, we need Bossi here." The same maid who had delivered the food was dispatched to find the advisor, who arrived quickly. Light from the morning sun hit his hair as he entered, and Caterina noticed how much older he looked. Shaking the sudden feeling of despair, she smiled at him.

"There is something I must do." She turned to Luisa. "I need you to stay here and remain with the children." To Bossi, she said, "And you'll need to remain here too."

"I don't care where you're going, Madonna, but I am going with you. Nowhere is safe right now."

"I need you here."

"I'll see that my best men are left here, if that will ease your mind." He waited, watching her face.

"Fine. But I am resolute and will brook no argument nor hear words that will sway me from my path." Bossi nodded his agreement. "This is the only way to ensure my husband will live through these next days and assure I still have some control." They looked at her expectantly as she turned to a mirror to put on a pair of riding gloves. Turning back to them, she smiled grimly.

"I am going to capture the Castel Sant'Angelo."

"You're going to storm the stronghold?" Bossi asked incredulously.

Caterina smiled. "No. I'm going to walk in and ask for it."

On August 14th, 1484, a woman dressed in a rough woollen cloak appeared in front of the Castel Sant'Angelo accompanied by a larger man.

"Are your men ready?" Caterina had borrowed a cloak from a maid who'd loaned her clothing when she'd snuck out to visit the Pope. Not knowing what her mistress needed the item for but sensing Caterina's urgency, she'd simply handed it over with a bowed head and whispered, 'God speed, my lady."

"They are, Madonna. I brought my best. They are hidden nearby, ready for your call."

Nodding, Caterina finally uncovered her head. She'd worn the cloak to better ease her journey through the city. Her pregnant belly meant it hadn't covered her completely, but it had proven its worth by keeping her hidden from enemies looking to harm her. As they travelled through the streets, she'd seen the evidence of the violence that always occurred during the *sede vacante*, the days when the throne of St Peter sat empty.

Now she needed the guards at the fortress entrance to recognise her, or else all would fail. She glanced at the forbidding citadel: three massive stone towers surrounding a fortified centre. After the fall of Constantinople thirty years earlier, the place had been strengthened for fear of Turkish aggression. She nodded to herself and, taking a deep breath, started walking across the Pons Aelius bridge over the Tiber to the Castel. The bridge typically provided a pleasing view of the river's left bank, but today all Caterina focussed on was the statue of St Michael, the archangel who gave his name to the structure.

Rising atop the mausoleum, the angel held a sword aloft, and Caterina crossed herself as she approached the door, taking strength from the familiar weapon. Bossi stood beside her. "Those who took pleasure in mocking my family name will now feel the power of the name Sforza." Standing taller, she pounded on the door.

A gruff, older man opened the door with a shout. "What do you want?!" Then, seeing Caterina, bowed. "My lady, I apologise. Please, come in."

With a thankful look up at St Michael, she and Bossi entered the Castel. "I'm here on behalf of my husband, the count."

The man looked confused. Sweat trickled down between Caterina's shoulder blades, and she fought the urge to shrug her arms, instead remaining still. Adopting an imperious façade, she looked the first guard in the eye and continued. "While my husband follows his orders as head of the papal army to protect the city, he has sent me to hold the fortress until he can arrive." She looked around as if comfortable that her words wouldn't be contradicted. Inside, however, her stomach roiled.

While the guard considered her words, Caterina thought she might be ill. Her brain raced in case her body betrayed her. Her pregnancy, the ride here, the frailty of a woman, any would serve as an explanation. Her fears were finally allayed when the man nodded. "I understand. Let me show you to the common room."

As they arrived at a large room in the centre of the citadel, another man entered, this one with a much finer uniform and kempt appearance. "My Lady Riario. What are you doing here?"

"Who are you to ask?" she replied, hoping her voice would hold.

The man bowed cursorily. "I'm Innocenzo Codronchi, the vice-governor of the Castel."

Caterina saw Bossi flinch and make a move to step toward the man. She put a hand on his sleeve to stop him and, turning to Innocenzo, repeated her story.

"This is highly unusual. No one should be out right now, it's too dangerous" he looked at Caterina's stomach, "especially for a woman in your condition." He shook his head. "No. I must send word to the count." He turned to leave, and this time Caterina didn't stop Bossi when he stepped forward and grabbed the man's shoulder from behind.

"What do you think you're doing?" The vice governor tried to shrug off Bossi's hand, but her advisor held firm.

"You are relieved of your position," Caterina said, then nodded at Bossi.

"But why? At least tell me that."

Caterina considered his words. What harm would there be now? "You were appointed by my husband, and you know of his many sins." The man's face softened, but he admitted to nothing. "Of all his failings, the worst is his cowardice." Feeling the ache in her feet, she started wandering around Bossi and Innocenzo. "A new Pope must be elected soon. Many clamber for the role, and many are deserving of stepping into Sixtus' shoes." Her face hardened. "But there are those who would do everything in their power to destroy my family. Rising to the papal throne would be an act of vengeance for these people, not one of virtue. They would strip away anything my family owns because of their hatred for my husband, leaving us penniless and completely at their mercy." She looked around. "Is there no wine at the Castel?"

The man's eyes flickered toward a large wooden cupboard. She nodded and spoke as she walked to it. "Girolamo is not man enough to fight for what is his, what was granted to him by his uncle." She opened the cupboard and found a sealed jug with a few plates and goblets. Opening the jug, she inhaled the rich earthy scent of red wine and proceeded to pour herself a cup. "The only way to ensure my family is protected is to insist on promises be kept and that they are recorded in writing in front of the entire college."

"And how do you plan on achieving that Olympian task?" Innocenzo asked sarcastically.

"With God's help, of course." She nodded at Bossi.

"Please come with me. This will go easier for you if you comply." As Bossi spoke, he removed a hidden dagger from the folds of his cloak. Light from the flickering candles that illuminated the room danced off the blade as he held it for Innocenzo to see.

With an angry scowl, the man wisely decided to obey and allowed himself to be locked in a secure room. The cavernous area beneath the Castel had been repurposed as a prison complex and everyone in Italy knew of the horrific questionings and punishments that occurred below ground. Understanding the alternative, the vice-governor sat on the bed glaring quietly as Bossi locked the door and returned to Caterina.

"What next?"

Pleased that her plan had succeeded so far, she forged on. "Bring in your men from outside and raise the drawbridge. Have the men round up my husband's men and talk them over to our plan. If anyone disagrees, deal with them gently but firmly, as we did with the vice-governor." She thought for a moment. "Remind them of their treatment by my husband, of the lost wages and lack of food. Offer them gold and tell them fresh food supplies from my own stores will be arriving soon." Sighing, Caterina finished. "If we can't win their loyalty, we'll need to buy it. We have no choice."

She looked around the main hall and frowned at a large wooden door at the opposite end of the room. "Where does that lead?"

The guard who had answered the door had been watching the entire time. When he saw the vice-governor's treatment, he decided to support Caterina. "To the Vatican, my lady."

Bossi walked over and found the door unlocked. Behind it, a long tunnel led into the darkness. He stepped aside and held the door open to show Caterina.

"A passage, I should have known. It must be blocked immediately."

Bossi nodded and hurried to the entrance to let his men in. Once inside, he instructed them to find the guards and then turned to the first one. "What's your name?"

"Ercole Miniati." He glanced to the side where Caterina stood and quickly added, "Guard at the Castel for two years."

She narrowed her eyes at him. "Where are you from?"

Turning red, the man stammered, "Everywhere, wherever I can find work." He hesitated. "But I was born in Milan, my lady."

Caterina smiled. "Then I think we understand each other, yes?" When he nodded gratefully at her, she continued. "Work with my man Bossi to block the passage. Be quick about it, for there is other urgent work to be done and time is of the essence."

As he hurried to join Bossi, Caterina watched with interest which of the Castel's existing guards would join her and which would continue to support the count. How many resented her husband's ill-treatment of them, she wondered, and how malleable were their loyalties? She was surprised when a quarter of the original guard sided with her husband. But that left her with an expanded personal army within the walls. And she intended to put them to work.

When the route to the Vatican had been blocked, she called Bossi over. "Come with me to the roof."

Together they climbed the ancient stone steps to the roof of the main building. From here, the three remaining towers of the fortress stood proudly, making Caterina smile. "The last set of renovations were done well." Looking around, she saw the cannons and walked to the roof's edge. "You see there," she turned, "and there?" Pointing into the distance, she continued. "Train the cannons on those roads, as well as any other that leads to the Vatican. I want to get the attention of the college of cardinals. This should do nicely." She accompanied Bossi back down the stairs.

By now, her body was complaining about the amount of activity, and Caterina collapsed into a chair. Uncomfortable as it was, for her husband's tastes in decoration and luxury hadn't made their way to the fortress, it was still a relief. Her body sagged, and she closed her eyes, putting her hand over her forehead.

"Madonna, there is a room prepared for you upstairs, away from the area where the guards are kept. Perhaps you should rest for a while and let me see that your orders are obeyed."

Caterina dragged herself out of the near-sleeping fugue that was settling over her and smiled. "Perhaps. It has been a long day." She rose and, grabbing the goblet and a second jug of wine, headed toward the stairs. Turning on the third step, she said, "Wake me if there is anything I should see to."

At Bossi's nod, she pulled her body up the stairs and went down a corridor where a young soldier stood waiting. He bowed deeply at her, and his whispered "Madonna" followed her into the room. With a weary smile, she closed the door after her and collapsed on the bed, still dressed in her riding clothes and borrowed cloak.

Chapter Twenty-One
1484

Before she'd even ridden to the Castel, Caterina had ensured the food and supplies she'd promised her new soldiers would be delivered soon. Unsure how long she'd be here, she also insisted on a trunk of clothing being sent.

When the supplies arrived two days later, a note from Luisa was at the top of the trunk when Caterina opened it.

"The children are well, I pray to God and Mary for your success. Love, Luisa."

Hugging the note to her chest, she thought of her children, just now rising for the day. Pushing the images her mind conjured of their faces to the side, she picked an outfit and changed, feeling better for being out of the same clothes she'd been wearing since she walked up to the Castel door. There was a knock on her door as she pinned up her hair and put on a simple hair cap.

"Enter," she called out through lips that held a long silver pin.

The door opened slowly, and Bossi peered in. He looked around nervously, fearing what he might see, then entered. "My lady, I hope you slept well."

'I'm getting used to the location. So much noise outside. Are the riots still occurring? Has my husband done nothing?"

Bossi shook his head. "No, Madonna. The men who accompanied the supplies tell me your husband hides in the corridors of the Vatican, occasionally issuing an order that is never obeyed."

"And the cardinals?" She took a last look in the mirror that had been found and placed in her room and turned.

"They have promised the count his lands and titles, as well as eight thousand ducats and payment for damages done to your homes. He is also to keep his title of Captain-General of the papal army."

"And you trust this information?" She tilted her head toward the door, and they proceeded out into the hall.

Bossi nodded. "I do. I chose only men I could depend on to deliver our supplies, and those I knew had their ears open to any news."

They walked the hall to the main area, where Caterina had had long tables set up so she and the men could eat. Already her small changes had made a difference in the mood of those who had sided with her, with more and more bows and respectfully murmured 'Madonnas' delivered as she passed by. She'd found a small cooking area and had instructed Bossi to find those guards most amenable to cooking for the others. Three men had been selected and had proven themselves with their first meal.

Sitting across from Bossi, she nodded at the men around her. After a first awkward dinner, the men had understood that she'd be eating with them, and now just bowed their heads in acknowledgement and continued with their meals.

"A generous promise. But a promise made to the air is worth nothing. Do you know what my husband's response was to such a lucrative offer?"

"I don't, sadly. That was all the information I was able to obtain."

She shook her head as one of the guards she'd assigned to cook brought them a tray of meat, cheese, and bread. As she tore a chunk of bread from a mishappen lump, she said, "In that case, we'll have to be patient, and pray the count did the right thing. I'm certain we'll hear soon."

Caterina had found a room filled with old military documents and maps and was leaning over a table studying one, her hand supporting her lower back, when Bossi entered.

"My men have spied someone waiting to cross the Pons Aelius bridge toward us. I've lowered the drawbridge as there is only one man."

She hurried to the door with him as a hand banged on the outside. Caterina nodded at Ercole to open the tiny window built into the door, then peered out at a young man dressed in the clothing of a Vatican page, wringing his feathered hat in his hands as he waited.

"Who are you? What do you want?" she demanded.

"My lady, I am Amato Allesi and am here on behalf of my master, Cardinal Riario. My master wishes to arrange a meeting with you and the cardinals."

Caterina made a dismissive noise. "I'm sick of cardinals. If not for cardinals, I wouldn't be in this place."

The man's face fell, her reply unexpected. "But my master..."

She interrupted him. "Your master and I know each other, and I consider him a friend. I will allow him and only him to enter the Castel."

"My lady, I must protest your arrogance and foolishness in these matters!"

Caterina's eyes narrowed. "So, such deeds, done by a man, are heroic and to be celebrated, but when a woman does the same it's arrogance?" She shook her head violently. "You dare match wits with me? Have you, any of you, not realised by now that I have my father's intelligence and am as stubborn as he ever was?"

"You are holding up conclave! No cardinal will enter Rome with your guns pointed at every road into the city."

"That's all I have to say. I know Cardinal Riario and will meet with him. Until I know where the loyalties of the rest of the College lies, I refuse to see them."

She started slowly closing the window, waiting for her words to garner a reply. "Wait." Sliding the window panel open again, she looked down at him with a raised eyebrow.

"I will inform my master of your kind offer of a meeting," the man said through gritted teeth.

"And I will wait for his reply." She shut the door, ending any further conversation. Nodding at Bossi and Ercole, she smiled to herself, enjoying the feeling of power as she walked back to the main hall. A tiny part of herself that could never comprehend some of her father's actions suddenly burst into fragments of understanding. The sensation was intoxicating.

Bossi re-joined her at the table and stared at her while his food sat waiting. When she began to eat her own meal, he shrugged and ate. As they were finishing, the door guard interrupted them. "Madonna, there is another visitor."

"That didn't take very long," she said to Bossi as they returned to the door. Peering outside, she saw Girolamo's nephew, Cardinal Raffaele Riario, Camerlengo of the Vatican, standing waiting.

"Let him in," she ordered, stepping back as one part of the massive door swung open.

The cardinal smiled at Ercole and then stepped forward and bowed. "My lady, thank you for agreeing to see me."

"Raffaele, please come in." She ushered the cardinal to a room that led off the main hall. She'd had a few chairs and a large table set up so she could work in peace. Without needing to be told, Bossi followed and shut the door behind them. He stood nearby with his arms crossed over his chest as Caterina and the cardinal made themselves comfortable. Caterina smiled and waited.

"My lady, I'm here on behalf of the College to ask you to stand down, surrender the Castel to our hands, and go home."

"I hold the fortress for my husband, who was granted governorship by Sixtus. I will only hand it over to the next Pope."

"And how are we to elect the next Pope if you continue to terrify the cardinals?"

"Surely God will aid you in your efforts?" she replied sweetly. "I'm only doing what any obedient wife would and protecting my husband and family." She shifted in her chair. "Can the cardinals not meet elsewhere? I'm certain God will guide their hands just as easily outside of the city."

"That's not fair. You know the Vatican has already been selected for the next conclave."

"Do I?" Caterina had, of course, heard this valuable bit of news.

Exasperation nearly getting the better of him, Raffaele kept his voice even. "What do you want, aunt?"

The sudden informality surprised her. A small wave of pity for the man washed over her. He would have to be the one to tell the other cardinals of their meeting. She hoped they would be kind but knew better. "I told you, I'm here for my husband."

Knowing there was nothing else he could say, the cardinal stood. "I hope you'll reconsider." He bowed at her and started out of the room on his own, with Bossi following close behind.

Caterina waited as news of the families of her enemies flooding back into Rome arrived daily. The remainder of the Colonnas had arrived with two hundred soldiers and had sent word to Caterina that her children wouldn't be harmed as they passed by their old home. The Orsinis had men stationed near the Vatican, and the other great Roman families had given their armies free rein over the city.

Finally, on the 23rd of August, more positive news arrived. Bossi knocked and entered Caterina's new study, where she'd met with Cardinal Raffaele a week ago. "The cardinal's representative is here to see you."

Sighing, she nodded. "Bring him to me."

She spent the time waiting by clearing a few of the books off the table and re-shelving them. Turning as the man entered, she smiled. "Don Allesi, I hope you bring good news." She waved him toward a seat. Bossi must have told someone about their guest, and a tray of wine and glasses appeared.

"I do, my lady. Your husband the count has made a decision."

Caterina filled their glasses. "Finally. Did he accept their offer?"

Allesi nodded. "He did, my lady. He is promised the eight thousand ducats, titles and properties, everything."

Caterina crossed herself. "Thank God it's over." She frowned, a sudden thought hitting her. "Were these promises obtained in writing?" She remembered thinking this very thing not long ago.

Allesi lowered his head. "No, my lady."

She sank into her chair wearily, feeling the now familiar rough side dig into her leg. "So, nothing has changed."

Sitting straighter, Allesi smiled at her. "Not at all, Madonna. The cardinals' words are sacred. There is no need for you to worry about any of that now. Your job is done. Go home to your children."

Frustrated yet again by her husband and infuriated by Allesi's tone, Caterina stood. "What else was the count given?" She saw that the man was concealing something by the way he glanced away. "Tell me. What did the cardinals give my husband?"

Allesi finally broke. "Gold. Many bags of gold. He has gathered his men and belongings and has left Rome to head north. You are abandoned. You must see your cause is an impossible one. It's over."

His sudden confidence was disconcerting. "Until I receive proof of these promises, in writing, I will not leave."

"But my lady..."

She cut him off. "No. I've been involved too long now to think mere words are sufficient from any man. My husband is selfish and boorish, but my children are young and still need a father for protection." She knew Girolamo would never actually fight and didn't mean protection in that way, but a living father contributed to his children's standing in other, less tangible ways. Walking around the table, she reached the door and held it open for him. As he followed a guard toward the main entrance, she called out after him, "The count may have forgotten he has a family, but I have not."

When Bossi had returned, she poured him wine. "Shall I prepare the horses, my lady?"

"Whatever for?"

His glass paused halfway between his lap and his mouth. "To leave. To go home."

Caterina drained her own glass. "Nonsense. I want you to send word to my men waiting at home that they are needed here. Tonight."

Overnight, one hundred and fifty men loyal to Caterina and the Sforza snuck into the Castel Sant'Angelo under cover of darkness and without the notice of the infrequent guards the College sent.

As the sun began to rise, Ercole watched as fresh men appeared around every corner. "How did you do this?"

Caterina smiled. Standing in the main hall, she was aware of everything going on around her. "There are ways. The older guards know a thing or two about the fortress, and my father taught me that all citadels have a weakness. I've had my men out looking since we arrived."

Bossi arrived at that moment. "Every man has been assigned a role and a place to bed down."

She nodded, and the sudden motion threw her off balance. Taking a step forward, she reached out her arm.

"Madonna." Bossi took the outstretched hand. "You are unwell."

Careful not to move her head this time, she smiled. "No. It's just the child and perhaps the fetid air in this part of the city."

"Can I do anything for you?"

Caterina looked at him, seeing the alarm in his eyes. "I'll lie down for a while. I don't think there's anything else we can do until we receive word. From my husband, the cardinals, someone." She patted his arm and headed toward the staircase, feeling Bossi's and Ercole's eyes on her back. Walking as steadily as she could, Caterina waited until she closed the bedroom door before collapsing on the bed. Like she'd done on her first night, she fell asleep in her clothes.

As Caterina had predicted, there was nothing to do but wait. Exhaustion threatened to overwhelm her, so she had an easy day sitting and reading while Bossi took care of the fortress. Even reviewing an old building plan for the fortress, something that had kept her gripped for days, now tired her. After a light meal and a few friendly conversations with the soldiers, she slipped back to her room and bed.

A knocking on her door the next morning roused her from her sleep. "Wait," she replied. Wrapping a blanket around her shoulders, she hurried to the door and spoke through it. "Who is it?"

"Bossi, my lady. There is someone downstairs."

From the tone of his voice, Caterina knew the visit wasn't trivial. "I'll be there shortly." She heard Bossi's footsteps recede, then went to the storage chest and withdrew one of her last clean outfits. Whoever had descended on them so early in the day would at least be presented with an appearance suggesting control.

She started speaking as she hurried into the main hall. "Good morning..." Her eyes widened at the sight of her uncle Ascanio standing before her in all his ecclesiastical glory.

"Good morning, Caterina."

Rushing over, she threw her arms around him. "Uncle!" His grip reminded her of her father, for all three Sforza brothers had been blessed with muscular figures. Releasing him, she waved toward two chairs that Bossi had arranged at the end of the table. "Please sit. Why are you here?" She looked around the room and only now noticed her uncle's retinue.

"I've come to give you this." He motioned at a priest who stood by nervously. The man handed a scroll to Ascanio, which he then handed to Caterina. Before she could unroll it, he summarised the contents. "Inside, you will find all the promises made by His Holiness Sixtus IV and the College of Cardinals to Girolamo Riario written out in full."

Caterina had unrolled the document and read it eagerly as her uncle continued. "At the bottom, you will see the signatures of the witnessing cardinals, including Cardinal Riario, Camerlengo."

She finished reading, taking in every detail. The promised money and repayment for the destruction of their property, Girolamo's continued leadership of the papal army, and, most importantly, Imola and Forli. The two words nearly brought her to tears, for the scribbled handwriting guaranteed not only their ownership of both but also that of her son and his sons after him. Clearing her throat, she carefully re-rolled the paper and grasped it tightly in both hands. "Thank you, uncle. I know you must have had some say in this."

He laughed harshly. "My dear, who would believe the word of another Sforza when one already threatened them so." He shook his head. "No. The doing was all yours. My brother taught you well, he would be proud."

Knowing the tears would start flowing, she smiled. "I'm glad it was you they sent to deliver the news."

"I was happy to do so. You may leave whenever you wish with all your men, no harm will come to any of you, and none will suffer any repercussions." He rose. "I have a lot to attend to, I'm sorry I can't stay longer." With Caterina's victory, conclave planning could begin in earnest.

The next day the drawbridge to the Castel Sant'Angelo was lowered and remained so. Caterina and her men rode out from the fortress to the thunderous cries of Roman nobles and ordinary citizenry alike. At the bottom of the ramp was Girolamo, waiting on his horse.

He must have ridden back when he knew it was safe, she thought. Keeping her suspicions to herself, Caterina smiled. "Husband," she nodded at him as she waved to a crowd of people. The mania that had swept the city when Sixtus had died was over, and a fatigue had settled. No one wanted the violence and crime to continue any longer.

"My lady," he replied through gritted teeth. "I'm here to accompany you and our unborn child home." His words were terse, the edge on his tone revealing the anger he was trying to hide.

Now he thinks of his children, she thought. Putting on a smile, she nodded. "Of course." They rode together away from the crowds, Caterina waving and nodding and Girolamo scowling.

When they were far enough from the people, her husband turned to her in his saddle. "Why? What was," he motioned backwards at the citadel as it receded into the distance. "I don't have the words to describe your actions. What did you think you'd accomplish by such a stupid act?"

"I had to do it." She turned to him. "You're weak. I knew of the deal you'd accepted."

"You weren't there," he growled.

"No, I was protecting YOUR inheritance, and that of our sons!" Caterina shifted in her saddle, the child in her stomach choosing that moment to kick.

"Watch your tone, my lady."

"Or what? You'll beat a pregnant woman? Knock me from my horse?" With a disgusted noise, she continued. "All of Rome knows of your cowardice so it would hardly be surprising to hear of such an act of petty violence from you."

Girolamo rode closer and began to raise his arm. Lifting her chin, Caterina stared coldly at him. Daringly. Defiantly. Glaring at her, he moved his mount to the side and rode a few steps away.

"I thought not," Caterina urged her own horse forward. "I'm going to pack what little we still have in Rome. Thank God I thought to send our belongings ahead to Forli." She stopped her horse and turned it to face her husband. "I'm leaving tomorrow. I can't stand to be in this Godforsaken city another day."

Chapter Twenty-Two
1484

"The building looks abandoned," Luisa said, peering into a cracked window.

Caterina nodded, stepping back to survey the damage to the apothecary shop. "I knew Isach was planning on moving his family from Rome. The city's violence must have finally forced him out." She moved a piece of glass with her foot. "We should get back. The carriages will be packed by now. We shouldn't have waited so long to leave. It's still not safe for us." Turning, she nodded at the guards that had accompanied her. They made their way through the market square, empty except for the same signs of chaos they'd seen everywhere. Litter and debris blew through the space and caught a piece of torn green silk, blowing it in a circle before depositing it a few feet away.

Shivering at the sight, Caterina quickened her pace. Soon they'd arrived back at their old house. The destruction done to the Riario's properties was worse than Caterina had expected. After thirteen years of Girolamo's cheating and lying, the city had had enough. Now that the count had no uncle to protect him, the pent-up anger held back for so long was released. Torn down almost to its base after the crowds had dispersed, the house was a skeleton, a mocking monument to the count's failures.

After finding only a few children's toys, she'd picked through the remains and had stood outside gazing at her former home sadly. Luisa took her arm, and they stood side by side for a moment, lost in individual memories of the time they'd spent here, both good and bad. Then Caterina shook herself. "It's time to go."

Caterina had done all she could to ensure the journey to Forli would be without drama. With the men protecting her, Girolamo, and their children, they weren't approached by anyone the entire way. Stopping at a large farmhouse on their first night, they were cautiously welcomed by the owner and his wife. The next morning, they said their gracious goodbyes and continued on their way. Bossi had gone on ahead to arrange accommodation for them, and with Caterina wanting to put as much distance between herself and Rome and insisting on as few breaks as possible, they made the journey in just over a week.

It was a relief when the towers of Ravaldino came into view. "It's as if the troubles of Rome didn't matter here," Caterina remarked as they rode through the main gates of Forli.

The townspeople cheered as they had before, and the path to the palace was lined with men, women, and children waving coloured cloth and ribbons. Thankful for their love, Caterina waved and smiled graciously the entire way to her home but was nevertheless relieved when she could finally dismount and stretch her legs in private.

The palace was ready for them, and all Caterina wanted to do was bathe and rest. She turned to Girolamo as he handed his horse over to a guard to ask if he had any plans but was ignored as the count strode inside without a word.

With a glance at Luisa, Caterina followed her husband inside. She walked slowly as her legs and lower back grew more comfortable, then quickened her pace as he traced the familiar path to her rooms. Sitting on the bed and lying back, Caterina sighed and breathed in the fresh air the open windows allowed. So different from her chambers in Rome, she thought. Smiling, she sat up.

"I've arranged a bath for us both," Luisa announced as she arrived a few minutes later. "I'll help you then I'll wash the smell of horse from myself. I fear if I wait any longer, it'll be a part of me forever." She cautiously sniffed her arm and wrinkled her nose.

Two pages arrived carrying a large copper tub and placed it near the fireplace. Thankfully, despite the Autumn heat, someone had had the good sense to light a fire. Shortly afterwards, the first of a long line of maids arrived carrying jugs of hot water. Luisa had removed her offending sleeves and now stood bare-armed as she helped Caterina from her own clothing. "Just put them over there. We can see to them later."

Nodding, Luisa carried her friend's travelling outfit to a chair and laid the items across the back. She helped Caterina into the tub before it was entirely filled and moved to one side as the maids continued pouring jugs of hot water over and around the countess.

"That feels so much better," she said as she held her back to allow the water to cascade down her hair. "I'm going to stay here for a while." Caterina stopped a maid. "Can you ask the kitchen to bring me wine and something to eat? Put it there," she pointed at a small table nearby, "and drag it closer so I can enjoy a glass while I bathe."

The maid bobbed quickly and scurried out. Caterina turned to Luisa. "Why don't you go clean yourself up. I'll be fine here. If I finish before you, I'll ask one of servants for help."

"Are you sure?" Luisa's voice crept up a tone at the end, her hopefulness making itself evident.

"Of course. Go." She waved a hand and settled back into her tub as more water was added. After a few moments, she heard a splash of water and a deep sigh as her friend got into her own tub in the room adjoining Caterina's.

There was a peaceful calm as each woman soaked. Caterina ensured Luisa had wine and, after a few sips decided to break the quiet. "What should we do tomorrow?" She called over her shoulder.

Luisa's faint voice replied. "Perhaps look at the garden? I don't know if the instructions I left last time we were here were followed. It could be in quite a state."

Caterina nodded. "Good idea. There may yet be something worth salvaging from the plants I had before. I want to see my workroom; it'll need to be fully restocked now that we've returned."

They chatted about plans and the days ahead until the water filled the tubs and no more could be added. Luisa dried, changed into a clean linen shift, and hurried to help Caterina out of her tub. Once they'd arrived, Caterina had insisted on the house being closed for the night. She was too tired to entertain; that could be started tomorrow or the next day. Tonight, they'd dine in her rooms alone and continue planning.

By the time Caterina went to bed, she felt more hopeful than she had in ages. She and her children were finally safe and away from that accursed city, and a new baby would arrive within a month. Smiling happily, she settled down into the covers.

Three days after they arrived in Forli, the count and countess received a messenger from Rome. He was announced as Caterina and Girolamo ate a midday meal together in one of the private dining rooms.

"Please, come in. What news have you brought?" Caterina wiped her mouth and waved her hand at the tired-looking young man.

"Signor, Madonna, there is a new Holy Father." He spoke as he stepped into the room and bowed.

Girolamo stood suddenly and, in two steps, was close enough to grab the messenger's shirt front. "Who is it? Tell me!"

"Signor," the man choked, "it is Giovanni Battista Cibo."

Releasing the shirt, Girolamo returned to his spot at the table. "And what is he calling himself?"

With a glance at Caterina, he said, "Innocent the Eighth."

"Innocent." The count spat the words out bitterly. "Innocent as an old whore."

Caterina knew as much as anyone about the new pontiff. Born in Genoa, he'd risen through the ecclesiastical ranks in Naples until he was made a cardinal. His reputation was one of peace and fairness. Still, there were whispers about his behaviour, and even the king of his own adopted home, Naples, had supported Cibo's rival Cardinal Roderigo Borgia.

"Husband, please." She ignored his frown and turned to the messenger. "Is there anything else?"

"Yes, Madonna, this." He reached into his leather satchel and withdrew a heavy rolled parchment tied with a red ribbon. "A papal bull, confirming all agreed between the Count of Imola and Forlì and the College of Cardinals."

This time when Girolamo rose, it was eagerly and with a smile. Reaching out, he tore the document from the man's hands and unrolled it on the table. After skimming through the contents, he nodded at the papal seal at the bottom, satisfied.

"Signor, there is more." The messenger held out another document. This one was smaller and lighter.

Taking the second missive, Girolamo read it, then slammed his fist on the table and crumpled the paper up. The messenger had jumped back a step at the noise and eyed the count warily.

"What is it? What does it say?" Even if he didn't tell her now, Caterina would find a way of discovering the source of her husband's rage. She always did.

Fortunately, this time he chose to share. "The cardinals, while still naming me as head of the papal armies, have dispensed with my services and insisted I remain in Forli, and forsake any thoughts of returning to Rome."

Caterina's eyebrows rose, but she quickly hid her surprise. She waved the messenger away and received a grateful smile in return. After he'd gone, she turned back to Girolamo, who had sat back at the table. "What does this mean for you?"

Shuffling the remaining food around on his plate, the count threw his knife onto the table. "It means I no longer have the loyalty of the papal troops, for how can any soldier respect a leader in name only?" He sloshed a bit of wine from the side of his goblet as he snatched it from the table. "Cibo is no friend. That accursed Florentine, Lorenzo Medici, has been a close supporter of our new Pope for years. And now that the protection my uncle's office offered is gone, my enemies will gather and strike."

He turned to Caterina and shared a rare truth. "Rome has abandoned us."

A few weeks later, as Caterina and Luisa were walking the grounds and re-planning the garden for Caterina's medicines, a commotion at the front of the palace disturbed them.

"Now what?" Caterina muttered to herself. She was tiring of her size and of waiting for the birth of her child, and as hard as she tried, she couldn't let her impatience creep into her tone. "Wait here." With a glance at Luisa, she made her way around the corner of the building to the front.

"What are you doing?" She rushed toward a guard, one of her husband's, who held a plainly dressed man by the back of his cloak. "Leave that man alone!"

"My lady, he came asking for you. Says he's a friend." The man sneered but released his grip.

Caterina went to the man. "I'm so sorry you were treated poorly."

"I'm fine, Madonna." He turned and smiled.

"Isach! You're here!" In her excitement, she forgot the soldier standing nearby, watching the exchange. "And your family? They are here too?"

Isach laughed. "They are, my lady. And all well."

She turned at the sound of the guard shuffling his feet. "You. I don't know who ordered you to treat people this way, but it stops now." Taking a step toward him, her height allowed her to meet him face-to-face. "This is my home, and this is my town." She waved a hand over the square. "Anyone who seeks me out, for any reason, will be treated with respect. Do you understand?"

The man nodded, his face turning bright red. "Yes, countess."

"Ensure the rest of the men know." Caterina nodded her dismissal and turned back to Isach. "Are you sure you aren't hurt?" She glanced at the retreating form of the soldier.

"I promise."

She turned back at Isach. "Why have you come? Is there something you need?"

He shook his head. "No, nothing like that. I wanted you to know that I'm here, should you need any supplies." He winked at her. "Not only have I brought my stores from Rome, but also my list of connections."

Caterina laughed. "Will you come in? Have some wine? I'd love to show you my workroom if you have time."

"It would be an honour, Madonna." He bowed at her and followed her into the house.

After instructing a passing servant to bring wine and that morning's fresh bread to her workroom, Caterina wound her way through the palace halls with Isach in tow.

A maid had informed Luisa of Caterina's visitor, and she joined them outside the room as they arrived.

"Signor, you remember Luisa."

"I do." He bowed at her. "Dama Tommasa, it's a pleasure to see you again."

"Please, call me Luisa."

He nodded his agreement. "Shall we go in?" Caterina held an arm out for Isach to enter first.

Inside, the room still smelled of the herbs and other ingredients Caterina had left here the last time they visited. "I haven't had a chance to clear out all the old things yet." She grimaced and grabbed her stomach.

"Are you well, Madonna?" Isach stepped forward worriedly.

Caterina waved him away. "Just the baby, kicking to remind me he's there." After a moment, she nodded. "Over here, I want to store my local ingredients, things I grow myself. What do you think?"

Isach nodded, his practised eye taking in the space the moment he'd entered. "It's the farthest wall from the light, an excellent place."

They spent half an hour walking around the room and exchanging ideas and recipes before it became evident to both Isach and Luisa that Caterina was tiring. "Madonna, I have kept you on your feet too long. And my family will be wondering where I am. If Dama Luisa would show me to the front door, I will leave you in peace."

With a grateful smile, Caterina nodded. "I'm glad you came to visit, even if the start was shameful."

Isach took her hand and, in a fatherly gesture, patted it. "I have already forgiven the man, for he was only protecting you, Madonna."

"Thank you, my friend." With a nod at Luisa, she smiled at him. "I'll come and visit you soon. Say hello to your family for me." She watched them go, a feeling of happiness welling up inside. While she had done everything she could to discard mementoes of her time in Rome, Isach's visit had only prompted pleasant memories for her. Humming to herself, she searched the shelves for a few more minutes, then walked to her rooms.

Caterina's pain started early in the morning of the 30th of October, and by the end of the afternoon, her fourth child, a son, was born.

"He looks like your father." Luisa stared down at the bundle in Caterina's arms.

"Nonsense. All babies look alike." She peered down at the wriggling child. Perhaps he did look a little like Galeazzo, his eyes? Shaking her head, she smiled. One could imagine any new-born to be an exact image of almost anyone.

"What will you call him?"

Caterina had already discussed this with Girolamo.

"If the child is a boy, he must be named Francesco," the count had demanded.

"Francesco." Caterina had stared at him. He'd entered her chambers unannounced and had walked over to her bed. "After your uncle." Her tone had been flat.

"Yes. He was a great leader and a true man of God. There can be no other name." He had turned to leave, thinking the matter settled.

"No."

Lying in bed with her son, she remembered the shocked look on her husband's face and nearly laughed. But her baby had fallen asleep, so she kept still but returned to the memory.

"I will not name our child after a man so vilified his name is still slandered more than two months after his death. Nothing but misfortune can come of such an association for our son. Not while our enemies still bay at our doors and the wounds of the past still bleed."

Instead of storming out, the count had stopped and considered his wife's words. He'd been more settled than usual as of late and was enjoying a rise in popularity after making a few key decisions upon arriving. "What do you suggest?"

Even when happy, he couldn't keep the sullen tone from his voice. Not for the first time, Caterina had wondered what his childhood had been like.

She had thought for a moment, and thanks to the amount of reading she'd recently done, an answer had sprung to mind.

Now lying in bed, Caterina saw that Luisa was still waiting for a reply. "Giovanni Livio Riario. After the founder of Forli, Gaius Livius." She looked down at her son and whispered to him. "A strong name for a strong son."

"And very politic." Bossi peered into the room from the adjoining one. As one of Caterina's closest friends and advisors, Gian Bossi was allowed access to most areas of the palace, within reason. Formal standing on ceremony was infused into every inch of skin on the older man, and, after all these years, Caterina still saw him struggle to be more relaxed with her.

"Gian. Come in. Why do you say that?"

Bossi walked to the countess' bed, where she sat propped up by pillows as she held her son. The birth had been two days ago, and her advisor still had not been to visit her boy or update her on any news. "It's a clever move. The people of Forli will love you for it."

"That's a part of my plan," she smiled.

"I thought as much. I came to tell you that there is nothing to tell you." He peered down at the baby, whose eyes had opened upon hearing his deep voice, and made a face.

Caterina stifled a giggle and pretended she hadn't seen this basic human gesture made from one so enigmatic. "Nothing at all?" She frowned. Was this good or bad?

"I'm sorry, my lady. Apart from a few balls..." he shrugged and made a mock frowning face at Giovanni, then stuck out his tongue.

"Thank you for the update. I'm relieved. I was worried some sort of punishment from fate would follow us from Rome. But I see all is peaceful." She nodded at Bossi, watching him cross his eyes at her son. "Would you like to hold him?"

Blushing deep red at having been caught, Bossi mumbled a no and backed away. "I must leave, there are, I have horses."

"As do I." Caterina could barely keep herself from laughing. "Why don't you go and see if they require anything."

Bowing gratefully, Bossi turned and hurried from the room just as Caterina and Luisa broke out into good-humoured laughter.

When she recovered enough, Caterina's first job was to continue organising her healing supplies.

"I need to go out," she announced at breakfast.

Luisa walked to the window and peeked out of the shutter. The sun shone down, but a crisp November wind had forced many to stay inside. "It's cold."

"I have a cloak," Caterina replied reasonably. "Let's finish eating. I want to get out and back without wasting time."

After a few more bites, Luisa nodded and got their heavy cloaks and gloves. She wrapped her head in a scarf to keep the wind from her ears as Caterina stretched the leather gloves over her fingers. "Where is my basket?" she said, looking around.

"Downstairs, near the door," Luisa said with a nod at herself in the mirror. "Where are we going?"

"To Isach's. Now that the colder weather is here, I'll need to restock supplies for coughs and chest complaints." She picked up her basket as they headed outside. The wind stole their words as they hurried across the empty square to the opposite side. Once there, they made their way down a narrow alley where many wealthy merchants had set up their shops.

When they arrived, it took all Luisa's strength to hold the door for her friend and not let it fly open.

"Madonna! What are you doing out in this weather?" Isach wiped his hands on his apron and came to kiss her hand. "A pleasure of course."

"Thank you Isach. Your store is close enough for me to risk the walk." Caterina removed her gloves and breathed in the warm herbal air. "As you know, my garden was neglected while I was in Rome, and I have nothing ready for the winter ailments I know are shortly to arrive."

"I see. Very wise of you, my lady. I'd expect nothing less. Do you have a list?" He looked at Luisa, nodding at her, then back at Caterina.

"I do." She handed him the list she'd been working on for a few days and waited as he scurried around his new space.

"I'm sorry, Madonna, for making you wait. I haven't gotten used to the layout. I've stored everything as close to my shop in Rome as I could remember, but, as you know, memory is a fickle thing, and I can't always recall the exact placement." He picked up a glass jar. "Ahh, here you are." He added the pot to the growing armful and took it to the counter. "I think I have everything. If not, Madonna, I can always order it for you. With the move to Forli, I'm more centrally located and find that my access to exotic ingredients has improved."

"I'm glad you settled here." She watched him put the jars and containers in her basket. "Promise me you and your family will come dine with me soon. I'd like my children to meet Sarra and I'd be honoured to show Ricca my library."

"I promise. Now," he put a last clay pot in the basket and covered it with a cloth. "You're ready."

"Will you send me the bill? The same arrangement we had in Rome?"

"I will, Madonna. Be careful outside." He bowed at her, and she smiled, happy to have gotten everything she wanted, but a little sad her visit was over.

"Anywhere else?" Luisa refastened her cloak as they stepped outside.

"No, let's go home."

They hurried back the same way; their speed hindered this time as they travelled into the wind. The ends of Luisa's scarf started blowing, and twice she had to stop and turn her back and fix it.

"Who's that? Who else would be foolish enough to be out in this wind?" Caterina pointed to someone approaching them. "Is that Cobelli?"

"It looks like him. Even with that, what is that? A women's scarf wrapped around his head?" Luisa asked.

"It's lovely, I'll give him that," Caterina laughed. By now, Cobelli had seen them and was removing the scarf as he headed over at speed. Caterina grabbed Luisa's arm and squeezed before putting on a calm façade.

"Countess! Of all the people I thought I might see today you are the very last."

"Signor Cobelli," she remembered a conversation they'd had when they'd first met and corrected herself. "Signor Lione, I mean, did you expect to see anyone today at all?" Caterina waved her hand in the air. To emphasise, a sudden gust swept past them all.

"Well, Madonna, when the weather changes, so do the people."

"Very mysterious of you."

"I enjoy observing people, you know this." He smiled and changed the subject. "I had heard you were back. I was waiting for word, some gracious crumb of an invitation to view your radiant visage again, my lady."

Caterina laughed despite herself. This man had a way of lightening any mood or day. "I'm sorry, I've been busy and surely you know of the birth of my child."

Cobelli looked away, a chastened look replacing his hopeful one. "Of course, of course. You are a busy woman, and my hopes often grow larger than they have any right to. Excuse my impudence." By now, the smile had returned to his face as he held his head low but raised his eyes to meet Caterina's.

Smiling graciously, Caterina nodded. "You are excused. Now, I'm sorry to cut what I'm certain is an accidental meeting short, but as you see, I must get home." She held up her basket.

"I said before, I must come better prepared, my wits are no match for yours. I confess to having seen you cross the square earlier and hoped to intercept you on your way back."

"Your wits are fine. It's your timing, Signor." The wind blew furiously across the square. "Expect an invitation from me soon." Caterina curtsied at him and turned back toward the house with Luisa. She didn't see Cobelli's face after delivering her last line, but the thought entertained her the rest of the way home.

When they'd moved back to Forli, Girolamo had assured the nobles that promises made to them about their lowered taxes would remain in place for the foreseeable future. But the city relied heavily on taxes, as all cities do, and soon the lack of monies intended for the upkeep of the town began to show.

To maintain the city's expenses yet still keep his promises and, thus, his finally favourable reputation, Girolamo had made several decisions without consulting Caterina.

"You cut the number of guards at the main city gate in half?" Caterina stormed into her husband's room, not caring about the servant who waved at her desperately to stop.

Girolamo looked up from his journal, a bemused look on his face. "How else am I to keep the city running if not by cutting unnecessary expenses."

"City guards are hardly unnecessary." Caterina thought of the enemies that still lurked everywhere.

He dismissed her concern with a raised eyebrow. "I cut the gate guards but there are still my personal condottieri. They will ensure our protection should the need arise."

As long as they're paid, Caterina thought but kept the words to herself. "I've witnessed their 'protection'," she replied, remembering Isach's rough handling.

Ignoring her, the count continued. "The people are in favour of my tax measures. Everything is running smoothly, and I'll change nothing." He returned his attention to his journal, abruptly signalling the end of their meeting.

Caterina didn't have much time to worry about the city's finances. Shortly after she met with Girolamo, and with the year coming to an end, Caterina fell deathly ill.

Chapter Twenty-Three
1484 - 1485

For a month Caterina lay in bed delirious with fever, chills, and sweats. She complained of the pain in her head during her rare lucid moments and vomited up anything Luisa tried to feed her.

"It's quartaine fever again," Luisa explained as she wiped Caterina's face and arms with lavender-infused water.

Girolamo stood by his wife's bed, gazing down at her. Luisa had never seen the count look so helpless but had no time to wonder at the change in his behaviour. Watching her friend was her priority right now, and Girolamo was just getting in her way, standing there wordlessly.

"My lord, perhaps you'd be more comfortable elsewhere. I will send word if there is any change." Luisa tried to speak kindly but struggled. It was difficult to pity the man, knowing him as she did.

He nodded and slowly walked from the room. Luisa chose a maid who had entered with fresh linen to stand watch over Caterina as Luisa hurried down to the workroom. She'd been practising her own healing skills along with Caterina and, while not as gifted as the countess, could concoct effective remedies for several illnesses. To treat Caterina, she selected some mint leaves from Isach's shop, a vial of almond oil, and a smaller glass bottle containing extract from poppies which Caterina had brought with her from Rome. Crushing the mint, Luisa breathed in the scent and allowed it to clear her head. When it was ready, she added a few drops of almond oil and mixed the two ingredients. The earthy mint smell mingled with the cherry aroma of the almonds, and Luisa wondered if this combination might work for other purposes. Shaking her head, she refocussed.

When the mix was done, she carried the small mortar bowl to another table and strained the mortar's contents through a piece of fine gauze. She waited impatiently for the mossy green drips to slowly form and fall into a cup she'd placed beneath the gauze. Squeezing the mixture as the dripping stopped, she got as much as she could out of the bundle before discarding it. She gathered up the cup and the vial of poppy and, careful not to spill any, returned to Caterina's room.

"I'm back," she announced, hopeful her voice would garner a reaction from her friend. She hurried to a table and poured a glass of wine. Reaching for the cup of green liquid, she added everything to the wine and stirred it with her finger. Looking down at the dark liquid, Luisa wondered if she needed to add the poppy.

As if in reply, Caterina began coughing behind her. Turning in alarm, Luisa ran to the bedside and helped her friend sit up enough to swallow some water. The decision made, she returned to the medicinal wine, added a few drops of the poppy mixture, and carried it back to Caterina.

"Drink this. It will help your cough and head." She held the glass to Caterina's lips and watched as the countess took a few sips before falling back exhausted. Luisa turned to put the glass on a bedside table, and when she turned back around, Caterina was already asleep.

Early in the new year, Caterina was feeling well enough to return to her usual household duties, which included arranging the ball that so many of the Forlese anticipated. Enjoying being up and around again, Caterina saw to every detail: the food, the music, the decorations, and the invitations.

"Should I hold back Cobelli's invitation for a day or two?" Caterina smiled wickedly.

"The poor man would have a fit if he thought everyone else was invited and he wasn't." Luisa laughed. "Best send it with the others."

Caterina sighed. "That's no fun at all." She walked to a long cupboard near the main entrance and looked over the silver and gold. Goblets, cups, plate, and other expensive items shone back at her. She nodded, pleased the servants had done so well with their polishing, for everyone would pass this display of wealth, a signal to all that the rulers of Forli were well-off.

"What else is there to do?" Luisa asked.

"I think that's it. A final check on the kitchen." Caterina smiled.

"You're in high spirits today."

Her smile widening at her friend's words, Caterina nodded. "I am." She started walking down the hall.

"I've noticed the count paying particular attention to you since you've recovered."

"He has. He's finally come to appreciate how important my connections are, and thus how important they are to him." She stopped and turned to Luisa. "I genuinely think my illness scared him." They started walking again. "I always say I'm not ready to be a widow, that my son is yet too young to rule. But I never imagined Girolamo wasn't ready to become a widower."

With a formal bow, a page approached and looked up at Caterina. "My lady, the count, your husband wishes to see you in his rooms. You are to make all haste." He bowed again and scurried away, glancing back at Caterina as he turned a corner.

"Wishes? He really is being solicitous." Luisa raised an eyebrow in surprise.

"I'll see what he wants. Can you start planning our outfits for the ball? Whatever my husband needs, I'll not see it ruin the evening. The nobles have been waiting long enough, and their expectations will be high."

"I already have a few ideas." Luisa smiled and continued down the hall.

Caterina turned and made her way to Girolamo's rooms. When she arrived, a guard bowed at her and held open the door.

"Caterina, thank you for getting here so quickly. I have news."

"Nothing serious, I hope?" She sat in an empty chair and noticed her husband had cleared the room of the papers and journals he usually had scattered everywhere.

"It could have been, but no." He poured them both wine and sat across from her at his worktable.

"I don't understand."

"The governor I put in place in Imola has sent word of a foiled plot to take over the city and move south to attack Forli." He hesitated. "And us," he added.

"What?" Caterina stood, knocking the table. A few drops of wine splashed over the side of the glass rim.

"Sit. Please." Girolamo waited until Caterina had settled herself. "Taddeo Manfredi, the former ruler of Imola, from whom your father acquired the property, decided to launch an attack."

"While I was ill and we were distracted," Caterina added.

The count nodded. "It would seem so, yes. My governor discovered the plot and stopped it before it could start."

"And the conspirators?"

"Likely backed by that bastard Florentine and his Medici lackeys. Thirteen men were hanged. Manfredi managed to escape."

Caterina let out a relieved sigh. Her relief lasted only a moment before she sat up again, alarmed. "Were any of these men people we know?"

Girolamo shook his head. "No, none of our nobles were involved."

"That's a small comfort but a comfort nonetheless." She took a sip of wine. "They see us as weak, unable to rule without the support of Rome."

"I agree. But I have an idea."

The count's plans came as a pleasant surprise to Caterina, for she agreed with them all. Over the next few months, Girolamo would devote all his energy to fortifying and expanding the fortress of Ravaldino. A new, more luxurious home was to be built for Caterina and her family within the fortress walls, and new barracks were being added that could hold up to two thousand men.

While her husband was busy with the building, Caterina saw to her own duties. That included the upcoming ball. She and Luisa stood in the main hall, taking a final look around before the guests arrived that evening. "We've done the best we can with our limited resources."

Caterina nodded, pleased. "Girolamo has pulled all available funds into the building work, and with the reduced taxes coming in, money is short." She sighed. "It won't compete with the dinners I held in Rome, nothing here does. I've hired locals to work in the palace, the families of the noble girls who accompanied me from Rome demanded too much for their children's upkeep. And I do miss meeting the new artists who grace Roman walls with their genius." Caterina gave in to a rare moment of regret, not for the city's drama but for its often-overlooked innovations in art and philosophy.

Shaking the nostalgia away, she smiled. "I think we're ready."

Despite her words, Caterina insisted on a final visit to the kitchen before hurrying to her room, where Luisa was waiting. "Where have you been? I've had enough time to arrange your clothes and dress myself."

"In the kitchen."

"It's late. We need to get you ready. You know how some guests arrive frustratingly early." Luisa held up a mossy green coloured gown. "As it's warmer, I thought your dress should reflect the season." She put the gown down and picked up a sleeve. "With a darker green sleeve and your silver hair net, the one beaded with emeralds."

"I'll be the embodiment of spring!" Caterina walked to the gown and held it up to her neck. "I think the next ball I hold will be costumed."

"Excellent idea, but right now there's this one to dress for." Luisa took the gown with a raised eyebrow. Caterina laughed and allowed herself to be dressed. When she was done, she turned to her friend. "How do I look?"

"Like a wood nymph from the old myths." Luisa tilted her head toward the mirror. "See for yourself."

Caterina walked to the mirror and gazed at herself. The way Luisa had done her hair, in braids fixed elaborately around her head and then hanging down her back, she did look like something from antiquity. "It's perfect."

The noise of conversation floated up to them from the main entrance. "Frustratingly early," they both said at the same time before breaking down laughing.

More noise reached them. "Let's go."

Caterina sent a servant to instruct the musicians to start playing, then hurried to the main door as quickly as she could manage and still maintain the dignity expected of her. Luisa went to check on the food in case any last-minute issues had arisen. Caterina started greeting guests as soon as she arrived, and each new couple brought the stark realisation of just how different the nobility was here. But despite having less lavish clothing and fewer jewels, the attitudes of the gentry weren't really that far removed from those she'd cut her teeth on in Rome. No matter their outward appearance, people with wealth were very similar inside.

Still, the privileged and powerful of Forli put on a dazzling display that night, dressing in their finest gowns, waistcoats, and overcoats. Every colour Caterina could imagine flashed through the room as each family strove to outdo the rest. Like peacocks displaying their tails, each person's goal was attention. From their peers and, more importantly, from Caterina.

She'd lost count of the people in the palace and assumed everyone had arrived. Stepping toward the main hall, she stopped at a noise behind her.

"Madonna!"

Caterina turned and saw Leone Cobelli, dressed in the brightest colours she'd ever seen, enter the palace. He swept his hat from his head and held it to the side dramatically as he bowed deeply.

"Signor Leone, I thought everyone had arrived. How remiss of me to not notice your absence." She held out a hand.

Cobelli rose and, taking Caterina's hand in both of his, kissed it. "My lady, you are the busiest woman in all the Romagna, my heart soars that you would deign notice me at all." He stepped back and gazed at Caterina, his eye narrowing as he looked her up and down. "Goddess, my apologies, for I thought I was speaking to a friend when here before me I see a being from Olympus itself."

"Leone, you go too far in your adulations. You've gotten your invitation already." Caterina mock frowned, then laughed. "I must go. My guests are waiting." She nodded to a page nearby, who showed the writer, or chronicler as he preferred to call himself, to the main hall.

Caterina waited a moment, then, after taking a breath, entered through a different door. The crowd began applauding as soon as she entered, a sign of respect for their hostess, but all Caterina saw was Girolamo standing at the front of the gathering, smiling at her. It was apparent he'd made an effort: his clothes were new and shaded green to match hers, his hair had been trimmed, and his face cleanly shaven. She'd have to ask Luisa about his choice of clothes, she thought to herself. He nodded at her almost imperceptibly and stood waiting with the rest.

"Nobles of Forli, my dear guests, it's my honour and pleasure to welcome you to my," Caterina corrected herself with a glance at Girolamo, "our home. The count and I hope you enjoy yourselves tonight, we will try to speak to every one of you and look forward to calling you friends."

The crowd erupted in applause again, and Girolamo stepped forward and took Caterina's hand. Holding it high, he tucked his other arm behind his back and led her through the crowds to the large dining room off the main hall.

He leaned toward her as they stood in the middle of a long table, waiting for their guests to settle themselves. "You look very well," he said gruffly.

Caterina knew that while her husband's words could not compete with even the poorest poet, his feelings were genuine. "Thank you, my lord. I see Luisa has betrayed my confidence and told you what colours I would wear tonight."

Girolamo's eyes grew wide, and Caterina felt a rush of tenderness for her husband and his effort to please her. "Don't be angry with her. She isn't to blame. I insisted that she tell me."

Given what the count had called her friend in the past, she could imagine poor Luisa's reticence at revealing anything to him. "I won't say a thing to her. Now," she looked around, "everyone seems to be here. Shall we begin?" At his nod, Caterina held up her hand at a servant near the door, his only task watching for this signal. He nodded and disappeared. The musicians had set up at the far end of the room, and strains of their compositions could be heard between snippets of conversation that filled the air. Caterina had timed everything down to the minute and prepared herself as the smell of food wafted through the room.

The noise in the room rose as the courses were carried in on silver platters, one after the other. Sweetbreads and fried kid's liver, veal pastries, stuffed pigeon stewed in plums, boiled veal and cheese, and artichokes with vinegar and pepper, all leading up to a spit-roasted lamb served with slices of lemon. The wine flowed as much as the conversation, and soon the servants began placing bowls of rose water before each guest so they could wash their hands, and small sticks of fennel to scrub their teeth. It was time to move to the ballroom.

Caterina had left the room more unadorned than the others, realising decorating would be a waste of time as her guests had already seen her credenza filled with precious items. And, after dinner and wine, they would probably be more interested in dancing than tapestries. Still, she'd seen that the existing frescoes were freshened and that stands of candles were placed every few feet, close to chairs and small tables.

Once the musicians had moved from the dining area to the dancing hall, Girolamo led his wife to the middle of the room. As the first strains of a courante started, the count bowed low to Caterina, then took her hands and started the dance. His steps were clumsy, but his efforts were rewarded by the cheers from the crowd of guests who encircled them as he took Caterina's waist. After the first few steps, others drifted with their partners onto the floor, and soon, the room was filled with quickly twirling people.

Girolamo, more used to activity while sitting in a saddle, started to lag after his third dance.

"Why don't you sit and talk to the families? I know they would appreciate a word from their count." Caterina was rewarded with a grateful smile and watched while men surrounded him immediately as he walked away.

"Does this mean there is hope of a dance with you, oh celestial one?"

Caterina turned to find Cobelli standing before her, the tiny jewels sewn into his waistcoat glittering in the torchlight.

"Leone, it would be my honour." She inclined her head at him and held out her hand. They moved to the floor along with others. "What would you dance to?"

"A saltarello, if Madonna is up to it." He smiled wickedly, his eyes glinting with the challenge.

Caterina laughed and sent a passing page to inform the musicians. She received a pleased nod from the recorder player and stood facing Leone. His face lit up delightedly when the song started, and he proved himself a true match for Caterina's dancing skills. There was no time to talk as they moved through the fast, hopping steps and as the music finally ended, it took them a few minutes to catch their breaths.

"Signor, I applaud your talent," Caterina led them away from the other dancers to a table set off to the side of the room. She glanced over at Girolamo and found him engaged in a conversation with a rotund man who looked like his waistcoat had given up trying to encase him and hung open in resignation.

Caterina sat and waved her hand at the chair opposite. Cobelli sat quickly as if afraid the countess would change her mind. A maid brought them glasses of wine and a plate of vanilla wafers as they settled comfortably to watch the others.

Leone leaned forward. "That man your husband is speaking with? He doesn't know it, but his wife is sleeping with his brother."

Caterina's eyes widened. No one had ever started a conversation with her in this way before. She glanced over at the well fed man again and giggled. "Is that true?"

He nodded vigorously. "It is, Madonna. I take my job as a chronicler seriously. I don't deal in rumours or falsehoods."

She looked at him critically. Was any man capable of such a feat? "We'll see," she replied. "I've heard many who make that claim."

"Because they all wanted something from you, Lady. Whereas all I want is to see that the truth is told. And, perhaps, another invitation to revel in your presence again?" he suggested hopefully.

Caterina laughed again. "You can be certain of it." She turned and looked around the room, narrowing in on a tall thin woman wearing too much tint on her lips. "Now, tell me about her."

Turning the World to Stone

Cobelli's smile turned wicked once more. He proceeded to share details about most of the nobles of Forli, including things they, themselves, weren't aware of. While Caterina rose and danced occasionally, she returned quickly to Leone to continue their conversation.

At the end of the night, after Girolamo had gone to bed and she'd bid goodbye to most of her guests, she turned to Cobelli. "How do you come to know so much about everyone and everything, I wonder," she said.

"People enjoy talking to me. I'm a good listener." A servant helped him into his cloak.

She watched as he fastened the intricate silver pin. "I'll have to be careful what I say around you, Signor."

Leaning forward to kiss her hand goodnight, Leone fixed his eyes on her. "Your words, Madonna, will always be safe with me. I know your story. It arrived here before you did. And I would never betray the trust of one as fearsome as you."

Unsure of whether he was teasing her, she curtsied and said goodnight, wondering if she'd found another ally.

Chapter Twenty-Four
1485

"You see there?" Girolamo pointed to another room deep within the fortress walls. "There are storehouses for food and ammunition, should anyone be brave or clever enough to cross the moat." He beamed proudly at Caterina.

He suggested they tour the now-finished project, and she saw just how industrious he'd been. "Everything has been seen to." She nodded. "It's a fine fortress, strong and well provisioned." She took her husband's hand. "You should be proud, my lord."

Clearing his throat gruffly, he continued. "Upstairs in the living area are rooms enough for us, the children, retainers."

Caterina laughed at his enthusiasm. "I'm pleased by all of it."

"It's nearly ready for us to move in."

"Good timing.

Caterina had realised she was carrying another child only a few weeks ago and was anxious to move her family to their new home.

When they finally did move, the streets of Forli were lined with people hoping to get a glimpse of the Riario's fabled wealth. People offered them help, but Caterina had planned everything to the last detail, and the move went smoothly.

Over the months, Girolamo's determined efforts for his wife continued, and he shared in her joy of their fifth child. When the weather allowed, he accompanied her on rides and hunts around the Romagna countryside. While Caterina revelled in the attention she received from her husband of twelve years, all she would say when Luisa asked was, "He needs me." That that need was political was understood, but she could permit herself to hope that a small part of the count did want her for more than the diplomatic connections and contacts she'd made over the years.

Although Caterina had found her social engagements had dwindled since their move to Forli, there were still essential visitors passing through the area who needed to be entertained.

"My nephew Raffaele will be visiting soon." Girolamo had stopped by Caterina's rooms to deliver the news. "A messenger just arrived with word."

Looking in a small tabletop mirror, Caterina finished smoothing a whitening cream on her face, one she had made for herself. "When will he arrive?" She stood and, tugging her dress over her swelling stomach, sat beside her husband.

"Next week." Girolamo poured them both wine.

"So soon? That doesn't leave me much time to plan. How many will he bring with him?"

The count sighed. "He's a cardinal and Camerlengo, what do you think?"

Caterina immediately started calculating the cost. While they had room for many in the fortress, feeding them would be another matter. And the entertainment, depending on how long they stayed. She shook her head. "We can't do it like we used to, he must understand that. This isn't Rome, and most of our resources were put into Ravaldino." She waved her hand around the room.

"I know. And you can also argue that he's a holy man and shouldn't expect anything lavish, but you know better." He raised an eyebrow.

They sat silently, each involved in their own thoughts. Finally, Caterina stood. "I'll see what I can do, starting with menus. Will you be dining with me tonight?"

"I will."

She nodded at him, pleased, then headed out into the hall and toward the kitchen to start planning.

By the time the cardinal arrived the following week, Caterina had, with Luisa's help, organised everything. Even with her limited resources, Caterina's inventiveness had ensured that all was fit for such a high-ranking official of the church, relative or not.

"Your Grace." Caterina curtsied. Despite her increasing figure, she still balanced herself gracefully and, smiling, rose.

Girolamo stepped forward and bowed. "Nephew."

"Caterina, my dearest aunt. It's good to see you looking so well." Raffaele waved his hand at Caterina as she reached to kiss his ring, dismissing the hint of any obsequiousness around him. Girolamo witnessed the exchange and stood watching.

Looking past his shoulder, Caterina frowned. "Your retinue is small, your Grace."

The cardinal turned. "Yes, I insisted that only those I need be with me. The others I have placed in inns around the town and just outside." He glanced back at Caterina, the sympathy obvious in his eyes. He knew of their financial difficulties.

Her face burning, Caterina cleared her throat of the shame she felt. She avoided looking at her husband, unsure if he had said anything to his nephew. "Please, you've had a long ride. Come inside, refreshments wait, as do your rooms and a bath if you so desire."

Their unspoken understanding, and Caterina's gratitude, were acknowledged by a small nod from the cardinal. "Some wine would do us all well I think." There were murmurs of agreement from the half a dozen men who stood waiting. Prelates mainly, from what Caterina could tell, with one or two civilian advisors in tow.

The late spring sun shone down, blinding them as it reflected off the newly refurbished walls of the fortress. Inside, the temperature was cooler, and the dimness welcomed.

Once his eyes had adjusted, Raffaele looked around the main hall, where wine and wafer stood waiting on a long table. "A very large room, and so," he hesitated, "sparce."

Caterina felt her humiliation burn across her face once more. "We are still acquiring pieces, your grace, and have only just moved here." This time she looked at Girolamo, who had headed further into the room.

"Of course." He brightened when he saw the wine. Walking over, he waved away Caterina's attempts to serve him. "You are a gracious hostess, aunt, but I am capable of pouring my own wine." He walked around the room, holding his glass and looking at the tapestries adorning the walls. Caterina's and Girolamo's love of the hunt was evident in this room, with each piece of art depicting deer, dogs, and rabbits, along with men and women in equal numbers riding on horses.

Raffaele put his goblet on the table when he had finished his wine. He'd already sent his followers up to their rooms and had received grateful looks as they had filed out. "I would like to accept your offer of a bath, aunt. I fear I have spent too long in your presence still smelling of my horse."

Caterina laughed. "It's an honest smell, your grace, and one I welcome in my household." She bowed her head at him, knowing that all the Riarios were at least skilled on a horse.

Showing him to his room and arranging for hot water to be carried up from the kitchen, Caterina made her way back downstairs.

"I'll go to my study, there is business I need to attend to." Girolamo bowed at her formally and walked toward the back of the fortress.

"Is the cardinal settled?" Luisa stood as Caterina entered the main hall.

She nodded. "He is. He's bathing and will sleep for a while before tonight's meal." Caterina sat in an oversized, padded chair, the brocade cover sighing as she sunk into the material. Looking around the hall, she exhaled her relief.

"Are you well?" Luisa handed her a glass of wine and sat in the chair opposite.

"I am. And pleased with the reception." She took a long drink. "Somehow, the cardinal was aware of our situation. He placed many of his men at inns instead of having us entertain them here."

"Did the count say something to his nephew?"

"I wondered the same thing. I don't know. I doubt it, for who would openly discuss their pecuniary difficulties?" She shrugged. "The fact remains that Raffaele is aware and accepting." Caterina took another sip of wine. "Which makes my work a lot easier."

The cardinal stayed for two weeks, during which time Caterina saw to their meals, their daily activities, and their nightly entertainments. More than once, Raffaele begged off, pleading exhaustion, but Caterina knew he was saving her further cost and loved him for it.

Halfway through the cardinal's visit, Caterina had taken Raffaele outside to watch Ottaviano at his swordsmanship lesson.

"You must hold your arm straight, little condottiero." Her son's teacher, Don Fallaci, demonstrated by holding up his own arm, sword in hand. He was a man local to Forli and less expensive than the teachers she used to be able to afford from Rome or Milan.

The five-year-old boy raised his arm again, the small wooden practice sword gripped tightly in his hand.

"A strong child. You should be proud, Madonna." As the words left his lips, Ottaviano lost his balance and stumbled to the side, dropping the sword. He looked down at the weapon and then up again, his lip trembling and eyes filling with tears when he saw her watching.

"No no, mia cara, it's all right." Caterina hurried over and knelt beside him. "There's nothing to cause tears." She reached over and picked up the wooden sword. "Here. You'll get there." She looked at his face earnestly. With a raised eyebrow and a nod at him, she rose.

Ottaviano stood still, holding the sword.

"Perhaps you could show me your garden again, aunt. Leave the boy to his learning." He winked at Ottaviano and, taking Caterina's arm, walked away with her.

"He looks like you."

"He looks like my father. Pity he has none of my father's military qualities." Caterina's voice sounded weary.

"He's still young," Raffaele added.

Caterina nodded, hoping it was true. But she had started showing promise early on and hoped she'd see the same in her children.

The cardinal left a few days later, thanking Caterina for her hospitality. The count and countess mounted their horses and escorted Raffaele's group out of Forli and a short way along the road to Florence, the papal representative's next stop.

"I wish you well with your child, Madonna." The cardinal kissed his aunt on the cheek as they both still sat astride their horses. Holding out his hand, he grasped Girolamo's. "Uncle." With a nod, he turned his horse and set off down the road. The Riarios watched until all they could see of the man was the dust his horse kicked up behind him.

The remainder of the year passed quickly, with Caterina busying herself with her plants and, when it got too cold, her remedies. Every day she saw to the running of the palace, as well as managing her children's educations. By the time her fifth child arrived in mid-December, Ottaviano had turned six, Cesare five, Bianca four, and Giovanni had reached his first year successfully.

"I want to call him Galeazzo, after my father."

Luisa smiled down at the babe, asleep in his wooden cradle. "A good name. The duke would have approved."

"And Bona, I hope." Caterina sighed. "I know she's well and living in a convent. I've had no word from her, she's not allowed any contact in her order, but I think she's happy away from court, now that all her children are grown."

"I'm glad." They stood together silently, the shared memories of Caterina's stepmother and their childhoods in Milan hanging between them. Without turning, Caterina grabbed Luisa's hand and squeezed it before releasing it.

A few days later, Caterina sat with her husband in her room, finishing their evening meal. It would be a few weeks until she could resume her usual activities, particularly with the vigour she was accustomed to using. Until then, Caterina had been enjoying the peace, using it to get caught up on her correspondence and housekeeping records. One subject kept rearing its head, no matter how much she tried to push it away: their finances. Caterina knew she'd have to say something to Girolamo, and soon.

Wiping her lips with a linen napkin, Caterina leaned back in her chair comfortably. "There is something we need to discuss."

"What is it? Are the children well?" Girolamo looked up from his boiled boar.

Caterina held up her hand. "They are all fine. What isn't, however, is the city's coffers."

Sighing deeply, the count threw his knife onto the table. "I know."

"We need to reinstall the dazi. People must start paying taxes again." Caterina raised an eyebrow at her husband expectantly.

"It won't be a popular move," he countered.

"Since when are taxes ever popular," she snorted, then grew serious again. "The city no longer has the luxury of relying on subsidies from your uncle. And the new Pope isn't a friend, you know this. People must be made to understand why the monies from them are important."

Girolamo sighed. "I'll talk to the town council." He stood. "But not until after Christmas. I'll not have that ruined too." With the sullenness Caterina had thought gone, her husband left the room.

With the meeting of the Council of Forty, the governing body of Forli, hanging over their heads, the Riario's Christmas celebration was subdued. Caterina did her best to ensure every visitor was offered warmed wine spiced with the last of her cinnamon and cloves and that the children didn't notice the feeling of anxiety hovering around each corner of the palace.

Two days after Christmas, the meeting took place in the town hall. A notary named Niccolò Pansechi argued passionately in favour of taxation, reminding the council of the terrible rule of the city's previous count and the generosity of the Riarios.

"Sixtus, whose munificence saw to the running of the city, is no longer with us and the new pontiff cares little for anything outside of Rome. The count and countess have used their own money to fund the city and pay our wages. Would we force them into bankruptcy so that all can enjoy the city's resources? Isn't it fair that all who live and work in Forli should pay for the upkeep of their home?"

Half the attendees applauded the speech. The other half frowned and looked at their neighbours to gauge their reaction. Girolamo sat by silently, observing and feeling the same burning shame his wife had felt creeping up the back of his neck. He said nothing as, one by one, the men in attendance walked to the front of the room and placed a stone into a dish: white for yes and black for no. No man could see what his neighbour dropped into the bowl, assuring anonymity.

Pansechi had done his job well, and the vote passed. Taxes were reinstated in Forli.

Chapter Twenty-Five
1486 - 1487

The assassination attempts started early in 1486. While the council may have agreed to the taxes, the people did not. Many saw it as an opportunity to invite the ousted Ordelaffi back to rule, their memories clouded by their anger.

"A new plot has been uncovered." Caterina wrapped her shawl around her shoulders more tightly. While her workroom was heated by a fire, the March winds still found their way into every room in the palace.

"Against the city?" Bossi asked. Even her grizzled advisor had been forced inside, and Caterina wasn't sure if it was the winds or the weariness she'd seen in him lately that had cracked his usual fortitude.

She shook her head. "Against Girolamo and me." Walking to a shelf, Caterina took down a clay pot and opened the lid, sniffing it. Nodding to herself, she put it on the work table. "A man was caught carrying letters from one of the Ordelaffi brothers. The letters had instructions for the takeover of Forli and the execution of the count and countess."

Luisa covered her open mouth, her eyes wide in horror. Bossi grunted. "Why wasn't I informed?"

"I'm sorry, Gian. It only happened this morning. There wasn't time."

"I may be getting older, my lady, but it is still my duty to protect you." He sniffed dismissively.

Caterina understood the man's distrust, even now, of her husband's soldiers. "I promise next time to inform you first. You're right of course, you must be included in these things."

Mollified, Bossi nodded. "Is the count readying for more conspiracies?"

Sighing, Caterina picked up a small knife she used to cut plants and started tapping the edge on her finger. "I don't know. Since the taxes were announced, he's gone back to his old ways. I can no longer get him to leave his rooms, and he won't allow me inside."

"But the taxes will now be collected. Surely the count is pleased with such an outcome?"

"Not at all." Caterina put the knife down and ran her hand over the tabletop, brushing a few bits of dried greenery to the floor. "When my husband is adored and admired, whether deserved or not, he can be charming. The opposite is true of any negative feelings directed toward him. He shuts himself away, as if a door will keep his problems from finding him, and shouts angrily at any who would help."

"Can anything be done?" Luisa asked helplessly.

Caterina shook her head. "No. Taxes must be available for the town's upkeep and people must pay those taxes. There is no other way. Every city in Christendom operates in such a manner and it's time for Forli to re-join the others."

Summer arrived in a blaze and the heat added to the unrest in the city. More attempts were discovered, some the half-thought-out schemes of fools, others to be taken more seriously. At least no one had heard from the Ordelaffis since their failed attempt to seize the city earlier that year.

Making matters worse, Girolamo's trusted castellan in Imola had decided to leave their service to join the Venetian army.

"The ingratitude of the man! After all I've done for him!"

Caterina had caught up with her husband as he rushed down the hall toward the stables. He hadn't invited her to ride. In fact, his invitations to ride and hunt had stopped completely. Servants scattered when they saw him approaching, and Caterina had to nearly run to match his pace, so urgently did he want to get outside and ignore his life. Finally, she put her hand on his arm. As if suddenly realising where he was, Girolamo stopped.

Caterina was astounded at his tone. "What do you mean, after all you've done for him? I've been informed the poor man hasn't been paid for over six months."

The count's mouth twisted into a sneer. "Oh, and I suppose you heard from your Bossi?"

"I did." She continued her point. "Is it any wonder the man left? No one can survive without money. No matter how thick their loyalty, that cloth wears thin with each slight or betrayal."

"But the Venetians?"

"Why not the Venetians? They'll pay him well." Seeing the look of petulance on Girolamo's face drew Caterina's ire. "And what man with experience and a good few years of fighting left in him wants to wait on a petty noble who no longer has any power."

Girolamo glared at her, his mouth sputtering as he tried to form words. All he managed to spit out was, "That includes you too, my lady."

The hard tone he adopted for the last two words had little effect. Caterina just shrugged. "But the difference, my lord, is that I've accepted what must be done, popularity be damned. We are not friends or family to these people." She waved an arm in the direction of the centre of Forli. "We are their rulers, and they look to us to make decisions that will serve the city best, no matter how difficult those choices might be."

The only reply she received was an angry noise made deep in the back of her husband's throat. She necessarily turned the conversation back to money in case Girolamo decided to argue the finer points of ruling with her. "I've also accepted that we are close to having no money ourselves, much like the town. Until the tax proceeds come in, we must live more frugally."

He raised an eyebrow at her. "And what have you done to contribute to our simpler lifestyle?"

"I've cut my staff to almost nothing. I see that the kitchens only use food from sources close to Forli, instead of sending for supplies from Rome. My clothing is made by seamstresses down the street from my own house, and not in the finer establishments with whom I used to do business and whose shops I used to frequent. I now make my own medicines and beauty supplies instead of ordering from abroad. Shall I go on?"

The count held up his hand. "Please, no. I had no idea the Countess of Forli suffered so and it would pain me too much to hear more of her tales of sorrow," he mocked.

Caterina closed her eyes and turned her head upward, resisting the urge to reply. When she opened them again, the count was hurrying outside.

Girolamo's behaviour continued to worsen until he was fully back to his Roman ways. He no longer dined with Caterina, and when he came to her room at night, she decided it was best to humour him than to start another fight. She knew the servants whispered about their bickering, which seemed to happen every time they bumped into each other. Each encounter left the palace heavy and listless.

By the time the winter winds started blowing through the town again, Caterina barely saw Girolamo, each having decided independently to avoid the other. She devoted her time to her children and her alchemical work, as she'd started calling it. "I don't want to make gold. I leave that up to the men and their lofty aspirations. Let them spend their time pursuing the distillation of life itself. I choose to be more practical and distil medicine," she had explained to Luisa.

It was only through her friend that Caterina learned of her husband's insult. Knowing Girolamo had reverted to his past behaviour, the news she received from Luisa should have come as no surprise.

"He did what?" Caterina stood, knocking her sewing from her lap to the floor. She was sitting in the library, enjoying the solitude.

Luisa hurried forward and picked up her friend's work. "It's true. One of the count's men told me, he was in the room when the count spoke with the ambassador from Milan. A noble called Francesco Visconti." She put the sewing on a nearby table and waited for Caterina to sit again. Once she had, Luisa lowered herself into the chair beside it.

"The ambassador arrived to invite me to my sister's wedding to the son of the Holy Roman Emperor himself and Girolamo said no?"

"That's what I was told."

Caterina shook her head. "Why would he do such a thing? Without even speaking to me? And for my own sister's wedding?" So many questions flooded her mind. An invitation to any event involving the Emperor was not to be refused, never mind the wedding of his heir.

Turning the World to Stone

Luisa took her friend's hand, and Caterina's stomach suddenly hardened in preparation. "The count said he spoke with you and that you said you couldn't attend because," Luisa hesitated, looking down.

"Go on," Caterina prompted, feeling the heat of the other woman's hand on her own.

"The count told the ambassador you couldn't attend because all your jewellery had been pawned and you said you were too ashamed to appear unadorned."

"What?" Her stomach may have been prepared for the blow, but her head had not. "He lied to the ambassador, and put words into my mouth as an excuse?"

"He did."

Caterina started pacing, her hand on her forehead. "Did my husband tell the ambassador where all my jewels are? I would certainly like to know."

"Mainly in Bologna and Ravenna," Luisa whispered.

"I see." She strode back and forth across the room a few more times, then turned to her friend. "Come with me." Caterina headed toward the door.

"Where are we going?" Luisa stood and straightened her dress.

"To pay the ambassador a visit. Let's see how my husband likes it when I tell falsehoods on HIS behalf."

"Madonna, slow down, please. I can't understand you." The Milanese ambassador, an older man with a rotund frame and thinning black hair, held up his hands as Caterina walked frantically around the room, wringing her hands. She occasionally brought her forearm up to her forehead and moaned. Luisa had followed Caterina from her rooms to the guest rooms in another part of the palace.

It was late, and Ravaldino slept except for the soldiers on duty, who had nodded at her as she'd passed.

Caterina had snuck up to the ambassador's room and listened at the door. When she'd heard movement indicating he was still awake, she'd taken a breath and knocked loudly. Without waiting for a reply, she'd burst into the room and started wailing at the startled man.

Now, he held his hand high as if the action would somehow calm the frantic countess. Unmarried, he had no idea what to do and stood there watching as Caterina continued wandering around. Luisa stood just inside the door and held her hand to her mouth, concealing her failed attempt to keep from smiling. She wondered how much more dramatic her friend would become.

"Don Visconti, I'm a poor woman treated terribly by her husband. His abuse knows no bounds." Caterina threw her arm over her forehead again dramatically and sank wearily into one of the chairs closest to the fire. No point in going through this charade and being cold, she reasoned.

The flustered ambassador pulled out a handkerchief and held it out to Caterina, then pulled it back and wiped the profuse sweat running down his forehead. He sat across from her and leaned forward, his face a mask of concern. "Madonna, I had no idea. I don't, can I," he stumbled over his words, "is there anything…"

Caterina interrupted him with a soft wail, ignoring Luisa's stifled giggle from the far corner. "Signor, I fear I am beyond help." She opened her eyes as wide as she could and held them, feeling them tear. "I envy those who have already died, for they are beyond their pain, as I would be. My husband has killed many men in battle, but me he destroys slowly." Her words tapered off to a whisper.

Out of the corner of her eye, Caterina saw Luisa turn and face away, her shoulders shaking as she laughed silently. Frowning momentarily, Caterina focussed on the ambassador, waiting for his reply.

"Countess," he leaned forward even more until Caterina thought he might fall from the chair. Taking her hand, he patted it awkwardly. "Caterina," he said tentatively, "you are a proud Milanese woman and must take heart that your illustrious ancestors watch over you. You must rely on the strength of their blood in your veins to help you through your current misery." His hand had grown moist as his nerves frayed, and he hastily pulled it back.

Unable to bear the torture she knew she was inflicting on this innocent man, Caterina relented. "You are very wise, Signor. I see why my uncle chose you for so lofty a position in his court. Your words do my broken heart good and I will heed them." She stood and curtsied to him as Luisa composed herself and turned around. "I thank you for your wise counsel."

Standing, Visconti smiled self-consciously. "You are very welcome, my dear. We'll keep this visit our little secret." He winked at her, and Caterina forced a chaste giggle before heading out into the hall and heading back to her rooms.

"Do you really think he'll keep his mouth shut?" Luisa asked.

"While he's in the city, yes. But once he returns to Milan, he'll report all to my uncle Ludovico," she said dismissively, "for that is his role in life."

By the end of the year, the expected taxes had neither been paid voluntarily nor collected by the officials. The city suffered through a harsh Christmas and New Year, none more so than Caterina.

"The taxes must be collected; how can my husband not understand this basic fact?" Caterina's mood was dark that day, and her frustration spilled over into all she did. She'd discovered in late January 1487 that she was pregnant with her sixth child. Her husband's brusque affections had done their job. This baby was making her more ill than all the others combined had ever done, and her usual daily activities were completely interrupted as the nausea, which usually subsided by mid-morning, had decided to plague her throughout her days and into her nights. Caterina had also learned that her sister's engagement to the emperor's son had been dissolved, a situation she was forced to accept without knowing why or what happened.

Bossi, uncomfortable with his mistress' condition, fidgeted with his belt a short distance from Caterina's bed. "I think he knows that, my lady, but awareness of something doesn't make it so. The people refuse to pay, and utter death threats against anyone the count sends to collect. A few of the collectors have returned with bloody and battered faces for their efforts."

"This can only get worse, especially if our enemies take advantage of the situation." She shivered, not knowing if it was the February cold or nausea that constantly caused her trembling. Slipping down deeper in her bed, she pulled the heavy wool blanket up to her shoulders. "It's no longer safe here for my children. I think we should move to Imola until this situation with the taxes can be resolved once and for all." Caterina turned to Bossi. "Do you agree?"

Bossi nodded. "I do. I've felt the tensions outside the walls of Ravaldino and the resentment that those inside must be better off than those outside. In my professional opinion, it wouldn't take much to send the townspeople down a path they'd certainly regret."

Caterina closed her eyes as another wave of nausea crashed over her. When it had rolled back out again, she sat and reached for a vanilla wafer that Luisa kept constantly supplied by her friend's bedside. After nibbling a bit, she sighed. "That's that. We'll move to Imola. I'll speak to my husband. Given the growing anger in Forli, and his disinclination for a fight, I'm certain he'll agree."

As she'd expected, Caterina received no argument at all from Girolamo when she offered her suggestion. He jumped at the idea of a safer place and of leaving his trouble behind, and within a few weeks, all was prepared.

The day was frigid when their wagons headed out of the northern gate of Forli and onto the road to Imola. Few people came out to see them off, and Caterina comforted herself with the fact that it could very well have been the weather that kept them away. The journey took most of the day, and when they finally arrived in Imola, the children were tired and crying. Seeing that they were handed over to their nurse, Caterina climbed down from her horse to find Domenico Ricci, the Governor of Imola and Girolamo's brother-in-law, waiting for them.

"My dear brother and sister." Ricci held his arms wide in a welcoming gesture. "It's good to see you both again and looking so well." He glanced over at the young Riarios being unloaded from their wagon. "And the family, also healthy I see."

Caterina nodded at the man and looked around expectantly.

"My wife is not here, Madonna. After her uncle passed, she, uh, thought it was best to return home to her mother. The connections she once revelled in cast her into the shadows after the Pope died, and it was a place she found too cold for comfort." He shook his head sadly, then smiled again. "But you are here now, and all is well in the city. Come inside. Your house is always kept ready for you."

They headed into the centre of town, taking the same route as their last visit, but without the fanfare or celebrations. Once at the palace, Caterina checked on the children. Finding them tended to, she supervised the unloading of her clothing chests as Luisa saw to her room furniture. That night Caterina collapsed in her own bed in a half-filled room, not caring that most of her belongings had yet to arrive.

The Riarios were so used to moving they settled into the palace in Imola quickly. Within a couple of weeks, the entire house had been set up to Caterina's exacting specifications. She was pleased to see that her garden had been well tended while she was gone, and when April rained down its showers, it did so on the first green seedlings of the year.

The move had woken something in Caterina, a longing for home. Twice now, she'd been denied the opportunity of travelling north to Milan, and the thought of a third attempt was too inviting to ignore. The change of location had improved Girolamo's mood enough for Caterina to bring up the topic.

"I'd like to visit Milan before our child makes it too unwieldy for me to travel." Caterina rubbed her hand over her barely visible belly and hoped her husband would forget that she had been seven months pregnant when she had taken over the Castel Sant'Angelo in Rome. She hated feigning weakness, but right now, it was a means to an end. She grimaced a little and shifted herself from one foot to the other for added effect.

"I'm on my way to meet with the nobles of Imola to discuss the town's business," he added quickly. "I have no time right now." He resumed his rapid pace down toward the door. Caterina moaned at his retreating back and was pleased to see her husband stop. Girolamo hesitated, then turned around. "Are you well, countess?"

Caterina walked slowly to the side of the hall and reached out her hand to a wall hanging to balance herself.

"My lord, this child is troublesome and uses my energy before I realise it's gone." She looked up at Girolamo through her lashes. "A few weeks in the north would still the babe and ensure his safe passage into the world."

"You think it a male?" While her husband hadn't been very interested in his first couple of children, the number of boys Caterina had produced in so little time had caused rumours to surface about the count's virility, rumours Girolamo did not deny.

"I do, a warrior, like his father." She stood waiting, still leaning on the wall, feeling the rough stitching of the tapestry gathering beneath her clenched fingers.

The count frowned, his eyebrows twitching as if in silent conversation with himself. Finally, he bowed his head. "If you feel a journey north would be beneficial, then I agree." He looked back up at her. "I am, of course, too busy to leave the city, there is important work to be done here but will ensure you are well protected on your travels."

Or too terrified of my family, she thought to herself. Caterina smiled and curtsied deeply. "My lord, it already does my heart good to hear your agreement. I will leave you to your business and see to my own." She watched as Girolamo nodded at her uncomfortably and turned away.

When he could no longer see her, Caterina laughed and hurried back to her room to prepare for her long-awaited and much-needed visit home. The last time Caterina had travelled the Via Emilia, it had been when she was a child, and she'd been heading toward her future in the opposite direction. Now, she headed back to her past.

Chapter Twenty-Six
1487

Caterina entered the main hall in her Milanese home, aware that the eyes of the entire court were fixed on her. She'd left Luisa and Bossi in their rooms; she wanted to do this reunion alone.

"Uncle." Caterina curtsied deeply. She'd had short meetings with all her siblings except her sister Chiara, who had married well since Caterina had left, and now ran her own household. Enlisting the help of her youngest sister Bianca, Caterina had obtained clothing and jewellery enough to impress even the most discerning Milanese noble.

"Caterina, how well you look!" Ludovico came forward from his dais and lifted his niece by the elbows. Taking her hands, he held her arms wide as he spun her around slowly. "Let me see you."

When she'd last been with her uncle, she'd had to look up into his face. Now she stared forward, her Sforza blood giving her a height to match his. Glancing around the room, Caterina saw a few faces she recognised, more wrinkled than she remembered, with more grey hair. But most of these people were strangers to her, no matter their smiles and nods.

Ludovico finally dropped her arms and turned to the court. "The countess is an honoured guest and will be shown the respect due to both her birth and her elevated position." Turning back to Caterina, he smiled kindly. "If you require anything, you need only ask and it's yours." He held out an arm. "Please, enjoy yourself in my home."

Caterina bit her lip. He may be acting benevolently now, but she knew her brother, the true Duke of Milan, was still firmly under Ludovico's control. "It was also once my home, uncle."

A flash of annoyance flitted across the man's face, immediately hidden by years of practice. Caterina, however, saw the emotion. Then he smiled again, a genuine show of respect. "You're right. And you will be treated as if it still is, countess." He bowed at her.

Feeling like she'd accomplished something intangible, Caterina curtsied again and made her way out of the room, begging exhaustion because of her condition. By the afternoon of her first day home, everyone knew of her pregnancy and everything else there was to share. She and Luisa had discussed their visit along the way to Milan and had agreed to reveal as little of Caterina's private life as possible with the courtiers. "A secret about a drop of water whispered at one end of the palace will become a biblical flood by the time it reaches the other end," Caterina had said.

Her uncle left Caterina to herself most of the time. Apart from dinner invitations and the balls for which Milan was famed, she was free to wander the palace and grounds, work in the garden, or read in her father's beloved library.

"Let's go and see the artist," Luisa suggested one morning. She helped Caterina into her dress.

"We were told not to disturb him." Caterina turned and smoothed her hands down the front of her gown.

"I think that means other people. You said your uncle told you to do what you will."

"That's true. And it would be interesting to see what he's up to. My uncle was very mysterious on the subject when I questioned him." She picked up a simple hair net and fastened it. "Let's go."

The April sun shone down warmly, and Caterina lifted her face, feeling the heat as it soaked into her skin. She'd have to remember to use something to protect against freckles, she reminded herself. They left the back of the palace and, linking arms, made their way around the side toward the front.

"His hair is very long," Luisa whispered.

"So are many men's." Caterina continued spying on the artist. She'd been told his name was Leonardo, from a small town to the west of Florence called Vinci. His hair was overly long, and he wore it tied at the back with a simple leather thong, but it suited his thin face. She could see his focus, the way his eyes narrowed in fierce concentration and wondered what it would be like to be stared at in such a manner.

"Let's go and greet him," Luisa said. "All artists enjoy talking about their work." Before Caterina could say anything, her friend had stepped out from behind the corner of the building and was striding toward the man.

Caterina hesitated and took a few steps, then stopped. Leonardo had heard Luisa and was now looking up at them both from the far end of the courtyard. She had no choice but to follow her friend.

"Countess." He bowed his head at her as she approached. The movement caused his bound hair to fall over one shoulder, and he unconsciously shrugged it back.

"You know who I am?"

"Of course, Madonna." Da Vinci tilted his head and raised his eyebrows. "Your adventures in Rome do not go unnoticed by the rest of us, be assured."

Caterina acknowledged his recognition with a nod as Luisa hovered nearby. "This is my friend Dama Luisa Tommasa."

Luisa stepped forwardly nervously. "I hope you don't mind us interrupting you. We've heard courtiers speaking of your work and hoped to see for ourselves."

Leonardo's face registered his disgust. "Courtiers, bah. Fools, all of them." He focussed on Caterina's face. "Except for you, Madonna." He swayed to the left and right, scrutinising her visage from every angle. "You are worth painting." Turning to Luisa, he did the same, considering her facial features. "And you, Dama."

Luisa burned bright red as da Vinci turned to a makeshift table made of a wooden board balanced across two shipping crates. Waving them over, he said, "This is what I've been working on."

On the table were piles of pages held down with rocks to keep them from blowing across the courtyard. Each one had a detailed chalk sketch done in brown or red of the different parts of a horse. Some showed legs in various positions: standing, running, and rearing up. Others showed close-up images of heads. She saw the mournful look of one as it stared out at her and could almost feel the velvet softness of the hair around its nose and mouth.

"They're remarkable. I see why my uncle asked you to Milan." Caterina gazed at the pictures. The more she looked, the more details caught her eye. A chipped hoof, a scar on a flank, the individual hairs of a mane.

"Those are the easy part, Madonna. What the duke has planned for them is the challenge."

"He wouldn't share any details," Caterina prompted. Beside her, she saw Luisa gazing at the artist more than the art.

"Ahh, well, as it's you, I'll let you in on the secret. He's asked me to take these drawing and create a giant bronze statue of a horse, in honour of your grandfather." Leonardo raised his arms in the air, pointing out the imagined beast. "Its head will point out, there. Its front right leg will be raised, like this." He looked through the drawings and found the one he wanted, of a horse's raised leg and nothing else. "It will be the largest horse sculpture in all of Italy."

Caterina nodded her appreciation of the idea. "As my grandfather would have wanted." Seeing the artist's interest in entertaining them waning, she put her hand on Luisa's shoulder. "We should leave Signor da Vinci to his work."

Disappointment flooded through Luisa, but she reluctantly agreed. "I hope to see you again, Signor."

"I will be here, Dama." Leonardo lowered his head and quickly turned back to his work, his eyes already clouded with another image that must be drawn.

With a final longing gaze, Luisa turned and walked back with Caterina the way they'd come.

"He's married to his work," Caterina whispered sympathetically to Luisa. She'd seen the effect the man had had on her friend. She'd also seen how intense the artist had become the moment they were out of sight.

"Oh, I know, I just..." Luisa shrugged. "His hair."

Caterina stopped walking and stared at her friend, puzzled. After a moment, they both burst out laughing and continued back to the palace.

Caterina enjoyed her time at home. Milan's wealth was evident: lavish balls, exotic entertainment, and heavenly music. Nothing was beyond the duke's means, and that included people.

Like his brother, Ludovico carried on with the wives of his courtiers. Unlike his brother, he kept his relationships civil and manageable, not needing the special funds Caterina's father had to maintain just to pay off angry husbands. The deals were agreeable to all involved, with the men receiving wealth, land, and position and their wives the recipients of valuable gifts of gold and silver tapestries and clothing, jewellery, and plate. Often the wives would be given their own homes, close enough to the palace should an assignation be required on short notice.

"Who's that?" Caterina was walking down a long gallery filled with paintings of her ancestors and current family. A new one hanging close to her uncle's had caught her eye.

"The duke's current mistress, Cecilia Gallerani. Her husband was given a commission and is away from court." Bossi had accompanied Caterina, preferring to be by her side even while she was in a familiar, albeit still foreign, city.

Caterina stepped back, considering the image. The woman was simply attired, her hair and sheer veil held in place by a black lenza. The plain cord matched the set of ebony beads she wore around her neck, and in her arms, encased by the cut velvet sleeves of her blue and red gown, was a white ermine. The thing that puzzled Caterina was the position of the woman's head. Instead of staring out at the viewer like the usual, more formal works, Cecilia looked to her left, in the same direction as her pet. Caterina felt as though she was secretly watching something hidden from view.

"It looks like someone has just entered the room and she's turned to see who it is," Caterina remarked. "Very unusual. Do you know who the artist is?"

Bossi smiled widely, a rare act, pleased he could answer the question. "That da Vinci fellow outside." He pointed in the direction of the courtyard.

Caterina nodded and moved on down the hall, still carrying the image of the painting with her.

Over the next few weeks, she enjoyed all that Milan had to offer. The entertainment rivalled only Rome, often surpassing it as the city had many artists and musicians. Unlike Forli, her uncle had collected taxes and used the monies for public buildings, churches, and monasteries in and around Milan. She would certainly be taking this example back to Girolamo.

Each dance she attended was a triumph. Still only twenty-four, and despite her pregnancy, Caterina impressed the Milanese nobles with her energy and skill. Learning new steps quickly, she performed them flawlessly soon after being shown. But her major success was ensuring the support of Milan for herself and her family against any aggressors.

"The count will be pleased, surely," Luisa said. It was late, and she accompanied her friend to her rooms after a meeting with Ludovico.

"It's difficult to say. He's clever enough to appreciate the benefits of such an alliance, but he distrusts Milan and will be suspicious of any deals handed to him, especially one I have negotiated." She shook her head. "He'd be a fool to listen to his fears."

As they walked up the staircase and turned, they saw a young maid lingering outside the door to Caterina's room. When she saw the countess, she hurried forward.

"My lady, this message just arrived for you." She lowered her head and held out a paper made heavy by the red wax used to hold the folds in place. Turning it so she could read it, Caterina saw the seal of the city of Imola. Puzzled, she tore open the parchment and read.

Seeing the sudden panic on her friend's face as she read, Luisa put her hand on Caterina's arm. "What is it?"

Caterina let the letter fall to the ground. "Girolamo is gravely ill. We must return to Imola."

Leaving most of her belongings to follow in carts, Caterina rode hard along the Via Emilia with Luisa, Bossi, and a handful of soldiers loyal to her. At six months pregnant, she was undoubtedly showing but was used to riding her horse with the extra girth and could complete the ride home with a little extra effort. By the end of May, Caterina was back in Imola.

"What's wrong with him?" she asked a physician she found in the fortress, presumably brought here by one of her husband's guards.

"A fever, my lady. A fierce one. I've done all I can, we must now wait and see if the count is strong enough to fight the illness." He shook his head and quietly left.

"Look at this place," she said disgustedly. Luisa followed Caterina into the dark room. Incense burned on a table in the middle of the room but did nothing to dispel the musky odour of Girolamo's body as the sweat seeped out of every pore. "Push aside the tapestries and open the windows."

With Caterina now back in charge, the room was cleaned from top to bottom and Girolamo bathed while his bed sheets were changed. The fresh summer air blew into the windows, carrying the scents from Caterina's garden below.

"Someone must be in attendance on the count at all times," she said to Bossi. "Can you find one among my husband's men who can follow instructions?" Gian nodded and hurried away.

"What can I do?" Luisa stood by helplessly, watching her mistress tuck a blanket around Girolamo. He had woken and thrashed incoherently as they'd bathed him, but now, back in bed, he slept peacefully.

Caterina next moved to a nearby table, where clay pots and glass vials filled with coloured liquids and a foul-smelling paste stood waiting. "These," she pointed, "get rid of them all. I can identify most of the ingredients the healer uses. The ones I could identify are useless for such an illness, and the ones unknown to me could cause more harm than good."

Luisa started collecting the jars, opening one and wrinkling her nose at the smell. Shaking her head, she wordlessly transferred the various shaped vessels onto a tray and put it on a table to be carried downstairs by the next available maid.

Caterina filled a bowl with lavender-infused water and bathed her husband's forehead. It was the best she could do until she could take stock of her healing supplies. Luisa busied herself with unnecessary tidying until Caterina finally spoke again.

"My son is too young to lose his father."

Luisa moved to her friend's side and looked down at the count's pale face. "We'll see that he doesn't."

Caterina nodded, swallowing her panic. If the fever took Girolamo, her son would be too young to take his place as count. Even the most generously natured of the nobles of Imola and Forli would not accept a seven-year-old boy ruling over them. She would have to rule as regent. Would they accept her? Caterina shook the thought away. "Can you go to my workroom and look around. I haven't had time to visit myself, but I'm hoping there are still stores from my last visit. Look for anything that can be used for fever and pain."

Luisa nodded and, squeezing Caterina's shoulder gently, left to perform her task.

Caterina knew there was only so much she could do against such an illness. She also understood that much of the healing depended on the count. Panic welled up inside again. Pushing it to the back of her mind, she instead focussed on wiping her husband's forehead and repeating lists of helpful plants in her head.

The count's illness was more severe than anyone could have imagined, and for months Caterina divided her time between caring for her husband and running their territories. The work distracted her from the visions of the uncertain future she saw should Girolamo die, and gave her a rigid focus.

"Is there any change?" Luisa entered the count's room. She'd gotten used to Caterina rising earlier than her and often found her friend already dressed and seeing to the count's needs.

Caterina replied to the same question she had heard every day from everyone. "No." She sighed and put the washcloth down. She patted the excess moisture the lavender-water left behind on Girolamo's forehead and looked up at Luisa. "It's been too long, and I have never witnessed an illness last as many months as this."

"You have no ideas?"

She shook her head. "None. At least none involving the body. The spirit, however, is another issue." At Luisa's frown, she continued. "I fear my husband can no longer live with the shame of his actions. The guilt and remorse are devouring his will to survive."

Luisa pressed her lips together and looked at Caterina sadly. "And there is nothing to be done?"

"A priest, perhaps, to pray for his soul. Other than that, I can think of no other remedy except to keep doing what we're doing. And wait."

Caterina, raised to run a large household and already a master of organisation when it came to her family and their homes, took to administrative life quickly. Her classical education stood her in good stead, and she easily and quickly grasped the crux of matters before an explanation was finished. Her reputation also served her well and, after a particularly productive meeting with the ambassador from Bologna, had been assured of their support in addition to Milan's.

"The town taxes are finally coming in?" She had summoned Niccolò Pansechi from Forli to ensure her orders were being followed.

"They are, Madonna. Your idea to offer a month free of taxes next year to anyone who paid on time this year was inspired. Most of Forli have already paid in full." He sipped from his wine glass. "And the citizens remember that it was you who sold your own personal property to buy blankets and firewood for the less fortunate over the past harsh winter."

Caterina waved her hand airily, brushing the man's words aside. They sat in the count's study, which was already set up and situated close to the front of the palace. "It's my duty to see that my people are well cared for," she said simply.

"And I assure you that your care, in particular, is noticed." With the emphasis he put on his words, Caterina knew the man spoke of her and her alone. "You have many supporters in Forli, Madonna. Both you and your son."

Caterina nodded her understanding of his words. Smiling warmly, she stood. "I'm relieved to know there are those whom I can trust in my life. Such people are few and far between."

"Always, Madonna." He leaned forward to kiss her proffered hand and left the room.

As if blessing the event, the summer heat abated as Caterina gave birth to her sixth child. Her visit home had her feeling nostalgic, and she named the boy after her grandfather, Francesco. She remembered that Girolamo had suggested it before to honour his uncle. This time, however, it was her choice and she made it clear that her son was named after her relative, not the still-disgraced old pope.

"He was a mighty warrior and leader of men, as you too shall be, won't you?" she whispered to the bundle sleeping peacefully in his cradle. "It's a big name for such a little one, but you'll grow into it as quickly as your brothers and sister are growing." She sighed, remembering the day Ottaviano was born. The love she had felt and didn't believe could be matched had been equalled and multiplied with each new child's birth. And here before her was more joy.

After the entire court had nearly given up, Girolamo's body finally recovered from his illness. His mood, however, did not. Lethargic and ever ill at ease, he inserted himself into the only element of ruling that still interested him: soldiers.

"Is it true you've increased taxes in the city?" Caterina walked briskly into the private chapel they shared in the Imolese palace, not caring if she disturbed her husband's devotions.

The count muttered a few words and crossed himself before standing. "Yes, it's true," he replied as he walked past her.

Caterina followed him out of the candle-lit room and into the hall. "Why would you do such a thing? All was going well, and everyone is living peacefully."

"You forget, our enemies are still out there, plotting our downfall, waiting for their chance."

Wondering how much further they could fall than rulers of two small towns, Caterina sighed. "And this extra money will be used how?" Servants bobbed at them as they passed. Caterina would normally nod back, but this time she ignored everyone except Girolamo.

"To hire more guards. And before you ask, I've told the city counsellors that four hundred should be enough."

"Four hundred extra men?" she asked incredulously, the number stopping her.

The count turned. "Yes. Four hundred. Now please leave me alone, you know all there is to know." He scowled and continued toward the back of the house where the horses were stabled. She knew better than to ignore his command, for once her husband had set his sights on a ride, there was no stopping him.

"One hundred."

"Are you sure?" Caterina frowned at Bossi. Immediately she was embarrassed by her own words. Of course, he was sure. When did he ever report anything back to her that wasn't true? She shifted in her library chair, feeling the fire's heat blanket her left side.

He ignored any insult, seeing the confusion on his mistress' face and knowing her question didn't indicate any doubts. "I am, my lady. The count has hired one hundred new guards for protection and shows no signs of obtaining more."

"But he told the city he wanted money for four hundred." Realisation dawned on her. "He kept their money."

Bossi nodded. "Yes, Madonna. And the people are not happy about it."

"No, I don't imagine they are. My husband has just proven himself as greedy as his predecessor. Will he never learn the art of politics?"

The older man knew to keep silent. "I have overheard conversations in the market." Caterina raised an eyebrow at him. "Only when I am unnoticed, for no one speaks anything of consequence directly to my face unless I ask them."

His words sounded ominous, but she understood his meaning. Gian Bossi was a well known figure in Imola and Forli, and people were often guarded around him. "And?"

"The word tyrant has been whispered."

Caterina placed her book on the arm of her chair and stood. "You heard that word being used? Specifically, that word?"

"I'm sorry to say I did, my lady."

She shook her head and gathered her shawl from the back of the chair. "I need to see my husband. I don't know what else he's been up to, but if that word is being used, things are worse than we thought."

Caterina raced down the hall toward Girolamo's rooms but was interrupted by one of her husband's pages. "My lady, the count sends me with a message: make haste and prepare, for you, the count, and your children leave for Forli tomorrow."

Caterina barely spoke to her husband on the return to Forli. Each time she tried, her fury choked her words back, so all she could do was glare her frustration.

Finally, she could hold back no longer. "How dare you continue to endanger our family? What do you think you're doing, making the same mistakes over and over? Does your greed know no bounds?"

Her husband looked disdainfully at her, then urged his horse forward and ignored her the rest of the way home. Once again, when they arrived, the children were upset and crying, not understanding the sudden upheaval to their young lives nor why they had to leave some of their favourite toys behind. Caterina decided to move her family into the palace overlooking the market square in the town centre rather than the fortress. If Girolamo wanted to continue on there, he could go alone. For reasons she couldn't fathom, the count, still not speaking, walked past her into the smaller palace.

The winter winds weren't the only reason the halls were cold that November. With little to no communication between the Riarios and Caterina feeling too weary to throw the large ball she knew was expected, the palace felt more like a crypt than a home. The maids and pages soon grew tired of the messages passed between the count and countess, mainly because they involved mundane topics like food and the children. Even the arguments that kept them entertained stopped.

The time apart gave them both time to think. While vowing to himself that he was in the right, Girolamo allowed himself to see how it might be different from his wife's point of view. Caterina had grown used to her husband's shortfalls in Rome and had only to remind herself that while he may have seemed changed when they left the city, underneath, he was the same man she had married.

By the time Christmas arrived, both had reconciled enough to sit together and share a meal. While the count had been brooding in his rooms, Caterina had arranged gifts for the entire family. New clothing and a new saddle brought a twitch of a smile to Girolamo's lips, and her son Ottaviano was excited to receive his own armour.

"I was your age when my father gave me my first breastplate," Caterina explained as she helped fasten the shoulder buckles. "I thought it high time you had your own."

All the children were delighted with their gifts, and Bianca, in particular, now six, told everyone she loved her new gowns more than anything else in the world.

With things seemingly settled between her and her husband again, Caterina looked forward to the new year.

Chapter Twenty-Seven
1488

The invitation arrived by papal messenger, its contents shocking both Caterina and Girolamo.

"The Holy Father, Innocent VIII, has invited us to attend the marriage of his son Francescetto to the daughter of our worst enemy, Lorenzo Medici? Is this a prank?" Girolamo turned the invitation over and back again.

Caterina took the paper from her husband and reread it. "No, it's an actual invitation to the wedding."

"And it's to be held in Florence," he said flatly.

She nodded. "Yes, so it would seem." Caterina threw the paper onto the table in Girolamo's study.

"We certainly will not be attending. Our two enemies joining? Creating a blood connection?" He shook his head. "No. If it's not a joke then it's a trap. Or else they invite us to mock us."

Caterina couldn't help but agree with him. It was an odd thing to receive. When her husband had been ill, Caterina had tried making subtle overtures to Florence, as she had with Milan and Bologna. But her efforts had been rewarded with silence. Not even the ambassadors could explain Lorenzo's lack of tact. And now this? She couldn't fathom what had warranted it, but she agreed with Girolamo: they could not attend. It was just too unpredictable a situation, no matter that cities and countries around Europe would be sending representatives.

Perhaps they had sunk so low in society their presence wouldn't even be missed, she thought miserably.

But to not attend such an event, and the chance at the new connections she'd miss making! She shook the self-pity she felt creeping over her away. There was no point in the feeling; it served no one.

"I concur, and I can see no good coming from our attending." Shaking her head, she turned and left Girolamo's room. They rarely agreed these days, so she was relieved when not going had been his idea. He could still surprise her sometimes.

Ultimately, Caterina thought it best to at least send a gift to the new couple and chose a set of six goblets made from silver and engraved with vines and flowers. A local craftsman had designed and created the group, and Caterina hoped the rustic charm would delight the pair.

"Will you tell the count?" Luisa asked as Caterina had seen to the shipping of the gift.

"I don't think so, he's still furious at the contempt he believes was the invitation's purpose." They watched the wagon drive out of the palace and turn toward the road to Florence. "I've been trying so hard to deal with Florence, I see no point in burning a potential bridge by snubbing the bride." They turned as the January wind hit them, and went back inside.

That spring a group of farmers came to the palace to petition the count. Caterina was told by her husband that she need not attend, but the incident with the invitation had soured Girolamo's mood even further, and she was taking no chances. Standing outside the barely open door, she listened as puzzled servants passed her in the hall.

"My lord, we are but poor farmers, and the dirt in which we toil to grow food for the town and its people doesn't even belong to us. The nobles own the land, yet it is we who are required by law to pay taxes on it." The man elected to represent them all wrung his sweat-stained hat in his hands as he spoke.

Caterina could hear noises of agreement amongst the other farmers. She could understand why they were so angry. The system was unfair, and she hoped her husband would realise that too.

She heard the deep murmur of Ludovico Orsi, one of her husband's advisors, and then Girolamo clearing his throat.

"Thank you for bringing this to my attention. I see the hypocrisy in such an arrangement and, from now on, the people who own the land will pay taxes on that land."

The room erupted in cheers, and Caterina heard scuffs and conversations as the farmers exited the main entrance. She prepared to leave. No one would come this way, but it wouldn't be clever to be caught by Girolamo lurking in the shadows. As she turned, Ludovico's raised voice reached her from inside.

"Are you mad? Has the devil led you to this foolish decision? One that will surely see you hanged and us too?"

Caterina could detect other noises and suspected that Ludovico had brought a few of his men with him. No one walked around alone these days.

He continued his chastisement. "Why stir up trouble like this? It will lead to the nobles and the artisans of Forli revolting against you and for what? So a group of men already used to paying taxes can save a ducat over their entire pathetic life times?"

There was silence, and Caterina imagined the petulant look on her husband's face. It must have angered Ludovico further, for his voice rose.

"Are you even listening to my advice? I'm a noble and my words deserve to be heeded."

This finally prompted a response from the count. "Don Ludovico, you may be noble, but I believe you begrudge my life and all I have. You should take more care with your words." The last sentence was delivered quietly, and Caterina strained to hear. Her heart jumped when she understood the threat being made.

Ludovico apparently did as well. Footsteps making their way toward the main door and away from Caterina echoed in the quiet room. Caterina left quickly, hurrying down the hall and out of the count's path.

The next day Leone Cobelli arrived at the palace unannounced.

"Madonna." He rushed in and took Caterina's hands, kissing them one at a time. With a practised movement, he removed his cloak with one hand and swept it around his body and onto his waiting arm.

"Signor, did we have an appointment I've forgotten about? If so, please excuse me." Caterina led the man in and up the main staircase to a small room she used to receive guests.

"You did not, my lady. It was presumptuous of me, I know, but I had to see you on a matter of the gravest importance."

Caterina frowned at him. His usual light-hearted manner was gone, replaced by this deadly serious man she barely recognised. They'd reached her room, and with a wave at a passing servant Caterina had ordered wine for them both. "Please, sit." She nodded to a chair and took the one opposite.

Cobelli glanced down, the movement hanging uncomfortably on him. He withdrew a small silk-wrapped parcel from his pocket and handed it to Caterina. "I wanted to give you this for your new baby. It will hopefully go some way to softening what I must share with you next."

Caterina unwrapped the red silk and found a finely engraved silver baby rattle. "It's beautiful. Thank you."

The wine arrived, and Leone nodded in reply to Caterina's raised eyebrow. She poured them both drinks, and the dance master took a long sip before continuing. "Yesterday, I was at the home of Checco Orsi, brother to Ludovico."

"I know of him, and Ludovico was here only yesterday, discussing taxes with my husband."

Cobelli nodded. "I know, Madonna. After that meeting Ludovico visited his brother. I was there to give Checco's young daughter a dancing lesson when the elder brother burst in. I would have left but I was unnoticed, for who sees the dance master." He sighed and then, glimpsing Caterina's frown, continued. "I stepped back behind a column and was able to hear all that transpired."

Reaching out for the glass again, he drained it. He smiled gratefully as Caterina refilled it and took another drink as the countess waited. "Ludovico was angry. He marched around the room shouting obscenities I'll not repeat about your husband. Called him," Leone flushed red, "I'm sorry, my lady, but they called him low-born and ill-bred."

Caterina sighed. It was nothing she hadn't heard before. "Go on," she encouraged.

"Checco tried to calm his brother down but struggled with the task. Eventually he said he had a plan that might work."

Gripping the rattle, Caterina spoke evenly. "What plan? When will this happen?"

"I don't know, Madonna."

"What is this scheme meant to accomplish?" Caterina's fingers began to ache from her hold on the silver toy.

"I don't know that either, my lady. I found an opportunity to finally sneak away before I was caught. I couldn't determine if indeed a plot was developed or if it was merely men throwing angry words to the wind."

The way he delivered this lack of information made Caterina relax for a moment. His next words, however, chilled her to the bone.

"What I believe is that they wish to punish your husband and reclaim the Orsi family pride."

"Ottaviano, finish your food please. You can play with your toy horse afterwards."

Caterina sat with the children in a small room off their nursery along with Luisa. That side of the palace had been rebuilt, so it now housed the small beds Caterina's elder children slept in, but also had a room for the cradle Francesco, or Sforzino as she'd started calling him, still needed. It had been a few days since Cobelli's visit, and with each passing hour since he'd left, Caterina had managed to convince herself his warning had been an overreaction. He was, she thought, overly fond of drama. Gradually Caterina had let herself breathe normally again.

"It's market day. If you finish everything on your plate, we'll go out and visit the vendors if you'd like."

Ottaviano's eyes lit up. He'd begun showing an independent streak lately and would do almost anything for a trip away from the house, even to the market.

"You too, Bianca." Caterina nodded at her daughter. "I'll leave Sforzino here and we can enjoy the sun." She smiled at Cesare, Giovanni, and Galeazzo. "All of us."

"What about papa? Will he come with us"

She glanced down to where she knew her husband was enjoying his daily nap in the room below, and she shook her head. "No, he's too busy right now. But Luisa will join us." Caterina nodded at Luisa, who held her youngest son in one arm and touched his nose with the finger of her other to make him laugh.

Before Bianca could say another word, a loud banging rang through the halls and up the stairs. The noise continued, and Caterina stood, her stomach clenching. The children looked up at her, their wide eyes suggesting they were more startled by their mother's sudden movement than the growing commotion below. Voices that had risen in indignance now started shouting. A scream made the hairs on Caterina's neck stand up and soon, the shouting had taken on a manic tone. She exchanged a worried glance with Luisa.

The noise and shouting grew louder. She recognised the sounds of fighting, and the pounding that hurried boots made as they approached. The children had started to whimper, and she looked down at them. "Shh, not a word. I must listen."

Caterina focussed on the different sounds, trying to piece them all together to form a picture. Unsure of whether to stay here and wait or head outside, her decision was made for her when a blood-curdling scream reached her from just below their room. The space in which her husband had been sleeping. The moment the terrifying sound had reached them, Ottaviano had stood motionless as the others ran to Caterina and hid their faces in her gown. She tried holding them close but knew she must leave the room immediately for there was only one door and becoming trapped here could prove deadly.

She untangled her arms from her children's grips and spoke softly. "Stay here. I must go outside."

"No, Mama! Don't leave!" Bianca burrowed her face more deeply into her mother's dress.

Caterina gently pulled the girl away and knelt in front of her. "I need you to act like a hero from the stories. Remember what I told you before."

The terrified child looked at her mother with tear-filled eyes. She nodded almost imperceptibly and whispered, "A Sforza is always brave."

"That's right my darling." She kissed Bianca's head and stood as the girl joined Ottaviano, then walked to the door. As she reached for the handle, Bossi rushed in.

"My lady, the palace is under attack. You must flee."

"What's happening? Where is Girolamo?" Caterina's voice rose higher with each word as she fought against the panic that threatened to overwhelm her.

"The Orsi have gained control of the palace." He stopped for a second. There was no time to be anything but blunt. "The count is dead, as are his guards. Ludovico Orsi convinced his brother to join him, along with two of your husband's men who hadn't been paid for months. The Orsi family are downstairs as we speak. Cousins, nephews, and more." He stepped outside and then back in. "You must go upstairs. There is no way you can sneak your family out, it's too late for that and you're certain to be found. The west tower is the least penetrable. You might have a chance there."

Bossi started gathering the children. Caterina stopped him. "I may not be able to get away, but you can. You know the secret ways in and out of the palace. A lone man can sneak out more easily than a family."

He shook his head. "No. I won't leave you."

Knowing she had little time left, Caterina put her hand on the older man's arm. "I need you to leave. You must contact the Bentivoglio family in Bologna, they will come to my aid. And my brother and uncle in Milan, they must also be told of this attack against their nephew." She wrapped her free arm around Ottaviano's shoulder. "Please. Do this for me. It may be our only chance."

Nodding reluctantly, Bossi saw the wisdom in the plan. "I'll either send help or bring it back myself if I have to." With a curt bow, he turned and swiftly walked down the hall, his soldier's senses glancing around as his form got smaller.

"Children, follow me. We're going up to the tower."

"The one where you can see the whole square?" Bianca hiccupped through tears.

"That's the one. Come on now, quickly." She heard a noise behind them as they made their way up the narrow stairs to a thick wooden door at the top. Caterina stopped to help Giovanni, who had tripped on a stair and screamed in pain as his knee hit the stone.

"Hush, we're nearly there." She lifted him up and held his hand as they ascended the last of the stairs behind the rest. Luisa got to the top first and held open the door with her free arm as she gripped baby Sforzino in her other.

"Everyone in," Caterina said. The noises were getting closer, and footsteps ran up the stairs toward them. "I'm closing the door now."

Caterina slammed the door shut and locked it as the face of Ludovico Orsi rounded the last curve of the staircase. The mask of hatred he wore only fuelled Caterina further. She looked around the room and saw nothing of use. There were no food supplies or water stored here, so any length of stay was impossible.

"Stand back from the windows," she instructed as she waved her arm at them. Risking one of her children getting hit by a thrown rock or bottle at this point would be foolish. Opening the window and leaning out as far as she could, she shouted to the market below.

"People of Forli! The palace is under attack by traitors! The count is dead and even now they threaten the life of your new count, Ottaviano Riario!"

The banging started at that moment, and Caterina hoped it could be heard by those below. Word had spread, and both traders and buyers alike milled about in shocked confusion. Luisa nodded at her.

Caterina continued. "If there are any among you who are still my loyal followers, arm yourselves, protect yourselves and your families at all costs, and head to the fortress of Ravaldino!"

She stopped, seeing that her words were getting through. A few people had started running from the square. At the far edge, she spotted Bossi. He nodded and disappeared into the crowd.

"Gather at Ravaldino! Defend it! Do not surrender to the traitorous Orsi family and their accomplices!"

Caterina leaned inside as a blurred object fell past the window from which she'd just shouted. Stepping back instinctively, she held out her arms to ensure none of her children, now silent with terror, would get hurt. Seeing nothing else fall, Caterina approached the window again and peered out cautiously.

A mangled body lay in the square beneath the tower, a growing crowd gathering around it to investigate. When the shrieks started, Caterina knew it was the duke's body lying torn and bloodied below her.

Fighting a wave of nausea, she looked into the sky and took a few breaths. Added to the commotion outside were the ever-rising sounds from inside. The noise at the door was almost deafening; someone had found an axe and was hacking at the thick wood. The sound bounced around the walls of the small room. Splinters flew as the children screamed and clung to their mother. With a final glance outside, Caterina saw that her words had been heeded. The square was emptying. She could only hope and pray now that the fortress would hold until Bossi got word to her allies in Milan and Bologna.

She turned as the door broke from its hinges, shuddering as her nerves departed.

"Countess." Ludovico mockingly bowed. "Please gather your children and come with us."

Chapter Twenty-Eight
1488

As soon as the word 'children' came out of Ludovico's mouth, Caterina felt her momentary panic dissolve into anger.

"How can one such as you possess the audacity to enter my home? You and your ruffian family?" She stood in front of her children with her arms spread wide. "If you should dare lay a hand on any of us..." Caterina left the threat hanging between them.

"What? What will happen, my lady?" He sneered and looked behind him at the men waiting. Their laughter spurred him on. "So, you're saying, if I do this." With a wide grin, Ludovico reached out and grabbed Luisa's breast.

The sound of Luisa's slap rang through the room and stopped the men's laughter. Caterina glanced sideways at her friend and smiled smugly as she saw the man raise his hand to the cheek Luisa had hit. She nodded at Luisa as the other woman shook the stinging out of her hand.

"Is that enough, or do you wish to see a further demonstration of what a member of the house of Sforza can do?" As Caterina had suspected, mentioning her name had the desired effect. Ludovico took a step back. To underline her warning, she added, "My eldest son, the Duke of Milan's nephew, is braver and more skilled in weaponry than all your men combined."

With a scowl, Ludovico stepped back. Motioning for his men to enter, he turned to face Caterina. "You're far from Milan, my lady. By the time your brother hears of our conquest, it will be too late. We will run the city. You had best keep that in mind." He turned to Checco. "Take them to the Orsi palace."

Checco took Caterina's arm and led her from the room, roughly shoving her through the doorway. The sound of her children's wails behind her broke her heart, but she dared not look back or show any maternal affection. She knew any sign of weakness would be used by these men, and while she was hopeful her family name would protect them all, there was still doubt.

As the family was led back downstairs and through the palace, Caterina nearly cried as she saw the destruction of her beloved home. The looting that inevitably followed a rebellion had taken place quickly; all her belongings were either gone or destroyed, the walls hacked, and tapestries torn and lying dirty on the debris-filled floor. They encountered a few who still loitered, men staggering around grasping half-filled wine glasses and empty decanters of Caterina's finest crystal.

Checco stopped Caterina outside a room and pushed her in. Blood splattered the floor and walls, and chairs were overturned. A dark stain slowly dripped blood from the couch where Caterina knew Girolamo had been napping. As she looked in horror, a voice whispered in her ear, "Your husband begged for mercy."

Turning angrily, Caterina held her arm to strike the man, but he grabbed it and laughed. "I'm not as ill-prepared for a woman's tricks as my brother." Yanking her by the arm again, he dragged her from the room. They continued as a huddled group, Caterina and Checco in the lead and her children gripping each other behind her. She heard Luisa murmuring to Bianca and Sforzino and took some comfort that her children at least had a familiar voice to calm them while she couldn't.

As they approached the door to the square, Caterina turned to help her children but was pulled back by Checco.

"Children should not see their father's dead body lying in the street."

"I thought Sforza children were fearless. Let them see what real life is."

Fortunately, the count's body had been removed by the time his family stepped outside, and all that remained was a bloody smear on the stones. Caterina glanced at Checco and saw him frown in disappointment but kept her satisfaction to herself. They were led across the square, and the few people who had still remained after her shouted warnings scattered upon seeing Caterina directed toward the Orsi palace.

Remembering her husband's room and the blood-spattered tapestry, Caterina shuddered and pushed the image away. Instead, she focussed on why Checco had bothered to stop and display his handiwork rather than take them hastily to their prison. The man obviously enjoyed attention. A second son always striving to outdo his older brother, she thought. This was something she could use.

"You won't get away with this," she said calmly.

"We already have."

"When other states hear of your actions there will be consequences." She hoped her feigned confidence would aggravate the man enough for him to give away some important detail of the brothers' plan.

"What other states? We've sent riders to Florence and Venice, informing them of our plans. With their support, they'll put the Ordelaffi family back in charge of

Forli and reward us with important positions on the council."

Ah, thought Caterina. So Florence and Venice would know of her plight by now. She knew there would be no help for her from Florence but was uncertain where Venice's loyalties lay. Seeing that they neared the Orsi palace, Caterina tried to keep Checco talking.

"You think the Ordelaffis will reward you? They haven't been seen anywhere near Forli for years."

"I know they will." He didn't elaborate, infuriating Caterina. They must have been in contact for some time, she guessed. By now, they'd reached the building, and Caterina and her children were ushered in by Checco and his men and forced into a small bedroom on the top floor.

"This is where you'll keep us?" Caterina asked incredulously. She looked around and saw Ottaviano standing in a corner with Cesare, both looking miserable, Bianca gripping Luisa's dress, and Giovanni and Galeazzo cowering together near an old worn chair. The room had a chair, a bed, and a table. A cold fireplace lined one wall, and the space felt like it hadn't been used in years. There was barely enough room for two or three people, never mind two adults and six children. As if just as shocked by the inadequate space as his mother was, Sforzino let out a loud howl.

Caterina rushed to the baby, taking him from Luisa. She turned toward Checco. "This is no place for children! How long do you intend to hold us here?"

"You're lucky to be alive, all of you." He scowled at them all and waved his men out. "I have a meeting to attend."

Caterina's anger at their situation boiled over as he began shutting the door. "What could you possibly add to any meeting? And what meeting would want you there?"

Checco's face appeared in the space between the door and the frame. "Not that it's any of your business, but my brother and I have called a meeting of the Council of Forty to plan what happens next to the city and its people." He glared at her before continuing. "That includes you."

Caterina felt the noise in her chest as he slammed the door and locked it. Waiting until she heard his footsteps echoing down the hall, Caterina finally allowed herself to collapse. Sitting heavily on the bed, she grasped Sforzino in one arm and held out her other for her children. "Come here, all of you." Cesare held his older brother's sleeve as he and Ottaviano climbed onto the bed beside their mother. Luisa gathered Giovanni and Galeazzo and, together with Bianca, ushered them over. When the children were assembled around her, Caterina spoke, choosing her words cautiously.

"You must all listen to me very carefully. Do you understand?" Small nods met her words. "You must try to be brave. I know it's very hard, and the men around us uncivil, but remember what I told your sister. A Sforza is always brave." Bianca looked up at her mother and nodded vigorously. "The men may take me away and leave you here. You must not worry. Your brother will look after you." Caterina drew Ottaviano closer to her with her free arm. "And Luisa. Do what Luisa says. If anyone says anything you don't like, tell them your uncle, the Duke of Milan, would not be pleased."

Passing the baby to Luisa, she grabbed her friend's hand and squeezed it before using both arms to embrace her children. Their crying had lessened, and she heard soft murmuring and snuffling. Releasing them, she looked at them solemnly. "I know God has not forsaken us; I want us to all pray now that he sends help soon."

She got on her knees and waited until the children did the same before tightly clasping her hands. There was much to pray for, and Caterina hoped her life of good deeds would persuade the Lord that her cause was worthy of His attention.

While the Orsi servants should have shown loyalty to that household, more and more found themselves sympathetic to Caterina. Imprisoning a man was one thing, but a woman and her infant children were quite another.

Overnight and into the next day, water and wine, blankets, and wash basins had been snuck into the room by considerate maids and even a few guards. A cradle had arrived for Sforzino, and Caterina, in her gratitude, made a note of every person who helped them, down to the young maid who had shyly brought them a chamber pot.

The visitors were few, however, and Caterina and Luisa spent their time trying to keep both their emotions and the children under control. The two friends' knowledge of stories from the libraries in Milan and Rome was a significant resource from which to draw, and when the children weren't being told tales of knights and ladies, they were sleeping.

Caterina had finally gotten them all asleep at the same time and was about to sit with Luisa in one of the extra chairs provided when a knock startled her. Looking at the children to ensure they were all still sleeping, she stood by the door until she heard the lock scrape open, then cracked the door open and peered out. A man stood there in bishop's garb, smiling kindly and holding his mitre in both hands.

"Countess Riario, may I come in?"

Having little choice, Caterina opened the door further and stepped aside to allow the stout man in.

She closed the door and waved her hand. "Your Grace, as you can see my circumstances are reduced and I have nothing to offer you."

Turning the World to Stone

The man looked around and took in the sleeping children and Luisa, still sitting nearby. "I'm not here for refreshments. But first, an introduction. I am Bishop Giacomo Savelli, papal governor of nearby Cesena. Please, sit," he waved his hand at the chair Caterina had just vacated, "I will answer your questions as best I can, for I'm certain you have many."

He waited until Caterina was settled, then sat on the edge of the bed, nearly missing Bianca's foot. She moved and folded her leg toward her body under the cover but stayed asleep.

Caterina decided to be honest about what facts she knew. It would save the bishop time and repetition. "I know my husband is dead, murdered by Ludovico and Checco Orsi in some misguided attempt to reinstall the Ordelaffi as rulers." She raised her eyebrow at him and waited.

"All you've said is true." He took Caterina's hand, and she hid a flinch of disgust at the dampness she felt. "I am sorry, so sorry your husband has departed. To be left a widow, and one with such young children..." he shook his head.

Caterina took advantage of his silence to slip her hand out of his. She lay it on her knee, feeling her dress absorb the man's sweat.

Savelli continued. "The Orsi brothers called a meeting of the Council of Forty to discuss their next steps." He held up his hand. "I only report what was told to me." Lowering his hand, he went on. "You are correct when you say they want the Ordelaffi family back, but the brothers met with much opposition when they suggested it."

Caterina interrupted. "People remember what it was like under them."

"Indeed. Some spoke for the idea, others against. A long argument ensued until someone suggested Forli become one of the papal states. That's where I enter this story." He looked around out of habit for wine, then remembered where he was. Standing, he went to the door and ordered the guard outside to bring them food and wine. He stopped a moment to gaze at the sleeping children, so like their mother, it was startling. Girolamo's ruddy colouring had not affected the lightness they had inherited from Caterina.

By the time he'd moved to his chair and sat down again, a servant had arrived and carried in a tray with a jug, glasses, and plain wafers. After a bite of wafer and a mouthful of wine, the bishop continued his story.

"The council agreed, and a messenger was sent to me in Cesena. I heard the news but could barely believe the council were serious, it was so sudden!"

Caterina took a sip of her wine and stared at the bishop wryly over the rim of her glass. "They did just murder the nephew of the previous pope AND the uncle of a high-ranking cardinal." She knew the man would recognise the reference to their nephew, Raffaele.

"Quite, quite. You understand the reticence I felt, trusting the report of these events. As soon as the messenger from Forli had updated me, I sent my own emissary to speak with the council and determine their plans. When I learned late last night that everything reported was true, and that the city was agreeing to be ruled as part of the papal states, I determined to ride here first thing this morning."

So, he'd been here all day and was only now visiting her, Caterina thought. At least she now knew where his loyalties and priorities lay.

"I came to see to your comfort and to assure you of your and your children's safety." He patted her hand in what she guessed was meant to be a fatherly gesture.

She raised her eyebrow again and looked around the room crowded with her children, sharing the bed and sleeping on blankets on the floor, and at Luisa, whose exhaustion was only partially hidden by the hair that had come loose and now hung in her face.

The bishop glanced away nervously, then back at Caterina. "I will see that you're treated well. You have my word." As if suddenly uncomfortable under Caterina's scrutiny, he stood. "I must leave you, but I will return." He put his mitre back on and headed for the door but hesitated. Caterina wondered if he would offer more of his bland assurances. Instead, he just opened the door and left them.

The bishop's words did nothing to alleviate Caterina's concerns for herself and her family, resulting in only a few hours of sleep and only because her body forced her eyes closed.

The next day Ludovico unlocked and burst through the door without knocking, and strode to where Caterina leaned against a wall. "Come with me."

"Where? Where are you taking me?" She fought for time but was unsuccessful.

"You'll find out. Your famed skills of persuasion are required." He smirked, and Caterina realised the look of disdain was plastered permanently across his face.

Rushing to her children, she held them one by one and whispered words of strength into their ears. Then she was dragged from the room by her forearm and out of the house past servants who turned away in sympathy.

Checco joined them outside, and, with one Orsi brother on each arm, Caterina was marched to the foot of the fortress of Ravaldino. She knew inside there were people who'd fled but had no idea how many had followed her advice.

Turning the World to Stone

Still holding her arm, Ludovico shouted up into the fortress. "Tommaso Feo! Show yourself!"

Tommaso was the castellan Caterina herself had put into place, and she was relieved he was still in his post. The tall, thin man appeared on the wall and looked down at them. Caterina stared intently at him, hoping he could see her expression from this distance. When he nodded at her, the look on his face confirmed that he was still a supporter.

"What do you want?" Feo shouted.

Ludovico pushed Caterina forward so hard she nearly stumbled. Righting herself, she turned and faced him, but he pointed to the fortress before she could say anything. "Tell Ravaldino to surrender to us. If you fail, it will go more harshly for both those inside and you."

Caterina took a deep breath and turned back to the castle. Raising her eyes to Feo, she began composing her words on the spot. "Tommaso, you are a great friend to the Riarios and to me personally. This is known by everyone. As my friend, I ask you to surrender the fortress to me." She wasn't certain, but Caterina thought she saw a twitch at the side of Feo's mouth. "My life is in danger, as are those of my children." Caterina's throat was dry, and the last word came out roughly, but the effect of a terrified widow worked in her favour.

"Madonna, it's true my loyalties lie with the Riarios, so you'll understand that I cannot hand the fortress over to you."

Caterina held up clasped hands and dropped to her knees. "Please, I beg you, give these men the castle so they'll free me and my children!"

"I cannot, my lady. I am holding the fortress for the heir of Count Girolamo, Ottaviano Riario."

By now, Caterina was confident in the ruse being perpetrated between them. She cried out loudly, "They will kill us!"

Still, Tommaso held firm. "I loved your husband. The count and the law state that the fortress must be handed over to his legitimate heir, Ottaviano, the nephew of the Duke of Milan."

Caterina nearly smiled. The mention of her brother was a clever touch, and she knew it had ended their conversation.

Sure enough, a moment later, Checco came forward and grabbed her arm again, raising her to her feet. Withdrawing his dagger from the sheath on his belt, he held it to Caterina's chest. "There is some mischief here. You and this knave," he moved the knife and pointed at Feo, who watched from the fortress walls, "have somehow managed to communicate and scheme." He returned the knife tip to Caterina and held it against her throat. "Do you know, if I wanted, I could move this blade from one side of you to the other, and you'd fall at my feet dead."

She waited only a moment before leaning into the blade, feeling its point nearly puncturing her skin. "You can hurt me, but you will never frighten me, for I am the daughter of a man who knew no fear. Do what you want, you've killed my husband, you can certainly kill me." Caterina adopted a mocking tone. "After all, I'm just a woman."

The armed guards who had accompanied the Orsi brothers looked at each other, unsure of their role. To kill an unarmed woman was a shameful act, not one the Orsi soldiers wanted to damn their souls with.

Caterina's nerve held, and Checco dropped the hand holding the dagger. "You are lucky there are so many witnesses. Otherwise, things may have gone differently for you," he whispered in her ear.

Taking a deep breath, Caterina allowed herself to be led back to the Orsi palace and into the arms of her children. After their tears of relief had ebbed, Luisa had them all down on their knees, praying their thanks for Caterina's safe return.

The afternoon passed in prayer and storytelling, and Caterina, exhausted by her ordeal, managed to get the children asleep. It amazed her that, after so short a confinement, they had already adapted to eating and sleeping patterns. "I wish it were so easy for us," she remarked to Luisa as the two stood gazing down at the smaller Riarios.

Again, Ludovico arrived without knocking and threw open the door. The children woke as a group but stayed frozen at Caterina's stern look.

"Madonna, I have a visitor for you. The good bishop has forbidden any contact between you and others, but I still have a soul and feel for your situation. I have brought a priest to comfort and advise you."

He delivered his words with a laugh, and Caterina prepared herself for anyone to enter the room. As Ludovico said, a petite man in black robes entered, a rosary and a bible gripped tightly in his hands. Were the Orsis having an attack of conscience? she wondered.

"I'll leave you to talk." Ludovico nodded at the priest and left the room, slamming the door closed and causing those inside to jump.

"My lady, I'm Father Lucchesi, the Orsi family have asked me to speak with you."

Still unsure of the priest's intent, Caterina remained silent, unwilling to give up anything her enemies could use against her.

The holy man waited for a moment, then his face grew red, and he frowned. "I am here to help you, Madonna, for I know your history and all your sins, and those of your husband. There is no place for people such as you in heaven, your behaviour has seen to that. No," he shook his head, "your place is reserved in Hell, besides Satan and other creatures of deceit. Your flesh will peel from your body and your hair burst aflame along with the others who turned away from God and the natural order of the world. You must hand over the fortress of Ravaldino if you have any hope of saving yourself and your immortal soul."

Caterina remained silent and steadied herself by watching Luisa go to the children and hold the youngest, trying to cover their ears. A vision of herself in flames terrified her, and she choked back the acid she felt in her throat.

The priest, now encouraged by her silence, continued. "I know of your husband's deed, the thieving and cheating and killing. So many of the commandments broken, his pain will be great for eternity."

She knew of the count's sins and had tried to make up for them with her own behaviour but always suspected it was never enough. Now, this man was confirming her worst fears.

"The count was murdered for his sins, you know this. Through the will of divine justice. You, yourself, have lived off the spoils of your husband's destruction of churches and maltreatment of so many nuns and priests, so will share in Riario's fate someday. But you can do something right here and right now to regain God's blessings. Give us Ravaldino."

Holding her words lest they betray her growing fear for her soul, Caterina remained silent. Father Lucchesi's face turned from a sunburned to a deep beet red, and he scowled.

"You are stubborn, Madonna, and while it may have served you in the past, it only harms you now. You and your children will starve to death locked in this room and your souls will forever be consumed in the fires of Hell unless you give up the fortress!" Both his words and the vehemence with which they were delivered broke something in Caterina. Hearing her children start to cry, she ran to the door and pounded on it with her fist, not caring about the pain she felt each time she hit. Crying out now, she hammered the door until her hand felt numb. Finally, Ludovico arrived and, sneering at Caterina, motioned for the priest to exit.

"I trust the good father has given you something to think about." He laughed and left the room, shoving past Caterina and shutting the door.

Caterina took a moment to calm herself and then the children. Luisa sang softly as Caterina ran her hand over Giovanni's head. Soon they were all asleep again, and, with a nod to her friend, Luisa covered herself with a blanket and closed her eyes.

While the outward appearance Caterina had adopted for her family was calm and composed, inside, she felt more fearful and raw than when she'd seen her husband's body lying below her window in the market square. Shivering, she drew a blanket around her shoulders and tried to sleep.

Chapter Twenty-Nine
1488

Caterina never learned the identity of the person who told Bishop Savelli about her visit from Father Lucchesi, but she would be forever grateful to them. The day after the priest had terrified her and the children, Savelli had arrived with papal guards to escort Caterina and her family to the tower of Porta San Pietro at one of the main entrances to Forli, and under the bishop's direct control.

The move went smoothly, and although the family found themselves in an even smaller room than before, Caterina allowed herself to relax a bit, knowing the Orsis couldn't get to them here without being recognised. Servants and guards here were as sympathetic to Caterina and her children's plight as those at the Orsi palace, and she soon found food, toys for the children, and fresh clothing for them all being delivered by maids.

When they were settled, and Caterina thought the servants had finished their deliveries, a knock came on the door. Caterina was about to respond when the lock slid open. The door opened, and a man rushed in. Peering back out into the hall, he closed the door behind him. His clothes and boots were caked with mud, and his head was covered by a hood, disguising his face.

Caterina's sense of danger made her stand. "Who are you? What do you want?"

"Only to deliver good news, my lady." The man pushed his hood back over his head onto his shoulders and smiled kindly at her.

"Bossi!" Unable to control herself, Caterina rushed over and hugged him. Feeling his body stiffen in embarrassment, she released him. "How did you get in?"

"I snuck in a back door behind a butcher delivering meat to the kitchen and broke from him when I saw the stairs. With my hood and rough appearance," he waved his hand over himself, "I was unlikely to be noticed. I hardly look like anyone official with all this dirt covering me."

Caterina grabbed his arm. "Sit. Tell us what you know."

"There isn't enough time for me to get comfortable. If I'm discovered, it'll be worse for you." He looked around the room, seeing the children staring up at him, a familiar face. Satisfied the family he served was at least clean and being provided with food, he turned back to Caterina. Luisa had joined them, and he acknowledged her with a nod.

"Your messages to Milan and Bologna have been delivered. I sent one of my most trusted men to Milan and took your message to Bologna myself. The council assures you of their support."

"Thank God." The relief was evident in her voice, but there was still much to be done. "I'm certain my uncle will send his army. In the meantime, I must hold out against the Orsi demand to surrender Ravaldino. If the fortress remains under Riario control, we have a chance. If it falls, we all fall."

"What would you have me do?"

Caterina thought for a moment. Tommaso Feo had already proven his allegiance, and he was quick-witted enough to understand what Caterina needed when she'd begged him to surrender Ravaldino. Now she needed him again and had no doubts about his participation.

"I have an idea."

The next day Caterina suspected that her plan had worked. She was once again taken from her children and marched to the same place she'd stood only yesterday, in front of the fortress. Then she'd been forcing her bravado; today, she felt more in control.

"I don't like this," snarled Checco as he gripped Caterina's arm.

"You don't like what?" Caterina asked innocently.

"This plan! You!" He spat the words at her, and she kept her pleasure hidden. She was still in danger, and there was no point antagonising the man.

"Let her go."

Bishop Savelli stared sternly at the younger Orsi brother, who scowled and backed away. "If this fails it'll be your fault," he muttered as he walked past.

The bishop waited until he and Caterina stood together, then called into the fortress. "Tommaso Feo! Come out! We wish to speak to you further about your demands!"

Caterina sighed in relief when she heard the bishop's words, for it was proof Bossi had played his part. She also heard the Orsi brothers grumbling behind her and wondered what had transpired between them, the bishop, and Bossi. At that moment, Feo appeared on the ramparts and looked down at them.

Savelli shouted up again. "Tommaso, we've met with your messenger."

"And you agree with my demands?" Feo replied. "You'll pay my back wages and provide a letter of recommendation stating I am a loyal servant and a fierce protector?"

The Orsi's complaining grew loud enough for the bishop to turn and gesture for them to be quiet. Chagrined but still angry, they quietened as Savelli turned back to Feo.

"Your demands will be met. I have the agreement here." He reached into his robe and withdrew a folded paper. Holding it up, he added, "See?"

Feo smiled widely from his position above them. "Excellent. Send the countess in with the agreement and I will sign it and surrender the fortress."

"No!" Two voices shouted at once. Ludovico and Checco rushed to Savelli. "You see!" Ludovico waved his arm at Feo, then pointed at Caterina. "There is a plot between these two, as we told you earlier! Now we see the proof!"

The red-faced bishop glanced up at the still-smiling Feo and then back to the Orsis. "Please. We are so close to achieving our goal. Anger and frustration have no place in these talks."

"But," Checco was cut off.

"But nothing. I know what's best and I say the countess will deliver the agreement." Before they could speak, he held up his hand. "However, she will take someone with her." He turned his face up to Feo. "Will you allow Checco or Ludovico to accompany the countess?"

"No!" Savelli waved the brothers' objections aside as Tommaso continued. "The Orsis are no friends to me, and I do not trust them!" With a quick glance at Caterina, he continued. "I will, as a gesture of good faith, permit any one person other than the Orsis or their supporters to accompany the countess in."

The Orsis threw up their arms and turned away. A large man lingered nearby, shuffling his foot enough to catch the bishop's attention.

"You. Who are you?"

The man stepped forward, a surprised look on his face. "I'm Luca, your lordship holiness." He grabbed his rough woollen hat from his head and bowed.

"Stand up, man. And I'm 'your grace'. What do you do?"

"I'm a farmer, your grace," he enunciated the words, "same as my father before and his before and,"

"Yes, yes, I understand." Savelli looked the man up and down. "Do you comprehend what's happening?"

Luca shrugged. "It's the business of the lords and council, nothing to do with me." He quickly added, "Your grace."

"Perfect. Right. I want you to accompany the countess into the fortress and bring her back out in three hours. Do you understand?"

"How will I know when that much time has passed?" Luca asked.

"Don't worry, we'll let you know. But you won't be in there that long, I'm positive." He smiled with the little confidence he still had, then looked at Caterina. "Take this," he handed the agreement to her, "and get it signed."

She nodded and looked at Luca as he returned his hat to his head. They stood together, waiting as the bishop backed away. Once Savelli had joined the Orsis, Feo shouted to someone below, and a loud groaning noise made them jump. Slowly the drawbridge was lowered, and Caterina held her position until it had come to a complete stop before stepping ahead of Luca and walking into the fortress.

A guard met them at the entrance, his helmet tilting over his face so much that Caterina didn't recognise Bossi until she stood in front of him.

"My lord the castellan is expecting you, countess."

"Thank you, soldier." Caterina started walking past Bossi but stopped, a sudden idea crossing her mind. Making a fist with her right hand, she pinched her thumb between her first two fingers and spun to the Orsis. Fighting the urge to smile, Caterina flashed her hand at them and then turned before witnessing their reaction at her obscene gesture. She did, however, catch a glimpse of Bossi's lip twitching as he controlled his grin. Satisfied, she nodded and made her way into the fortress. Before the last glimpse of Caterina's dark blue dress disappeared into the doorway, the drawbridge began rising, blocking the view of those still outside.

"It worked." Bossi took off the helmet as one of his rare smiles appeared. He turned to Luca. "You did well." He slapped the man on the arm.

Luca took off his old hat and threw it on the ground. "I'm just relieved the bishop chose me. I didn't know if my twitching foot would attract or annoy the man."

"We had another plan, in case someone we didn't know was chosen." Caterina nodded her head at Luca as he went to join his fellow soldiers and followed Bossi to the main hall of the fortress. Inside she saw temporary beds on the floor and families sitting on and near them and smiled at those she passed as she went to the main table.

Someone arrived behind her with a wine jug and glasses as she sat. She turned to thank the person and saw Tommaso Feo grinning at her. "Countess, I thought you could use something to refresh you. Your room is waiting for you, and, as we speak, a bath is being prepared and fresh clothing laid out."

Reaching up, Caterina grasped the man's arm. "Thank you, Tommaso. My children and I will be forever in your debt. Your efforts will not go unrewarded."

He nodded graciously and sat when Caterina waved at a chair. "I hate to bring up such a delicate topic, my lady, but are your children safe? Do you think it wise to leave them?"

"Your concerns are noted, and I appreciate you voicing them. Luisa is still with them and would rather die than see any harm befall them." Bossi nodded at her words as she went on. "As foolish as the Orsis are, I don't believe they'd harm the children, especially the niece and nephews of the Duke of Milan." She shook her head and took a long drink, savouring the rich flavour, so much better than the cheap wine the Orsis had been supplying. "My children are also the cousins of Cardinal Raffaele. Despite his dislike for my family, Pope Innocent would not allow the relatives of such a highly ranked cardinal to come to any harm."

She'd been so used to sitting the past few days that her body felt restless and, rising, Caterina continued as she paced. "What were my choices? If we surrender, then we have nothing left with which to negotiate and the Orsis win. My children and I would be put into prison somewhere secret and fall victim to suspicious accidents, of that I'm certain." She stopped and drained her glass. "My family's best chance is to keep doing what we're doing."

Bossi refilled their glasses and spoke. "Bologna is on our side, as is Milan of course." He nodded his head at Caterina.

"Then we need only wait. Milan will send troops, but Bologna is closer, and we may see their forces sooner. It all comes down to who will arrive first, our supporters or the Vatican forces Innocent is sure to send." Caterina sighed. "I'm going to bathe and change. I'll be back soon."

"Do you need anything from us, my lady?" Feo stood as Caterina turned to leave.

She turned back. "Pray that God gives our allies swift feet and an easy path."

Caterina had changed and tidied her hair and had re-joined the men downstairs as the minutes ticked by. They all held their breath, waiting as the three-hour deadline approached and passed.

After waiting a while, Caterina nodded to Feo. "Go outside. Do what you must with conviction."

He nodded at her, and they listened from the hall as his footsteps echoed up the stairs to the battlements. At first, there was silence, then the sound of Tommaso shouting.

"I have taken the countess as my captive!"

Caterina and Bossi heard murmurings but couldn't discern words.

Feo replied. "She was told to run when her husband was killed but, instead, she showed herself a true ruler and stayed behind to administer to her people. I would offer her further protection, for, as a woman, she hasn't fully considered her options."

Bossi and Caterina looked at each other, and Caterina imagined Tommaso trying his best not to grimace as he delivered his words. Caterina raised a wry eyebrow at her friend.

"I will hand the countess back to you in exchange for the cousins and nephews of Ludovico and Checco Orsi!"

This time the uproar was loud enough for those resting on the floor in the hall to look up. When the noise had died down, Caterina heard the sound of a lone reply, then Feo's angry footsteps pounding back down the stairs toward them.

Caterina gripped the table, preparing herself. "What happened?"

"They said no. There were other words, but I'll not repeat them in front of you, my lady."

She nodded and released her hold on the table. "Did they give any indication of what they'll do next?"

Feo shook his head. "I'm afraid not, Madonna. But we must be ready for anything."

Ready since her husband's first scream, Caterina looked around the room again. A young family caught her eye, a woman and her husband huddled together with their three children. They smiled gratefully at her, and one of the children looked so much like Ottaviano it nearly broke Caterina's heart. She repeated the words she'd told her children: a Sforza is always brave. It sounded so unconvincing without her family around her.

Returning her attention to Bossi and Feo, she smiled grimly. "I don't know how long it will be before they're back. Go and sleep where you can, for as long as you can." When neither man moved to leave, Caterina nodded her gratitude and prepared herself for the wait ahead.

The wait was shorter than any of them expected. Within an hour, raised voices reached them from outside. "Madonna Riario! Come outside! We would speak with you!"

Caterina wondered what new way they had devised to get her to surrender. Sighing wearily, she muttered something under her breath.

Bossi and Feo had heard her words, but all it took was a quick look between them, and an agreement to remain silent was reached. Caterina mounted the steps and walked to the edge of the fortress wall. What she saw horrified her, and, covering her mouth, she took a step back and turned away.

"They have Ottaviano," she whispered as Bossi and Feo joined her. Reaching for more will than she'd ever summoned before, Caterina returned to the wall's edge.

"Countess, as you can see, we have your son and Dama di Corte." Ludovico Orsi gripped Luisa's shoulder as he forced her forward. Beside him, Ottaviano struggled to escape from Checco's arms, and as soon as she caught his eye, her son began calling out. She glanced at Luisa, and while her friend's face was blank, Caterina could see that Luisa had been crying.

Caterina had hoped these men wouldn't resort to violence against her children and had actively pushed away any thought to the contrary. But now, faced with the threat, she hesitated for a moment. Her son's cries filled her ears, and she nearly gave in just so she could run to him and give him comfort. But then Checco's laughter reached her, and her resolve hardened once more.

"How dare you lay a hand on my son? Do you understand the consequences of such an action? At this very moment, my uncle's men are marching here. You would be reckless enough to present them with the body of his nephew upon their arrival and yet still hope to placate them after such an unnatural deed?"

Her words stopped the younger Orsi brother's laughter but brought about something much worse. At his nod, four men stepped forward with raised swords and daggers and pointed them all at Ottaviano. As they approached, the boy screamed like an animal trapped.

She started to reach her hand toward her son, but as her arm moved, Bishop Savelli stepped forward. "Enough!" The brothers turned, puzzled looks on their faces. Scowling at them, Savelli stepped forward and shoved his way through the circle Ottaviano's guards made around the boy. "My God, this is but a child! Put down your weapons and leave. All of you."

With a quick glance at Checco, the men backed away. "This is not how Holy Mother Church treats its weakest and most innocent members." He nodded to one of his retainers. "Take these two back to their room and see they receive water and clean clothing. I want my own guards posted outside their door at all times. No one is to move them without my saying so." When Ludovico started to protest, the bishop held up his hand, his face stern with anger. "No. I trusted you when you promised to obey my orders to treat the family better. I gave you permission to visit them only, but you've shown yourself unreliable and cruel. The family is under my protection, you will remember that." He glanced up at Caterina, who still stood watching from the fortress wall, and received a slight nod of acknowledgment. With a final glare at the Orsis, he strode away.

The Orsis stood watching him, then turned and stared up at Caterina. Ludovico stepped forward, his face red, and pointed his dagger at her. "I don't care what the bishop says, I will drag each of your children here and kill them in front of you!"

Anger engulfed her body and forced itself out with her words. "Do it then, you fools! I am already pregnant with another child by my husband, Count Riario, and I have the means to make more!" Without waiting to see their reaction, she turned and hurried back into the fortress.

When they'd locked the heavy wooden door behind them and sat at the table, Bossi cleared his throat. "My lady, did you speak truthfully when you said..." He stopped, and his reddening face finished his question when his words could not.

"No, I am not with child. I felt such anger, like never before, and the lie created itself." She shook her head. "An immature boast, not worthy of a warrior."

Bossi patted her hand, surprising her. "You are more warrior than most men. And, now, worthy of a rest. I'll remain here with Tommaso if you should like to sleep awhile. I feel we may be waiting some time for the Orsis to make their next move."

With a grateful nod and a small squeeze of his hand, Caterina left Bossi sitting with Feo. Her exhaustion overtook her, and once she'd undressed and climbed under a blanket, Caterina fell into a troubled sleep filled with visions of her crying children.

Two days later, a group of exhausted townspeople arrived at the fortress rather than the Orsi messenger they'd all been expecting.

"We were forced out of our homes and the lives of our families threatened if we did not proclaim our support for Ludovico and Checco. When we had no more money to give them, they sent their men to destroy our shops and homes."

The same story was repeated by more and more who arrived, and it became clear just how desperate the brothers seemed to be to hold onto what little power they had.

"What does this mean?" Feo and Caterina looked down from a tower and saw more people arriving.

"It means the Orsis are weak. They no longer have the support of the town, if indeed they ever did. Even those who preferred to remain impartial are being attacked." Caterina turned and walked back to the hall. "Make sure we have space." She looked around at the already crowded hall. "I suspect more will arrive soon."

A shout from the far end of the room caught her attention. "Madonna!"

Caterina turned and saw Isach waving at her. Smiling, she headed in his direction and saw that he had his wife Ricca and daughter Sarra with him.

"Isach! I'm glad you're safe." Looking at Ricca and Sarra and seeing the terrified look on their faces, she added, "All of you."

"We are relieved to see you so well, Madonna. No one knew what was happening, or if the Orsis had committed some offence against your person..." He let his words fall away.

"I'm safe and well. I don't know what lies have been spread about me but you can see for yourself." She held her arms wide. "Will you sit with me and have a glass of wine? Perhaps some food?"

"That would be very kind of you." Isach gathered his family in his arms and followed Caterina to the main table. There were always glasses and bottles of wine waiting, and Caterina served Isach and Ricca before herself.

"Tell me the news. I trust you more than anyone who's arrived to convey all you know truthfully."

"Madonna, I will try. What do you want to know?"

"Has the pope sent his army yet? Is there any sign of their arrival?" Caterina stared at him earnestly. The more she knew, the more she could prepare.

"You don't know? There will be no papal reinforcements. Innocent decided not to send any help."

"Indeed." She paused for a moment, savouring this good news. "Did the Holy Father give any reason?"

Isach shook his head. "Not that I know of. Perhaps that's why the brothers became more aggressive in their actions toward us." He waved his hand at his family.

Ricca finally spoke, her eyes wide with horror at the things she'd seen. "No one is safe. In the artisan quarter every shop was entered, and all work destroyed. The pawnbrokers had all their belongings taken and were left injured when they tried to protest. Some of us were more harshly treated than others." She shivered and held Sarra more closely.

Caterina could see the poor girl's eyes closing as they spoke. "I've kept you long enough. We'll find you a place to sleep." She waved at one of Feo's guards, who walked over and waited until the family had stood.

"Thank you, Madonna. God will see that your efforts are rewarded." With a bow, he followed the guard and his family upstairs to the private bedrooms.

"The Orsis must be punished for what they're doing to my people." Caterina now held her meetings in a small room. The main hall had become too crowded with the continued flow of citizens into the fortress, and while she trusted most, there was still a chance an Orsi supporter snuck through.

"There's nothing we can do from here except offer aid to anyone who needs it," Bossi replied reasonably.

"I know, but there must be some way we can make their continued foolishness more difficult." She frowned, thinking. Sending someone out to spread rumours would be too dangerous. As was having poison find its way into their food, she thought cynically, then shook her head. Others may take this dishonourable route, but she preferred to face a problem directly. "Noise," she said suddenly.

"What?" Tommaso was also with them and had been included in all their meetings.

"Cannon fire. We know where our enemies' houses are. If we shoot cannons over their roofs, the noise will be enough to distract even the most patient of saints."

Bossi nodded his head. "It might work. We'd have to be careful with our aim."

Feo spoke up. "That won't be an issue, my men are the finest in Italy."

Caterina nodded appreciatively at him. "Can you see to it?"

Smiling widely, he nodded. "I will, my lady." He hurried from the room while Caterina and Bossi watched.

"An interesting idea."

"We won't know if it works but the amusement of terrifying our enemies will keep me distracted while we wait for something to happen."

Caterina was provided with regular reports on their blasting efforts. She insisted the cannons only be fired during the day, hoping people would remember her kindness when they were able to sleep at night.

Three days passed, and soon everyone, Caterina included, was weary of the booming sounds from above them. When the noise suddenly stopped, all were relieved except Caterina, who had not ordered them to cease.

Bossi, who had been standing with Feo on the fortress walls, rushed into Caterina's meeting room. "My lady, Giovanni Bentivoglio's banners are flying in the distance."

Caterina stood and, without a word, ran through the hall and up the stairs. Shielding her eyes from the mid-day sun, she allowed her vision to adjust and then scanned the horizon. Riding toward the fortress were the flags of Bologna's ruling family. Bossi had joined her and, together with Tommaso, watched as the riders grew closer.

"So many! There must be at least eight hundred riders."

"And even more infantry. The Bentivoglio family are well known for their forces. Thank God they've come to help us." Caterina crossed herself and mouthed a thank you to the sky. She'd spent so many hours in the fortress chapel that the skin on her knees had hardened, and she promised she'd spend even more time there once this was over.

"The first of them have arrived, over there." Tommaso pointed at a town gate.

"Clever. They're setting up camp at the main entrance into Forli. No one will get in or out without Bologna saying so."

At that moment, the gate swung open, surrendered by Orsi supporters easily and without a fight. A dozen men rode in wearing the red and yellow of the Bentivoglio family. Caterina rushed to a side wall to watch them ride through town without stopping until they arrived outside Ravaldino.

Seeing her staring down at them, one of them urged his horse forward and swept his hat from his head. "My Lady Sforza, my lord, the most exquisite Giovanni Bentivoglio, sends his greetings and his support!"

Caterina's heart leaped at his words, and she would have hugged the man if she'd been closer. Maintaining her composure, she instead smiled down at them. "Thank you, Signor, for bringing me glad tidings," she shouted.

"That's not all, my lady! We also bring word from the Duke of Milan that you also have his support and that his men are on their way!"

Hope and happiness like she hadn't felt in ages flooded through her. "You are an honourable man, and my uncle was right to trust you as his messenger!"

The man bowed at her and put his hat back on, then turned his horse and rode toward the centre of town with the others following.

Turning to Bossi and Feo, she smiled. "They will ride into town and proclaim to all that Milan and Bologna back my cause." Her relief got the better of her, and Caterina rushed toward Bossi, grabbing his arm and squeezing it.

"Finally, some good news."

Chapter Thirty
1488

The next day the emissary from Milan arrived in Forli. A meeting was hastily arranged, one to which Bossi had been invited.

"Why me?"

"Both Milan and Bologna know how important you are to me. I cannot leave the fortress, the minute I do Forli will fall, so you'll go in my place."

"And how shall I conduct myself? Do I repeat our demands? That you be reinstated, and your children released? And that the Orsis leave?"

Caterina shook her head. "No. Remain quiet but listen to everything, and watch the faces of those who speak, for men give away information unawares. I have been assured that no harm will come to you, for harming you would be harming me." She held up the message that had arrived, outlining the time and place for the meeting. "Representatives from both Bologna and Milan will be in attendance, let their voices be heard and report back all when you return."

Bossi nodded. "I will, my lady." He bowed and hurried toward the main door as Caterina watched. More waiting was required of her, and she was growing impatient. There were gardens in the fortress, but Caterina was tired of walking around the same place, and yearned to be on one of her favourite horses running through the fields outside the city wall. Shaking the melancholy such imaginings brought on, she stood from the small table in her workroom and went outside to see her people while she waited for Bossi to return.

When Gian Bossi returned a few hours later, Caterina could see he was flustered.

"I've been a soldier all my life and never professed to having any great understanding of the ways nobles, but men are men, and the intelligent ones learn from their mistakes, and know when they have lost. But these Orsi brothers," he threw up his hands in disgust, "have no idea what they're doing and not an ounce of wit between them."

"Come. Tell us what happened." Caterina had met him at the door, and they walked to her workroom, where Tommaso waited. He rose when Caterina entered and nodded at Bossi before they all sat.

"As you know, representatives from both Bologna and Milan were present, as were Ludovico and Checco Orsi and Bishop Savelli. The bishop introduced himself and the Orsis to the ambassadors, then wasted no time explaining why your son should relinquish his claim to Forli."

Caterina had poured wine and made a dismissive noise as she sat again. "I can only imagine what he said about us."

"Now that Forli is under papal control, the good bishop stated that the presence of you and your family were unwelcome. And unneeded. He told everyone that the Riarios had already given up their right to rule due to their refusal to pay tribute to Rome."

Making another derisive noise, Caterina took a long drink of her wine. "The situation was different when my husband was alive."

"Indeed, my lady. Nevertheless, the Orsis were nodding like fools and agreeing with everything Savelli had said by this point. The bishop went on in this manner, eventually arriving at a solution: to ship you and your family out of Forli to live as private citizens in Imola."

"What?" Caterina stood, her face red.

"Ludovico and Checco had a similar reaction." Bossi waited until Caterina was sitting again before continuing. "Both men started shouting at the same time and it became clear they didn't want to negotiate at all. They complained of the compromise bitterly."

"Only victory on their terms is acceptable to men such as these," Tommaso said.

"What happened next?"

"The Milanese representative stood and waited until all voices were silent, then proceeded to question the bishop, asking why your claim would be denied in one place yet not another a mere half-day's ride away. He said," here Bossi imitated another, more deeply voiced man, "will you allow them to live peacefully, or will you force them to give up Imola too? Where does your vendetta end? For I have seen evil before but never such cruel vengeance directed at a widow and her children. Have you no conscience?"

"Strong words. Did the brothers show any shame at all?" Tommaso frowned.

"The words had the exact opposite effect than they should have. A moment after the representative spoke his piece, Ludovico leaped from his chair and shoved the ambassador over, then proceeded to kick him while he lay on the ground. Checco joined his brother before any could stop him and soon both men were beating the envoy. I was closer to the back of the room but hurried forward and grabbed Ludovico as one of the councilmen who was there stopped Checco."

"My God, is the poor man badly injured?"

"Fortunately not, my lady. I managed to stop Ludovico before he could do real damage. Apparently, the brothers' bites are as ineffectual as their barking. Still, the man was shaken. Another of the councillors led him away and the meeting ended. Nothing was accomplished. A waste of time."

"I wonder if that's true. News of the Milanese envoy and his treatment will spread fast. In fact, I'm certain the story is already on its way north. And the ambassador from Bologna witnessed the Orsi's manner of ruling first hand, it can only lower them further in his opinion."

"So now we must wait. Again." Bossi sighed. "I'm a soldier, not a rat, the infernal entrapment inside this fortress is maddening."

"It is for us all, Gian." Caterina rose and placed her hand on Bossi's shoulder. "A little more patience. I hope this is nearly over."

For two days, Caterina aided the citizens living within Ravaldino, seeing to their needs the best she could. A fever had started spreading, and, fortunately, her garden at the fortress provided everything she needed to prepare a treatment. So far, it'd been working.

While tidying her physick room, she heard Bossi's heavy regular footsteps echoing down the hall toward her.

"My lady, there is someone here to see you."

"Who is it?" She turned, wiping her hands on her apron, and was surprised to see her nephew standing beside Bossi. "Raffaele! What are you doing here? Doesn't the college need you close?"

Cardinal Riario entered the room smiling and with his arms held wide. "Aunt, it's good to find you looking so well." He released Caterina and nodded. "As you know, there are so many rumours in Rome, and one in particular troubled me."

"Let's go to the hall. Are you hungry? I was about to eat, if you'll join me?"

The cardinal shook his head. "I'm sorry, aunt, but I can't stay very long." They sat at the main table and were served wine before Raffaele addressed Caterina's confused face. "The Holy Father has appointed me his representative here. As I say, rumours have reached us, many about Savelli himself, so Innocent felt it best to send someone he trusts.

"And the story that worried you?" Caterina asked.

"Checco Orsi claimed he had killed all of the Riario children and had ridden around town boasting of it." Raffaele looked down.

"What?" Caterina stood, her arms raised in alarm. "My children? Where are they? Did he do it? Because if he or his brother dared to lay a finger on ..."

"My lady! Your children are safe. I visited with them before coming to you. Your friend Luisa is also safe and still with the children."

Caterina sank back into her seat in relief. She had believed his lie for a moment, and a vision of her children's dead bodies had flashed across her mind. Sitting, she allowed her breathing to slow before speaking.

"Thank you, nephew. Are you certain you can't stay?"

Raffaele shook his head. "Now that I am the pope's representative, I must be seen to be neutral, I can't be accused of showing more favour to one side than that other. You understand." He raised an eyebrow.

"I do." They rose from the table, and Caterina accompanied the cardinal to the main door. "I'm happy you came. It does my heart good to see you well placed and putting peace out into the world."

"And I am pleased you and the children are better than I had expected." He hugged her briefly and whispered into her ear, "Keep your faith strong and you will succeed."

Raffaele stepped away and smiled at her, and the sudden resemblance to his uncle brought the horrors of Girolamo's death to her mind. She blinked back the tears threatening to fall as the cardinal smiled kindly. "All will be well, aunt."

With a nod at the few men who'd been waiting near the door for him, Raffaele turned and left without a glance back.

At the end of April, after days of watching the horizon for their much-needed help, help that would tip the scales in their favour, their wait was rewarded.

"Banners! To the west!" One of Feo's men shouted from the wall.

Caterina, Bossi, and Feo hurried up the stairs and peered in the direction the man pointed at. "Where? I don't see anything." Bossi frowned as he stared.

"There, to the left of the forest."

"Is it the papal army? Has the pope decided to send his forces?" Feo asked.

It was Caterina who recognised the banners. "It's not the pope's army. It's Milan!" As the soldiers marched closer, Sforza colours and flags could be seen everywhere. Caterina and Bossi watched all day as the men continued arriving and setting up camps outside of each of the city gates. No one could now leave or enter without permission of Bologna or Milan.

"I estimate at least ten thousand men, possibly more." Bossi waved a piece of bread at the men. Feo had left him and Caterina to attend to other duties.

The day had been mild, and Caterina was elated enough to enjoy food and wine on the fortress wall. Watching her city's troops and their manoeuvres would also prove educational for her. Nodding at Bossi's guess, Caterina smiled. "These movements are of interest to me but don't feel you need to sit here if you have other business to attend to."

"Madonna, my business it to attend to you. And I'm a military man, of course the workings of other armies interest me."

With a smile, Caterina welcomed his company, and the two watched until the early evening when torch lights appeared in the camps. They spread across the darkness one by one, giving an even greater sense of just how many men her uncle had sent. A large force prepared. And waiting.

The Milanese army seemed to have grown even more by the time Caterina appeared on the fortress wall the next day. Walking with Feo, she learned that a rumour had started of an imminent attack on the city by Milan.

"Good. Perhaps the Orsis will finally relinquish their futile hold on my town and give way to superior numbers."

The late April sun beat down on the fortress walls, forcing Caterina inside. The hall was noticeably cooler, and although she'd rather watch events unfold from outside, the relief from the heat was welcome. Frustrated with waiting, she walked around the hall, greeting people she knew and introducing herself to others.

"Madonna, how are you?" Isach sat in a chair beside his wife while Sarra sat at his feet.

"Isach, I'm well, thank you. And your family?" Caterina stopped and smiled at them.

"Just reading stories to keep our spirits lifted." He leaned forward and lowered his voice. "I'm sorry, Madonna, I borrowed one of your books. When we fled our home we weren't able to carry much. Your man, over there," he looked around the hall and, spotting Bossi, pointed, "he said you wouldn't mind."

"Of course, I don't mind, not at all." From the corner of her eye, Caterina saw Feo gesturing at her from the far side of the room. "I'll leave you to your stories. Perhaps when this is over, I'll visit, and you can include me when you read." With a nod at Isach, she winked at Sarra and hurried toward Tommaso.

"What's wrong?"

"Something is happening in town." Feo waited for Caterina to run up the stairs before following her. From the direction of the town, she heard the cries. "The Church is here!"

Turning to Feo, her eyes wild, she asked, "Is it true? Has Innocent finally shown his hand?"

"I don't know. As soon as I heard the commotion, I ran to find you." By now, Bossi had joined them, and together they watched as a crowd of people gathered, cheering.

"Did the Orsis persuade the Holy Father? Is there something they know that I don't? Something I missed?"

The crowd of shouting townspeople grew closer to the fortress as they surrounded a group of riders flying the crossed keys of the papal flag. As the group of fifty or so men arrived at the drawbridge of Ravaldino, one man rode forward. "Countess Riario!"

Caterina hurried to the wall overhanging the main door. "I am here. What do you want?"

As if on cue, every papal banner was lowered and replaced a moment later with the yellow and blue of the Riario family. The soldier who stood ahead of the others continued. "I want to tell you that your nephew, Cardinal Raffaele Riario, sends his regards to his beloved aunt!"

"Lower the drawbridge! Immediately!" Caterina rushed downstairs to the main door to welcome her nephew's men. They were sent to a larger door toward the stables as Caterina watched, nodding her appreciation at them all. As the last one rode in, the one who had called to her, he smiled and added, "The cardinal thought you could use some help."

"My nephew is astute. And also has a sense of humour. I'm guessing it was his idea to carry the papal standard until you reached the fortress?" The man's wide grin was reply enough. "See to your men then join us in the main hall. Our supplies are low but, still, a celebration is in order."

"My lady." He bowed his head and urged his horse on to join the others.

The feast lasted all night, and Caterina finally went to bed as the sun's rays had begun to soften the hard blackness surrounding Ravaldino. As she undressed, she recalled her conversation with Feo and Bossi.

"If this is the great papal army the Orsis were holding out for, they must have been shocked when they saw so few numbers then devastated when the army turned out to be our friends." Caterina had laughed.

Bossi had snorted. "I wish I could have seen their faces. One wonders what they'll do next."

"Nothing." Her sudden seriousness had surprised them. Caterina had continued. "There is nothing left for them to do. They have no allies. Florence and Venice have obviously deemed it beneath them to get involved in what they believe a petty squabble, Innocent chose the cautious path because of my nephew I'm sure of it, and anyone foolish enough to offer arms would have been scared off immediately by Milan's and Bologna's armies." She'd shaken her head. "No, I don't believe they have any avenues still open to them. No one will help them."

"No one," Caterina repeated to herself as she climbed into bed. She'd been resting only a few hours when shouts from downstairs woke her. Rising with a start, she was already out of bed when Bossi rushed into her room.

"Excuse the intrusion, my lady, but you must come downstairs, there's something you must see."

The excitement on Bossi's face, and the fact that he'd burst into her room without knocking, told Caterina something significant had happened. Wrapping herself in a dressing gown, she hurried behind Bossi as she tied the silk cord around her waist. Hope grew quickly, and, in her haste to get to the hall, Caterina forgot her shoes. Feeling nothing but her rising expectations, she began running as she reached the top of the stairs and nearly stumbled in her haste as she reached the bottom.

Regaining her balance, she stood and looked across the room. There, standing with a dozen city council members, was Ottaviano.

With a shriek, Caterina flew across the hall and wrapped her arms around her son, feeling his warmth and the contours of his body against her own and the smell of him under her nose. The room was still, with everyone watching the reunion of mother and child with awed silence.

Finally, Caterina felt Ottaviano begin to struggle against her embrace and reluctantly released him. She looked him up and down, then around at those who'd accompanied him. "Where are my other children? And Luisa?" Caterina's voice rose in panic.

"Mama, my brothers, and sister are all well and are with Dama Tommasa." He looked at her, and she saw his eyes had taken on a new hardness that hadn't been there before. "They are safe."

Relief flooded through her, and she hugged her son again, unable to stop herself. This time he held her back just as tightly.

Holding his head and kissing the side and top, she heard chanting outside. "Ottaviano! Ottaviano!" Caterina finally let her tears flow and, clutching her child, whispered, "We did it."

End of Part One

Turning the World to Stone

Author's Note

Caterina Sforza

I used primary sources as well as current history books to create Caterina as accurately as possible. The major events in the novel ie marriage, relationship with Pope Sixtus, her husband's participation in the Pazzi Conspiracy, and the defence of Ravaldino at Forli are all actual events from her life.

Girolamo Riario

As with Caterina, I used as many primary sources as I could to bring the pope's nephew to life. Reports of his low breeding and sour looks are accurate, as is his participation in the Pazzi conspiracy (for which he really wasn't punished) and the disaster at Campo Morto. His death is also accurate.

Luisa Tommasa

I made Luisa up as a friend for Caterina. There are no documents listing any particular friends or confidantes and I felt she needed someone sympathetic with whom to share her journey.

Caterina's Children

Caterina had given birth to six children by the time she was twenty-five. All names and birthdates of her children are accurate, including nicknames.

Gian Bossi

Bossi is a real person but wasn't as involved in Caterina's life as I've written. His role in her life was to accompany her to Rome to see her settled then return to Milan.

Botticelli and Da Vinci

There is no record of Caterina ever having met these men, but she was at the Vatican while Botticelli worked and was visiting Milan when da Vinci had been hired by her uncle, Ludovico the Moor, to paint his mistress and create a giant statue of a horse in front of the Milanese palace. Sadly, while da Vinci's designs for the horse still exist, the bronze meant for the statue was eventually used for war and the statue never built.

The likelihood of Caterina meeting Botticelli is greater: he may have needed both her and Girolamo to sit for him for their inclusion in his fresco in the Sistine Chapel called The Healing of the Leper, part of the Temptation of Christ cycle.

Others

Most of the characters are all real people who lived and interacted with Caterina, including her family, the Riarios, the College of Cardinals, Leone Cobelli, and all the Italian families mentioned. Minor characters including the apothecaries are all my own invention.

The Siege of Forli

While the siege of the fortress of Ravaldino in Forli is well documented, the accuracy, as always, depends on the source.

Two of the most well-known stories told about the siege, one of which is oft repeated as an example of Caterina's inappropriate behaviour and thus unsuitability to rule, are
1. her giving the fig to the Orsis and
2. her lifting her skirts from the top of the fortress and flashing her genitals, then grabbing them and proclaiming she had the means to make more children, should hers be killed.

The first story is likely true and is verified by several sources. (Giving the fig was an extremely offensive gesture similar to giving someone the finger).

The second, however, needs a little explanation. While there are differing claims as to what Caterina did when her children were presented to her, none of the actual eyewitness accounts mention her lifting her skirt, which is why I've excluded it from her story. It was only after, in letters to ambassadors, that this scene was reported and embellished by those trying to illustrate Caterina's unsuitability to rule, including Niccolo Machiavelli.

Caterina and Medicine

Caterina was a skilled alchemist. She focussed on the more practical elements of alchemy involving treatments and cures that involved careful and repeated distillation of numerous ingredients. Her reputation was well known, and she was consulted by other alchemists around Italy. Her book "*Gli Experimenti*" is a compilation of all her cures and treatments, including those for plague, scrofula, sleeplessness, and wounds of all sorts.

Her collection also includes beauty treatments for bad breath, lightening hair, creams for the face, thin beards, and sunburn. There is also a sneaky recipe for making tin look like silver and one for adding weight to a shield. It's amusing to think of her fooling her enemies with fake silver, although no record of her doing this exists that I could find.

Food

All of the recipes used in Turning the World to Stone are authentic to the period, and are taken from "The Opera of Bartolomeo Scappi". Scappi was Europe's first 'celebrity chef', and cooked for cardinals, bishops, and popes. His 'Opera' is a compilation of recipes, divided into sections ie meat, fish, dairy, vegetables etc, but also sectioned into meat and non-meat days. Scappi also provides woodcuts of what a kitchen at that time looked like and the food being prepared.

Acknowledgements

Many thanks first to Julia L. Hairston for her help and encouragement. Her support was very much appreciated! Also big thanks to my eagle-eyed editor Max Evans and my lovely mapmaker, Lorena Cosimo.

My beta readers, as always, weren't shy in pointing out what needed to be changed and for that I love them all: Rose Brown, Mercedes Rochelle, Allan Pringle, MJ Porter, and Elizabeth Andersen. Miss Rochelle, Miss Andersen, and Miss Porter are all authors, you should check out their work!

Turning the World to Stone

About the Author

Born in Canada of Scottish extraction, Kelly Evans graduated in History and English then moved to England where she worked in the financial sector. While in London Kelly continued her studies in history, concentrating on Medieval History, and travelled extensively through Eastern and Western Europe.

Kelly is now back in Canada with her husband Max and a rescue cat. She writes full-time, focussing on illuminating little-known women in history with fascinating stories. When not working on her novels, Kelly writes Described Video scripts for visually impaired individuals, plays oboe, and enjoys old sci-fi movies.

Connect with Kelly:

Website: https://www.kellyaevans.com
Facebook: https://www.facebook.com/kellyevansauthor
Twitter: https://twitter.com/ChaucerBabe

Printed in Great Britain
by Amazon